HIGH PRAISE FOR BONNIE VANAK!

THE COBRA & THE CONCUBINE

"When a heroine haunted by her brutal past finds new hope and love with a hero torn between two cultures, their passion for each other proves to be as scorchingly hot as the desert sands in the latest of Vanak's vivid, lushly sensual historical romances set in colorful nineteenth-century Egypt."

—*Booklist*

"Vanak's latest novel recalls the big, exciting historical romances of the past—ones with lots of adventure [and] exotic locales."

—*RT BOOKreviews*

"Ms. Vanak sweeps the reader away with a fast-paced tale of adventure, intrigue, betrayal and the healing power of love. With love scenes that are hotter than the sun-scorched sand of the desert that surrounds the lovers, this is a book you won't want to put down until the final page."

—Fresh Fiction

"If you aren't a fan of Bonnie Vanak's novels, you should be. *The Cobra & the Cocubine* is a must read for all historical romance fans."

—A Romance Review

"*The Cobra & the Concubine* has more delightful twists, turns, and plot excitement than a Cairo alley, and around each bend, there is a surprise."

—Romance at Heart

"The lush backdrops of England and Egypt set the tone for this wonderful and at times, heart-wrenching story."

—: Heart

"*The Cobra & t*   need in
a summer roma   eviews

LIKE SHIFTING SAND…

"A considerate man could make you happy," Graham observed.

"Perhaps. But you are the only man who was ever considerate of me. Last night…" Two scarlet roses bloomed on her cheeks.

"A man who is otherwise is a fool. You deserve tender, careful consideration," he growled.

She glanced shyly at him from beneath those incredible long lashes. "I did enjoy our dance."

"Both?" he teased.

"Both. You would never tread upon my toes." Jillian smiled.

Wistful regret coursed through him. For her, forced to marry a man she detested. For him, forced into an act where he'd surely hang. Graham brushed a knuckle against her petal-soft cheek, feeling the dampness still there.

"Good-bye, Lady Jillian," he said quietly. And he left her standing alone in the moonlight.

The Panther & the Pyramid

BONNIE VANAK

LEISURE BOOKS NEW YORK CITY

A LEISURE BOOK®

September 2006

Published by

Dorchester Publishing Co., Inc.
200 Madison Avenue
New York, NY 10016

ISBN 0-8439-5755-7

The name "Leisure Books" and the stylized "L" with design are trademarks of Dorchester Publishing Co., Inc.

Printed in the United States of America.

For Dawn Neumayer,
who enjoyed blueberry pancakes with Steve every
morning, caring for animals, and life itself;
and my uncle, Edmond Fischer,
a gentle soul dedicated to caring for his family.
You both made the world a little brighter
with your presence and your love.

The
Panther
& the Pyramid

Prologue

The red hair haunted him, as it always did, in his deepest nightmares.

Red. The color of blood. His blood. The hair . . . its crimson shock flapping in the air like a warning flag. The thick tangle of red-gold billowed from the force of the wind whistling across the desert sands. Always the desert, the harsh yellow sun searing his sweating body, mocking his dry, childish screams for help. Green eyes, brilliant as glossy emeralds, stared at him with scornful challenge.

He moaned, tossing and writhing. Hands clawed the air in a desperate attempt to fight his attacker—his attacker who wanted the magic wishing casket buried deep in Egypt's sands. He tried, oh, he tried so hard to wrest it away, to keep its awesome power hidden, but his tormentor grabbed the box. Then, words drifted from those mocking lips.

"There's no escape from the truth. You can't hide from what you really are."

With a strangled yell, he sat up. Sweat dampened the

soft Egyptian cotton sheets beneath his naked torso. His hand shook uncontrollably as he wiped moisture from his forehead with the sheet's edge. An ominous foreboding shook him.

It wasn't the red hair this time, nor the words that caused him to tremble. It was the face. This time, it wasn't the face of the man who'd abused him that one day in the desert. It was the face of a woman. And she would make him scream until only hoarse cries wrung from his dry throat. Only this time, his screams wouldn't stop with a dirty rag frantically shoved into his mouth.

This time his screams would not end. . . .

Chapter One

London, 1896

The Duke of Caldwell had chosen a most unusual way to lose his virginity.

Graham Tristan stood quietly in Madame LaFontant's wine-colored private receiving room. Sweat trickled down his back, gathered in the waistband of his fine buff trousers. Summoning all his courage, he faced the brothel owner and said in a quiet, commanding tone, "She must be . . . untried. And not a redhead. My brother assures me your establishment is the most discreet in London."

The saucy, chestnut-haired madame gave him a slow, thorough assessment. "Of course, Your Grace. I pride myself on discretion and fulfilling the deepest desires of many of your peers. Your request was not unusual." She paused and tapped an elegant nail thoughtfully upon the back of the horsehair settee. "That is why I sent my note. The type of woman you want just arrived. Not quite young. She's twenty-two. A honey-blonde. Very well-spoken. Quite lovely. Is that acceptable?"

A tiny puff of air escaped his lungs. Graham forced his face into an expressionless mask. "Is she a virgin?"

"Most assuredly. Of course, for such a jewel I'll have to charge double."

"Of course," he murmured, his heart galloping with a mixture of excitement and dread.

Madame LaFontant's corset stays creaked as she rose from the chaise. "Remain here and I'll prepare everything. Please, make yourself comfortable. There's brandy on the sideboard."

And with a swish of starched taffeta skirts, she whisked out the door. Graham ran a finger along the soaked white collar of his otherwise immaculate dress shirt. He eyed the sideboard with its gleaming array of crystal and decanter of amber fluid. He'd never drunk alcohol before, either.

"There's a first time for everything," he muttered.

In three strides, he was pouring two fingers of brandy into a snifter. Graham gulped down the liquor, coughing violently. He wiped his mouth and set down the glass. Good God, he hoped sex was going to be a hell of a lot more pleasurable than drinking.

"Is there such a thing as a monkish duke? Or a dukish monk?" he asked himself and laughed.

All the debutantes who'd eyed him as the Season's parties and balls began, marriage glinting in their eyes at the thought of snaring the very eligible, very rich duke, would be scandalized to know he was as innocent as they. A twenty-eight-year-old virgin.

But no longer. Knowing full well he'd hang for the crime he planned to commit, the revenge he would take, Graham vowed he'd experience pleasure in a woman's soft arms for the first time. Tonight, no skilled whore who would detect his inexperience. He wanted a woman as inexperienced as he, a woman too nervous to notice his awkward fumblings and hesitation. A virgin who would not ridicule him if last-minute panic flowered and he decided he couldn't bear to be touched after all . . .

Graham fisted his hands, staring at the scarlet silk-paneled walls. The man who'd robbed him of his boyhood was long dead. Graham had killed him with his scimitar in a duel, ruthlessly avenging the abuse he'd suffered after having been taken captive by an Egyptian tribe at age six. But that other man, the redheaded Englishman who'd wanted the same—*he* still roamed free. The man who'd promised a desperate eight-year-old that, if he wouldn't struggle, if he would do something very despicable, he would be freed from his tormentor and returned to England. Graham had closed his eyes and sold his soul to the devil. That devil with red hair and green eyes . . .

And then he'd screamed in anguish as the man rode off in a cloud of dust, leaving him behind to face his laughing captor and the nightmarish stench of the dirty, gray sheepskins grinding into his face each night.

Graham's eyes flew open. "Never again," he whispered fiercely. "I am not that same child."

Abandoning the sideboard, he paced the fine wool carpet, trying to contain the restless agitation welling inside. He stopped, forcing himself to remember: He would not be the only virgin in bed tonight. Surely his first lover would be very nervous. Think of her, he admonished himself. Focus on her.

Kenneth, his brother who had relinquished the family title to him upon Graham's return to England last year, had given him a few very explicit words of advice. He'd also loaned him explicit books with illustrations. "The key to arousing a woman's passion is to make love with your mind, not merely your body. Woo her with words, not just touch," he'd suggested.

Woo her. Graham scanned the room and spotted a slim china vase holding a bouquet of fresh roses. He went to it, studying the blooms. Instead of a full dozen of one color, they were mixed. White, yellow, red and pink. How curious.

"Take one, please. You may give it to her."

Madame LaFontant's voice startled him. Graham frowned at the vase, then glanced over at the woman in the doorway.

"Why the different colors?"

A mysterious smile touched her mouth, but she gave a casual shrug. "I like color," she said. "Go ahead, choose one to give to your lover."

He went to choose and hesitated. Kenneth frequently gave red roses to his wife, Badra. Red surely meant love. Graham knew no woman could ever love him. Yet the rich, deep crimson called to him. Maybe, just maybe, he could pretend at love. It would make this very personal act less impersonal. But he would add a white rose, to minimize the apparent meaning.

"Might I have two?"

Madame LaFontant's smile deepened. "But of course."

Graham hesitated, then selected a long-stemmed crimson bloom and a white one. As he withdrew them from the vase, a thorn pricked his thumb. Recoiling, he glanced at the scarlet bead on his skin.

"Roses have thorns. Like life, Your Grace. Sweetness and beauty come with a price."

He sucked on his thumb and gave a wry smile. "I don't mind paying a price—as long as I'm not entirely drained."

She laughed and gestured to the door. Graham held

the roses carefully in one hand, his heart hammering with anticipation.

He fiercely hoped the nightmares would end tonight. Holding a woman in his arms, feeling her soft body beneath his naked one, plunging into her wet warmth . . . No more bitter shame or painful memories.

Tonight he'd be a man at last.

Jillian Quigley was one step closer to her dream.

She touched her blond wig, adjusting a stray curl. In this disguise, no one could identity her. Madame La-Fontant's establishment was discreet and paid its women well. And none possessed her most precious commodity.

Virginity. Tonight, for one hundred pounds cash, she would lose it. Anonymously. In the dark, with some uncaring stranger.

Hugging herself, she walked about the expansive room. An ironic smile curved her lips. Losing her precious virginity in a whorehouse—now wouldn't that make Father howl? His daughter he'd ordered to marry the wealthy Bernard Augustine, no longer possessing her saleable asset. Dull Bernard, who constantly cleared his throat and laughed when she began discussing Marshall's economic theories.

After tonight she'd have money to sneak off to America. All her life she'd had one shining dream tucked into her heart. She closed her eyes, inhaling the dusty scent of chalkboards, hearing the bass rumble of the professor's voice, feeling the hardwood seat beneath her. Two years ago, Harvard College had created a women's annex. Radcliffe called to her like a well beckoning a weary, thirsty traveler. Jillian itched to drink from its knowledge. And unlike her father, the teachers wouldn't reprimand her for being smart and a woman.

Long ago Jillian had vowed never to marry a man as emotionally remote as her father. College offered the only hope of escape from the gray shadows of her silent, oppressive home.

She went to the heavy blue brocade drapes, which were drawn against the night and prying eyes from the street below. Her appreciative gaze swept the room, taking in the polished satinwood wardrobe, the delicate tables with their inlaid marble, the soft glow from the leaded crystal lamps. Madame LaFontant specialized in pampering her wealthy clients with surroundings as elegant as their own domiciles, and women who provided every fantasy their wives could not. She glanced at the bed with its rich, soft cotton sheets, and shivered delicately. She hoped her client would be fast, indifferent and uncaring. She just wanted to get it over with, and move on.

Jillian caught sight of herself in the gilded mirror above the gleaming dresser. The lovely peacock-blue gown Madame had loaned her made her exotic, almost attractive. Jillian fingered the low décolleté, flushing at how it revealed the generous, rounded halves of her bosom. Father insisted on her dressing modestly in dull gray. If he could, he'd keep her in sackcloth. Father's invisible, dull Jillian, her reputation sterling, her morals rigid as his own.

Cosmetics now altered her appearance, shadowed eyelids making her eyes appear more blue than green. Dim lighting aided in the disguise. Not that it much mattered. No one would expect to find the earl of Stranton's daughter in a whorehouse.

Heavy footsteps, accompanied by a lighter tread, sounded on the wood floor outside. They paused outside her door, voices murmured, then the lighter steps resumed, walking away. Jillian bit her lip and gathered her courage. Smoothing down her gown, she steeled her spine and faced the door as it opened.

Please don't let him be fat, ugly or make any disgusting noises, she silently prayed. Last-minute panic gripped her in an icy fist.

The door opened and her client stepped inside, slowly closing it behind him. He stood, hands behind his back, quietly gauging her.

Breath seized in her lungs. Jillian stared, spellbound.

She had prayed for a man not too ugly. She hadn't expected one so handsome.

A shock of black hair brushed his starched white collar, spilled across his forehead. His face was classically handsome, yet held strong character in the tempered steel of his jaw and proud nose. His chin was firm and strong, but the mouth hinted at softness with a full, sensual lower lip. A mouth made for kisses.

Jillian pulled back, uncomfortable with the thought. Clearly this was a nobleman of fine breeding. But what had she expected?

He was of medium height, a few inches taller than she, and a hint of muscle showed beneath his finely tailored suit. His eyes were onyx, blacker than the night, and they studied her as intently as she studied him. Dark, soulful eyes with secrets.

Fresh dismay coursed through her. She only wanted to get the deed over with and banish the memory to the deepest corner of her mind. How could she forget this man?

Her mouth went dry. She felt awkward and uncertain. What now? She wasn't sure what he expected. Let him set the pace. If he rushed forward, ripped off her clothing . . . Her quivering hand stroked her beautiful blue gown. He had a commanding presence, but no cruelty shone in those dark eyes. They looked . . . watchful. Speculative.

Finally, he spoke. "Hullo. I'm Graham."

His voice melted over her like warm honey. Dark and deep, but with a rough note. So masculine and solid, like granite. So different from the men in her life. Strikingly solid, especially contrasting to Bernard's pudding softness.

Jillian pushed back a lock of her fake hair, hoping the assorted pins would keep it in place. "I'm Christine." She gave him her middle name.

He nodded and approached, his heels making muffled noises on the thick carpet. "I brought these for you," he said softly.

A slight trembling affected his hand as he gave her the roses. Jillian melted. She closed her eyes, inhaling the flowers' sweet fragrance. "Thank you," she said shyly, opening her eyes to smile at him.

A thoughtful look entered his eyes as he touched a rose petal, then with the same finger stroked her cheek. "Exquisite," he murmured.

He took a rose back from her hand and brushed her cheek with it. "An English rose," he said, "with delicate soft beauty."

Her lips curved into an ironic smile, though her heart skipped at his poetic words. "English roses have sharp thorns," she said. Then Jillian bit her lip, dismayed by her tone.

But he seemed unperturbed. He held up his right thumb, showing a small puncture marked by a rusty dot. "I've already found out. Wounded in the line of duty."

She smiled. "You're quite brave, sir, to risk injury to bring me such a gift."

He nodded. "Yes, quite right. Do you suppose the Queen will knight me for my courage?" A twinkle in his eyes belied his serious tone.

Jillian laughed, her tension fleeing. Graham smiled, showing gleaming white teeth. His entire face had changed, the severe lines softening and making him appear boyish. It was such a drastic difference, and Jillian found herself utterly charmed.

Graham took the other rose from her hand and set them both on a nearby dresser. His smile vanished, replaced by an intent look. He framed her face with large, warm hands.

When he kissed her, so gently she felt as cherished as a bride on her wedding night, Jillian closed her eyes and pretended. Her lips moved beneath his.

Graham deepened the kiss, drinking in her mouth, sipping and tasting. He curled one hand about her nape, holding her still. His tongue probed the closed seam of her lips. Flicked lightly, tracing. A question.

She opened to him like a flower unfurling its petals. An answer.

His tongue slipped inside; he deepened the kiss, tightening his hold on her nape. Like an eager adventurer, he explored her mouth, tasting and nipping at her lower lip. Breath fled her lungs as she melted into him. An odd fullness pooled in her loins.

He broke their kiss, tearing his mouth away with ragged breaths. Jillian stepped back, a little woozy and startled. Her hand flew to her swollen mouth.

"Oh," she whispered.

She hadn't expected to be aroused tonight. Satisfaction gleamed in his gaze.

Knowing what was expected of her, she reached for the fastenings on her gown. Graham slipped behind her and assisted. His fingers felt fumbling, and once he uttered a low curse.

"How the hell do you women manage these things?" he muttered.

Jillian gave a sharp, nervous laugh. "They have men do it?"

A warm chuckle teased her suddenly exposed back. She shivered again as he slid the gown free.

Her stays came next. She loosened the front laces with practiced ease and then shimmied awkwardly out of her chemise and underdrawers . . . and stood before him, naked and unsure.

She was very cold inside.

The woman's body gleamed like alabaster in the dull lamplight. Graham felt his breath hitch.

So beautiful. The face of an angel, with high curved cheekbones and a red, inviting, kiss-swollen mouth. Blond hair hung down to her shoulders—those lackluster curls the only tarnish on her beauty. Huge luminous eyes met his. Blue? In this light, hard to tell. He guessed their color to be a deep sapphire. Her breasts were full, tipped by rosy nipples. Pale, creamy skin begged for his touch.

Her hips were rounded, and there was a slight curve to her belly. Her woman's mound, he noted with surprise, was shaved, showing an inviting glimpse of the treasure between her thighs. That damp hollow he'd dreamed about, dreamed of sinking into wet warmth and feeling a pleasure he'd never experienced . . .

Blood rushed to his groin, causing his slight erection to grow. He hardened to stone. He dimly felt grateful for the reaction. The first hurdle was cleared.

Just kissing her had aroused him. And he'd been pleased at her look of dazed wonder. Although he was a virgin, Graham had some experience with kissing. The widow he'd visited once back in Egypt had been an expert, and had taught him a few very pleasurable things—but when he'd started to undress to complete the act, he'd frozen.

That was years ago, he reminded himself, silently watching Christine blush to the roots of her blond hair. *You can do this now.* Indeed, his eager body assured him he could.

Graham sat on the bed and unlaced his shoes, then began to shed his clothing. When he stood nude, a shiver wracked his body. He hoped she wouldn't notice.

The last time he had stripped before another person . . . Memories asserted themselves. The dirty sheepskins, the stench of old smoke in his flared nostrils. The wrenching pain from behind . . .

His harsh breaths filled the silent room. *I can't do this*, he thought frantically. *She'll know. She'll know!*

Then a sudden, small noise jerked his attention away from his inner torment. Graham realized it had come from her. A tiny, squeaking sob.

He studied her, realizing she shivered more than he did. As if a severe chill or fright had seized her. His nervousness fled. God, she was more scared than he was.

Stepping forward, he took her into his arms and kissed her.

Graham's powerful body frightened Jillian, with its strapping muscles and thrusting phallus. Never before had she faced such intimidating maleness. He seemed carved from hard marble, a wealth of dark hair covering his muscled chest.

She had been unable to prevent a sob of fright from escaping her lips. This was a dreadful mistake. How could she do this? She held no love for this man. No emotions. She'd thought a lack of emotion would make it easier.

Instead, it made it more difficult. She should be doing this with a man she loved. Her lover would take her into his strong arms and kiss her, arousing her passion and easing her fears, and they would unite their bodies and hearts.

No, not this impersonal stiffness, this chilled room with a total stranger. Flesh to flesh. No feelings. No affection. Nothing but an exchange of cash.

13

But then he took her in his arms and kissed her again. Her fears melted a little from his warm, authoritative lips. She closed her eyes and let that tiny bud of sensual pleasure blossom.

Graham lifted her into his arms as if she weighed no more than a feather. With gentle reverence, he laid her on the bed.

She was more beautiful to him than a full moon shining upon Egypt's sands, this woman. Graham marveled at her lush body, the soft places and sweet curves. So soft, compared to the hard muscles of his own body.

He touched her slowly, carefully, mapping her with warm hands, tracing each square inch of her skin. His fingertips trailed over her round, slender shoulders, caressed the knobby points of her collarbone. He sucked in a trembling breath, filled with fresh wonder. A woman's body was so different from a man's, so soft and round and supple, as giving and pliant as the rose petals he'd brushed against her cheek. Bending his head, he kissed the juncture of shoulder and neck, tasting her. He gave a delicate lick. Salty-sweet. A shudder coursed through her and she shifted beneath him. Ah, she was not indifferent to his caresses either.

Soft—so textured and giving. He continued kissing her warm flesh, tensing his own body for better control to keep from ruthlessly plunging into her like a callow youth. His body screamed for release, but his mind wanted to savor the slowness, the newness of his first woman. His mouth trailed a line to the top of one firm breast, and when he encased her hardened nipple with his mouth, she gave a startled cry and arched. Slightly alarmed, he drew back, then realized her cry had been one of pleasure. Instinct urged him on.

He licked and suckled, rasping his tongue over the

pearling peak. Wedged partly beneath him, Christine wriggled and moaned. Her hands fisted in his hair, holding him against her.

Graham let his hands roam her body, feeling each curve, the small ridges and indentations of her ribs, the roundness of her hips. Then his fingers delved into the cleft between her legs. He heard her gasp. Hiding a smile, he found the little jewel mentioned in the books he'd eagerly devoured. His thumb stroked once, twice.

Rewarded by a sharp whimper of pleasure, he continued. He summoned the famous control he'd learned as a warrior in Egypt and tightened his muscles, seeking to give her pleasure first. His tongue flicked hers in rhythm to the small strokes his fingers made. Dewy moisture soon coated them.

He slipped one finger inside her, pleased at her response. Her feminine passage was tight, oh, so very tight. The thought of his member inside her damp, slick sheath nearly drove him crazy. His finger found a barrier—her maidenhead. He drew in a deep breath and thought of something innocuous, as Kenneth had instructed.

Finances. Stock futures they had in the American railroads. He thought of steam locomotives chugging merrily along as she writhed and sobbed and wriggled beneath him as his finger thrust in and out of her, accompanied by wild strokes of his thumb.

He increased the tempo, encouraged by her tiny, excited cries. Then suddenly she tensed and arched. Her flesh convulsed about his finger. Clutching his head to her, she sobbed out.

Jillian gulped down deep breaths, feeling so worn and dazed that she couldn't move. She felt Graham shift, part her thighs with his hands.

He mounted her swiftly, covering her naked body with

his. The roughness of his thick chest hair rasped her tender breasts. Dawning fear mingled with wondrous pleasure as he raised himself above her, his intent gaze locked to hers.

Then he lowered his head, planted a singularly sweet kiss on her brow. She felt an enormous hardness probing the sensitive hollow between her legs and gulped down a steadying breath.

"I'm sorry," he said quietly. Then he pushed into her. The pressure between her legs increased. It felt like a thick iron bar invading her body.

Breath fled her in a startled sob. She tried relaxing, but the sudden pain caught her unexpectedly.

"Hold on to me," he whispered, touching his forehead to hers.

She did, gripping his back, digging her nails into the hard muscles as he pressed deeper. He pushed and pushed and then gave a mighty thrust, sundering her maidenhead.

Jillian gave a small cry. Madame had urged her to, warning gentlemen who liked virgins expected it—but this had not been pretend. Her nails burrowed into Graham's back. A tear slipped from her eye.

Warm lips descended to her cheek, chasing the droplet, kissing it away. The tenderness of the gesture touched her.

Graham remained utterly still. Waiting. Deep, ragged breaths and coiled tension in his muscles warned her how far he'd been pushed. How much control he exerted.

Experimentally, she rotated her hips and felt herself relax around him. Graham let out a rough growl and began moving.

His heart wanted to explode as he sank into her. Ah God! Never had he felt such raging bliss. Never would he forget it, either.

She was hot wet satin encasing him, so tight and warm he wanted to die with shuddering pleasure, as if the sun had wrapped around him, coating him with molten heat. Graham groaned with the effort to remain still. Male instinct nudged him to move, to push and thrust. But concern for her stilled him.

And then he felt the tiny muscles gripping him so tightly relax the slightest bit, and he could wait no longer.

With a strangled groan, he thrust forward once and the floodgates burst. He hoarsely cried out, pumping his seed deep inside her.

The man lay upon her, his muscled weight pressing her into the bed. Deep breaths filled the pillow where he rested his head beside hers. Jillian shifted slightly, marveling at the newness of the experience. Her limbs felt languid and heavy. A burning soreness throbbed between her thighs.

Finally, he lifted his head. His heavy-lidded eyes, gleaming from spent passion, regarded her with pleasure, then widened. "I'm afraid I'm crushing you," he murmured.

"It's quite . . . all right."

Rolling off, he lay beside her. Jillian felt a sticky dampness between her legs. Her blood and his seed. She felt naked and exposed and suddenly chilled, stricken by a wild longing for him to take her back into his arms. But this was a business arrangement and not love, she firmly reminded herself.

To her shock and pleasure, Graham turned toward her and gently drew her into an embrace. Jillian found herself instinctively curling her body against his, burying her face into his broad shoulder.

So he, too, craved warmth and closeness afterward. How simply marvelous that he wasn't cold and indifferent. Regret pierced her. How tragic that they would never see each other again.

Graham shifted and touched her cheek. "Are you in much pain?" he murmured.

Embarrassed by such an intimate question, Jillian made a noncommittal answer. Graham shifted and left the bed. She heard water splashing in the adjacent water closet. When he emerged, he held a clean, wet towel and a fresh dry one.

Before she could utter a protest, he gently parted her legs and pressed the towel there. Her cheeks burned, but the cool dampness soothed the sting.

His thoughtfulness threatened her with fresh tears. Jillian murmured her thanks and lay still. She felt him remove the towel and gently dry her off.

"Are you all right?" he asked, his dark eyes filled with concern.

She offered a contented smile. "The last part was not quite so nice, but the first part . . . I felt like I waltzed in heaven."

He gave her a thoughtful look. "Yes, I suppose dancing in paradise is an apt comparison."

It was over now. He'd leave and she'd follow soon after, perhaps giving herself a few minutes to collect her bittersweet thoughts. But instead of pausing to pull on his clothing, Graham lifted the sheet and slid back into bed.

He gathered her in his arms again and lay there, staring at the ceiling, silent.

Her natural shyness had faded during the act with this stranger, but this seemed even more intimate than sharing their bodies. But as his big, powerful body radiated warmth, she naturally drew closer, curling herself about him like a sleepy kitten.

Her eyes closed and she struggled against sleep . . . and lost, drifting away in a hazy cloud. A thought nudged her, that she must do something before she slept, but it was gone as she found slumbering contentment.

Graham woke up to the light of a grayish dawn peeking through a slit in the brocade drapes. Startled, he blinked and tried to assess his surroundings. Something soft and warm lay beside him. A woman. Now he remembered.

Far more shocking than spending the night in a whore-house was a delightful realization. He'd slept the entire night deeply. No dreams!

Wild joy surged through him. Not one single nightmare. He'd slept at last!

Filled with happiness, he gave a small shout then quieted, realizing she still slept. Graham grinned and turned toward the woman who'd made this wondrous possibility come to life. It was *her*; he knew it. Making love with her had banished his nightmare of the emerald-eyed redhead that haunted him these few months past. Hungrily he caressed her face with his gaze. Relaxed in sleep, she appeared more youthful and childlike than the previous night.

Lush pink lips parted slightly as she breathed. Long, sooty lashes feathered her pale cheeks. He gently touched one winged, dark brow.

When he pulled away, black dusted his thumb. Graham frowned and rubbed a little harder. He stared at the red-gold brow. His gaze drifted to her hair. Sudden dread pooled in his gut. One shy strand of golden fire peeped out among the coarse blond strands—a wig.

Small wonder her hair had felt stiff and coarse compared to the rest of her! With a growl, he ran a finger up her brow and encountered a rough-edged surface. Graham pulled out the stray lock of golden flame.

The woman woke, blinking sleepily at his look of dazed horror. Eyes wide, she grasped her blond locks in a futile attempt to keep them planted.

In a moment he'd rolled atop her. Sex was not his intention as his frantic fingers grasped her head covering. He sought the pins holding it in place and yanked them free. A strangled breath caught in the woman's throat as he yanked the wig away.

Flame-colored tresses tumbled down, free at last. Graham stared wildly at the woman's face then rolled off, running for the window. With a hasty yank of the drape cord, sunlight flooded the room. He ran back, scanning her face.

Red-gold hair. Green eyes—not the blue eyes he'd imagined last night.

"Oh God! It's you!" he rasped, his heart thundering in his chest.

The nightmare hadn't ceased, after all. It had only just begun.

Chapter Two

Caught. Fully awake, Jillian touched her hair in panic. He knew. He knew who she was! She stared at him with a plea in her eyes, and he backed away as if she were Medusa with snakes wriggling in her head.

"Please," she said, hating the tremulousness of her voice. "I can explain."

He jerked away from her, snatching his rumpled clothing from the floor. He shoved his legs into his trousers and fastened them, then donned socks and shoes.

She couldn't bear him running off like this—as if she were his worst nightmare and the sweetness and passion of last night did not exist. If he did, she'd truly feel what the experience of selling her virginity made her: a whore.

"Graham," she said in a stronger tone. "Look at me!"

He turned, thrusting his arms into his shirt. Anger shone in his dark eyes, turning them to chips of onyx. She shrank back. His voice was ominously quiet, controlled and more threatening than if he'd shouted.

"I explicitly requested not to be with a redhead. Any woman but a redhead with green eyes."

Bewilderment mingled with relief. He did not know her identity.

"I know," she admitted quietly.

His icy gaze riveted to hers, he went still. This eerie motionlessness scared her more than his previous anger. She clutched the sheet to her breasts.

"You tricked me," he said.

"I had no choice. All arrangements were made previously with Madame. I was desperate."

He moved with ruthless power onto the bed and seized her chin in one strong hand. The tender lover had vanished, replaced by a dangerous stranger whose iron grip held her captive. Her insides quivered in remembrance of those strong hands touching her with slow gentleness, rousing sweet fire. His fury scared her, but she did not drop her gaze.

"Why were you desperate? Who are you?" he demanded.

"I needed money. I must remain anonymous. I dare not reveal my real identity."

He studied her. "You cannot hide being a well-bred lady. Do I know you?"

Jillian hoped he didn't hear the wild thudding of her heart. "Perhaps, my lord. We move in the same circles. So let us remain as we are now—two strangers sharing one night, faces in the dark. A memory best forgotten."

"Forgotten," he echoed. His gaze narrowed. "Damn it, I want to forget you. But bloody hell, I know I will not."

Then he drew her face to his and kissed her ruthlessly. His lips moved over hers, coaxing a response. Jillian released a frustrated sob and flung her arms around his neck, dragging him closer, needing his heat, his passion.

When Graham tore himself away, Jillian put a hand to

her kiss-swollen mouth, longing tearing through her. How could one man make her feel this way? He aimed a look at her so piercing, it arrowed into her like a knife.

Gulping in a harsh breath, he said, "We must never see each other again." And grabbing his jacket, he whirled and left, slamming the door with such violence the hinges rattled.

Jillian was left alone, naked on the bed. A chill seized her. She was a whore.

In the Egyptian desert, he had been known as Panther, the silent cat that hunted prey alone. Never socializing with other warriors, never joining them around the crackling bonfires at night to laugh and exchange boasting tales of virility and fearlessness in battle. He'd stalked, keeping to the periphery of the fire's reddish glow, just outside the circle of men and light and warmth. Always hiding in the shadows, a nocturnal creature who hated and feared the night but ultimately could not resist it.

Like the panther, Graham was smaller than other predators but had powerful muscles that could strike an enemy with quick, killing blows. He had adapted out of a pure instinct for survival. This ability had served him well when he finally accepted his heritage and came home to England, leaving the desert, its draining heat and bitter memories, to shapeshift into the role of duke.

He'd forced himself to transform from a simple desert warrior into a sophisticated duke. Yet inside, he had not changed. He prowled the margins of a different campfire now—the glittering balls and London fetes, with their sparkling crystal and equally sparkling conversation. Smiling and nodding, he maintained an aloof yet polite presence. It had created an aura of mystery that ladies found irresistible, and it hid his inner torment, camouflaging his pain much as a thorn tree's leaves disguised a panther.

But once in a great while, his carefully cultivated composure cracked. A face seen in a crowd could cull shameful memories, and the duke would dissolve from fierce jungle cat into wounded kitten; a scared little boy trapped in Egypt, sobbing for the parents he'd seen brutally killed, who'd been dragged into the dark interior of a black tent where an evil predator had pounced upon him. A terrified child who only wanted to scream and scream . . .

During those times, Graham would shudder. He'd fight the childish compulsion to shriek; he'd gulp down deep, calming breaths. He'd flee to a deep place inside himself where no one would witness his shame, and would force the outside world to see only a man with a tight smile.

He had not experienced one of those episodes, outside of the usual dreams, in more than a year. Until now. Until the woman he had taken in the fierce heat of desire turned out to be his living nightmare.

The violent tremors affecting him since fleeing Madame LaFontant's had ceased. By the time the hackney cab reached his home in Mayfair, he was able to present his usual quiet control to the stiff-spined footmen attending the massive oaken door. Disappearing upstairs to his expansive rooms at the end of the long corridor, he firmly shut the door behind him. Graham shoved a trembling hand through his damp hair.

The redhead in his dreams. Emerald eyes. How could it be?

Fate, his inner voice mocked. She is your fate. Your destiny. Yes, said his superstitious Egyptian upbringing. His formative years had been spent molded by tales of wicked jinn haunting the desert sands. His English side scorned such ideas and pushed the thought aside.

Striding to his dressing room, he stripped off his clothing, balling it up and tossing it onto the floor. Nude, he padded over to the adjoining water closet and splashed cold water into the basin. Graham doused his face and flung back his head, spraying droplets onto the mirror. His face, pale and drained, stared back at him.

He glanced downward and flinched at the dried scarlet on his thighs and his soft member. Her virgin's blood marked him.

With a low curse, he wet a towel and scrubbed himself vigorously, but guilt assailed him at the thought of taking her innocence and the callous way he'd abandoned her, lying in bed, looking at him with those wide green eyes stamped with hurt. Treating her like a whore.

But she tricked me!

Graham tossed aside the towel, padded naked into his dressing room and snagged the fresh clothing his valet had laid out the previous night. He dressed quickly in a crisp white shirt with a starched collar, black and gray silk trousers, black cravat, a double-breasted charcoal gray and black vest, a gray morning coat and patent leather shoes. The gilded mirror showed a dark-haired, dark-eyed, expressionless aristocrat in proper English dress. It did not show the violent turmoil churning inside.

He went downstairs in search of food and calming routine.

The pale yellow, cheerful breakfast room was empty. On a polished sideboard, silver hot plates contained his favorite dishes. Graham selected freshly scrambled eggs, a warm muffin dripping with golden butter and four strips of crisp bacon. He sat and picked up the *London Times* lying in its accustomed place and buried himself in it.

"Tea, Your Grace?"

Graham peered around the paper at the footman. The servants knew he drank strong, bitter Arabic coffee each morning, one reminder of his Egyptian life he'd not relinquished.

"There's no more coffee?"

"I'm so very sorry, Your Grace. Your brother drank it all. Cook is sending someone to the market for more. I can go myself next door right now and borrow some if you want. . . ."

"Never mind." Graham ducked behind his newspaper again, scanning headlines. Another aristocratic London family was auctioning off their valuables. A wealthy American named Henry Flagler had built a railroad from Jacksonville, Florida, to some godforsaken place called Biscayne Bay.

Graham devoured this second piece of news with interest. American railroads were a good investment. But the family's losses in the Baltimore & Ohio were beginning to pinch; they needed to recoup their money. Still, things weren't too terrible. He was rich enough to buy a virgin for one night of enchanting pleasure . . . and then wake to the horror that he'd eagerly bedded the witch of his nightmares. His fingertips trailing over her skin, soft as rose petals . . . His heart pounded as he remembered her throaty cries of pleasure, the searing heat as he took her.

It was just sex, he firmly admonished himself. As hot and sweet as it had been, only sex. Nothing more. Surely he'd feel the same with any other woman.

He returned his attention to the paper, forcing himself to concentrate. A clanking noise made him set down the broadsheet. Graham glanced up as the downstairs maid shuffled past, carrying a coal bucket. Her head was down. Shy and timid. He remembered Kenneth's warning about being friendly with servants and dismissed it. A civil greeting couldn't hurt.

Graham lowered his paper and watched her set the bucket down. She began to shovel coal into the grate, her head turned away like a shy bird.

He offered a brief, friendly smile. "Good morning."

The little maid stared, then a hesitant smile touched her lips. She bobbed an awkward curtsy. "Good morning, Yer Grace. I'll have yer fire all nice and cozy soon."

Fires in the summer—a necessary luxury after living in Egypt for years. He watched the delicate blue flame catch and the coals begin to glow. His thoughts turned back to this very room where he'd shared breakfast with his indulgent parents. Graham smiled, lost in memory. Raspberry tarts. He'd loved those.

"A warm tart . . ." he mused aloud.

He heard a gasp and, glancing over, was startled to see the maid's blue eyes widen. "Ye like tarts, Yer Grace?"

"Oh yes." He smiled, remembering. "Licking their centers, having that delicious sweetness flood your mouth . . ."

She moistened her lips. "Ye like to tongue tarts, Yer Grace?"

"Yes. Perhaps I should ask Cook to accommodate me."

A look of comic incredulity filled the maid's face. "*Her?* I can serve ye, Yer Grace. It'd be my pleasure."

And to his astounded shock, the maid set her shovel down and bustled to his side. She leaned down, pressing her ample breasts against him. "Yer Grace. Yer such a fine, strapping man, fit to warm a girl's bed. It's so cold in the attic."

Graham felt a strangled breath escape. "I'll fetch you a blanket," he said.

Her hand reached into his lap and fondled him. He gasped, but his cock gave an interested twitch.

"You like tarts. I like yer sausage," she purred. "Care for a table-ender? Right quick?"

"I beg your pardon?" he gasped. Beneath her eager, massaging hand, his cock jerked again.

"Cor, blimey—it's a big, thick sausage," she said with an admiring gaze. He didn't know whether to reprimand or thank her.

She rubbed her generous breasts against him. His body tightened, but not with the raging desire he'd experienced last night. Last night had been tender, passionate. This felt lustful, tawdry. The knowledge filled him with fresh dread. He needed to forget that redheaded witch, but his body could not.

He grabbed the maid's hands, trying to escape the hold she had on his nether parts. "There's been a misunderstanding," he said.

Firm footsteps sounded on the hardwood floor, clicking toward the breakfast room. Graham looked up as his brother appeared in the doorway. The little maid released a shocked gasp and fled, snagging her coal bucket as she ran. Kenneth's puzzled gaze followed her, then shot back to his brother. He slid into a chair next to him.

"What happened?"

"The downstairs maid . . . squeezed my sausage," Graham rasped.

Kenneth gave him an exasperated look. "The help? Surely you wouldn't . . ."

"I would not," Graham shot back, offended. "All I did was mention how much I once loved tarts. . . ."

Kenneth stared. "Good God, Graham! Didn't I warn you about being friendly with servants? Don't you know that in street language, tart means a woman?"

Graham felt a flush flood his face. "Obviously not," he muttered. "She thought I wanted to lick her . . ." He buried his head in his hands and groaned. He peered out through splayed fingers. "What's a table-ender?"

"Sexual intercourse on a table."

Graham groaned again.

Kenneth grinned. "It can be quite the thing, but I wouldn't recommend it on a table with dishes. Rattles the china, you know. Speaking of, er, the topic, any news to share?"

Forcing himself to recover his composure, Graham gave his brother a level look. He drank some tea, grimacing. An Englishman he might appear, but he hated this insipid drink. Oh, for a cup of strong, bracing coffee . . . "Only the news that you drank all my coffee. Again."

His brother shrugged and picked up Graham's muffin, nibbling the edges. He said, "I'm an expectant father, what do you want? I'm drinking for three. Myself, Badra and the baby."

"You must store coffee like a camel stores water. And you're clearly eating for three as well," Graham admonished, snatching the muffin away and tossing it back on the blue-veined plate. "Keep eating like that and you'll grow larger than this house. Or your wife."

Kenneth lifted a mocking brow and patted his flat stomach. "Always room for more. And as for my wife—as soon as we're done with this one, we're going to have another."

Graham shook his head. "Give the poor woman a rest, man, in between filling all those empty nursery rooms upstairs," he advised. A fond smile touched his mouth, then he glanced at the ceiling, frowning. "How is Badra? She hasn't been down for meals in two days. Is she well?"

He knew his brother well enough by now to discern the worry darkening Kenneth's eyes. "Tired. Fretting. The doctor said the baby should be here any day. She's ready. More than ready." He blew out a breath. "So am I."

Graham felt awkward. He sensed Kenneth's anxiety, but didn't know how to offer reassurance. "She'll be fine," he said crisply.

"I know she will. Enough of this." He stretched his legs and tapped fingers on the white lace tablecloth. "How did you fare last night?"

The question, asked casually, masked Kenneth's anxiousness, but Graham knew it was there. He leaned back with a rueful smile, remembering the act. "I fared . . . quite well."

Delight shone in his brother's eyes. Graham felt a deep wave of affection. This brother he'd only just begun to know this past year. This brother he'd once considered an enemy. This brother he'd never see again once the deed was done and he swung from the gallows. . . .

Kenneth gave a great shout and slapped him on the back. "I knew it! Congratulations." Then he looked around hastily and reddened. "Sorry. So tell me, did everything go as planned? No mishaps?"

His smile slipped as Graham fisted his hands and said, "Just one or two. She had red hair. Green eyes. Like the nightmare."

Kenneth looked shocked. "Damn it!"

Graham nodded. "She—the woman—was wearing a wig. And in the dim light, the color of her eyes was difficult to discern."

"I'm sorry, Graham. I didn't—"

"Why should you apologize? If not for you pushing me into this . . ." He shrugged. "The goal was accomplished, and most pleasantly, I might add. Of course, I woke this morning and realized I'd been duped."

His brother's glance was sharp. "You slept there?"

"All night." Graham sighed. "All night through," he said significantly.

Kenneth's eyes widened to saucers. "No nightmares?"

"None."

Kenneth clung to the topic like a puppy with a bone. "Perhaps . . . It sounds like she's the *answer* to your dreams," he suggested, studying Graham.

Graham snorted derisively. "My worst nightmare?"

"Graham, there's a reason why things happen the way they do. I believe it. And you do as well. Destiny."

Graham started to protest, then stopped, staring at his plate. Both he and his brother, raised in separate Egyptian tribes when their parents were murdered during a caravan attack, held fast to their superstitious Bedouin upbringing. They could no more erase that than they could change their English genes.

"You're still attending the Huntlys' ball tonight?"

"Yes," Graham said quietly. "Social obligations."

"Well, you've trained enough. You almost sound completely English again. You eat like an Englishman—you even waltz far better than I. No one can tell you were raised in Egypt. And heaven knows you're as stiff-spined as an Englishman," Kenneth joked.

When Graham was reunited with Kenneth last year in Egypt, he had agreed to return to England with him, his new wife, Badra, and her daughter, Jasmine. They'd gone to the family estate in Yorkshire. From there, Kenneth circulated an elaborate story about Graham's past to make his acceptance back into society more secure. In the quiet countryside, Graham studied English mannerisms, etiquette and lost most of his Egyptian accent. The first few balls and parties in London this past month had proven successful. But waltzing with debutantes was far easier than dancing with the devil of his nightmares. . . .

Kenneth's blue eyes were sharp. "You think he will be there, now that the Season has fully arrived—that redheaded nobleman . . . what did you say the al-Hajid called him? Al-Hamra?"

31

"Yes. *The red one*. I have other names for him."

"He might not be there tonight."

"The entire *ton* attends the Huntlys' fete. I'm certain he'll be there. He lives in London, Kenneth. I'm positive it was him I saw last year in the square."

Last year, before he'd set aside the life of an Egyptian warrior and revealed his true heritage, Graham had visited London. While walking in the park he saw a red-headed nobleman he felt certain was al-Hamra. Unable to stomach the idea of facing his tormentor, he had fled in shaky panic back to Egypt, where he'd remained hidden, vowing never to return to England. It had taken a great deal of encouragement from Kenneth and Badra to coax him back. He had too much shame, too much fear.

Now that he'd returned and begun relearning the English life, his shame had slowly dissolved into bitter anger. Al-Hamra must be stopped from preying on other desperate, helpless children. And an idea had suddenly crystallized, like a caul lifting from his face. He'd seen the installation of himself as duke with fresh purpose: to mingle at the balls of his first Season, and then reveal his past . . .

"Graham, all the *ton* thinks you were raised by an eccentric, doting English couple who traveled throughout Arabia. Besides, you were only eight years old when he . . . when . . . you know. He couldn't possibly recognize you."

Graham lifted his tormented gaze to his brother. "I'm not worried about him recognizing me. I'm worried that . . ."

He'd nearly slipped. He compressed his lips.

His brother leaned forward, his look compassionate. "Are you worried you'll run away like you did before?"

The words were not intended as an insult, but Graham felt their piercing sting. "I'm not worried I'll run. This time, I'm worried that once I recognize him . . ." He gave a smile as chilled as he felt. "I'll kill him."

She had always been a good girl. Proper, quiet and polite. *Yes, Father*. No outward temper. Spine straight, molded by her father's will. A ghost of herself. A red brick wall hiding silent fire. Inside, how she burned and raged. Never outside. Never.

Jillian tapped her morning egg with the knife edge, hard quick taps like a chick trying to break free from the shell.

There were always hard-boiled eggs at Lord Stranton's household, because her father wanted only hard-boiled eggs for breakfast. One day, she promised herself, she'd have eggs scrambled. Perhaps with a dash of pepper tossed in, and hard cheese. She'd taken a far greater step toward freedom last night.

The Earl of Stranton grunted as he whacked his egg with neat, precise strokes. His shock of red hair going gray was balding, and he had a body that was razor thin and a pasty complexion. His brilliant green eyes were like her own. And they missed nothing. Jillian felt her pulse quicken with dread. Could he know what she'd done?

She thought of the money earned, carefully hidden in her room. So much money, all for a night of passion in a stranger's arms. A stranger she could not forget.

Her jaw clenched and she stared with nausea at her egg. In tiny bites, she began to eat. Jillian thought of the loose board upstairs in her room hiding other secrets. Soon she'd be in America. Adventure. College. Life. That dreadful finishing school Father had insisted would mold her into a model wife for a rich aristocrat had only whetted her appetite for learning.

Surely in America someone would listen to her thoughts, be respectful. In this house, Jillian felt like furniture covered in Holland sheets—preserved under drapings of civility until her father could marry her off to the highest bidder.

She tried filling the uncomfortable silence with talk: "I understand that the Americans built a rail through Florida, Father. Mr. Flagler ended the line at some dreadful swampland they call Miami. It's fascinating how they continue to expand. Do you think any development will follow?"

Silence still. One might as well talk to the wallpaper. Jillian tried again, pushing back an ache in her throat. Her father never listened. . . .

"Mr. Dow in America has created a fascinating new standard called the Dow Jones Industrial Average. I do think the American depression will end soon, with their presidential election. Father, do you think diversity is an important factor in maintaining one's finances? Aunt Mary says if her husband had diversified his American investments more, she'd not be in such dire financial straits. . . ."

Now he did turn and look, his piercing gaze homing in on her. Silence hung in the air once more, razor sharp and deadly. Jillian shrank back.

"Yes, your aunt Mary. Jillian, you failed to ask me permission to spend the night at her house. When I returned last night and your mother told me, I was very upset."

The lie she'd told her mother, using her favorite aunt as an alibi, was about to meet its reckoning. Jillian gathered her courage and boldly met his look. "I'm twenty-two, Father, and not a child. Surely I may be allowed out for a night now and then."

There! She'd done it. Her palms grew clammy as she fisted them in her lap. The deed was done. She felt both exhilarated and fearful. Never before had she spoken back.

Lord Stranton set his coffee cup down very carefully

and placed both hands upon the table. He smiled at his wife from across the endlessly long table. But Jillian knew that smile; the Earl of Stranton never raised his voice. He only gave a chilling smile that struck terror into her bones. . . .

Jillian's frantic gaze whipped to her mother, who blanched. Oh, dear God, no, please . . .

"Sylvia, you've been neglecting that rose garden you claim to love so much, as you've neglected controlling our child in my absence. The bushes are quite overgrown and thorny. Disciplined pruning is necessary for growing anything, be it a garden or a willful child. Isn't it, my dear?"

"Please, Reginald." Her mother's voice quavered.

Lord Stranton beckoned to the attending footman. "James, fetch the pruning shears. Take all the downstairs staff with you to the garden. I want every single rosebush cut down. Immediately. To the roots."

She could not allow her mother to take her punishment. Ignoring her racing pulse, Jillian forced herself to speak. "Father, please—it's my fault. I should have told you. Don't blame Mother, she had nothing to do with it."

The earl focused his attention on the footman. "Immediately, James. Cut them all down. And burn them."

"Yes, my lord," the footman responded.

A lump rose in Jillian's throat as she watched the servant march out of the breakfast room. Her mother lowered her eyes to the table, but not before Jillian saw a faint glimmer of tears. Yet Lady Stranton would not allow her husband to see them.

Familiar bleakness filled Jillian. She concentrated on eating, but could not push back her anger and fear. Darkness pressed behind her eyelids. The old nightmare bobbed to the surface. A door quietly closing, a key turning in a lock, a low cry of pain . . .

Jillian bit her lip, willing away the darkness. She must keep that door closed forever. She didn't want to know what secrets lay behind it.

"Now, Jillian, your schedule. I'm freeing you from your usual visits this afternoon. I want you primped and polished for the Huntlys' ball tonight. And for Mr. Augustine." Her father regarded her mildly over the rim of his coffee cup, but there was no mistaking the iron will in that tone. This was an order, stated as precisely as by a military commander.

"Yes, Father, I will be at the Huntlys' ball tonight."

"Good. Mr. Augustine has formally asked for your hand, and I have accepted. I told him I will announce your betrothal tonight."

Jillian's mouth went dry. Something inside her cried out. *Tell him you cannot marry Bernard! Say no, just for once!* The linen napkin crumpled in her sweaty palms. She moved her lips, then heard herself saying in a small voice:

"Yes, Father."

Revulsion clutched her stomach. She stared at her egg, the cracked shell. She was not a silent fire roaring inside. She was an egg, whose fragile outer shell hid even greater softness. So weak. Oh, so very weak.

This is why I have to leave.

It was too late for her mother. Jillian glanced at the silent countess, aching at the purple shadows beneath the woman's large blue eyes, the hollows in her cheeks. Jillian could not bear to leave her, yet Aunt Mary promised she would be watched over. Her father's sister, who'd encouraged Jillian to seek out Madame LaFontant to earn the money she needed to flee. They had worked out the arrangements together, waiting for the time when the earl would be gone from his house on one of the excursions he took to settle matters at his estate in Derbyshire.

"She owns one of the most elegant brothels in London. You'll be well-treated, Jillian," Mary had assured her.

Now, one more ball and then she'd leave.

But until then she must be scrupulously careful not to arouse her father's suspicions. Act as normal as possible, be the obedient, mindless daughter he knew.

Soon, she promised herself, clutching her napkin in her lap, twisting and turning the linen. Soon she would be free.

When breakfast was over, Jillian politely excused herself and fled into the quiet sanctuary of the library. Closing the door, she leaned against it with a trembling sigh, inhaling deeply the scent of leather-bound learning.

Here was peace. Here was knowledge. Her haven.

She settled into an overstuffed wing chair with a volume of Alfred Marshall's *Principles of Economics*. Her fingers lovingly stroked the heavy tome. Yet for once, the words failed to hold her attention. Instead, she kept seeing the man from last night. Graham.

A burning soreness existed between her legs, and thoughts filled her head. Passion unleashed in a stranger's arms, her keening cry filling the air as he brought her to mindless pleasure. One night with a handsome man who'd paid dearly for what her husband would have had for free. Graham's face, taut with desire, swam before her. His tender care. His hard body nestling into hers.

His angry face when he'd discovered her trick. Jillian's insides clenched. Who was he? A nobleman with a taste for innocence? Whatever he was, his handling of her had been gentle, tender, with none of the harshness or dismissal she'd expected.

She thought of his seed inside her, of a secret, tiny bud begun in a moist garden. But her monthly courses had just ended and she had taken the herb mixture Madame assured her prevented conception. She had not taken any chances.

Soon, she promised herself. Very soon she would be free and in America.

"You can't kill him, Graham."

Kenneth would not give up. All day he had hounded Graham, chasing him down, trying to coax him into talking about the subject Graham was determined not to discuss. Oh, how he regretted having let those words slip!

His brother leaned against the closed door, worry crinkling his brow as they stood in Graham's expansive dressing room. Graham studied his reflection in the gilded mirror. The evening wear hung in crisp lines on his frame. He looked English, but inside he was still Egyptian—a warrior trained to exact swift, certain revenge.

Thick silence hung in the air between them. Graham ran a finger along his tight cravat. All these years remaining hidden, a panther lurking in disguise, fearing to show his true identity. That panther was ready now to strike.

The valet returned, silently gathering up discarded clothing. Kenneth switched to speaking Arabic, a language both brothers knew and none of the servants did.

"You can't do it, Graham. You're not a warrior anymore. You can't just brandish your scimitar, demanding justice."

A humorless smile touched Graham's lips. "Yes, a pistol would be more efficient." He considered. "Though not as painful."

"You can't kill him. As much as that damn bastard deserves it." Kenneth's voice remained mild, but two lines channeled his brow. He looked very troubled.

"Perhaps not. Castration is much more appropriate. Are there any redheaded eunuchs?" But the little joke did not cause his brother to smile.

"Hire someone," he blurted out. "Have the bastard beaten senseless or even killed on a street corner, but don't do it your—"

"No. This is personal. I must do it myself."

"Then what, Graham? Damn it, I don't like the idea of this jackal walking the streets free and untroubled any more than you. But this is England, not Egypt. There are laws." His brother was nearly shouting.

"There are laws in the desert as well," Graham quietly reminded him. "The punishments a bit more primitive, one might say, but quite effective."

"If you're caught, you'll be imprisoned and hanged." Kenneth's lean, handsome face twisted with grief. "All those years thinking you were dead, Graham. All those damn wasted years. I won't lose you again, not like this. You're family, and I love you as much as I love my own wife and child."

His brother freely admitted now how much he cared. He didn't deserve such affection. His soul was as dark as the interior of a cold Egyptian tomb. He had ruthlessly killed before, and he would kill again. Any woman who dared to grow close would cringe in disgust if she knew who he was inside. Yet Kenneth and Badra, and Jasmine, they all kept trying to coax him into their little happy place of life and love. Graham resisted, allowing them only to crack open the door so he could see inside.

It was for the best. Because when English society knew Graham's secret, only Kenneth's wealth and position would enable him and his family to hold their heads high. In this society, money mattered more than honor, Graham thought cynically.

Worry gnawed at him. The family finances had been so shaky as of late. Losses in the Baltimore & Ohio truly had been staggering. Agricultural prices were down and the harvest had been poor. Yet, Kenneth seemed optimistic they would recover. They must, if Graham's plan were to succeed. They must for his brother's sake.

Though not born to his deep sense of Bedouin honor, it flowed in his veins. He wanted to protect his family from scandal. Yet his only chance for redemption was eliminating the beast. Al-Hamra would die, shamed before his peers, his vile behavior revealed. Even though exposing him before the beau monde would mean exposing Graham's own shame.

That shame would die with him on the hangman's gallows. While he did not covet death, he welcomed an end to the pain.

Graham studied the worried blue eyes meeting his in the gilded mirror. He swallowed past a thick lump clogging his throat. Kenneth had Badra and Jasmine. They could not understand the blackness inside him.

He forced a smile and spoke in English. "Don't fret. There promises to be quite a crush at Huntly's. If he is there, I'll probably not see him."

But as the valet moved to adjust his cuffs, he caught his brother's expression in the mirror. They both knew it was only a matter of time.

Graham waited until both the valet and his brother departed; then he glided to the far wall of his bedchamber. Depressing a notch in the pine paneling, he sprang the mechanism that revealed the hidden compartment. The old house was filled with such secrets.

A large cedar wood casket sat in the wall niche. Graham fished a key from the tallboy drawer and opened the box. Riches lay inside: half of a papyrus map that led to buried treasure but was useless without its missing mate, a yellowed photograph of his parents, stacks of pound notes. Graham had resolved never again to be caught without money. Glancing at the photo with familiar grief, he caressed it. His mother's serene brown eyes stared back at him.

Such a lovely child, your Graham, her friends had said. He looks like you, dear Miranda. So pretty.

Such a pretty boy, the low, evil whisper taunted.

Graham's stomach clenched. The papyrus map led to a gold statue and a priceless emerald buried deep in the Egyptian desert. Al-Hamra had the missing half.

Graham pushed aside his anger and regrets and dug to the box's bottom. He unwrapped a palm-sized oblong object from its shroud of indigo, set it on the tallboy then replaced the casket and closed the wall panel. Then he picked up the leather-sheathed object and studied it.

Unlike the *jambiya* he'd carried in Egypt, this knife had been custom-made. It was small and thin enough to hide inside a man's cuff. And to slip down into his palm.

He pocketed the dagger and walked out of the dressing room, then stalked down the hallway to attend the Huntlys' ball.

Chapter Three

A gray ghost stared back at her in the looking glass as Jillian regarded herself draped in dull gray silk. Tiny beads of perspiration dotted her forehead. She tried to take a deep breath but was restricted by her whalebone corset.

Her maid finished tugging the fabric into place. Jillian suppressed a grimace. The unfashionable ball gown had a high-necked bodice and rigid lines. Just once she longed to wear emerald green, to show off her bare shoulders and the faint sprinkling of freckles across them. Freckles that had been concealed by the brothel's dim light.

Did Graham like freckles? In a different life would his lips caress each one, blessing the tiny spots with the heated brush of his mouth?

Graham, that handsome nobleman who'd taken her virginity. His voice had held a slight accent she didn't recognize, but his bearing and stature convinced her he held a position of great wealth and importance. How terribly embarrassing if he were there tonight.

How terribly delicious as well.

Jillian smoothed her gown. Ivory lace dripped from the capped sleeves. Her hair, drawn up, was arranged so tightly her head pounded. Lord Stranton insisted on severe hairstyles to overcome the handicap of red hair. She rebelliously tugged free a few strands.

At Radcliffe, she wouldn't wear a corset, she decided.

In the carriage, she sat across from her father and next to her chaperone, Aunt Mary. Her mother had remained in her room all day, begging off with a headache. Jillian eagerly turned to her aunt, the only person who ever listened to her.

"I read that Mr. Dow has published his industrial average. He also created a railroad average," she remarked.

Her aunt gave her a questioning look. "Do you think railway stocks are still a worthy investment?"

"I don't think they all will lean toward receivership like the Baltimore & Ohio. I'm more interested in the United States presidential campaign. That will be quite telling."

Her aunt glanced at Jillian's father, who was staring in brooding silence out the carriage window. She lowered her voice. "How so?"

"Mr. Bryan is advocating the silver standard. Mr. McKinley supports the gold standard."

"And whom do you think will win?"

Jillian frowned. "Mr. McKinley. He supports American mercantile and industrial interests, and those remain the real power in America. Besides, ever since the Sherman Silver Purchase Act was repealed, how can anyone seriously consider backing currency with silver?"

"Gold, then, is what Mr. Pepperton should consider?"

"Mr. Pepperton was wise to sell his shares in the silver mines when he did."

"Mr. Pepperton received good advice," Mary murmured.

Jillian hid a smile. The mythical Mr. H. M. Pepperton

was a character Mary had created after the death of her American husband. Horace had left her a small inheritance, from which Mary's solicitor allocated her a very modest income. Jillian began fantasizing that Mr. Pepperton had already doubled Mary's money by sinking it into various investments or selling stocks accordingly.

"Mr. Pepperton receives good advice because he listens to his counselor—even if she is a woman," Jillian suggested.

As if he'd finally caught on to their conversation, her father turned to Jillian with a frown. His harsh gaze rested on her. Critical. Judging. Assessing her as if she were artwork at auction.

"How many times must I warn you to stop this prattling, Jillian? Nothing offends a man more than a woman who pretends to be as intelligent as a man. I expect you to be a paragon of respectability tonight. Your betrothal to Mr. Augustine is important to me. I need his help getting my reform bill passed in the House of Commons. I've a chance to advance my political career if it is approved. In return for your hand, he's promised a healthy marriage settlement."

Jillian felt more like a whore than she had last night, sold to replenish her father's dwindling coffers. She felt a palm rest atop her gloved hand and glanced down. Mary gave her hand a quick, comforting squeeze.

The carriage halted abruptly. Jillian disembarked and her kid slippers trod noiselessly upon the red carpet leading to the Huntlys' front entrance. She forced a smile as she passed through the portico of the elaborate Mayfair mansion, flanked by her redheaded father in his white tie and tails, and her dark-haired aunt in black bombazine. In the withdrawing room, she removed her outerwear, feeling like a bird stripped of its feather, but her smile remained frozen on her face as they descended the sweeping mahogany staircase into the ballroom, and as the majordomo announced them in booming tones.

Crystal chandeliers sparkled overhead, casting soft light upon the dozens of couples swirling around the dance floor. Women's skirts billowed in graceful arcs of silk, satin, lace and taffeta. Like colorful flowers unfurling, Jillian thought dimly.

Guided by her aunt, she settled near a cluster of tight-lipped matrons. The chaperones sharply eyed their young charges for hands straying too far, or for gentlemen desiring to kiss more than simple gloved fingers.

Her lace fan, its ivory sticks clenched tightly in Jillian's hand, remained folded. Her dance card dangled from her white-gloved wrist. Surrounded by a herd of matrons in severe black bombazine, she was a corralled horse, already bought and purchased. Bernard stood near, chatting with a few others.

One last ball. One last dance, then freedom. The steamer for America left in five days. Five days more and she'd be on its sloping decks.

But as Bernard approached, and Father shook his hand heartily, Jillian had the sinking feeling that wouldn't be soon enough. The businessmen were clearly making a profitable transaction.

Jillian stared in dread at Bernard's florid face and waxed mustache. She imagined him looming over her on their wedding night, his body straining, his breath harsh, his flabby belly rasping hers. She forced her smile back to her lips as he approached.

"Mrs. Huntington." He acknowledged Jillian's aunt with a formal bow.

"Bernard." Mary gave him a cool look, but he ignored it and turned to her.

"Jillian, my dear." He bent over her hand, kissing the glove. She squelched her revulsion. "I've formally asked your father for your hand, and he gave his blessing and told me you will accept. We'll marry in July. Then a honeymoon in Bath. Delightful, eh?" he boomed.

Ah, Father. My opinion counts for naught.

"How delightful indeed," Mary said tonelessly.

Jillian swallowed her distress. "So soon?"

"The sooner the better, eh, my dear? I've no desire to wait." He lowered his voice. "I know how shy and maidenly you are, but you have nothing to fear from me on our wedding night."

He simpered. Bernard, with his lewd gaze, thin lips and waxed mustache . . . Jillian thought of the passion she'd found in Graham's arms. How reckless she'd been, how daring. And remembering Graham's lips upon hers, the desire she'd felt . . .

"Of course she has nothing to fear," Mary commented. The barest smile touched her lips. She shot Jillian a sideways look, filling Jillian with courage. Jillian tossed back her shoulders, prepared to tell Bernard she could not marry him. But the words froze on her lips as she saw her father approach.

The spines of her fan nearly cracked under the pressure of her fingers. When he at last moved off with Bernard, leaving the ballroom, she released a trembling breath. They would indulge in a game of whist with political cronies. Father would lose, but consort with high-powered officials. Now, with Bernard's money, he could afford to lose.

How weak Jillian was! All but that one night in Graham's arms, when she'd felt all the passion and life inside her come boiling to a turbulent bliss. Never again.

He arrived late, as would be expected with his rank. Inside, Graham searched for a redheaded enemy.

Like a panther he prowled the perimeter of the ballroom. Not listening to the feminine whispers fluttering in his wake, ignoring the admiring stares and hastily dropped curtsys as he approached. As always, he lightly clasped his white dancing gloves. Rarely did he dance, and when he did, it was with a select few. Graham did not want to encourage speculation as to the possibility of a future bride.

Last year, his brother had consorted with these same people. Kenneth had come before them with his Egyptian accent and his Egyptian past. Money and rank had won him acceptance. Still, he had stood out like a pyramid. A savage, they had thought him.

Graham did not stand out. He blended, his accent nearly gone, his habits very English. He was already respected as one of them, thought to have been raised by his proper English parents. The truth would rock them back on their delicate heels. That he had been captured by a warrior Egyptian tribe and learned to kill to survive, that he was far more savage than his brother . . .

Faces swam before him in a blurred haze. Detached, he dropped a smile here, made polite small talk there, and moved on. Tonight, his restlessness was too great to be assuaged by chitchat.

His eyes scanned the ballroom for a flash of red hair. He saw none. Until . . . he turned and his gaze alighted upon a tall mass of red-gold curls. His heart raced. It was *her*.

He spotted her across the crush of people. She stood out like a living flame on a smoky horizon. Graham could not breathe. He could not think, nor act, but simply stood, lips parted. The red hair mesmerized him. He had not seen the full glory of those tresses, nor anticipated how the strands would wind around his heart like a spider's sticky silk.

He remembered her, naked before him. Skin to skin.

Sweat slicking their bodies as they strained against each other, strangers forging a brief fleshly bond.

Shared passions. Hidden secrets.

Self-discipline and control shattered like glass. Graham began striding forward, mindless of the fawning stares cast his way.

Barely six feet away, he stopped, daring her to see him. She turned. Their gazes caught and held. They could have been the only two people present.

Intense hunger filled him. Like an opium addict's deep craving, it took hold with steely claws. Graham stared, remembering the sweetness and passion in her arms. He wanted to hold her in his arms again, even for one mere dance. She was his worst nightmare. And yet he could not help wanting her.

Though all instincts screamed a protest, though his senses urged him to stop, to turn and leave behind the sweetness of last night, he paid no heed. Graham, the aloof duke who rarely danced, tugged on his white dancing gloves, making his intentions perfectly clear.

"Look at the Duke of Caldwell. How striking Graham is," Mary murmured.

The breath caught in Jillian's throat. The Duke of Caldwell? She put a trembling hand to her coiled hair. Graham. Her lover.

Clad in elegant black evening dress, he cut a regal, imposing figure. Women pivoted to stare. Ivory and lace fans waved madly as erratic butterflies. Whispers were everywhere. Several pairs of admiring eyes affixed to him as he wended his way toward her. Young girls preened. Older women simpered. Jillian simply stood motionless. Her heart thudded erratically against her chest.

She remembered the male glory of his nudity. The

powerful muscles of his shoulders, the clean lines of his back.

His body was now draped in severe black silk, a white waistcoat and tie. His thick ebony hair was swept across his forehead. Those piercing, dark eyes remained guarded.

Regarding her, he advanced. His loose-limbed, graceful stride reminded her of a powerful jungle cat. The fleeting image of a leopard came to mind. A black leopard, sleek, stalking. She was his prey.

Jillian braced herself, forced a smile to her face.

An amazing change came over the matrons as he approached. They tittered and curtsyed, and a sparkle lit their eyes. When he stood silently before Jillian, she glanced at her aunt. Aunt Mary's stern look softened. She swept down in an elegant curtsy.

"Your Grace. How good to see you again. It was indeed a pleasure meeting you at the Knightsbridge assembly."

Graham nodded, his eyes searching Jillian's face. "Mrs. Huntington, might I have the acquaintance of your charge?"

His voice was smooth and deep, the burn of whiskey sliding down a parched throat. The burn of whiskers rasping across the tender flesh of a throat, as heated as his kisses . . .

Jillian automatically put a gloved hand to her flushed neck in remembrance. Her aunt's gaze was riveted to her. "Your Grace, Lady Jillian Stranton, daughter of the Earl of Stranton. My niece. Lady Jillian, His Grace, the Duke of Caldwell."

By rote she sank into a deep curtsy, knees wobbling so precariously that it was a marvel she didn't collapse upon her skirts. Graham nodded to her dance card, to the short pencil dangling from it.

"Might I have the pleasure of the next waltz?" he asked.

Her dry lips moved. Bernard had requested that dance. "I'm . . . afraid the next dance is taken, Your Grace."

"Then I must take one that is available."

Graham seized her dance card and penciled in his name. His dark, knowing gaze transfixed hers. He dropped the card, gently grazing her gloved wrist with his hand. Heat blazed between them, a living, writhing thing. The pencil swung from her trembling wrist.

"Until then," he murmured.

With a shaking hand, Jillian scanned the card. Until then.

She waltzed with Bernard in a blur of delicious anticipation and awful dread. The Duke of Caldwell was her lover. *The* duke. The mysterious, dark-eyed duke who'd been causing whispers through the ballroom all night. The eligible, wealthy and enigmatic duke.

Her glance flicked to her partner's wide brow, broad cheekbones and again to the thick, waxed mustache above his thin, pursed lips. He danced with a slight stoop. A liberal dose of cologne barely cut his body's stench of sour sweat. Moisture beaded his forehead, though the waltz had barely begun, and as always Bernard cut a clumsy turn, nearly causing Jillian to trip. She recovered, tried to focus and stepped on his foot.

"Jillian, my dear, watch your feet," he cautioned.

She mumbled an apology and concentrated on her steps. Out of the corner of her eye she espied the duke talking with some matrons. He glanced up, caught her flustered gaze with a smoldering one. She hastily looked away.

"Bernard, what do you know of the Duke of Caldwell? I've never seen him at an assembly or ball before."

"Jillian, it's not polite to gossip."

"He requested the next dance. If I'm to converse with him, I do not wish to make any social errors."

Bernard gave an approving nod. "Well, the duke was orphaned at age six when his family journeyed to Egypt and a band of wild Arabs attacked their caravan. Heathens slaughtered everyone. He hid behind some rocks and saw it all."

"Goodness, the poor boy!" she said, horrified at the thought of a young Graham being forced to watch his parents being brutally killed.

"All thought he and his younger brother, Kenneth, the Viscount Arndale, were dead. A passing English couple rescued the duke and took him in. They were an older couple, eccentric, and liked to travel in Arabia. Kenneth was raised by some heathen Egyptian tribe. The old grandfather found him in Egypt and brought him back to England to train him as his heir. Last year, Kenneth became duke when the grandfather died—and when he went to Egypt to supervise an excavation, he found his older brother living in Cairo!"

"Found him, after all the years he'd been lost?"

"Apparently the duke suffered a memory loss when he saw his parents murdered. His memory returned when he met his brother. Kenneth relinquished the title. Good thing as well—the viscount married a heathen Arab girl, a filthy native woman with little social standing and adopted her daughter. However, the Tristan family is wealthy and the old duke was well regarded."

"You seem to know quite a bit about them."

"I make it my business to know of every family who has power and wealth. It helps me politically."

Jillian remembered the haunted look in Graham's dark eyes. "He seems tragic."

"Of course. Though he was raised by that English couple, they tainted him by forcing him to live in Arabia—among those repulsive, dirty heathens."

Jillian suspected the turmoil in the duke's eyes had nothing to do with living among the natives. She sensed deep secrets. And oh, how she knew about keeping secrets.

The waltz ended and Bernard escorted her from the floor. He scanned the ballroom for the duke.

"His Grace could prove useful to me in Parliament. Be witty and charming, and do not attempt to converse about anything intellectual." He chucked her under the chin. "None of your silly chatter about the woeful state of the English economy."

Resentment filled her. "Why? Isn't it rather woeful?"

He laughed. "Jillian, leave intellectual discussions to men. Such talk will tax your brain."

How would you know? Your brain has never been taxed, she thought. Bernard, if they opened your head they would find nothing but that dreadful Macassar oil you smear on your hair.

"Yes, of course, Bernard," she said.

He moved off, presumably to join her father in a game of whist. Jillian's heart pounded with excitement and disquiet as the duke approached.

Silently, he held out a gloved hand. Silently, she took it. Graham's grip settled upon her waist, his heat like a burning coal through the fabric of her gown. Jillian swallowed and they began the waltz.

In his arms again, this time in full view of society. Fully clothed. Her hand tightened on the broad shoulder encased in black silk, remembering her fingers gripping the hard muscles of his back as he thrust inside her . . .

Though extremely nervous, she found dancing with him much easier than with Bernard. Jillian glided along to his expert lead, and arched her neck to glance up at him.

"You expressly stated we must never see each other again. Why the dance?" she asked bluntly.

"Perhaps so we could talk without prying gossips eagerly eavesdropping."

"Very well. Talk then."

He chuckled. "You're very direct."

Only with you, she thought. With everyone else, she was a quiet, redheaded mouse. A shadow of her real self.

He cut a very smooth turn and she followed effortlessly. They matched each other well, as they had last night. A dull flush burned her skin as she remembered. She hoped he would not notice.

"You're very becoming when you blush," he remarked.

Jillian raised her gaze to his and cut off his pleasantries. "You need to talk to me, Your Grace? Tell me what you wanted to say."

He gave her an intent look. "Perhaps I merely wanted to compliment you on the real color of your hair. It is like golden fire, or the flare of an Egyptian sunset."

"Is that all? Praises of my hair? No poetic homage to the beauty of my eyebrows and how they resemble winged doves in flight? Or how softly rounded my elbow is, like a ripe rich peach?"

His lips twitched with amusement. "I fear I have no such eloquence within me. I must confess, I am not an authority on women's elbows—unless they be the kind that are rather pointed and jabbing me in the ribs."

Jillian laughed. Heads turned, stared. Her mirth died as soon as it began; she could not risk drawing attention to herself. She looked away from the duke, away from the man who had taken her virginity.

"I told you last night, it's best we remain strangers in the dark," she said, staring over his shoulder.

"It was best," he agreed. "But that was before we saw each other across the room. Then it became wiser for me

53

to ask you to dance, to acquaint myself with you should anyone sense . . . we know each other somehow. Pretense is not my strongest suit."

She gave a wry smile. "It *is* mine."

"Only when necessary, I think. You disguise yourself, but I sense you long to show the world who you truly are," he murmured.

Startled, she did now look at him. "But aren't we all in disguise, in some form or another? Don't we all hide our real selves from the world? Even you, Graham Tristan."

He nearly stumbled, but recovered quickly. "Who are you?" he asked.

"A stranger who shared last night with you. A nobleman's daughter who wishes discretion." Boldly, she looked at him. "And you, Your Grace? Who are you?"

A mysterious smile took his lips. "A duke, dancing with a nobleman's daughter. A stranger sharing a second night."

"Had I known who you really are . . ." she began.

"You'd have turned and walked away?"

Jillian compressed her trembling lips. She looked directly into his eyes. "No," she admitted. "I would not have."

Satisfaction filled his gaze. She did not stiffen as he pulled her closer than polite society allowed. The air between their bodies grew warm from their combined heat.

"Your Grace, would *you* have walked away had you known my identity? Had I stated my name and revealed all?"

The strains of violin and cello filled the silence as a second dance began. His scent teased her nostrils, a faint spice she could not identify, mixed with the smell of clean skin and shaving soap. Jillian awaited his answer. Some unknown emotion flickered in his eyes. Then his gaze darkened.

"No," he admitted quietly. "I could not have."

His gaze softened as they regarded each other. For a magical moment, she felt they were the only two people in the immense ballroom, and they had not met previously, but were starting anew. Filled with the wonder of discovering each other.

She smiled, fresh courage filling her. "Why would you not have walked away?"

But he made no reply. A distant look came over his face, as if he had shuttered himself off from her and desired no further contact. Jillian was surprised and hurt, but she resigned herself to finishing the dance in silence. She stiffened much as she had in Bernard's arms. Their steps became more halted and less relaxed.

Thankfully, the waltz ended. She curtsyed and Graham executed an elegant bow. She sensed impossible layers to this man, hidden to the chattering *ton* by his perfect manners and cool indifference. He wanted to blend, and so he withheld part of himself.

She had been physically intimate with this man, he had known every part of her body, and yet she did not know him at all. They were strangers.

Graham put a hand on the small of her back, guiding her through the crush. His touch was light and yet seared through the dress. He relinquished her to her aunt, whose soft smile held a hint of approval. Oh goodness, did her aunt think a man such as this charming, wealthy duke could rescue her?

She was beyond rescuing.

The duke's mouth quirked upwards as he took her hand, kissing her gloved fingers. "My thanks for the enormous privilege you accorded me, Lady Jillian. Our dances gave me great pleasure. It was like . . . waltzing in heaven," he said softly.

She stiffened, caught off-guard by the words. An echo

of the ones she'd spoken last night. Smoky desire darkened his gaze. She knew his true meaning, knew he spoke of the dance where they tangled and twirled and strained together in naked, blissful abandon. He wanted her yet.

Jillian tilted her chin up. "I experienced equal pleasure, Your Grace. It was indeed . . . paradise."

He studied her intently. She grew uneasy at the spark in his eyes.

"I trust you are well, Lady Jillian, and our dancing did not leave you feeling flushed or . . . sore in any way? I tried to be as gentle as I could, for I know strenuous physical activity can sometimes prove painful for gently reared ladies."

Damn him! Did he not know such talk could prove dangerous to them both? Why was he doing this?

Her aunt interjected, seemingly eager. "I assure you, Your Grace, my niece can well handle the duty of dancing. Even gently-reared girls are quite capable. And a dance may leave her sore, but such discomfort is easily overcome and should not cause undue distress."

"However," he murmured, his gaze never leaving Jillian, "your discomfort would cause me distress and an eager desire to amend it. I'd wish to experience the delights of another dance as soon as you felt comfortable enough to engage me."

Oh, damn the man! What was he thinking? Jillian tried to control her wildly beating pulse, her desire. She gazed at him coolly, but gave in to his fire.

"I am quite well, Your Grace. I am quite capable of dancing as often as any partner."

"It sounds as if you quite enjoy the dance," he suggested, his knowing gaze transfixing her. Jillian flushed.

"Every season I prove myself most competent," she retorted, this time refusing to follow his lead.

His dark eyes twinkled. "Do you?" he asked in a deep,

lazy drawl. Then he added; "I can imagine the man who was your first partner shared a very special moment, indeed."

She raised her gaze boldly to him. "Special indeed, good sir. I shall never forget."

His eyes widened and darkened, and a look of pensiveness came over him. Unsmiling, he regarded her. She could see a pulse beat in his throat. Her own heartbeat echoed its cadence. Thick tension hung in the air. What was happening? Jillian had never met a man before who made her feel this way—as if all her careful plans might crumble to dust and she'd care not a fig. Not even about Radcliffe.

The sweet tension broke as Bernard appeared. Murmuring excuses, Aunt Mary slipped away. Jillian felt herself shrink back into the old position. She stammered polite introductions, but misspoke, saying, "Graham, the Duke of Caldwell."

She'd called him by his first name. Flustered, she quieted.

Bernard shook his head mildly, haughtily amused. "Forgive Lady Jillian, Your Grace. She is usually not so gauche."

The duke did not return his smile. His eyes grew cold. "I rather think her introduction was correct. Graham *is* my name—a name I ask certain people to call me."

Bernard blanched. "I apologize. I did not realize Lady Jillian was familiar enough to address you by your given name."

"We shared a wonderful dance, and that certainly makes her familiar enough," he replied, glancing at her.

"I do hope she didn't step on your toes, as she did mine," Bernard said lightly, to Jillian's mortification.

"On the contrary, I found Lady Jillian quite accomplished at dancing. We thoroughly enjoyed ourselves."

Jillian shot him a warning look. Graham ignored it, his dark eyes dancing now.

"Do you dance often, Mr. Augustine?" he inquired.

"I'm afraid I'm not as skilled at dancing as some," Bernard admitted. "I do not enjoy it."

"Indeed?" The duke lifted his dark brows.

"Dancing is necessary, but it can be quite dull," Bernard continued, oblivious to the conversation's subtext. Graham refused to let up.

"I daresay you are wrong, Mr. Augustine. With the right partner—such as Lady Jillian—a man must find it a very pleasurable experience." His sensual, full lips lifted in a crooked half smile. A hot flush lit Jillian's cheeks.

Graham couldn't help biting back a chuckle. Bloody hell, Jillian had spirit. He sensed it brimming beneath her calm surface, stultified by her upbringing. The dull gray gown she wore hid everything. She looked like a stern governess. But the covering intrigued him as he imagined stripping it slowly from her to reveal ivory-white skin that gleamed as it had last night in the dull glow of the brothel's lamps, kissing each inch of her white skin, coaxing a throaty little cry from her long, slender throat now concealed in a froth of severe lace.

Ah, but the passion he'd coaxed from her last night . . . surely it still burned within her. He hid a smile, contenting himself with mentally stripping Lady Jillian nude, waltzing with her on the mattress, this redheaded woman with green eyes blazing with desire . . . laughing at him in the desert as she trapped him there—

His fantasy ended abruptly. Graham's smile faded. He must leave their liaison a secret and swear off ever meeting her again. Every cell inside him warned she was dangerous. Even the question she'd innocently asked: *Why did you not turn and walk away?*

It mattered not. After tonight, after he found his

quarry, nothing would matter. Not even one sweet night in her soft arms. Passion and heat. That would die with him as a memory when he hanged.

His icy composure broke. Never again to taste her, to experience such bliss as they had, tangled as one . . .

The self-important little prig who called himself Bernard was saying something. Graham forced a smile to his lips and inclined his head.

"Lady Jillian and I plan to honeymoon in Bath, Your Grace. Have you ever taken the waters there?"

What? Jillian was to marry this pasty-faced fop? Shock gripped Graham, but he managed a noncommittal answer as he stared at her. Two delicate roses of color stained her cheeks. She looked away.

An unexpected surge of male possessiveness shook him. If she'd known of her engagement, why had she surrendered her innocence to him, a virtual stranger? In a whorehouse?

Unless she had a good reason for not remaining a virgin . . . His troubled gaze returned to Jillian. Ah God, she was beautiful, her slender figure standing so proud, those delightful white shoulders he'd adored kissing now hidden by ugly, dull gray.

Jillian paled. She gave a curtsy and murmured, "Please excuse me." Then, pivoting on her heel, she turned and pushed off through the crowd, as if to leave the ballroom.

Bernard shrugged. "Wedding jitters. Every bride has them."

Graham watched her go. After a polite moment, he excused himself and wended his way through the crowd, following her discreetly. It was easy, too, after all the years learning stealth as a Bedouin warrior. His tread, despite his hard-soled polished black shoes, remained as light as sand. As Graham trailed her down the hallway to a set of double doors, she opened one and stepped inside. He followed.

A library. And silhouetted by glistening moonlight streaming through French doors on the other side of the room, Jillian stood gazing outside. Graham closed the door softly behind him.

"Lady Jillian," he said roughly. "There is more to say."

Dread pooled deep in her stomach. Jillian recognized the deep, confident voice, the tone demanding and expecting answers. Her trembling hand smoothed gray silk. Graham wanted answers she could not give him.

She did not turn but felt the heat of his body press near her, like a banked coal fire. A shiver born of longing raced along her spine. His voice was deep and angry.

"Are you quite mad? Why last night if you are to marry?"

Jillian closed her eyes. She inhaled a lungful of air. "It's none of your business . . . Your Grace. I have my reasons."

"None of my business?" His harsh laugh grated in her ear. "You give yourself to me, a total stranger in a whorehouse, and you dare to say it's not my business?"

Now she did turn, feeling desperation and anger rise within her. "You paid money for discretion, and conducted the transaction. Your business ended this morning when you left."

A rough note filled his voice. "It was a business arrangement where the executor failed to deliver on all the terms of the contract. I did not want a redhead."

Jillian shivered, his heat turning into a chill that frosted her. She whirled and met his stormy expression with a defiant look. Her words held the volcanic anger building inside her for a long while.

"If you feel cheated, then work out another arrangement with Madame. I gave you your money's worth, Your Grace. Now go away and leave me be!"

He did not move. She glared at him. "I told you to go."

The duke regarded her with a solemn look. "Such spirit. How strange. You appeared such a meek mouse standing next to your betrothed."

Jillian sighed.

Silver moonlight streaming through the windows sharpened the raw hunger on Graham's face. After a moment he said, "Our paths shouldn't cross again, but I can't resist whatever fate keeps us colliding together."

"You never wanted to see me again," she reminded him in a whisper.

"I did not. But my good sense takes leave of me when I see you. I can't think of anyone else," he said roughly.

"You must. I'm to be married. What happened between us is best left a memory."

Graham went still, studying her. His nostrils flared, as if he could scent her distress. Jillian felt a touch of unease. Instinct warned her this man was dangerous when crossed.

"A well-bred lady comes to a whorehouse, seeking to lose her virginity. The next evening, the same woman stands beside the man she's to marry . . ." he mused.

"Sell it, not lose it," she corrected bitterly. She bit her lip, wishing she could bite back the words.

A pained smile touched his mouth. "Of course. *Sell* her virginity. But why? When her father has money, and she has—"

"Nothing. I needed the money. Now please, I wish to be alone."

"Why would a well-bred young lady need money so badly?" He began circling her, making her ache with tension.

"Your Grace, please leave. If you're found here . . ."

"Why, when her father can provide her with every-thing she needs, and then her husband can? Perhaps she would need it because there's something she can't ask them for."

"A gown, a hair ribbon, fripperies," she agreed, whirling as he circled. Oh please, why wouldn't he leave her alone?

"But such a drastic means to obtain funds? Selling her body to a stranger? That sounds like the act of a truly desperate woman."

She joked weakly, "One must do what one must do to remain in fashion."

"A woman who wants to run away."

He halted. Her shoulders sank.

"That's it, isn't it, Lady Jillian?" Pity filled his voice. "Is that why you did it?"

Her voice broke. "Bernard is wealthy. He's to give Fa-ther a very large marriage settlement in exchange for me." In exchange for a pure bride. Ha! Pure no longer.

"Is your father in financial trouble?"

Jillian looked away, hugging herself. "Many families in England are during these trying times."

"And where were you running to?"

"Away."

"Why run off? Just tell him no."

"I cannot."

Graham gave a gentle smile. "It's a simple word, no. Very easy to say."

He was a powerful duke; he couldn't understand the restrictions of living under the iron thumb of a demand-ing father, or what it was like to be a female with a thirst for knowledge. He, like others, assumed women in her station lived only to marry well and produce children. Even though this duke appeared different, he would laugh at her dreams. Gently-bred aristocratic ladies did not attend colleges to improve their minds.

"Hasn't there ever been a time in your life when you wanted to but simply couldn't say no?" she asked brokenly.

Graham fell dumbstruck. How many times? *No.* He'd wanted to say the word to Al-Hamra. He had not. He breathed deeply to contain his emotions.

"My felicitations on your nuptials," he muttered. He started for the door then turned for one last look.

Silver tracks of tears shone in the moonlight on Jillian's pale cheeks. Taken aback, he went to her, touched a pristine drop. She scrubbed the rest away with a furious fist.

"Why are you crying?" he asked quietly.

"Nothing, it's nothing. Please leave."

He studied her, troubled by her obvious distress. Instead of obeying, he cupped her tear-streaked face in his hand . . . and kissed her.

Her lips tasted like warm honey. She jerked back slightly, but he bracketed her head with his hands and held her still, deepening the kiss. She responded, opening her mouth to the urgent, tiny thrusts of his tongue. Graham coaxed her mouth with his, boldly tangling their tongues. Intense thrill raced through him. Blood rushed to his loins, hardening him to stone.

No other woman had ever caused such an instantaneous reaction. Bloody hell, he wanted her. God help him.

Graham broke the kiss, stepping back with a feeling of self-loathing. He was secretly kissing another man's intended.

Yet, he had claimed her first. His blood stirred at the memory. Graham touched her mouth, swollen from their embrace. His first woman. His worst nightmare. Yet he had slept like a child with her in his arms. No more violent dreams.

"What will you do, Lady Jillian?" he asked.

She gave a half shrug. "What I must. A woman's life is ruled by her father until she marries, then she becomes her husband's property. Even if the husband is a pompous boor."

Her despondent tone roused in him a fierce protectiveness to shield her from pain. Graham had never felt such for a woman before. Even with Badra, when he had been her bodyguard before she married Kenneth, his protectiveness was not this consuming. He realized with rueful dismay that Kenneth was right. His brother had warned that you never forgot your first.

Kenneth had failed to mention she could also slip into your brain, infiltrating everything like tiny grains of sand.

"Not every husband is a pompous boor. A considerate man could make you happy," he observed.

"Perhaps. But you are the only man who was ever considerate of me. Last night . . ." Two scarlet roses bloomed on her cheeks.

"A man who is otherwise is a fool. You deserve tender, careful consideration," he growled.

She glanced shyly at him from beneath those incredible long lashes. "I did enjoy our dance."

"Both?" he teased.

"Both. You would never tread upon my toes." Jillian smiled.

Wistful regret coursed through him. For her, forced to marry a man she detested. For him, forced into an act where he'd surely hang. Graham brushed a knuckle against her petal-soft cheek, feeling the dampness still there.

"Good-bye, Lady Jillian," he said quietly. And he left her standing alone in the moonlight.

* * *

He paced restlessly in the hall before forcing himself back into the ballroom. Once inside, Graham snatched a glass of champagne from a passing footman. He sipped, grimacing. His years of not drinking alcohol among the Bedouin were hard to change.

And I don't make a splendid drunk.

But tonight, he just might change that.

Movement toward the front of the ballroom caught his eye. Jillian emerged, seemingly composed. There was no trace of her earlier distress.

The musicians had stopped playing and the pasty-faced Bernard caught Jillian by her elbow and led her to the dais to join Lord Huntly. A balding, redheaded gentleman in black formal wear emerged from the crowd and joined them. Their beaming host made introductions.

Graham choked on his champagne. He squeezed the delicate stem of the glass so hard it threatened to crack.

No. No. No.

It could not be.

Not him.

But there was no mistaking that face. He had seen it hundreds of times over the years in his darkest dreams.

Graham croaked in a whisper of disbelief. His champagne glass tilted. He vaguely felt chilled liquid splashing onto his trouser leg.

His heart thudded harder against his chest. He stared wildly at the red-headed Englishman on the dais: Reginald Quigley, the Earl of Stranton. *Al-Hamra.* The redheaded Englishman from his past—and the father of Lady Jillian.

Graham tensed. The little boy inside him—oh, how he wanted to run screaming from the ballroom and weep. The grown man wanted to howl with anger, to crush Stranton to a pulp with his bare fists. Instead he saw himself as if through a thick lens, very calmly watching his right hand dig into his pocket. He slid his miniature dagger from its leather sheath.

The handle felt cool in his sweating palm as he slipped it inside the left cuff of his jacket. It felt right. He had waited twenty years for this moment, which had now arrived.

It was time for the panther to move in for the kill.

Chapter Four

Trapped. Caught like a bird in a cat's claws, Jillian frantically scanned the ballroom. No escape. Father would make her betrothal public, force her to acknowledge what she did not want.

She had expected to escape—pleading an ache of the head—before Father made the announcement. But seeing the duke had severely rattled her, and by the time she recovered her composure, Bernard had summoned her father, consulted with their hosts, the Huntlys, and ordered the musicians to stop playing.

Her hands were clammy and damp. Jillian had tried to protest as Bernard hustled her onto the dais, but it was no use.

Lord Huntly's sallow face took on a new light as he faced the crowd. His voice boomed. "Ladies and gentlemen, I have a splendid announcement! It is my honor to announce the formal engagement of Lady Jillian Quigley, daughter of the Earl of Stranton, to Mr. Bernard Augustine!"

Bernard's pink face shone with glee. Jillian saw a life stretch before her: her father still ruling over her like a lord, her new husband joining forces with him, closed doors, dark secrets . . . Pain pressed behind her eyelids. No! She fought the darkness threatening, the cloudy haze of memories behind the thick oak door.

Jillian scanned the room for her aunt but could not find her. Oh, if only to find one single understanding face in the massive crowd to feed her courage to escape! To flee the wild applause and delighted faces. There was none.

Then she caught sight of an elegant figure clad in black silk. Standing alone, regal and proud. The Duke of Caldwell.

Jillian's gaze riveted to the duke. She forced a smile to cover her fear, but her mind mouthed a quiet cry. *Help me*.

Sweat dampened Graham's palms. His pulse quickened. The Earl of Stranton would die today. He must.

Forcing himself to take a tiny step, his eyes didn't leave the small dais. *Focus on your quarry. No emotions.* The words taught to him as a warrior echoed through his head. Graham took another step, then, out of the corner of his eye, noticed Lady Jillian standing beside his enemy. Her face was pale. Her smiling lips moved as if in a plea.

Graham hesitated. The terror shining in her eyes masked by a brave smile—oh, how he recognized it! He had seen it enough in the mirror. He knew that helpless fear of being trapped in an inescapable quandary. Bitter anger clogged his throat. No matter. The father would pay.

But her look—ah, so pitiful!

No one had taken pity on that eight-year-old boy twenty years ago. What if someone had?

The haunting possibility diverted him. Graham looked down at his elegant cuff, at the knife hidden inside. His muscles tensed for action, but his feet did not take any.

Jillian's wide-eyed look had summoned a distant memory, pulling him back. . . .

The al-Hajid tribe had called the visiting Englishman al-Hamra—The Red. Escorted by heavily armed warriors, he had arrived at the camp to purchase one of the tribe's beautiful, sleek Arabians. The eight-year-old Graham had stared at the Englishman, the first he'd seen since his parents died two years before. Fleeting hope took wing. Surely this man, whom they said was powerful in the land of the English, could rescue him.

He hovered silently near the circle of men as they talked. No one noticed him, the small, invisible child; he was ignored by most but the warrior who kept him like a prized dog. Graham held his breath, waiting for the chance to talk.

The opportunity came—when the redheaded Englishman went walking and stumbled off to rocks in a canyon to relieve himself. Graham trailed behind. When the redheaded man finished, Graham approached.

"Please, sir, help me. I'm English, like yourself, but a prisoner. I was captured by the al-Hajid as a slave. Please, get me out of here." Speaking his native tongue for the first time in two years, his voice had cracked, filled with so much desperation and hope.

The man buttoned his trousers. "And why should I believe you or help you and risk my friendship with the al-Hajid? Do you have money?"

"No, sir." Graham had felt sinking despair. "But I promise, I will get you some when I'm in England. My family is wealthy."

"Promises from a child. No good."

Graham bit his lip. He had no money. But he had that treasure map, his most prized possession. Torn in two, there was another half.

"Wait here, please," he begged. "I have something."

Then Graham had scampered to the nearby secret hiding place he had dug in the sand. He removed one torn half of the map and returned, offering it to al-Hamra.

"It's a treasure map. Do you know hieroglyphs?"

Al-Hamra snorted. "No, why would I know the heathen writing of the ancient Egyptians?"

"I learned a little. My father . . . he taught me. This map leads to great riches in a pyramid."

The man studied the ancient, cracked papyrus and sniffed. "Interesting—but not enough to risk getting caught. Do you know what the al-Hajid do to enemies, boy?"

Oh, he knew. He'd seen his parents' blood flow like water upon the sands for daring to cross land the Al-Hajid claimed was theirs.

"Please, sir—please, I beg you. I'll do anything." Graham fought to control his tears.

Al-Hamra stared at him. "Such a pretty boy," he said, an odd intensity lighting his green eyes. "So very pretty."

Graham had shrunk back. He had recognized that fierce, wanting gleam.

"What's your name, boy?"

A deep sense of self-preservation learned early among the savage al-Hajid had halted him from giving his real name, or his status as the Duke of Caldwell's heir. "I'm called Rashid."

"Well, Rashid. The map is nice. I'll tell you what. I'll help you escape, if you give me the map and something else. . . ."

And then the redheaded devil had invited him to a hellish dance. Horrified, he had refused—until al-Hamra slyly suggested, "What is one time with me, a fellow countryman, compared to a lifetime with your Arab master? Come now, boy. I promise, it will not take long."

70

And so Graham had closed his eyes and followed the man to his tent where he'd sold his soul.

Stop it! You're perfectly safe. Calm, man, calm. Graham jerked himself out of the past with forceful effort. Sweat plastered the white silk shirt to his skin.

"Sir? Your glass."

"What?" Graham started, then stared at the white-gloved servant in total confusion.

"Your champagne glass, Your Grace. Would you like another?"

Graham glanced at the crystal, which was tipped upside down in his left fist. He took a shuddering breath. "Yes."

He handed over the now empty glass and took a fresh one. Gulping down the contents, hardly noticing the bubbles tickling his throat, he dimly thanked English protocol that prevented servants from asking questions of dukes who spilled champagne on their trousers.

The moment was lost, his resolve weakened. The earl would live. For now.

Graham locked his attention on the dais, trying to control the wild beating of his frantic heart. His gaze flicked to Jillian. He tried to look away from the plea in her eyes, but they called out to him, begging for help.

He tried to tell himself it mattered not. Jillian would survive. Just as he had survived. But at what price?

Graham set down the empty champagne glass on a nearby table, fisting his hands. He stared at al-Hamra. The earl was nodding and smiling as congratulations were offered to him. Watching, Graham realized a terrible truth. The earl was firmly ensconced among society's most influential and powerful leaders, Lord Huntly among them. If he shouted to the assembled crowd what Stranton had done, they'd call him mad. No one would

71

believe. Thanks to the story Kenneth had circulated about his past, no one even knew he'd been raised by the al-Hajid. How utterly ironic that the very story fabricated to grant him respectability among his peers would be his downfall.

He had no proof of Stranton's crime. He needed proof.

The bastard was barking a syrupy speech to the crowd. Graham forced himself to listen. Good God, it sounded like political grandstanding.

"As you know, Mr. Augustine has joined me in campaigning to revive and restructure the Contagious Diseases Act. Not only will we register fallen women in our fair city, but the legislation I propose will heavily tax houses of ill-repute. The money will then be funneled into a fund to help these fallen women gain more respectful employment. The vile vices that plague our society are an affront to the flowers of virtuous English womanhood, such as my daughter here."

Graham nearly choked. Jillian's frozen smile looked ready to crack.

She had sold her virginity in one of those whorehouses. Wouldn't the earl's political influence shatter if anyone were to know? Graham smiled darkly. Yet, that wasn't enough. Stranton must suffer more than mere public humiliation. He wanted the bastard on his knees, begging for mercy. Begging as Graham himself had begged.

The answer came as an echo of the past, the words of the Khamsin sheikh who'd advised him as Graham took the oath of loyalty and became a Warrior of the Wind. "Know your enemy's flaws. Be as a predator studying a herd of gazelles. Disguise your scent and cloak your intentions. Learn his secret desires, then use those to weaken and defeat him. Knowledge is a far more power-ful weapon than the sharpest scimitar," Jabari had said.

And Graham knew al-Hamra's weakness. But he needed to establish a trusting relationship with the earl to lure him into the right trap—a more difficult and terrify-ing prospect.

And once he succeeded? Stranton's family would suffer from the scandal. It would crush Jillian. If only there was a way he could protect her from the onslaught.

The answer came to him with the force of a sandstorm sweeping across the desert. Lady Jillian wanted out of a marriage she dreaded. He wanted a close connection with her father.

Surprisingly, he anticipated the solution. He would do it and damn the consequences.

Jillian sucked in a breath, imagining herself proudly ad-dressing her father, exploding with the spirit he had ruth-lessly squashed. Telling him no.

Caught up in the fantasy, she darted a glance at the man. Hard triumph shone in his gaze. Her shoulders sagged. She could not do it. Oh, she was too weak to stand up to him!

Movement in the crowd caught her eye. That tall fig-ure in elegant black silk, striding with commanding force. The Duke of Caldwell wended his way forward, the crush parting deferentially. He halted short of the dais, his obsidian gaze sweeping them. Lord Huntly greeted him in a booming, respectful voice, and to her amazement, the duke mounted the steps and stood be-fore the crowd, legs spread, shoulders thrown back in a proud stance.

And in a loud, authoritative voice that rang across the ballroom, he uttered words that froze her blood.

"If you truly mean what you say, Lord Stranton, then why is your daughter no longer a virgin?"

Breath caught in her throat. Oh dear God . . .

Bernard's jaw dropped. Her father looked comically shocked.

"How dare you insult her!" Bernard sputtered.

Graham's even gaze met hers. "Insult? I *know*, sir, because last night Lady Jillian and I became lovers."

Jillian stared in astonished shock. Oh God, what was he doing? Admitting such, and just after her father triumphantly announced his campaign against London's demimonde?

"Your Grace, my daughter is virtuous. I myself have safeguarded her maidenhead. Just where did this act take place?" her father asked.

The duke smiled.

Silently, Jillian begged him with her eyes. *Please, please stop. Don't tell them. No, don't tell them where you took my virginity.* If he did, she'd die of shame.

Graham saw her distraught expression. "That, sir, is a private matter between myself and the lady."

Jillian nearly collapsed with relief. But she felt her father's wrathful eyes burning into her like two hot coals.

"Jillian, what is the meaning of this?" he asked in a clipped voice.

Her lips moved in soundless protest. A humiliated flush crept up her burning throat to her cheeks. Murmurs rippled through the crowd. Graham's dark gaze transfixed her.

Bernard turned with a whine. "Jillian, why is he saying such things? Tell him to stop."

But she could not.

Graham gave Jillian's betrothed a gentle, almost pitying look. "In good conscience I could not allow you to marry her under false pretenses, Mr. Augustine. The fault lies solely with myself."

Then, with a note of husky admiration in his lowered voice: "I could not resist Lady Jillian's beauty, and I seduced her."

It was an apology without actually apologizing, she realized. And she was grateful.

"Jillian, tell me he's fibbing," Bernard pleaded.

Lips that had lied before moved to agree, *Yes, he is falsely accusing me*. She opened her mouth to deny the duke's words. Jillian's lips moved to whisper, "He's . . . not."

A dull flush lit her fiancé's face. Bernard shot her father a look of mortified disgust. "Under the circumstances, Lord Stranton, I cannot marry your daughter."

"No, Mr. Augustine, you will not," Graham stated. "Because I am formally declaring for her hand."

Jillian stared at him in astonished shock.

Lord Huntly rubbed his mustache, looking flummoxed. "I'm quite confused. Er, which engagement am I to announce?"

"Mine," the duke said gently. "But first a few details should be worked out before any congratulations are offered."

Jillian's father's mouth worked violently. For the first time in her life, Jillian saw him at a loss for words. The duke had commandeered all the space in the room. His powerful, imposing presence made all other men look diminished. His shocking confession and daring declaration of intent had made every marriage-shy bachelor look weak-spined.

Suddenly Jillian became aware of the flock of young, eligible women staring with barely disguised interest at Graham. With his confession, he had increased the stakes, transforming from an aloof spectacle to a dashing rogue. Sighs of regret from the eligible girls—and even some prudish chaperones—rippled through the room. Murmurs of censure mingled with them.

Graham offered a humorless smile. "I think we'd best adjoin to a room where this may be discussed in private. But first, I beg a word with your daughter, Lord Stranton." And without awaiting her father's reply, the duke gripped her elbow and began escorting Jillian out of the ballroom.

"They shouldn't be alone! It's not proper!" Bernard protested.

She heard Lord Huntly's ironic reply, "I do believe it's a little late to worry about that."

Chapter Five

Jillian's mind whirled as Graham steered her into the expansive, pine-paneled library and shut the double doors. A brass key remained in the lock. He twisted it, locking them in. Or more likely, her father out.

He flicked a switch, flooding the room with electric light, and leaned against the door. Crossing his arms, he watched her.

"You disgraced me!" she said.

Unsmiling, he regarded her. "I rescued you, Lady Jillian—from that insipid fop determined to marry you. I did not mean to distress you, but I saw a solution best for both of us."

A flush burned her cheeks. Jillian gripped her gloved hands so hard she felt her nails digging into her palms through the thin silk.

"Why? *Why?*"

"I need a wife. You wanted to run away. Therefore, the solution: marriage to me."

"I hardly think that is a solution. And if you, sir, were in the market for a wife, surely you could find a willing candidate among the Marriage Mart without creating a scandal!"

"Perhaps I could find a bride among those giggling, whey-faced chits who circulate at these affairs. But I want you."

"I'm penniless. And you don't even know me!"

"We have a better beginning than many marriages. We already know each other's pleasures."

"You are quite mad," she snapped. "We spend one night together and you declare you do not want to ever see me again, and now you offer me your name?"

"I changed my mind."

"I have not. I will not marry you!"

"You have little choice now," he pointed out.

It was sheer madness. She felt caught in the vortex of some unstoppable force. "So you're forcing me into marriage by publicly telling society I'm not a virgin? You've ruined my father's good name."

The duke's expression shifted. His features became hard as granite, his eyes obsidian. She watched, uneasy yet fascinated. Jillian suppressed a shiver, reminding herself of the coiled power she'd glimpsed in the brothel.

"Ruined? I think not. On the contrary, he's gaining a duke for a son-in-law. And let's not forget finances. Your father is eager to make money from your marriage. I will offer the same marriage settlement Mr. Augustine offered."

Tears burned the back of her throat. "And the advantages for me, sir, once my father is paid? There are none."

A knock sounded at the heavy wood door. She started.

"Jillian? Your Grace?" her father called out.

The duke ignored it, watching her intently. She put a knuckle to her mouth, wanting to run away. Her nervous gaze darted toward the French doors at the library's far west wall.

Graham crossed the room to her. His voice was low and cajoling. "Running away isn't the answer, Jillian. I will provide generously for you and you'll have wealth and position. Just ask and I'll give it to you. Jewels. Furs. Gowns from the finest Parisian couturiers. Anything your heart desires."

"Anything my heart desires?" Jillian laughed. Oh, this was too priceless. Yes, he'd give her anything but the one thing she desired most: her freedom.

"What use is a fine gown and position when all of society sees me as a fallen woman? They can't wait to rip me to shreds."

The doorknob rattled—her father, trying to get inside. "Your Grace, a word please. I must speak with you," his disembodied voice called out.

Graham glanced at the door. "They'll forget about our rather questionable beginning once we're married."

"Forget? You know little about the *ton*, Your Grace, if you think they will forget. They have long memories."

His gaze narrowed. Once more she felt the coiled menace in this man, as if his polished exterior hid a dark core.

"No one will dare insult you if you are my wife. I promise you, I shall not tolerate one single affront."

"They won't insult me. They'll just ignore me," she demurred.

"They cannot ignore you if you are my duchess, Jillian. Think of it. I'm offering escape from being chained to the insufferable Mr. Augustine." He paused, a slow smile touching his mouth. "Wouldn't you prefer being chained to me? In bed, say, for long hours of delightful pleasure?"

Erotic heat shot through her. She tried to ignore it. "How do you know he's insufferable?"

"His mustache. Clearly he spends a great deal of time waxing it. Do you truly wish to become the wife of a man obsessed with his facial hair? His kisses must be as dreadful as the Macassar oil he smears on his hair."

"I wouldn't know," she murmured.

"He never kissed you?"

"He tried. I stopped him. It seemed to me as dreadful as licking beeswax off a staircase."

His abrupt, deep laugh nearly coaxed a smile from her. Jillian suppressed it. "Why do you wish to marry me? What possible reason could you have?"

"The most elemental one of all, Jillian. You're a beautiful woman and I want you in my bed."

A delicate shiver stroked her spine at the determined note in his voice. "S-sex is a feeble basis for marriage."

"Is it?" He advanced, a gleam in his dark eyes. She shrank back as his fingers found her cheek and stroked it in the barest of touches. Jillian closed her eyes, need shuddering through her. Ah, the power of his caress.

"I think it's a powerful reason to marry. It's how the duchy continues. I need a son." At this disclosure, her eyes flew open. Graham's level gaze flicked down to her flat abdomen. His large, warm hands settled on her clothed shoulders. She remembered them stroking and caressing, creating delicious heat. "I'm most eager to begin trying for an heir after we marry."

Warm breath tickled the sensitive back of her ear. He bent his heard toward her, and he whispered, "I'm afraid your options are quite ruined, Lady Jillian. There is no escape but marriage to me."

She swallowed, hard. Marriage was not the answer. Leaving England was. The duke had ground everything to a halt. Jillian worried her bottom lip. There was still the money hidden in her room. She could still escape. For now she'd pretend, to gain precious time.

"Very well," she muttered. "I'll marry you."

The barest smile touched his mouth. Then he dipped his head and kissed her lightly—a brief kiss promising sensual pleasures.

Yet it was pleasure she'd not experience, for she'd not marry him if she could run first.

Father might be appeased by Graham the duke instead of Bernard the insufferable, but deep down she had the uneasy feeling that Graham, with his dark intensity and dangerous charm, might prove the far more deadly choice.

Graham managed to rope in his raging emotions as he gripped Jillian's hand and prepared to face her father. Inside his head a voice screamed, *are you mad?*

Perhaps he was. Forcing her hand and ensuring his enemy would become his father-in-law sounded completely insane.

But keep your enemies close, his friend the Khamsin sheikh had once advised. How much closer than by making Stranton a relative?

Long ago, Graham had vowed to never marry. But this solution meant Jillian would remain under his care and protection when the larger scandal broke. Sexually she pleased him, and the thought of bedding her again swelled his body with pleasure.

And she could provide him with an heir. Having children would keep her occupied and out of trouble. And his dreaded nightmare would not come true as long as he kept her from the desert. Chances of her ever traveling to Egypt with him were as unlikely as him finding Khufu's lost treasure.

Graham tucked Jillian's hand into the crook of his arm. He forced a blank expression to his face and, inhaling a deep breath, unlocked and opened the door and stared into the enraged face of his enemy.

Graham had not confronted him for twenty years. Once, last year in London, he had run from this man in shameful fear. He would run no longer.

Blood roared in his head. He wanted to squeeze, to crush, to strangle. A bored smile played on his lips instead.

"Good evening, Lord Stranton. Your daughter has graciously agreed to marry me." Jillian pressed his arm in a warning.

Graham ignored it, his body taut and ready to engage the man in battle, verbal or otherwise. But Stranton just stepped inside and closed the door behind him. He did not look at his daughter.

"Whether or not she agrees is immaterial, Your Grace. Jillian will do as I tell her. She has disgraced me with her behavior and will not do so again."

Tendons stood out in Stranton's neck. The earl looked at his daughter with deep contempt.

"And I told you, Stranton, I take full responsibility for what happened. I seduced her."

Stranton smiled, his eyes cold. "I don't hold you responsible, Your Grace. I raised Jillian to resist, to not cave in to the sins of the flesh. She has failed me miserably."

Beside him, he felt Jillian tense. Graham realized the man was threatening her because she was a safe target who would not defend herself. He wanted to snap Stranton's neck. It would be so easy.

"We are all weak human beings, sir," he said politely.

"Weakness is no excuse for such a grave moral lapse."

Disgust laced the earl's voice. He narrowed his gaze at his daughter. She dropped her own to the floor.

"And *my* moral lapse?" Graham asked, studying the earl through hooded eyes.

Stranton gave him a fawning smile. "It is different for men, Your Grace. This is why my campaign to control the houses of ill repute is quite important. We must concentrate on regulating the behavior of wayward females. Perhaps you will take an interest."

"Perhaps." Graham had no intentions of a political career.

Encouraged, the earl went on. "I have lost considerable influence tonight because of her behavior. What she did goes beyond the pale. She publicly disgraced my name." The man had all the emotional depth of a turnip. He cared only that he'd been embarrassed before his peers. "And now she will make amends when you make her your wife."

Graham suddenly felt a pressing urge to toy with the earl, like a cat swatted a cornered mouse. "I could make her my mistress," he said. He smiled inside as Stranton recoiled.

"I must recover my reputation. You need to marry her!"

"I do not *need* to marry."

Stranton hesitated. "It is your duty as an English gentleman to marry her, Your Grace."

"I have no desire to be an English gentleman."

Panic flared in the man's green gaze. "But, you . . . you offered for her hand."

"Perhaps I have changed my mind."

How does it feel to be utterly powerless, you bastard?

Powerless as Graham had been.

No other man would marry Jillian now. She had been a ripe peach her father had carefully preserved to sell at an exorbitant price, but Graham had plucked the fruit, bit into its juicy center, savored its delicious taste and then replaced it in the bin. Without paying a single pence.

He stole a glance at Jillian. She stood, erect carriage, a silent wooden statue. Then she lifted her gaze to him. Moisture had turned her eyes to glistening gems. His heart twisted. He did not want to hurt her.

"Are you saying you will not marry Jillian, Your Grace?" Stranton asked.

Silence thin as the edge of his scimitar hovered. Graham let the moment linger. He glanced at Jillian. Her gaze was downcast, her shoulders slumped.

"I will marry her. But because I desire to marry her, and not out of any obligation."

Stranton's relief was audible. "Of course, Your Grace. Will you come to tea tomorrow to discuss the terms?"

The marriage settlement. Ha! "Yes."

The earl visibly relaxed. Graham suddenly remembered when he had escaped his Egyptian captor. The man had thought to easily defeat Graham, who was not accepted as a warrior. He had lowered his guard and . . . in that bare instant, Graham killed him.

Stranton's guard was lowering. It would be gone, completely, when Graham dealt the killing blow. He continued the effort to disarm him.

"Your campaign does intrigue me, Stranton. I would like to know more of your efforts."

The earl looked eager. "We could discuss my bill at tea."

"Of course," Graham murmured. He glanced at Jillian, and took her trembling hand, pressing a kiss to her gloved knuckles.

"Good night," he murmured, nodding to Stranton.

As he turned on his heel and left, Graham drew in a ragged breath. For a moment he was sorely tempted to march back and proceed with his original plan. It would be so easy to kill him. Making Stranton his father-in-law would be hard. This was going to be more difficult than he'd ever anticipated.

Much more difficult. But he hoped the reward would be sweeter.

All through the carriage ride home, Jillian remained motionless and silent. Punishment would be swift and exact. She knew her father too well.

They arrived home and the earl ordered the servants to assemble in the drawing room. Silent, efficient wraiths, they stood lined up in a row. Jillian tensed as he spoke.

"I called you here to see that my daughter does not leave this house from now on without myself as her escort. Only myself and no one else until she is married. The only exception will be her daily ride in the park with a groomsman. If I ever catch her leaving the house without me, I will dismiss you all. Without references. Is that clear?"

When they nodded, he continued. "My daughter is a whore. She publicly disgraced me tonight. I cannot risk further scandal should she decide to expose herself to more ruination."

He strode toward her. A cool breeze touched her back as he began unbuttoning her dress. He then ripped it from her shoulders, the sound thundering through the quiet room. Her faded corset and shabby chemise showed the outline of her full breasts as he ordered her to remove the garment. Jillian felt a creeping flush turn her skin crimson.

"From henceforth, to insure she does not stray from my house, she will be denied clothing unless accompanied by me when she ventures out, or for her afternoon ride in the park." His stern gaze locked on the head groom. "You, Beckett, will accompany her. Let her out of your sight and you're dismissed."

The groom blanched and nodded vigorously. Jillian stared ahead. Tears shimmered in her eyes, but she bit her lip. A tiny rivulet of blood trickled down her chin. She'd bit her lip so hard it bled.

Her father continued looking at her with contempt. "I want all her clothing removed from her wardrobe. But first . . ."

Dread filled her as he barked an order. When the servants returned, her heart sank. Oh God, please no . . .

In their arms they held a short stack of books. Her treasures. Marshall. A priceless edition of Adams's *The Economist*. The earl took them and marched toward the fireplace.

Jillian's lips finally moved. "Father, please, no . . ."

He tossed the stack into the fireplace.

The strike of the match was thunderous in the silent room. Flames soon caught, licked the pages. They curled, shriveling with the fire. Shriveling as her heart shriveled. Jillian stared in wordless agony. Her precious friends, dying.

"From now on, you will not read anything," her father ordered.

A single thought arose; it echoed again and again in her mind. *I will not cry in front of the servants.*

Her father gave her a look of disgust. "Retreat to your room and reflect on how you aren't fit to be anyone's bride, and thank the Lord the duke offered to marry you. And you had better not bore His Grace with your insipid chatter of economics and make him change his mind. Go. From now on you will take your meals in your room. The sight of you makes me ill."

Jillian managed to mount the stairs. Inside her room

she lay on the bed in her underclothing. She lay there for a long time, in numb silence as the servants paraded in and out of her dressing room, removing all of her gowns. She did not cry.

Chapter Six

Graham broke the news at breakfast the next day to his brother and his bright-eyed nine-year-old niece. Kenneth's look was of awed shock. Jasmine clapped her hands with delight.

"Oh, Uncle Graham—a wedding. Can I help?"

He gave her an indulgent smile. "It's going to be a very quiet, very quick affair, I'm afraid. The circumstances do not call for an elaborate wedding, Jasmine."

"I can imagine the circumstances," Kenneth said dryly.

"The circumstances are of no consequence."

"How well do you know this woman?"

"I knew her . . . quite well *the other night*," he drawled, knowing his brother would understand.

Kenneth looked deeply troubled. "Graham, really, I know how your first time can be . . . memorable, but marriage?"

Jasmine's sharp gaze whipped back and forth between them. "What's a first time?"

"Something you won't have until you're forty," Kenneth muttered. He studied Graham. "Do you love her?"

"I don't need love. I need a son."

"So you're marrying her for a broodmare? There's more to marriage than producing an heir."

"I daresay you're correct, but I hope you will respect my decision and leave off. If I wish to breed sons with her, it's my business and no one else's." Graham took a long sip of bitter, tangy Arabic coffee.

"Uncle Graham, if you're going to breed this lady, are you going to mount her like Prometheus did Cassandra in the stables?" Jasmine asked with interest.

Graham choked. Kenneth's jaw dropped. "Jasmine! What the . . . where did you get that idea?"

"From watching," she said practically. "I was in the stall with my kitten when I saw you leading Prometheus to Cassandra, Uncle Graham. It was most interesting. He started prancing about, and then this thing between his legs started growing very—"

"How is your pony, Jasmine?" Graham hastily interjected, before his precocious niece could ask how he compared to his favorite Arabian stud.

She launched into animated chatter about her favorite topic—riding her horse—and Graham's gaze met his brother's as she prattled on. It promised, *We will finish this later*.

When they finished eating and Jasmine vanished upstairs for lessons, he fixed on Kenneth again. There was only one place guaranteed to free them from prying ears.

"Shall we have a round?" He pushed back from the table.

Kenneth's worried gaze shot to the ceiling. "Badra . . ."

"Will never know. Come on, then," Graham urged.

They went to the exercise studio. Graham headed for

the row of weapons hanging from the wall. A raging restlessness gripped him. He ignored the fencing foils with their protective buttons and headed straight for the heavy pieces.

Kenneth stared at the curved scimitar in his brother's hand. "You know how she worries about one of us getting hurt. If she finds out . . . Badra will have my head."

"Not if I have it first," Graham mocked. "Come now, Kenneth, we haven't practiced in an age with these." He tossed the scimitar to his brother, who caught it by the hilt, one-handed. Kenneth examined the gleaming weapon's edge.

"Duller than a paper opener," he observed. "Still . . . we should use . . ." Kenneth replaced the weapon and handed a foil to Graham, who gave the foil a disdainful swish. They both stripped off their coats and waistcoats and eyed the nearby protective leather vests. Their glances shot to the rules written on a white board in bold letters by the fencing instructor Kenneth had hired: *Gentlemen always wear leather vests to protect their bodies.*

The two exchanged wry glances. "We're warriors, not gentlemen," Graham commented.

Then, with reckless abandon, both brothers set down the foils and pulled their shirts off. Bare-chested, they took the swords and faced each other.

Well-matched, they stood about the same height. Kenneth was less muscled, but possessed a wiry strength and was quicker on his feet. Graham had learned to pinpoint his brother's advantages and use his own. His blood thrummed with excitement. A similar gleam shone in his brother's eyes.

"Come on, let's see how your lunge fares these days. I'll wager your thrusts are too slow," Kenneth challenged.

"That's not what the lady said," Graham replied.

"And that's why you're marrying her. Bloody hell, sex isn't a good reason to marry."

They engaged. Kenneth launched a furious assault, clearly frustrated. Graham gritted his teeth, leashing his temper enough to parry and riposte.

"Really, Graham, marrying a prostitute just because you enjoyed bedding her—"

"A virgin," he corrected, effortlessly deflecting Kenneth's latest thrust. "And a lady."

His brother gave a loud snort of derision. "You must be mad about her if you're calling a prostitute a lady."

"A real lady. An earl's daughter, whom I saw again last night at Huntly's."

Shock twisted Kenneth's face. As he hesitated, Graham took ruthless advantage, and executed a perfect coup, knocking his foil aside and touching his brother's chest.

"Right in the heart," he said with satisfaction. "You'd be dead."

"I might still die of shock. You mean the woman you tupped—the *virgin*—is an earl's daughter? Good God, what was she doing at a brothel?"

"Pleasuring me," Graham said. "Now shall we continue, or are you too witless to defend yourself?"

In response, his brother lifted his rapier and attacked. Relishing the challenge, Graham concentrated on defending himself. Kenneth was an excellent opponent who had perfected his fencing moves. In Egypt, he had been called Khepri, a Khamsin warrior fearless in battle. He had killed many. But Graham had killed more.

Graham the warrior had taken the life of his Egyptian captor. Then he had sliced off the man's testicles, presenting them to the al-Hajid sheikh as a trophy.

"I gather you aren't going to tell me details," Kenneth panted, as Graham began a fresh assault.

"I am not."

Steel clanked against steel as they exchanged blows. Graham sidestepped Kenneth's lunge and moved to finish the match just as a startled shriek filled the air. Both men froze.

"Are you two mad? You could get hurt!"

Badra, Kenneth's very pregnant, very scowling wife, stood nearby. The brothers exchanged guilty looks. Red-faced, well aware of his half-naked state, Graham scrambled for his shirt, jerking it on hastily. While he drew on his waistcoat, his brother faced Badra, unashamedly bare-chested.

"Honey . . ." Kenneth began.

"It's my fault," Graham interjected. "I made him. I wanted a bit of the old thrill."

Badra swung her annoyed gaze to him. "No one makes him do anything. You're worse than a pair of children." Graham offered a sheepish grin and Kenneth hastily dressed. "It's too dangerous," Badra continued, waddling over to them.

An exasperated look touched Kenneth's face. "Honey, Graham and I fought as warriors. We've slain enemies in battle and have the scars to prove it. You think dueling with these"—he flicked a finger at his foil—"swords that couldn't cut warm butter on a hot day is more dangerous than that?"

"This is England, where men are civilized. There's no need to duel," she protested.

"How am I supposed to protect my family? What if some madman rages in and threatens my beautiful wife?" Kenneth inquired.

She rolled her eyes. "Do as every other Englishman does."

"Run?" offered Graham.

Badra scowled. "I can defend myself. You taught me, Kenneth, remember? You kick a man in the privates."

Both brothers cast her tiny but heavily rounded frame a doubtful glance. Graham restrained a smile.

"Kicking a man is a good idea, but my sword is far more effective," Kenneth stated.

"I agree. You can cut off his nether parts instead of kicking him," Graham suggested helpfully.

Badra rolled her eyes. "Wouldn't it be more sporting to simply shoot him?"

Graham nodded. "Shoot him in the privates, I suppose."

Badra laughed, holding her enormous belly. "Stop it," she gasped. "Or I'm going to have the baby right here."

Kenneth grinned. "Relax, my love. We were merely celebrating Graham's, um . . . little announcement. Brace yourself. My brother is getting married."

Badra's laughter stopped short. Shock dawned in her beautiful eyes. She stared at Graham, who shifted uneasily.

Badra knew his tortured past long before his brother ever did. When he'd been known as Rashid, Khamsin Warrior of the Wind, Graham had been assigned to protect her. They had forged a friendship sealed with the dark secrets of their individual pasts, and had both agreed never to marry. Kenneth's gentle, patient love had helped Badra change her mind. But both knew Graham's demons still tormented him, riding his mind as he once rode his mare, fast and hard across the sands.

"M-marriage? To whom?" she asked, still staring.

"Some beautiful damsel in undress," Kenneth said evenly. "She captured my brother's heart. Or another vital organ."

Graham shot him a warning look.

"Are you certain? Is she special? She'd have to be . . ." Her voice trailed off. Badra stared as if Graham were a jinni, a desert spirit. Graham felt flushed with humiliation. Bloody hell, he knew what she thought. What woman would want him?

Yet he had hoped for understanding from Badra. Without words he picked up the abandoned foils and their rubber tips, and carefully replaced them on the wall. Inside he felt like that little boy of long ago, aching and hurting. He forced a cool note to his voice as he studied the wall.

"You needn't worry I'm marrying some common tart from the streets. Lady Jillian is the daughter of a well-known peer. She's quite suited to become my duchess." He whipped about and faced Badra with a defensive look.

Badra put a hand on her immense belly, calmly regarding him. Once they had provided each other emotional support, had been friends and allies in the shared pain of their pasts. She'd been the only one he trusted. Still, he had withheld part of himself, never fully sharing. Now she was married to his brother, expecting his child, and had her own family. Life had changed so much.

Kenneth discreetly moved to the other side of the large room, tidying a pile of lawn tennis rackets. Badra waddled closer to Graham. So tiny, so delicate-looking, she was barely as tall as his shoulder. But he knew looks were deceiving. Inside, she was strong as a fierce desert wind.

"Rashid, talk to me about this. Don't shut me out. I sense you are carrying a heavy burden, and it has become much heavier these past months since we arrived in London."

Her use of the Arabic name he'd been given by the al-Hajid made him cautious. He folded his arms over his chest. "What do you want, Badra?"

Distress etched her face. "You've changed, Rashid. Once we were so close. Ever since we came to England, you've grown more distant every day. I hardly know my friend anymore. Why is that?"

"You and Kenneth urged me to assume the title. Of course I had to change. I'm no longer Rashid. Those days are gone."

"And our friendship, too? Once you would have done anything for me."

His voice softened. "As I would continue to do, but you're married to Kenneth now. He comes first in your life, as it should be. As it will be for me when I marry my new bride."

"Oh, Rashid." Badra's deep sigh indicated displeasure. "Your bride. Who is this woman? You never mentioned any woman before. How do you know she is the one for you?" She touched his chest gently. "How do you know she is the one to share your heart?"

Graham rubbed his face. "Badra, what you have with Kenneth is special. My expectations of marriage are not so high."

"Why not? Why shouldn't you expect to find a woman whom you can share every part of yourself with, who will fill that empty space inside you? No, don't tell me it's not there," she added as he started to protest. "I know, more so than anyone else, how empty that ache can make you feel. And I know how wonderful it is to finally have someone fill that void, and feel the peace of being loved and cherished for who you are."

Vastly uncomfortable now, he shrugged. "I'm glad it happened for you. Truly, Badra." *It just will never happen for me.*

Joining his wife, Kenneth slid an arm around her ample waist. His calm gaze met his brother's troubled one. "We want you to be happy, Graham. You don't deserve anything less. Can this woman make you happy?"

"She pleased me enough the other night," he repeated. He remembered what Kenneth had said and tossed it back at him. "You said that she was my destiny. And you can't fight destiny. I'm marrying her. Can't you both just try to be happy for me?"

Kenneth glanced at his wife. "Yes," he said. "We can."

"Yes," Badra echoed softly. "Please bring her to tea. I want to make her feel welcome here. Very welcome."

Graham managed a genuine smile as she disengaged from her husband and came to him. She kissed his cheek, her large belly bumping his hip.

Kenneth gave him a solemn look. "If this is what you want, then I am happy for you. I just want a woman who's good enough. You deserve the best." He looked wistful. "I would have given anything to see you happy before this, but we can't go back, only forward. So let us know what you need and we'll be there for you."

Struggling with his emotions, Graham nodded. After all these years of walking alone, he finally had a family who cared. He felt torn between wanting to grow closer, and his natural reserve. How much easier it would have been to simply remain in Egypt, masked by his indigo Khamsin garb, hiding from the world.

When Kenneth swung Badra into his arms—despite her protests she could walk—Graham felt even lonelier. Murmuring excuses, he vanished into his apartments. There he dressed to go riding in the park.

Slapping his riding crop against his thigh, he descended the polished staircase. Jasmine galloped across the hallway toward him. Her face broke into a beaming grin. A flurry of excited Arabic spilled from her.

"Uncle Graham! Are you riding? Can I go with you? Please, please! I haven't ridden my horse in two days!"

"English, Jasmine," he automatically corrected. "And hasn't your papa told you no riding without a groom? You're still not accomplished enough on sidesaddle."

Her face fell. "Yes."

"You'll get better in time," he encouraged.

In Yorkshire, Kenneth had taught his adopted daughter to ride the Bedouin way. Jasmine had ridden astride until two weeks ago, when boys in the park had teased her about her odd riding style, calling her a heathen. Deeply upset, Jasmine had quietly asked to learn the English way to ride.

Graham felt a tug of deep pity at her crestfallen expression. He gave an indulgent smile. "Go change into your riding habit, and I'll meet you at the stable," he promised.

Trailed by Charles—the silent head groom Graham trusted most—he and his niece rode to Hyde Park. Graham controlled his Arabian stallion with his knees, while Jasmine sat on her pony, struggling with the sidesaddle position. As they approached the Row, he noticed her stiff posture. Graham nudged his mount to a halt and leaned forward in his saddle.

"Listen to me, Jasmine—*relax*. Your horse takes cues from you. The more you feel comfortable, the more you are able to control your mount. Animals sense it when you are nervous. Bend your knees a bit and relax your posture."

"My governess says I must sit straight as a board."

"Have you ever seen a board ride a horse?" He winked. Jasmine giggled, and her shoulders relaxed.

As they rode into the park, Graham turned a curious eye again on his niece. Like him, she was a loner. He asked her about making friends. Her woebegone expression turned his heart over.

Glancing over her shoulder at the indifferent-looking Charles, she spoke in a hushed tone in Arabic. "Uncle Graham, I want to play with them, but they don't want to play with me. They say I'm too odd. Especially Tommy Wallenford. He says he's the Honorable Tommy Wallenford and I'm just a silly heathen girl from Arabia without a title."

So Jasmine had been snubbed for her imperfect English. Graham bristled with anger. "Listen to me, little one," he said somberly. "They think themselves superior. You must show them you are their equal. You are the Honorable Jasmine Tristan, daughter of a viscount. And the niece of a duke."

He saw her inner fight to bravely check her tears.

"But I did. They won't listen to me. They keep listening to Tommy. It hurts when he calls me names, Uncle Graham. Just because I'm Egyptian and my skin is darker."

Graham felt a twist of anguish, remembering his own difficulties when he returned to England, the whispers and curious stares in the Yorkshire community.

"What would you do, Uncle Graham?" she begged.

His natural caution broke at the sight of her trembling lower lip. He racked his brain, remembering. "When I first came to England, this one sod—er, fellow—mocked my accent. He had no respect for my title and called me a heathen of Arabia."

"And what did you do, Uncle Graham?"

He could not resist a wry smile. "I gave him what the English call a 'facer.' I punched him in the lip and told him, 'You stupid bloody sod, a heathen from Arabia can fight just as well as an Englishman.' And then I earned respect by relearning English customs and English ways. Eventually most have come to accept me."

Jasmine's wondering gaze held his. "Then I should focus on learning English ways and they'll accept me as well?"

Graham was attuned enough to prejudice to know firsthand the answer. Jasmine's midnight-black hair, large dark eyes and dark skin set her apart. It always would, no matter how perfect her English or how western her dress.

"Learning English customs and perfecting your English will help, but it's also important you don't sacrifice who you truly are, little one. Be yourself, and be confident in who you are. Worthwhile people will respect you."

Jasmine gave a solemn nod. "Thank you, Uncle Graham. Now maybe you should go ahead. I have to ride slower on my pony. I need to practice riding English-style, to prove to them I can do it."

Sooner or later, she would have to face her troubles alone. Graham promised to rejoin her as soon as he had a good gallop.

With a sigh he headed for the soft, tawny track designed to accommodate brisk riding. Once there, he let Prometheus have his head, relishing the power of the big stallion's working muscles. Graham steered the stallion with pressure from his thighs, just as he'd learned from the Bedouin.

Minutes later, he slowed the panting horse to a canter and let him cool down, then headed back to Jasmine. He trotted onto the lane, his keen gaze searching for an elfin-faced girl and the groomsman who resembled a melancholy hound. The sound of laughter pulled his attention to a small stand of oak trees. Lady Jillian was there, talking with Jasmine. Charles waited patiently nearby.

Graham's chest constricted. This was not how he'd intended to introduce Jillian to his family. He spurred the big horse forward, galloping until he reached them. He expertly pulled the stallion to an abrupt halt.

"Good day, Lady Jillian," he said.

"Good day, Your Grace." Her charming smile faltered.

Oblivious to the adults' discomfort, Jasmine glanced at Graham with a bright smile. "Uncle Graham! Miss Jillian has been telling me about horses and riding!"

"*Lady* Jillian," he corrected.

"And I was telling her about Egypt and how you, Papa and Mama brought me here last year."

Graham's blood went cold. How much exactly had Jasmine told Jillian? That he had been an Egyptian warrior—living, fighting and killing? Any hint of how he'd lived with a Bedouin tribe and Jillian might pass that on to her father, who might do some hard thinking about his future son-in-law and remember . . .

He managed a tight smile. "Did you now? What exactly did you tell Lady Jillian?"

"Oh, that Mama saw Papa last year in Egypt, and how he's not my real father but he adapted me . . ."

"Adopted," Graham corrected.

"And how Papa saw you in Cairo and we all had dinner at a nice hotel before we came to London."

Was that a wink? Graham bit back a grin. Precocious little baggage. She'd told much without telling anything.

"Egypt sounds terribly far," Jillian remarked.

"Oh, it is. But it's lovely. It has lots of . . . Arabic ponies?" Jasmine struggled with English, but she'd worked hard to master it in recent months.

"Arabian horses," Graham corrected in Arabic. Then he repeated in English for her benefit.

"I see you are quite fluent in the Arab tongue, Your Grace," Jillian remarked.

Dull heat flushed his body. "Quite. But I speak it only when necessary, so as to not offend the sensibilities of those who look down upon the land," he replied tightly.

She gave him a searching look. "I meant no offense. On the contrary, I greatly desire to travel abroad, and to see the fantastic sights of Egypt and other countries."

"Egypt has many such sights," he agreed.

A spark lit her green eyes. "Oh, indeed! And you must have seen them. I have never been beyond England, but for one journey to America as a child to visit my aunt."

"You desire to travel?" he asked.

"Yes. It must be marvelous to journey wherever you

please, to learn of new cultures and have grand adventures."

He stared at her. "Some might call my time in Egypt a grand adventure. I venture to call it something different." Thankfully, his bitter sarcasm was lost on her.

"Tell me about your travels. They must have been so fascinating. What is Egypt like? Did you travel up and down the Nile on a *dahabiya*? Oh, to smell the river water, to see the vistas of flowering trees and the lush, quiet date palms."

Graham shot her an amused look. "Where did you hear about Egyptian houseboats?"

"I escape to other places in books," she replied. She sighed, looking despondent. "Since I will never journey there."

"Never say never," he told her. "The Arabs believe in destiny—and you can't fight your destiny."

As well he knew.

For the first time since Father's harsh punishment, Jillian felt the caul of bleakness lift. Destiny. Yes, soon she, too, would have grand adventures. In America. Radcliffe. The halls of learning. What greater quest could life offer?

"Father traveled all over Egypt. He liked the pyramids. He said they were interesting, but he said the people were sly beggars. How did *you* find Egypt? Did you spend any time with Bedouin tribes? Father did. He speaks excellent Arabic."

Graham remained silent as they trotted along the lane. He looked as remote as the pyramids themselves.

Then she remembered. He'd lost his parents in Egypt, had seen them viciously murdered. "Oh, I am so sorry, Your Grace," she said. "I did not mean to remind you of any past pain."

He tossed her a quick, startled look. "What do you mean?"

"The attack on your caravan. When you were six and lost your parents to a Bedouin tribe."

Tension tightened his jaw as he looked away. "That was a long time ago. I remember very little."

She nodded. He seemed reticent, closed off to her. And as Jillian rode beside him, she wondered which of her words had caused his disquiet.

So, her father had told her the Egyptian people were beggars? What irony. Beggars, as Graham had begged Stranton? He imagined an outstretched dark-skinned palm and Stranton's superior laugh as he ignored it, just as he had ignored Graham's pleas.

But Jillian knew nothing of his past. He would keep it as such.

Jillian desired to travel. Well, perhaps when they married he'd take her to Greece. Or Rome. Anywhere but Egypt. Graham suspected Jillian was like a leashed yet spirited filly, anxious to run free. If given rein, she'd range far and wide.

And yet she'd appeared so lifeless at that ball, overshadowed by her father. Except while dancing with him, and then later, when cornered in the library. He sensed beneath her very proper, dull gray exterior the heart of a woman of great passion and a burning spark for life. A spark others managed to dampen, but not entirely extinguish. Suddenly he had a great desire to see it roar into an inferno. What would Jillian truly become if allowed the freedom to do as she pleased?

He glanced over at his silent niece. She looked very much a miniature of the other women who trotted along the lane: proper, reserved, her natural animation gone . . .

Suddenly he wished they had never left Egypt. Far better to remain in a land regarded as heathen than to mold spirited little girls like Jasmine into silent models of decorum. He could not bear her to become a quiet gray ghost or a mean-spirited gossip like many of the chits he'd met since arriving in London. The sparkling summer day in London had suddenly become more oppressive than Egypt's searing heat.

As they rode through the park, Jasmine stopped her pony and let loose a stream of excited Arabic. "Oh, Uncle Graham, there are some children I know. May I join them? Please?"

Torn between wanting to protect her from being hurt and knowing she needed to fight her own battles, he nodded. Accompanied by Charles, Jasmine primly trotted her pony toward the gathering of children bowling hoops in the park.

"She's a lovely child," Jillian remarked.

Graham studied his future wife. Clad in a dull gray riding habit, she almost faded into the background. The other ladies were all smartly attired in their fashionable habits, top hats perched at saucy angles. Jillian was like mist, camouflaged but for those flame-gold tresses. He wondered if she desired to hide, like sunshine shrinking behind dark clouds.

Graham let his mind drift. He envisioned Jillian nude on all fours. He was taking her, hard and fast, mounting her as a stallion did a mare, wringing throaty cries of hot pleasure from those sultry lips—

"You have a fine steed, Your Grace. An Arabian?"

Blinking, he started. Aware of his swelling erection, Graham shifted in his saddle to conceal it.

"Yes, Prometheus is a full-blooded Arabian. Spirited, and loves to have his head when he runs. Yours?"

"Daphne is gentle but fast."

"Let's head for the track and race," he suggested.

Her red-gold brows lifted. "Challenging me?"

"You say your mount is fast." He caressed Prometheus with a loving pat. "My own is restless for a gallop again."

She gave him a wry look. "Riding sidesaddle puts me at a distinct disadvantage."

"Then ride astride," he said recklessly. "If you are an excellent rider, you know how to control a horse with your knees. The saddle does not matter."

Those clear green eyes widened. She looked at her own impassive groomsman, who was trailing close behind her, and whispered, "I can't."

Graham studied the groom, then spoke. "You may leave us now, and wait for Lady Jillian at the gate."

The man looked nervous. "No, sorry, Your Grace, I can't. The earl ordered me to remain with her at all times for her afternoon rides. If I disobey, I'll be dismissed."

Hmmm. It was a slight problem, but easy to solve.

"Lady Jillian will need a good horseman when she marries me. If you remain in the earl's employ until then, I'll pay you whatever wages you earn now, plus a five-pound bonus if you agree to leave us alone when she rides in the park with me. If he dismisses you before then, I'll hire you."

Her groomsman looked eager. "Yes, Your Grace!" And he rode off, looking quite happy. Jillian looked after him with the air of a prisoner who'd been given parole.

"Well? Shall we race now?" he asked.

A spark lit her eyes. Raising herself up, she tugged up her loose skirts. Beneath them she wore leather trousers. Graham grinned in delight as she settled astride. Bloody hell, she had spirit! And as they headed for the track, his admiring gaze absorbed her long, shapely legs.

"Have I shocked you?" she asked.

"On the contrary, I rather prefer this. It puts us more

on an even level," he murmured. Jillian in this position sent a jolt of fresh desire through him.

"I daresay we are not, as my mount is not as splendid as your Arabian," she said, sounding wistful.

"Yes, Prometheus has generations of pure Arab blood. My breeding book traces the bloodlines back hundreds of years. I plan to begin a business breeding here in England."

"I do not know much of breeding Arabians," she confessed.

"It's a simple matter. When a blooded female comes into season, a selected stallion is chosen and mounts her. Nearly the same as the London Season, but for the weddings." He laughed at his joke.

Jillian shot him a withering look, but his words had set a wanton image dancing in her head. She quashed it, trying to ignore the naughty tingling between her thighs. Her open thighs, her damp feminine juncture pressed against the hard leather of her saddle, the itch to rub and slide as his hand had created such wicked pleasure the other night . . .

When they reached the track, with a daring look she dug her heels into her roan. Graham laughed again, letting her take the lead. She glanced over her shoulder and saw him follow.

They galloped down the long track, Prometheus barely breaking a sweat. Jillian's horse fell behind. As they reached the end, Graham let his mount slow to a trot and she joined him, panting from the vigorous exercise. A fine sheen of perspiration coated her brow beneath her dull gray hat.

"You have a fine seat," he told her. "You just need a better mount for a faster ride."

"But not before the wedding," she replied.

The duke threw back his head and laughed. Jillian flushed from both the exertion of her ride and the daring of her little joke. She glanced around and realized other riders were staring with avid curiosity.

They left the track and Jillian held out a hand.

"Would you help me, Your Grace? I need to resume my seat."

With effortless grace, the duke slid off his stallion. He helped her dismount, his large warm hands curling about her waist. A shiver raced through her. Bending over, he linked his hands together, helping her to mount the sidesaddle. Jillian arranged her skirts and took up the reins.

They rode back to where Jasmine had left them. As they approached the small stand of oak, they saw a defiant figure in a mussed green riding habit standing beside a pony. Graham's momentary enjoyment collapsed as he stared at his niece. Jasmine marched toward them as they dismounted. He noted with alarm her clothing was stained with grass and dirt, her face set in a mask of unhappiness.

"What happened?" Jillian cried.

"I was very polite, as you said, Uncle Graham—until the Honorable Tommy Wallenford arrived. He called me an ugly Arabian mare." Jasmine's lower lip jutted out in defiance. "So I did what you did. I gave him a facer and told him, 'I'm a filly, you stupid sod! I'm too young to be a mare!'"

Graham couldn't help a chuckle, but then he gave her a serious look. This would not help things. "Young ladies do not punch boys, Jasmine. If you wish to fit in, you will not hit anyone again."

His niece's face fell. She nodded glumly.

Jillian leaned over her mount and said, "But I'll wager that facer was worth it, wasn't it?"

Jasmine's crestfallen expression brightened. She gave a cheeky grin and nodded.

Graham studied his intended, who was clearly good

with children. At least Jasmine had taken an instant liking to her.

"Come to the house and meet my brother and sister-in-law," he suggested.

Jillian hesitated. "I'm not sure that would be proper."

His hand snaked out and snagged her reins, then tied them to his saddle. "Now you have no choice. Follow me."

Jillian protested as he trotted to the gate and they were met by her beaming groom. "I cannot—not like this!"

Graham shook his head. "No worries. They don't stand on ceremony."

"But I smell like horses," she complained.

"A delightful perfume. They like horses. They're from Arabia, land of the horse, remember?"

Jillian's exasperated groan mingled with the husky tenor of his laughter.

Chapter Seven

Despite it being his suggestion, Graham felt unusually tense as he introduced Jillian to Kenneth and Badra. He'd stripped Jillian of her damn bodyguard, leaving the groom in the stables.

They now stood in the informal drawing room, Jillian looking self-conscious in her dusty riding habit. Both Kenneth and Badra gave her steady, assessing looks. Graham became intensely aware of Badra's darker skin, her immense rounded belly; Jillian's pale white skin, her very English, albeit shabby, gray riding habit. He noted the differences between his little family and her, and the intense scrutiny Kenneth accorded her. He saw his brother's blue eyes devour Jillian and knew Kenneth's thoughts.

An earl's daughter selling her virginity in a whorehouse. Perhaps this was a mistake.

But Badra gave a friendly smile and held out her hand. "I'm so pleased to meet you, Lady Jillian. I look forward to becoming better acquainted, and I hope we can be friends," she said. Her expression was earnest, her words spoken in perfect, if accented, English. Graham tensed. If Jillian failed to accept his sister-in-law and snubbed her as others did . . .

Jillian visibly relaxed. "I also look forward to it, Lady Tristan. I've been eager to meet Jasmine's mother. She's quite an intelligent little girl."

A beaming smile broke out over the little girl's elfin face. "And I give an excellent facer."

Badra shot Graham a questioning look. "What is a facer?"

Graham reddened. "Something Jasmine won't do again if she wishes to learn to become a proper young English lady."

"I'm afraid I'll never be a proper young English lady, Uncle Graham," Jasmine said cheerfully. "But I will try to be more like Lady Jillian."

Jillian's smile wobbled. "Be yourself, Jasmine. There is more to life than aspiring to be like me." Kenneth gave her a thoughtful look.

Graham didn't like the calculating assessment in his brother's eyes. He glared. His niece tilted her head, looking very confused.

"I wish I were a horse. It seems so much simpler than being a girl."

Jillian gave a choked laugh, but Badra grimaced, putting a hand to her daughter's back. "If you'll excuse me, I'm afraid I must retire." She grimaced again, and Kenneth sprang to her side.

"Are you all right, my love?"

"Just some back pain I've had all night."

Kenneth murmured some excuses and they left. Jasmine's wide-eyed gaze met Jillian's. "My mother's going to have a baby soon. I can't wait to have a brother or sister. It will be better than when I saw my cat having kittens." She turned to Graham with an earnest expression. "Do you think I can watch, Uncle Graham?"

Graham ran a finger along his too-tight collar. "Uh, I don't think that would be wise, Jasmine."

"Why?" she demanded.

"Er, these matters are usually reserved for females."

"I'm a female," she pointed out.

A dull flush covered Graham's cheeks. His helpless gaze sought Jillian's. She offered only a serene smile.

"Older females," he explained.

"But I know how babies are made. So why can't I see how they are born?" The girl turned to Jillian. "Would you like to know how babies are made, Lady Jillian? I saw it with horses. First—"

"Jasmine, young ladies do not discuss such matters," Graham interjected.

Jillian flashed him a wicked smile. To his niece she said, "There is time enough for such discussions when you are much older."

"Maybe when I'm ten?"

"Maybe when you're forty, like your papa would want," Graham put in, and tickled her ribs. Jasmine screeched with laughter.

Suddenly, a harsh female scream ripped the air and Kenneth yelled down the hallway, "Graham, Badra's water just broke! Call the doctor!"

The blood drained from Graham's face. "Lady Jillian, stay here with Jasmine," he ordered.

For a wild moment he wanted to bolt from the house. Instead, he ran for the telephone. With trembling fingers, he picked up the receiver and called the physician. Dread shot through him as the doctor's housekeeper relayed that the man was at his club, but she assured Graham she would send a servant to fetch him immediately.

"Do it. Find him and bring him over, *now*," Graham barked into the phone, then he hung up.

Another harsh cry stung his ears. Graham raced upstairs, darting into Badra's bedchamber, and ground to a halt. She was sitting on the bed, Kenneth sitting beside her, the two equally pale and distressed. Badra's scared, wide-eyed gaze found his.

"The baby's coming. I thought it was just back pain, but my water broke."

Graham felt a jolt of dizzying alarm. "Right this minute? He can't come now—Dr. Andrews is out!"

The housekeeper rushed into the room. Graham turned to her, urgency in his voice. "Mrs. White, can you deliver a baby?"

Her eyes widened. "I've never done it before."

Badra uttered another moan and Kenneth went even paler, clutching her hand. "Have *you* ever delivered a baby?" he asked Graham.

"I've delivered a camel," Graham admitted, feeling a cold sweat break out on his back. "It can't be much different, right?"

Badra glared at him. "I'm not a camel!"

"Of course not, my love," Kenneth soothed.

Distress filled her face. "If I can't have Dr. Andrews, then I want to give birth the old way. Look under the bed."

Kenneth shot her a bewildered look, but he dropped to his knees and rooted beneath the massive four-poster. Slowly he stood, two dark mud bricks in his hand. Elaborate hieroglyphs were etched on the sides. Recognizing them, Graham drew in a breath.

"Birthing bricks," he said.

Badra looked at her husband. "Yes, Khepri," she said

beseechingly, using his Arabic name. "Squatting on the bricks. Just as I birthed Jasmine."

Kenneth's mouth hung open as he set the bricks down. "Y-you agreed to my request for an English doctor. You told me you wanted to give birth as an English wife did."

"If I can't have the doctor, then I want this. Please," she whispered. "I'm so scared. I need the familiar." Tears shimmered in her eyes and she grimaced, holding her stomach. Another contraction? Graham slowly counted, feeling rising panic as he realized how close the pains were.

Kenneth gave the housekeeper a desperate look. She backed off, arms waving in the air. "No, my lord. I can't. I don't know heathen ways of birthing. I've only attended one birth, and that was a proper English delivery, the mother lying on a bed. And no men were present. It's indecent, what she wants."

A low growl rumbled from Graham's chest. "Mrs. White, other cultures have different customs. That does not make them indecent. On the contrary, the method of birthing she describes has been used for thousands of years. If this is what Badra wants, then she'll have it. *I'll* deliver the baby."

Three astonished heads swung toward him. He shoved his hands into his trouser pockets and added, "I saw such a birth." Badra looked hopeful. Kenneth looked doubtful. Mrs. White looked scandalized.

"A duke acting as a midwife!" the housekeeper sputtered.

Graham racked his brain, remembering. "We'll need two people, one on either side, Badra, to support you as you push."

Kenneth kissed his wife's cheek. "I'll take your right side, my love. I won't leave you." Then they all glanced at the stricken housekeeper, who shook her head.

"It's shocking and improper. This is women's business!"

Graham gave the woman a hard stare. "A man helped create the child, so that makes it a man's business as well. Now stop squawking and assist." His voice, low and quiet, carried the lash of command. With great satisfaction, he saw her recoil.

"I'm s-sorry, Your Grace," she stammered. "What do you want me to do?"

Graham took a deep breath, trying to calm the rapid beating of his heart. "I'll deliver the baby the way the viscountess desires. In between pains, she'll lie on the bed and you must tend to her. I want her to rest as much as possible to save her strength for the delivery. I'll need your help to coach me through. Oh—and cleanliness, Mrs. White. Do not touch the viscountess without washing your hands."

He jammed a hand through his hair, doubtful he could entirely count on Mrs. White. However, he wanted her there should anything go wrong. Women died in childbirth. If anything happened to Badra . . .

He couldn't worry about that. He closed his eyes, recreating a scene he'd eavesdropped upon years ago in the al-Hajid camp. "We'll need fresh straw and linens. We'll deliver the baby in my bedchamber—it's more comfortable and private."

"Only the heirs to the duchy are born there. It's tradition," Kenneth protested.

He gave his brother an even look. "I'm well aware of that."

The chubby-faced housekeeper gaped. "Straw, Your Grace? The *viscountess* is giving birth. She's not an animal!"

He leveled a hard look at her. "Ring for the footmen and order fresh straw delivered to my bedchamber." She swallowed a protest and went to the bellpull.

Kenneth very gently lifted his wife into his arms, following Graham to the ducal bedchamber. Inside the room, Graham set the bricks on the antique Persian carpeting rather than the polished wood floor to keep them from sliding. Badra grimaced as Kenneth settled her onto the bed.

Looking at Mrs. White, Graham decided they needed another woman to support Badra as she delivered, one who could keep her wits about her and refrain from being severe and condemning. Jillian? Could he ask her to do something this personal? She was his future wife. Best they both learn if she could rise to a crisis. He looked at Kenneth, who was remarkably pale but calm.

"Talk her through the pain. Take deep breaths," he advised.

The viscount sucked in air.

"Not you! Your wife," he hissed. "She'll need to get undressed. Totally."

Kenneth gave him a blank look. "You want my wife to give birth naked?"

No, in a ball gown. Graham rolled his eyes. "Help her undress. I'll be back."

He sped down to the formal drawing room. He ground to a halt in the doorway, seeing Jillian sitting on the settee, Jasmine clutching her hand and looking scared. Seeing the way she talked soothingly to the child gave him fresh hope.

"I need your help, Lady Jillian," he said roughly. "Badra is in labor and we're going to deliver her baby. The physician is unavailable."

Jasmine bounced up and down on the seat. "Mama's having my sister or brother," she sang.

But panic flared in Jillian's large green eyes. "Me, Your Grace? I've no experience birthing babies!"

"All you need do is stay at Badra's side, support her weight and encourage her. She needs another woman."

"Surely the housekeeper . . ."

"Mrs. White is needed to assist me in delivering the baby."

Jillian's fingers gripped her seat cushion. "You don't know me. What if I'm the type to fall to pieces? Or swoon?"

His gaze was steady and unwavering. "You're not. I can see it in you. I need you. Badra needs you."

A scream ripped through the house. Jasmine stopped bouncing and looked scared. Worry scrunched her elfin face.

"Mama? Is my mama going to be all right?" she whispered.

Jillian put an arm about the child. "It's all right, Jasmine. It's perfectly normal and natural, and there's nothing to fear." She smiled, patted the girl's hand and drew herself up. "Tell me what I must do."

Relief flooded Graham. "Come with me."

And they left, Jasmine insisting on accompanying them.

For all her life, Jillian had longed to be needed, an active participant in life instead of a silent, gray observer. She had never anticipated being needed to help birth a baby.

Sweat dampened her clammy palms as she scurried down the hall behind the duke, whose long stride never slowed. At a room at the end of the corridor, he twisted the brass doorknob and went inside. Jasmine scampered after him. Jillian hesitated.

Courage. She sucked in a breath and joined them.

The dark-haired, beautifully exotic Lady Tristan lay on an enormous bed, its majestic headboard carved with the ducal crest. Her husband sat beside her, gripping her hand. She wore only a man's large shirt, knotted below her breasts. From the waist down she was naked, her legs spread. A dark thatch of curly hair showed below her immense belly.

A fierce blush heated Jillian's cheeks. She had never seen another naked woman, nor participated in anything so private. And so scandalous, two men with her who were not physicians!

Then she noticed the worried look of the viscount, and the grim set of Graham's jaw and the lady's own fear. What did propriety matter in such a crisis?

Badra suddenly moaned like an animal in pain. Her face contorted.

"Deep breaths, Badra," Graham advised. "Talk her through the pain, Kenneth."

As the viscount slipped an arm about his wife, crooning, the stern-faced housekeeper bent between Badra's legs. She put her hand into—goodness!

"He's coming, Your Grace. Better hurry," Mrs. White said.

The duke removed his pin-striped coat and swiftly unbuttoned and stripped off his gray waistcoat, tossing both onto a nearby chair. He rolled up the sleeves of his immaculate white shirt. A handful of worried footmen scurried into the room, carrying armfuls of straw. They dumped it between the bricks as the duke instructed, stole a quick glance at the woman on the bed and hurriedly left.

Jasmine went to the bed. Her lower lip wobbled precariously. "Mama? Are you all right?"

The duke gently pushed her away. "She'll be fine, little one. Now, can you do something for me to help your mama?"

Her large, solemn gaze held his. "What, Uncle Graham?"

"I want you to go downstairs and wait for the doctor.

As soon as the butler lets him in, I need you to send him upstairs. I need someone I can rely on. Can you do it?"

Jasmine glanced doubtfully at her mother. Graham squeezed her shoulder. "It's all right. Your father and I will make sure nothing happens to her. I promise."

The little girl frowned. "When my cat had kittens, we put her in a nice box with a blanket. Shouldn't you get mama a box?"

Jillian almost laughed. But the duke smiled gently at his young niece and said, "It's different than your cat."

"You mean, she isn't going to lick my new brother or sister like Cleo did?"

"She'll be fine, Jasmine. Now, say good-bye to your mother and go downstairs. We really need your help."

The child kissed her mother, then cast a dubious look over her shoulder and trotted off. Graham vanished into the water closet to scrub his hands.

Feeling out of place in her riding habit, Jillian removed her faded gray outer jacket and hat, carefully placing them on the dresser. But Lady Tristan looked relieved to see her.

When another low moan rippled out, the housekeeper announced the baby was coming. The duke returned from washing up, and they moved Badra to the bricks.

As Graham instructed, Jillian stood beside the laboring mother, who squatted on the bricks. Bending, she slipped an arm around Badra's waist, holding her upright.

The duke crouched before his sister-in-law, his hands positioned beneath the lady's bottom as he made encouraging noises. "You're doing splendidly, Badra. Keep pushing, gently."

Jillian didn't know what to do, feeling absurdly useless. Badra's trembling arm gripped her, and the woman's pain became her own. Her worried glance fixed on the viscount, who was bending his head to his wife, crooning softly to her as she whimpered and moaned. Supporting the laboring mother took all her strength. Leg muscles unaccustomed to the odd position began to ache, but Jillian ignored the pain. She focused instead on the viscountess, making encouraging sounds that made no sense but sounded right.

Her words had no visible effect. Badra's face contorted as the woman grunted and strained and screamed to deliver her child. Her husband gripped her tightly, murmuring soothing words while the duke squatted before his sister-in-law, his face fierce with concentration. Jillian fell silent, awed at how Graham's commands made Badra focus even as she cried out, how cool and steady he seemed. And suddenly, his big hands gently held a furry, dark head that emerged from between Badra's legs.

Fascinated, Jillian fell speechless, watching the duke slide a tiny bluish form from inside its mother. A bloody wash of water spilled out, bathing his hands and the child. He gently massaged the newborn's back, crooning softly to the squalling babe. A collective gasp rippled through the room.

The viscountess sagged against Jillian, who felt an absurd urge to weep. She squeezed Badra's arm instead and smiled. "You have a baby," she whispered.

"A strong, healthy boy," Mrs. White declared with surprised satisfaction.

Graham glanced up—not at the mother, but directly at Jillian. In his eyes she saw pleased wonder. Jillian smiled through her tears. This was the most thoroughly unconventional, unpredictable and wonderful man she'd ever met.

She could perhaps fall in love with him. Heaven help her.

* * *

His mind had worked like a steadily ticking clock, without emotion, allowing him to deal with the crisis at hand. He'd remembered all the details of seeing the birth, and had applied them with detachment. Even while calling out words of encouragement for Badra to push, Graham felt severed from the experience—detached and aloof, as always.

But when the baby slipped into his outstretched hands and he held the fragile new life in his palms, something deep inside him stirred. A connection he didn't want.

It came, nonetheless.

Graham held the squalling baby, staring in awe. The tiny, innocent and helpless life roused every intense feeling he had desperately sought to quash. He struggled to contain his emotions and maintain his composure, but he cradled his nephew to his chest, unmindful of the bloody fluid coating the baby's now reddened skin. He began massaging the baby's back and glanced up at Jillian. She looked at him as if he had performed a miracle.

He felt himself transformed, as if in the baby's new beginning, he too, could begin anew. And he would do anything, absolutely anything, to protect that new life.

Graham gently bent his head and pressed his lips to his new nephew's dark, furry head, feeling dampness suddenly burn his eyes.

Life, in all its incredible, brutal and awesome force, had taken place before her. Jillian stared in marvel as the duke kissed his nephew with all the tenderness of a new mother. Then his usual aplomb returned as he and the housekeeper briskly tied string about the bluish white cord winding from the baby to its mother. The duke sliced through the cord with an odd-looking, curved dagger with an elaborate silver hilt.

The viscount's eyes were wet as he kissed his wife. He said, "My dagger—remember, my love? The one you used to cut us loose last year when we were trapped in the shop."

"A fitting blade to welcome your new son into the world," Graham murmured, taking a fresh towel from the housekeeper and carefully wiping the baby.

Standing upright, her body trembling, Badra sagged heavily against Jillian and held out her arms. "Please, let me see him. Let me hold him."

"Not now, my lady. He needs to be cleaned up first and swaddled," advised Mrs. White.

Jillian felt the violent tremor that shook Badra. "No, I need to see him. Let me hold him. Don't take him away, no!" Badra screamed as the housekeeper plucked the baby from the duke's hands and began walking away.

Instantly, the viscount bounded after the startled housekeeper, retrieving his son. He brought the squalling infant back to his sobbing mother. Tenderly he folded the naked infant into her arms. "Here's your baby, my love. Our son."

Badra clutched her son to her breast and wept. Jillian stared uneasily. The duke's brilliant, dark gaze lifted to her, burning fiercely. Then he stood and fetched a blanket from the bed, gently draping it over Badra's shivering shoulders.

A flurry of activity sounded down the hall. The door banged open and Jasmine burst inside. "The doctor's here," she cried.

A chagrined Mrs. White quickly hustled the wide-eyed Jasmine from the room, then returned. The gray-haired physician calmly assessed the situation, instructing Badra to push out the afterbirth. Kenneth and Jillian resumed their positions, supporting her. The doctor took the baby. He started to hand him to Mrs. White.

"No," Badra cried. Her beseeching gaze sought Graham's. "Give my son to the duke to hold."

The doctor did so. Graham gently cradled the newborn to his chest, keeping him warm in his arms as the physician delivered the afterbirth. Then he carefully returned the baby to Badra.

The duke glanced at Jillian. "Let's give them privacy. Why don't you meet me in the drawing room?"

But Jillian instead trailed him into the water closet. The mood inside the bedchamber had dramatically shifted when the housekeeper had attempted to remove the newborn for cleaning and swaddling. She wanted to know why.

Graham stripped off his bloody shirt. The taut flesh of his broad, naked shoulders captured her gaze. He bent over the basin, used water to scrub his hands and arms fiercely.

"I don't understand. Why was she so upset?" Jillian asked.

Graham stopped. Soap lather coated the dark hair on his arms as he braced himself over the basin. Beneath the smooth skin of his back, muscles rippled.

His voice was low. "When she was born, Jasmine was taken away from her while Badra slept. When she awoke, they told her Jasmine had been too small and died. She only discovered her daughter was alive last year, in Egypt. She had been sold into slavery, trained as a future prostitute."

Jillian stared at him in horror. "Who would do such a cruel thing? Does it happen all the time in Arabia?"

The duke finished rinsing his arms and hands, and briskly dried off with a towel. He lifted his head, his midnight gaze piercing hers in the mirror. Cold anger tightened his face. "There are many people in this world who are cruel, Jillian. Including in this country." He threw down the towel. "Sometimes people in this country are even crueler."

Chapter Eight

The grating harshness of his rapid breaths thundered in his ears as Graham stood outside the Strantons' Mayfair home.

Jillian had proven herself composed and confident in assisting in the birth. Her huge green eyes signaled sympathy as he told her the story of Jasmine's ill-fated birth. And then she had told him something he would never forget.

"It's horrible what happened to Jasmine," she had said, "but she's happy now, and has a new life. We can't change the past, we can only build anew and reach for the future. If one dwells on unhappy memories, you destroy your chances for future joy."

At a loss for words, he had stiffly thanked her for her assistance. Jillian had then murmured excuses about needing to return home.

Her wise words now gave him pause. For a wild moment Graham wondered if he hadn't made a dreadful mistake in seeking to bring down her father. Wasn't he doing just what she warned against, destroying any chance for happiness? And he began to wonder if she truly wasn't his destiny, sent to rebuild his shattered life from fragments of his troubled past.

Graham hesitated as he went to lift the brass door knocker. For twenty years he had hidden inside himself. The silver-topped walking stick in his left hand felt like a lead weight. His hand shook as he fingered the knocker to summon the butler and be ushered inside. Into the den of the beast.

But would it be better, as Jillian asserted, to release the past?

He closed his eyes. An image of the sneering Stranton danced in his memory, saying words Graham could not forget. They consumed him, made him doubt everything.

"You liked it. You know you did. You can't hide from what you really are, pretty boy."

The words weren't true, he thought in agony. Or were they?

He pushed the hateful words from his mind. The course was set; he must follow it. But his hand shook violently as he tried to rap on the door. Inside, the little boy in him screamed to turn and run far, far away. He could still return home, live safely within his comfortable four walls and never have to face Stranton. Never make him his father-in-law.

For a wild moment he nearly did turn and walk away. But Jillian's face rose in his mind. He had ruined her, and on his honor he owed her marriage. Without honor, he was nothing. All those years growing up with the al-Hajid, he'd thirsted for honor as a warrior. Turning his back on Jillian would mean turning his back on everything he valued. Graham gave the knocker a solid, confident rap.

Shabby silver-and-green livery covered the butler who answered. He took Graham's hat, outerwear and walking stick, then escorted him to a drawing room. Graham sat on a threadbare wing chair. His practiced eye took in bright spaces on the wall that indicated missing portraits on the faded silk wallpaper. Like other English aristocrats, had Stranton been forced to sell his artwork to keep up his household?

One framed piece stood in stark relief on the wall. Graham stood and wandered over to it, a sudden feeling of dread pooling in his stomach. Even before he saw the telltale script, he knew. The papyrus was ancient as Egypt's sands, fragile-looking behind its glass case. The lines drawn in vegetable ink were faded and worn but discernable.

The missing half of the map! The one Stranton had taken from him in childhood.

Graham fisted his hands, nearly plucking it off the wall. *It's mine. Mine!* Fresh anguish filled him at the memories.

Hearing footsteps in the hallway, he resumed his seat. He forced himself to relax as the earl boldly strode into the drawing room, Jillian trailing behind him, accompanied by a dark-haired, fragile-looking woman. His fiancée wore a hideously ugly gray gown buttoned to her neck. Her brilliant red-gold tresses were tightly coiled. She kept her gaze cast downward.

Mystified, Graham studied her. Where was the assured woman who had helped birth a baby? Jillian had vanished back into her quiet grayness, mist slipping into mist.

The earl brusquely introduced his wife. Graham bent over Lady Stranton's limp hand. Her smile seemed strained.

As they all sat, Graham's discomfort trebled. Forcing himself to make small talk about weather, he then asked questions about Stranton's proposed legislation. The earl launched into a enthusiastic diatribe while his wife and daughter remained silent.

When Stranton obliquely asked about the marriage settlement, Graham interrupted, suggesting they retire to his lordship's library for a private business talk. He did not want Jillian listening to her father discussing her as if she were bartered goods. The earl did not look at his daughter.

"There's no need, Your Grace. This is private enough."

Jillian served tea silently as her father crudely laid out the terms for her hand in marriage. Graham listened in disgust to the earl talk of his daughter as if he were selling a horse. The settlement was quite healthy. For a minute he balked at paying, thinking of his family's precarious finances. Then he looked at Jillian, pale and trembling. She was worth every shilling. He would marry her, then crush her father like soft limestone.

The earl's green eyes were cold and hard, where his daughter's were sparkling with life. Though not now. Jillian kept her gaze downward, her emotions hidden behind dull gray silk.

"How did you meet Jillian, Your Grace? My daughter rarely ventures out without my permission. She said she'd spent that night at her aunt's house."

Startled out of his ruminations, Graham glanced at Jillian. Her hands shook a little in her lap.

"Mrs. Huntington asked me to her home for dinner. Afterward, Jillian and I went for a walk in her garden."

Anger flared in Stranton's gaze. "My sister clearly failed in her duty."

At the ball, the earl's sister had pulled Graham aside as he waited for his carriage, and told him the truth—how she was the one who'd sent Jillian to the whorehouse. She'd begged him to collaborate in a lie to protect Jillian from her father.

More lies. More deceit. While Stranton sat, back straight, disapproval filling his face.

You lied to me. You promised you would rescue me. I should kill you now. It'd be so easy to press his thumb against the hollow of that throat and squeeze. . . .

"Mrs. Huntington was distracted with a domestic problem while I was in the garden with your daughter," Graham lied.

Gratitude flashed in Jillian's eyes.

The earl sniffed. "She is a poor chaperone, and I have told my wife as much."

Lady Stranton flinched and Jillian went pale. Graham's unease grew. This household held dark secrets, like an Egyptian tomb.

Abruptly he murmured excuses about needing to return home. He kept a watchful eye on Jillian as he stood, pressing his lips to her trembling hand. Hatred boiled inside him as he shook the earl's hand, wishing he could crush him. It would be so easy.

As he left the house, Graham frowned. Something was amiss. Lady Stranton with her red-rimmed eyes and lethargic air had the drugged attitude of an opium addict. Jillian was silent, the spark of her laughter missing, the confidence displayed during the birth vanished. What had that bastard done to her?

Graham climbed into his carriage and rapped on the roof with his walking stick. When he got home, he went to his study and sat, thinking hard about the papyrus he'd seen. The map. He must have it back. Even if it meant breaking into Stranton's house.

Much later that night, dressed in black trousers, black shirt and a black coat, Graham walked to the Stranton townhouse. He stood in the street, staring up. A light blazed in one upstairs room, from which he could see the slender figure of a woman sitting in a chair by the window. Red-gold tresses shone in the light.

127

Graham sucked in his breath. The woman was clad only in her chemise. Darting a glance about the deserted street, he hastily crossed the lawn. He studied the balcony and tossed up the rope he'd brought. He double-knotted it the way he'd been taught by the Bedu, and shimmied up.

Lithe as a cat, he climbed over the railing and dropped silently onto the balcony. Jillian, sitting by the open French doors, gasped as she saw him.

Shrugging out of his coat, he was beside her in two quick strides. Graham forgot his purpose to steal the papyrus. Nothing else mattered at the moment but her.

"Why are you sitting at the window undressed?" he hissed.

She shrank back from him. Gooseflesh erupted on her naked, alabaster arms. He very gently placed his coat over her shivering shoulders. Graham repeated the question in the soothing voice he reserved for skittish mares about to be bred. Finally she lifted her luminous gaze to him.

"Father's punishment. I'm to be denied any clothing except when I venture out with him or for my supervised ride with the groom. Because he says I'm"—she gulped—"a whore."

His guts twisted in anger. "It's well past one in the morning, *habiba*," he said softly. "You must sleep."

Curiosity flickered in her lifeless gaze. "What is *habiba?*"

An endearment. But he didn't answer, instead taking her chilled hand into his warm palm. He began rubbing her hand to warm her flesh. "Why are you sitting at the open windows?" he asked.

"Father says a whore should display her wares to the world," she said dully.

Graham bit back a curse and focused his attention on his future wife. She sat still and stiff, like Jasmine's china doll.

He went to the bedchamber door and jammed a gilded chair beneath the knob to prevent anyone from intruding. Then he returned to Jillian and crouched beside her, wishing she could speak and release her anguish. Wishing he could help. But all he could do was marry her and remove her from this hideous household as quickly as possible.

Jillian felt as if she would shatter. A bone-chilling numbness struck her as he witnessed her shame. The duke stood and closed the French doors with a firm click. His large frame remained blurred by tears she refused to shed. Why had he come here? She hung her head, wanting to die from mortification.

"Come over to the bed where it's warmer," he said in a soft voice, hypnotic in its soothing tones.

Like a mindless puppet she obeyed, placing her trembling, chilled hand in his. The duke sat her upon the bed, which was neatly turned down for the night by her maid. She wanted to burrow beneath the covers. But he suddenly toed off his shoes and began unbuttoning his waistcoat, rousing her from stupor. Removing it, he did the same to his shirt. His bare, powerful chest with its thick covering of dark hair caused a little tingle between her thighs. Goodness, he couldn't mean to . . .

"W-what are you doing?"

"Since you're denied clothing, I've removed mine as well. It's not fair for only one of us to be fully dressed. I want you to feel comfortable." His midnight eyes twinkled.

But she could only stare in alarm and arousal. An intense yearning filled her as she drank in the sight of the smooth bulge of his hard biceps, of the swirls of dark hair on his hard chest. He sat beside her and held both her hands lightly in his.

"It's all right," he crooned. "I'm not going to make love to you. Not yet. Not until we marry."

Disappointment and shame replaced arousal. She

looked away. She was a whore, just as her father indicated. Lusting after taut male flesh without the sanctity of marriage to procreate. Her father's long, labored lecture rang in her ears:

"Sexual lust is reserved for the marriage bed, Jillian, and only then to create heirs. You will do your duty to the duke to give him a son, but before then I'll be damned if I'll let your lusty, tawdry nature shame me again. Do you hear me?"

He had not shouted, just looked at her with that cold grimace of disgust.

She was a disgrace.

"*Habiba*, don't shut me out. You're so cold," Graham whispered.

She forced herself to reply. "What are you doing here, Graham? It's certainly an odd time to pay a social call. I'm afraid it's a bit late for tea."

He did not smile at her little joke. "I want to steal something from your father."

Jillian looked at him, startled. "Steal what?"

"You. Leave with me, Jillian. Tonight. We'll run off and marry in Gretna Green. You can't remain here with him for a day longer. Not when he treats you like this."

Tempting, oh, so very tempting. She liked Graham, and the way he made her feel, but she also wanted to be her own woman, educated and independent. If she caved in and went with him, her dream would die. Just a while longer, a steamship to America and she'd be free. And she'd march naked to the docks if she must.

"Please go. Servants will find out, and they will talk."

"No," Graham said softly, brushing a finger along her compressed lips. "Not until you let it out. You're like china, *habiba*. And if you keep everything inside, you'll shatter. Don't let him break you. Let the pain out now, while he can't see."

Squeezing her eyes shut, trying to will away the enormous pressure inside, she shook her head. Graham's arms settled about her. He pressed his lips to her temple, murmuring soft words. His compassion undid her. Jillian felt a treacherous tear slip from one eye. Like with a leaky dam, the flood threatened. She pushed faintly at the muscled arms holding her close. He only stroked her hair. He would not let go. She did.

The dam burst in a violent gush. Tears flowed down her cheeks as great, choking sobs escaped. Jillian rocked back and forth, moaning as she wept into her hands, all the pain of past years finally spilling out. Graham continued to hold her, stroking her hair.

"Yes, let it out. Let it all out. It's all right."

The outburst did not last. Jillian felt utterly drained as he wiped her eyes and nose with a corner of her bedsheet. Well, he'd seen the worst. But the duke simply looked at her.

"Are you angry?" he asked.

God, yes, she was. She wanted to break things, scream and rage, but years of quietly suppressing her emotions held her temper in check. Her breath came in great, ragged gulps of air.

"I want to hit something," she gasped.

The duke picked up one of the bed's large pillows. "Go on, punch it," he encouraged. "It will feel good to release your rage."

She stared at the pillow in horror, her stomach clenching. "I can't. That's totally preposterous."

"Sod preposterous. Punch it," he ordered. "Hit it until all those emotions are out of you."

Jillian acquiesced. She took it and threw it on the bed, banging it against the edge with wild fury.

"Harder!"

She flung the pillow against the bed. The aging yellow

case suddenly split. Feathers burst out, covering him in a spray of white. She stared, goggle-eyed, at the duke. Graham blew out a breath. A feather floated upward from his lips. He gave a wry smile.

"Well, perhaps you're right. It does look preposterous," he said.

Jillian collapsed beside the duke and laughed.

"Feel better now?"

She nodded, realizing he had been right. But still, the shame crept back. He had witnessed her humiliation, and now this violent outburst. . . .

"Why did you do that?" she whispered.

"Because I know what it's like to be caught in a situation where you need to release everything bottled up inside you."

They both lay down on the bed. He enfolded her in his arms, which felt wonderful. She became aware of the hardness of his long frame, and of a different hardness below. Jillian tensed.

Graham gave a rueful smile. "Oh, right. That. Relax. It's a normal male reaction I have around you. But I promise I won't demonstrate my, ah, affection until we're married."

He pulled her closer. His muscled chest became her pillow. Jillian felt the springy hairs tickle her cheek.

"You smell so nice," she mumbled against his warm skin. "What is that scent?"

He caressed her hair. "Sandalwood soap. A leftover habit from my days in Arabia."

Jillian inhaled the delicious smell, utter exhaustion replacing her tension. "Graham, you must leave. Father . . . he cannot catch you here," she protested sleepily.

He placed a single forefinger upon her lips. "Shhh," he said softly. "Sleep now. All is well."

"But, Graham . . ."

He merely tightened his grip about her. "Five minutes. Five minutes more and I'll leave," he promised.

Graham listened as Jillian's breathing became deep and even. Why did he feel so peaceful with her, as if everything slid from his shoulders and he could sleep? No nightmares. No dreams. Just utter peace.

Just close your eyes. Five minutes, he told himself.

He closed his eyes and fell fast asleep.

Chapter Nine

Something was dreadfully wrong. In the dream she stood, as always, in the hallway before the heavy oaken door. The forbidden door. She wanted to touch the gleaming knob, but she was too afraid. Yet she must. She had to open the door!

Jillian quivered with terror as her fingers went to graze the pretty glass knob, and a disembodied voice drifted inside her mind, filled with savage anger. "Go away, or you will suffer the consequences."

A faint click sounded, and the brass key turned in the lock.

Jillian could not move or think; she could only stare in horror, knowing terrible things would happen.

And then it came. A faint, but high-pitched sound of distress from behind the door. A muffled cry from within. A cry that—

Jillian awoke with a loud gasp. Sweat drenched her body. Her heart pounded wildly as she slowly became aware of her surroundings. Willing herself to calm down, she counted slowly. The nightmare had returned.

She had not experienced it since childhood. Why now? Why had she started dreaming again of the locked door? Something was terribly wrong. The weight of another body pressed against her. She glanced over.

Muscled arms surrounded her. Jillian lay still, processing her thoughts. The duke. He had climbed into her room last night and he was still here.

Wildly she struggled to sit. A grayish, smoky London dawn shone outside.

Oh, goodness! Graham had slept the night away. Here, in her bed! Soon the undermaid would come to rouse her. Father always insisted on rising early and breakfasting together. Hysterical laughter bubbled up. What would the maid say upon seeing the handsome stranger in Jillian's bed?

She jostled Graham. "Your Grace, wake up! You've got to leave now!"

He roused so instantly she wondered if he had been sleeping after all. He lay back down, his finger tracing dampness on her cheek. He gave her a thoughtful look.

"Did you have a nightmare? You were crying in your sleep."

"Oh heavens, never mind that! Please, you must leave. Now!"

Graham rolled over and stretched, yawning like a contented cat. Taut biceps bulged as his large frame straddled her. She felt the hard bulge of his erection on her belly.

"Answer me, Jillian. Did you have a nightmare?"

"Doesn't everyone have nightmares? Please, you must leave!"

His heavy-lidded gaze caught hers. "Don't I deserve a good-morning kiss?" he drawled.

"Not until we're married. *If* we marry."

"Are you planning to run from me as well, Jillian?" he asked, looking surprised.

Her gaze automatically shot to the floorboards that concealed her hidden money. The duke followed her gaze, and he gave her a knowing glance. He sprang out of bed and walked on the boards, testing their weight. *Oh no . . .* At the board closest to the wall, he tapped his foot.

In minutes he had her hiding space revealed, the money in his hand. Graham fingered the treasure as dread seized her.

"Running away still," he observed.

"I don't wish to marry," she blurted.

He remained silent a moment, weighing the currency in his hand as if weighing something much heavier. When he spoke, his voice was low and earnest.

"I'll make you a bargain, Jillian. If you give marriage to me a chance, for three months, and you still wish to leave, I'll let you. We can obtain an annulment and I'll give you money enough to be free on your own, for good."

Confused, she stared. "You mean, you won't . . . touch me?"

"I didn't say that. If you're my wife, I expect to exercise my husbandly rights." He dropped the money into its hiding spot. "Money will secure the annulment. Money can buy anything."

Suspicion flowered. "Why are you so intent on marrying me?"

His expression remained blank. "Having an English wife whose father is well-regarded would be a tremendous asset to my family. My brother's wife is snubbed because of her Egyptian heritage. I fear little Jasmine will suffer the same. You can help Jasmine learn social graces that will help her gain acceptance when she has her coming out."

Jillian remembered Bernard's sneers about Lady Tristan. Her gaze met his. "I understand. But what if . . . I become with child?"

"The child remains with me. I'll raise him as my heir."

She thought rapidly. A chance for freedom. But she would be long gone before then.

"He won't let you get away before then, you know." Graham's gaze was sharp and calculating. Jillian drew the sheet up to her chin. A fierce intensity appeared in his eyes. She knew he would not let her escape. He would have her. Jillian swallowed hard.

"Is it a bargain? You'll marry me and become my wife, in every sense of the word, for three months. If you're not satisfied, you're free to leave."

"I will try to flee before then. I must," she whispered.

Silent and catlike, Graham crossed the room. He seized her chin with one warm, firm hand. "Don't run before my three months come due. I will find you if you do."

Startled at the deep warning in his velvet voice, she shivered. "You want me that much?"

He took her hand and gently placed it over the bulge in his trousers. Her eyes widened.

"What do you think?" he asked.

He bent his head and brushed her lips gently with his. Against her better judgment, Jillian's hands slid around his neck as she clung to his warmth. The hardness of his arousal ground against her quivering body. With wry amusement she realized she was equally aroused.

Gently he removed her hands and brushed her cheek with a knuckle. The duke turned, heading for the French doors, clad only in rumpled black silk trousers. She watched his taut, round bottom move with each elegant stride.

"What are you doing?" she cried.

"Leaving, as you asked."

"Not like that. Put on your clothing!"

He looked down. "Oh, quite right. I'm dreadfully un-attired. Perhaps I could ask your father to borrow one of your gowns since you're not presently using them."

Despite the gravity of the situation, she laughed, and the duke smiled.

"That's more like it," he said. He dressed rapidly. "Now then, I need a favor. The map downstairs, the pa-pyrus one framed in the drawing room. I need a tracing of it."

"Why?"

"Because I think I may have the missing half. I don't want to tell your father, on the odd chance I could be wrong. But if I have a tracing, I can tell for sure."

"You mean it actually might be worth something?"

Her fiancé looked pensive. "Yes. It is a map leading to an ancient buried treasure. A myth that could be true."

Excitement coursed through Jillian. Buried treasure? "I can do it. But having it delivered to your house may prove challenging, as Father is having my correspon-dence closely watched these days."

Graham smiled and lifted her hand, pressing a kiss to it. "Then hide it carefully among your things and bring it with you when you become my wife."

She almost sobbed. *But I will never become your wife, Graham.*

He kissed her, his lips hard and ruthless, and she sagged against him, clutching his coat lapels. Footsteps sounded on the carpeted hallway outside. Jillian started.

"Graham, you've got to leave."

He frowned at the door. "Perhaps I should remain and let him know what I think of his treatment of you."

The footsteps halted. Jillian's frantic gaze whipped to

the door. The knob rattled. "Lady Jillian? Why can't I get inside?" a female voice called out.

"Just a minute, Dotty." She bit her lip.

The sound of a familiar male voice made her blood freeze. The door rattled on its hinges as a heavy weight pressed against it. "Jillian! Let me in at once!"

Father.

Her gaze caught Graham's, which was filled with anger. Graham quickly laced his shoes. He stroked her cheek lightly.

"Stay strong for me," he murmured, then he ducked out the French doors.

Jillian looked frantically about. The room smelled of him, sandalwood and pure male. She ran to her bureau, took a bottle of heavy French perfume and spilled it, staining the wood and scenting the air. She pulled up the rumpled covers and ran to the door, snagging her wrap along the way.

Jerking the chair away and opening the door, she looked into her father's infuriated face. Jillian drew her wrap close about her shoulders. Her father stormed inside. His hard gaze scanned the room. It landed on the disturbed floorboard. He ran to it.

Oh no, no, no. The duke had forgotten to cover . . .

In his hands, her father held all her money. Her freedom.

"Why have you secreted money away?" Pound notes fanned the air as he waved them, a fan fashioned from selling her flesh.

"It's . . . it's mine, Father. I've been saving."

"There's no need to squirrel money away. I provide for all your needs. I'll take it."

A silent scream echoed inside her head. But she bit back her cries, watching in dumb grief as he pocketed her money.

Her hard-earned pounds and pence. Her education.

Her dream died, shriveling to a blackened crisp, just as those books had burnt in the fire.

Watchful green eyes, mirrors of her own, studied her. A chill seized her spine. "Jillian, were you planning on running away?"

Her mouth went dry. Wordlessly, she stared.

"You will not. You will marry as planned, Jillian." A cold smile slid over the earl's face. "Proper young ladies do as their fathers bid. As will you. Or else."

The threat hovered in the air between them, but a kernel of courage surfaced. Jillian thought of her passion in Graham's arms. She found courage to do what she must. What else could he do to her? Jillian forced a brave note into her voice.

"Or else what, Father?" she challenged.

Surprise flared in his eyes. The earl straightened, calmly assessing her. "You truly wish to know?"

She felt her courage flicker like a lamp flame. With all her strength, she fanned it. "I'm a grown woman, Father. Not a child anymore."

The corners of his mouth pulled downward. "You are my *daughter*, Jillian," he began. Then he stopped. The look in his eyes scared her. She had seen it before, once, a long, long time ago.

The creak of a door slowly closing . . .

Jillian swallowed hard. Sweat dampened her temples, cooling in the mild breeze wafting through the open French doors. Her heart thundered in her chest. She remained motionless, even when he pivoted, almost gracefully. He silently assessed her.

The crack of his palm against her cheek did not hurt as much as the words following. His face twisted in ugly anger as he said, "You will marry the duke, Jillian. You will, or you will find a cell in Bedlam very confining. Yes, very confining indeed."

"You wouldn't," she whispered.

"A father has every right to commit his daughter when her lusty, wayward behavior endangers her." He turned sharply on his heel and, at the door, spoke over his shoulder. "Think of it, Jillian. Marriage to the duke, or a cell in an insane asylum. The choice is yours."

Cold dread seized her as he closed the door behind him. The key turned outside. She was locked in.

Chapter Ten

The day after breaking into the earl's house, Graham paid Stranton a polite visit. He voiced two objections to the earl's marriage settlement. Graham told Stranton he wanted to marry by common license, preventing a reading aloud of the banns—it was better not to draw attention to Jillian. But the earl balked. He wanted the public to know exactly whom she married. He did finally agree, reluctantly, to Graham's proposal of a small church wedding with only the immediate family present.

That Sunday in church, Graham quietly watched from a distant pew as Jillian flushed in agonizing shame as the banns were read. Heads turned to look at her. They knew why she was marrying the duke.

Two weeks later, the earl, his wife and Jillian sat stiffly in the duke's immense drawing room for an engagement tea. Jillian had once more lost her inner spark. Her eyes were dull and lifeless. Graham shot a quick, hard look at the earl. Bastard. He wanted to wring Stranton's neck for the cruelties inflicted on Jillian.

Instead, he engaged the earl in talk of politics, pretending rapt interest in his proposed legislation. Then he struck, the first step to ensnaring his enemy.

"Perhaps your proposed bill would foster public support if you demonstrated the good it can do," Graham suggested.

Stranton leaned forward. "What do you suggest?"

He kept his tone deliberately casual. "Why don't you find a victim of the vilest of the sex trades—say, a young boy—and reform him? Teach him a trade and create a living model of the good the bill could achieve."

Silence filled the room. Graham ignored Kenneth's worried look. He focused all his attention on the earl. Stranton steepled his long, thin fingers and nodded.

"Excellent suggestion. A young child living in the streets, given a new chance and turned into a model citizen. Where would I find such a child, though?"

"I could help you find one. My groom, Charles, used to live in St. Giles, an area known for such wretched activity."

"I would greatly appreciate your support, Caldwell. But . . . I think it best our little venture remain between us. We should not tell the other lords, should it prove a dismal failure."

Graham fought to keep his emotions level. Oh, it *would* prove a dismal failure, when he presented Stranton with a gift the earl could not refuse. . . .

"I promise," he said evenly. *Like you promised me you would help me escape the al-Hajid, you bastard.* Promises could be broken.

He dared to sweep his gaze about the room. Jillian kept her gaze downcast. Lady Stranton looked as meek and distant as her daughter. But Kenneth shot Graham a wary look. *What the hell are you planning?* he seemed to say.

A shard of guilt speared him. Graham ignored it and turned to Badra, asking about the baby. The woman, bless her, picked up his cue and skillfully turned the conversation into small talk of children. Graham smiled and listened with half an ear, only growing wary when the earl's wife asked to see the newborn.

Badra rang for the nurse, who came into the drawing room with the boy, handing Michael over to his mother. Lady Stranton perked up at the sight of the sleeping baby. The earl leaned forward, his thin face sparking with interest.

"May I see him?"

Distress seized Graham as Badra went to the earl. As she lowered the tiny bundle for his inspection, Stranton smiled.

"Such a pretty boy," he crooned. Graham went perfectly still.

The words echoed in his head, a jagged memory piercing him. That voice, those words, as he shrank away in numb terror, hating himself for what he did. Hating that man . . .

Such a pretty boy. No. No. No. Not again. Not this time!

The earl reached out to touch the newborn. Graham bolted from his chair, mindless of the perspiration dampening his back. "Let the proud uncle hold him, Badra. He is my heir," he said, fighting to keep the tremulous note from his voice.

Bemusement darkened her expression, but she handed Michael over. Graham took the baby. He cooed over him as a proud uncle should. Inside, he quaked violently. Forcing a stiff smile, he regarded his guests.

"I think he needs to sleep now. Surely being about all

these adults is not good for him. I'll see him off to his nurse," he said, nodding as a means of good-bye.

Ignoring Badra's dumbstruck look, he forced himself to walk slowly out of the room, cradling the baby against his chest. *I must not let him touch Michael*, he thought. He had to shield him, protect the boy from Stranton. Michael, so vulnerable and innocent.

Graham held his precious nephew as he entered the nursery with its cheerful yellow walls and the elaborate, carved cradle Kenneth had made. The round-faced nurse in her crisp white apron and sensible gray dress sat reading at the window seat. She sprang up at his entrance.

"Your Grace?"

Ignoring her, he carefully laid the baby down in the cradle. Then Graham stood guard, rocking the baby, trying to quell the violent panic inside. The nurse watched.

Michael stirred, whimpering in sleep. Graham put a gentle hand on his head. "I won't let him hurt you, Michael. That's a promise. I'll rip him to pieces before he ever lays a hand on you," he whispered in Arabic.

He looked over at the nurse, who stood quietly nearby. "See to it that no one but the baby's parents, Jasmine and myself enter this room. Under no circumstances is Michael to leave the nursery until I give permission."

"Yes, Your Grace."

He quietly thanked all English servants, who always obeyed odd orders from their employers and did not ask questions.

A knock sounded at the door. His body tensed, Graham whipped around, his arms spread over the cradle as if to shield the baby. The doorknob jiggled. His blood went cold. Memories asserted themselves, piercing like knives. *Such a pretty boy . . .*

The *jambiya* he'd taken to hiding in his jacket since seeing Stranton slipped into his hand. Its steel edge gleamed. The nurse gasped and reached into the crib to take Michael.

Graham reacted swiftly, the blade slicing the air, stopping a whisper from her throat. "Don't touch him," he warned. Roused from sleep, the baby began a thin, reedy wail.

Graham swung back toward the door. A key turned, the door began to open. Assuming a defensive stance, he held out the knife and waited in wary dread for the intruder to enter. A man stepped into the room. Graham raised the knife.

"Graham, please put the *jambiya* down before you hurt yourself or my son."

Relief filled him as he recognized Kenneth and Badra. But he did not lower the knife or leave his post.

Blue eyes met dark brown. "Nurse, leave us," Kenneth said.

She floated past them out the door, a gray ghost in a crisp white apron. Gray like Jillian. Invisible.

"What happened down there?" his brother demanded. Badra put a hand on Graham's arm. Her gaze was unwavering.

"Such a pretty boy," she said in a singsong tone.

Graham trembled, the knife shaking in his hands. "No," he grated. "He mustn't touch Michael. Must not touch, don't touch, don't touch, leave him alone."

"Graham!"

He blinked, tried to focus. His sister-in-law. His brother.

"Oh God, no. It's *him*, isn't it? Stranton's the one. He's al-Hamra, your future father-in-law!" Kenneth spat a mouthful of Arabic curse words. "And you invited him *here*!" Repulsion tightened Kenneth's mouth. But repulsion for whom?

Graham stiffened. "I would not let Michael get hurt." *Never. Ever.* Either by Stranton or himself. Sudden grief squeezed his chest. Did Kenneth think so?

"Of course not. The baby is hungry, I imagine," Badra observed. She offered a gentle smile. "May I feed him?"

He stared at her then realized he still held the knife. The duke sheathed the blade and tucked it away, stepping aside from the cradle. With remarkable aplomb, Badra retrieved her son, nestling him to her breast.

"I know you were trying to protect him, Rashid. . . ."

Her use of his Arabic name jerked him back to the present. Graham took a gulping breath, struggling to regain his usual, detached self. As she walked over to the window seat with Michael, he forced his normally rigid control to return.

Kenneth was not so calm. He stared. "Why are you marrying Jillian if you know her father's al-Hamra? What is your purpose?"

"To know an enemy's weak spots, one must study them intently. Even infiltrate their defenses by slipping among them, blending and coaxing them out," he recited.

"Jabari always said that." Kenneth shoved a hand through his hair. "That's why you did it. You're marrying the enemy. Good God, Graham, are you insane?"

"Completely," he managed.

His brother stared, then threw his hands into the air. "Whatever," he muttered. "It's your life. Marry her. But I'm telling you this, Graham, I'm staying out of it and so is my family. Plot your revenge, but I will not have my family hurt. Is that understood?"

A hollow ache settled in his chest. He felt terribly alone once more. "You have my word," Graham said quietly.

Kenneth looked bewildered. "I don't understand you, Graham. I feel like I never will."

"No, you never can, Kenneth," he agreed. And thank God for that.

Mustering his resolve, he headed for the door. "Excuse me. I must return to my guests."

And to the ghosts of his past.

Chapter Eleven

Graham and Jillian were married in their quiet church ceremony. She wore a modest gray gown; her father expressly forbade her from wearing white. When Graham solemnly slid the thin gold band onto her finger, it felt like the jaws of a steel trap shutting.

The wedding luncheon was torturously slow. Hosted by Jillian's parents, the funereal atmosphere depressed her, with the heavy burgundy drapes shutting out the sun from the ominous, long mahogany table where they all stiffly sat. One only needed dirge music. Even Jasmine failed to fill the air with her excited chatter, for she was not present; Graham had thought it wisest to leave her home. The duke's brother kept studying her and then staring at her father as he talked with Graham. Badra's attempts at conversation with her mother withered and died.

When it was over, Jillian uttered a silent prayer of gratitude. Graham escorted her home and upstairs to the duchess's quarters. She gazed dully at the pretty blue and white bedchamber with its spacious sitting room.

"I'll leave you to rest. Dinner is at seven," he said.

"I'm not certain if my gowns have all arrived."

"I had them burnt," he said calmly.

Jillian raised her brows. "At least Father allowed me to wear my underthings. Do you wish me to walk about naked?"

He smiled. "That's the spirit. But no. I took measurements from the gowns your father had sent over, and had new ones made. I don't want you to wear gray. Wear emerald. Sapphire. Jewel colors to match what I know lies inside you. No gray."

"What lies inside me, Graham?" she asked. Today she felt only keen despair.

He touched her cheek. "Passion. A spirit that was nearly extinguished, and that needs encouragement to turn into living flame."

Disturbed at what he saw, she patted her head with a wry smile. "To match my hair? Father ordered me to wear dull gowns to suppress it. I prefer dark colors."

A somber look entered his eyes. "Don't, Jillian. Darkness can be terribly lonely."

He dropped a light kiss on her cheek. "Since you lack a lady's maid, I've assigned one of the more experienced upstairs maids as your attendant. Wear the sapphire gown. I know it will look lovely on you."

Then she watched him leave, wondering if the darkness he mentioned wasn't the reason for the secrets in his own eyes.

Too nervous about the night to come, Jillian barely tasted her dinner. The informal casualness here shocked her, especially allowing Jasmine to dine with the other adults instead of taking a tray in the nursery. Yet Jillian found herself growing wistful as Kenneth, Badra and Jasmine talked and laughed with each other. Here was the type of family she had always wanted—open, honest and affectionate, not remote and cold.

Only the duke remained slightly aloof, smiling now and then. Over the top of his wineglass, his brilliant gaze regarded her. Puzzled, she stared at Graham's flute as he set it down. A footman sprang to fill it with water.

"I don't drink," he said. "But I don't wish to ruin the table setting either."

Then he grinned, the same boyish smile he had displayed their very first night at Madame LaFontant's. Jillian laughed.

After dinner, the little maid he'd assigned as her personal attendant helped Jillian remove her sapphire gown. Jillian sighed as she caressed the smooth satin. Never had she owned anything more vibrant or luxurious. Emily helped her into a cream satin peignoir. Its heavy flowing lines draped her body.

"The duke had this made for you as a gift. He said his beautiful bride deserved to wear something special on their special night," the maid explained, gazing in admiration.

Jillian touched the nightwear with a trembling hand. White, for her wedding night. She wasn't a virgin, but he was treating her as honorably as one. Father called her a whore and shamed her in front of the servants; Graham called her beautiful and honored her before them.

She drew in a ragged breath, apprehensive and excited, as she sat on the massive four-poster. The bed was enormous, with waves of soft cotton sheets and piles of silk pillows. She swallowed hard, wondering what awaited her.

The duke had bought her virginity, but this was different. Before, there had been nothing but physical intimacy and a parting of the ways. Tonight her lover would not be a stranger, but her husband who expected to share her bed each night.

The door to their adjacent chambers opened. Graham stepped inside, wearing a black robe that stretched over his broad shoulders and fell to his bare knees. The sight of his muscled, taut calves with their thick dusting of dark hair seemed more sensual than when he had uncloaked himself in the brothel.

As breathless as their first time together, she studied his face. A thick sweep of ebony hair fell rebelliously over his forehead. Dark eyes, lit with fierce intensity. A proud, straight nose, sculpted cheekbones displaying his aristocratic lineage and firm, sensual lips. Her gaze flew to the thick muscles in his neck, the long, almost feminine eyelashes. Goodness, he was beautiful. Almost pretty, but for the hard line of his taut jaw and the slight bristle shadowing it. Graham prowled toward her with lithe grace, silent as a cat.

He held out a hand. "Come with me."

Confused, she stared. "Why?"

His deep voice, smoky with unspent passion, caressed her skin. "It is tradition that all the heirs to the duchy are conceived in the duke's bed."

Obediently, she rose. His large palm swallowed hers like a tiny bird. It mattered not, for he would take her where he willed. Her bedchamber or his, the results would be the same. No baby would be conceived.

The duke led her to his bed. Massive wood pillars thick as tree trunks dominated the oak. Graham swept her into his arms and laid her carefully upon the sheets. He stood back, unsmiling, and unbelted his robe. It parted and puddled at his feet, and he stood before her fully nude. The chamber was flooded with light, unlike her first time.

Suddenly shy, she shrank back. "Why so much light?"

"I want to see you this time. *Everything.*"

Trepidation filled her. She didn't love this man, but felt a deep sensual pull toward him. It made her scared and vulnerable. Jillian couldn't forget the unbreakable bond between them. He had been her first lover.

Yet, years of his sexual experience stood before them. She lifted her arms as he tugged the nightwear off her. Jillian lay on the bed, nude.

"You are truly a redhead," he mused, staring at the tangle of soft curls covering her womanly parts.

A heated blush covered her cheeks. He knew all. There was no deceiving.

Graham studied the contours of his wife's body, the firm, heavy breasts tipped with reddened, taut nipples. Her ivory skin lay smooth and silky, begging for his touch. A slightly rounded belly gave way to the flare of her curved hips. His breath hitched as he spied the red-gold curls hiding her womanly parts.

A becoming crimson blush, like a sunrise, crept from the horizon of her throat to her cheekbones. His breathing grew heavy and ragged. Fierce desire mingled with tender passion. Blood flooded his groin. Her lush, full mouth parted and her emerald eyes darkened with evidence of her need.

He joined her on the bed, one hand tenderly cupping her breast, the other caressing her cheek as she gazed up at him. Her hands rose, touched his face as if charting a map. He trembled.

Oh God, he wanted her so badly. Too much. He had

never wanted, not since childhood. Graham had learned to relinquish, to never permit his desires and wants to rule him.

Not now. He could no more prevent his furious need than he could force a Khamsin wind to halt. He let the wind envelop him in its hot, torrid embrace as he caressed her—his wife.

Her skin was pale and luminous, white as alabaster from the ancient ones in Egypt who carved statues in homage. Graham wanted to worship her, to cover her ivory skin with adoring kisses until she writhed beneath him. Cinnamon freckles peppered her pale shoulders. Intrigued, he bent closer, studying. He had not seen them in the brothel. Laying her down, Graham brushed his lips against one, gave a delicate lick then began kissing each one of the tiny, adorable dots. Hot anticipation curled inside him as she moaned and clutched his head. Graham pulled back, driven by a need to explore her soft body.

Jillian lay outstretched like a naked sacrifice for him. He stared, enraptured. Graham placed a warm palm upon her silky skin. Very slowly, he traced a line from the deep indentation in her trembling belly down to the soft tangle of red-gold curls. With gentle reverence, he placed a kiss upon her stomach.

His hands stroked the smooth skin of her legs. She recoiled as they slipped upward to the tight clasp of her clenched thighs, delving deep within. A startled look entered her eyes and Jillian jerked away.

He soothed her with a husky murmur of masculine reassurance, then continued his exploration, kissing his way down her legs, then kneeing her thighs apart and slipping between them. Her hands rose, shaking wildly, pushing at his chest.

"We made a bargain, Jillian," he told her softly. "Remember? You will be my wife in every sense of the word."

She didn't want this—didn't want him and his dark, exotic sensuality overpowering her. But hunger ate at Jillian, teasing her to open, to accept him. The burning need in his eyes echoed her own internal ache. Her loins felt heavy and wanting.

Jillian moaned as he kissed the hollow of her neck, stroked her skin in small, delicate caresses that filled her with hot yearning. Graham lowered his head and took her nipple into his mouth. She whimpered, her body growing taut as his tongue rasped the hardening peak. Her hips pumped upward in nameless need.

Graham settled between her legs, pinning her wrists to the bed. His muscled torso slid across her body, his springy chest hairs caressing her aching nipples.

He entered her in a hard, quick thrust. Blunt pressure between her legs, thickening and filling. No pain this time, just this endless stretching and pushing—oh, so incredible. She pressed her hands against his sweat-slicked muscles to urge him in further. He rose above her, his nearly black gaze pinned to hers.

He began to move, quick thrusts hinting of restrained power. She felt engulfed, surrounded, as if he tried to absorb her into himself. Or push himself into her. The part of her she protected flared into light. Jillian closed her eyes, afraid to let him see her secrets flickering there.

"Open your eyes," he ordered. "I want you to see me."

Her eyes flew open as she saw him straining above her, his fingers laced through hers. The soft mattress squeaked in rhythm to his pounding thrusts, her arching hips. The dance, she thought in a heated haze of pleasure. The dance of flesh meeting flesh.

She cried out as heat flared and exploded inside her. Graham groaned deeply and gave a hoarse cry, then gave a final thrust. His hot seed spurted inside her.

Jillian lay still, curled against her new husband in the aftermath. Regret funneled through her. If only this could be real. If only she loved him and he loved her and she could confess her heart's desire. But she trusted no one.

He stroked her hair in a gentle caress. She reminded herself there was no love between them. Physical intimacy did not equal emotional intimacy. Two silent tears slid down her cheeks.

Graham pressed his lips to one, kissing the salt water. "Jillian, why are you crying?" he asked quietly.

She made no reply, trying to resist the fierce impulse to turn into his shoulder and bury her head. Worry filled his gaze, and he sat, cupping her face in his large, warm palms.

"Did I hurt you?"

Overwhelmed at his concern, she shook her head. "I'm just . . . a bit dazed. I'm fine."

"I feared our dance might have taxed you." He grinned.

Her chin lifted in challenge. "Never."

"Of course. You're a strong dancer." His charming expression lifted her sadness. Jillian laughed as he pulled her against him. "You, my lady, are quite capable of engaging me."

They lay quietly a while, absorbed in the silence. Jillian pillowed her head against his chest. Graham was hard, firm and muscled—so different from her soft, giving body. Rapt with fresh wonder, she slid her hand through the dark hairs dusting his thigh, relishing their silky feel. She drew in a hesitant breath, staring at the thick flesh dangling between his legs. An instrument of some pain their first time, and of deep pleasure now. She touched it. It jerked violently, and she gasped.

Graham's eyes flew open. His amused gaze met her embarrassed one. "It's all right. You won't hurt me."

Encouraged, she gave another tentative stroke. It stirred and hardened before her fascinated gaze. His husky chuckle filled the air. "The Khamsin, the tribe I . . . stayed with once, call it 'the scimitar of love.' They say a woman's passage snugly fits a man's scimitar, much as a sheath caresses its sword."

Jillian sat up, frowning, peering closer at his male part. "It does not resemble a sword, Graham. Rather a very thick cucumber. Or a squash."

Dark brows quirked in apparent amusement. "Are you comparing my manhood to a vegetable, Jilly?"

"Or maybe a fruit. Perhaps a large banana."

Blood drained from his face as Graham anxiously glanced down. "A banana! Soft and spongy!" he sputtered.

"Well." She hid a smile. "It is curving to one side. . . ."

A rough growl erupted from his chest. He rolled over, pinning her to the bed, enfolding her in his tight embrace as she laughed. A sudden hardness probed her naked thigh.

She glanced down. "Oh my. It's no longer curving. . . ." Jillian dragged her captivated gaze up to meet his, fierce with desire.

"Not a banana, Jillian," he said thickly.

"No," she whispered as he feathered hot kisses over her flushed skin. "The Khamsin were right. Definitely a sword."

Intense triumph filled him. Jillian, his fiery redhead whose passion equaled his own. Sweat beaded his forehead. He could not resist the sweet calling of her flesh to his. He wanted her. Needed her.

In minutes, he had her beneath him again. Large green eyes, brilliant as rare jade, met his gaze. He kissed her, his tongue tracing her mouth, coaxing her lips open. Instinct pounded, demanded. He fought it, took his time, exploring her body with eagerness but not haste. Taking her nipple into his mouth he suckled the tender flesh, delighting in her little cries. Jillian undulated her hips, sending fresh heat through him.

Slowly, so slowly this time, he entered her. Jillian wrapped her long slender legs about his narrow hips, pressing him close. He teased her with small, gentle thrusts until she whimpered and pounded at the hard muscles tensing his back. "Graham, please," she gasped, bucking.

His low laugh filled the air. He rode her hard then, his hips slamming against her, darkly triumphant at the way she sobbed and writhed beneath him. His. All his. He'd taken her, claimed her, loved her with a hot madness. He had taken away from her father a virginal daughter and turned her into a wanton creature begging him for that burning, sweet pleasure.

She screamed and clung to him as the tight wet warmth of her sheath clenched in release. Graham groaned deeply as he poured himself deep into her. Ah, God, she was his. Part of her would always be.

He rolled off, cradled her to his chest, feeling their damp skin rub against each other. It was bad, this mindless lust whipping through him. He could not resist. And if he could not resist, he would have her again. And again. Love her until she screamed and begged and sobbed. Until she craved him like opium and thought no other would suffice. Bind her to him with lust and she would not leave him.

A chill went through him as he thought of her father. That evil half grin, the cold green eyes glittering like dead stones. Not green fire like Jillian's. Graham resisted a shudder. He would avenge himself, and all else be damned.

He had not intended this, but it struck him as perfect. Taking his enemy's daughter, claiming her body and causing sweet cries to wring from her pouty mouth.

The woman in his arms stirred, her silky tresses rubbing against his bare shoulder.

Mine, he thought. *All mine*. His hand splayed on her belly, caressing the soft skin. He had planted his seed deep inside her, twice. Perhaps she already was carrying his child. Graham felt a glow of fierce satisfaction.

Then she raised her head, regarding him sleepily. "Graham, we must talk. Please, I have something to tell you."

In her peignoir, Jillian reclined in the ducal sitting room, tightly clenching her hands. Graham had promised to return shortly to talk to her. He was downstairs, fetching a small snack.

He returned in his black velvet robe, balancing a plate of small, tawny cakes and a brandy snifter filled with white liquid. Jillian raised her brows in a questioning look.

"Milk and gingerbread," he explained, settling into a chair by the crackling fire. "Now, tell me what's troubling you."

"Graham, I want nothing but truth between us," she said earnestly. "I don't want a baby. I need to inform you I've been taking herbs to prevent conception. Considering my family is not very fertile, I doubt I shall conceive."

She expected an angry scowl. Instead, a thoughtful look entered his eyes. Graham set both plate and glass down on a small table beside the chair. "It's all right. Kenneth has a son who will remain my heir. I don't need a son right now."

Immense relief filled her. *Good. Because I also can't risk making love with you again. You'll make me lose my resolve to leave you.* "Then I need not share your bed," she ventured.

A slow smile twisted his mouth. He stood and yanked at his robe, shrugging it off. The duke resumed his seat. Naked. Oh goodness. A furious blush covered her cheeks.

"That's better. I feel more comfortable now. You were saying, Jillian, that you don't want to share my bed?" Her hungry gaze caressed the thick muscles rippling beneath his skin as he twisted to take up his glass again.

"Er, there's no need. I d-don't plan to remain with you," she stammered.

Over the rim of his snifter, his dark gaze pierced hers. "You still wish to run away after our three months are passed?"

Oh goodness, this was most peculiar. Here she was, having a serious conversation with her naked husband, a powerful and influential duke. Seeming perfectly at ease, Graham lounged in the overstuffed chair. His long legs, taut with muscle and dusted with dark hair, stretched before him on a blue ottoman. The plate brimming with gingerbread sat next to him on the spindly inlaid table. He took a small square of the dark cookie, licked it in slow, sensual strokes.

Jillian's feminine center tightened in memory.

Graham popped the cake into his mouth. He sat near the crackling fire, eating like a pampered pasha in his silken tent. His long, tapered fingers held a gingerbread square out to her.

Jillian stared as if he offered forbidden fruit. Shook her head. The duke tossed it up and caught it between his teeth.

A delicate shiver wracked her in memory: his teeth, ever so softly biting her nipple . . .

Remaining here was fraught with hazards. The longer she stayed, the more Graham lured her with his sensual snare. An inner sense warned if she didn't leave, heartache would follow.

"You want to run away from me, Jillian?" he repeated. The statement uttered in flat tones startled her. She felt as if he could see into the darkest part of her.

"Leave. Not run away," she corrected.

"You're not running away from me, Jilly." The endearing way he said her name in his smooth, silky tone made her quiver. He swirled his milk as if it were the finest brandy. "You're running away from yourself."

"I beg your pardon?"

Graham quirked a dark brow. "There's no reason to beg anything from me. We're husband and wife now. Stop this formality as if you're addressing royalty."

"Don't be silly. Usually when I address royalty, said royalty is wearing a bit more clothing. Or should I call you your naked grace?"

His loud, deep laughter rang out in the room. Amused, too, she smiled. Graham sipped his milk. "You're so delightful. Were you ever like this at home?"

Her mirth slipped away. "No."

His gaze dropped to her hands, which were clenched tightly in her lap. Graham set his snifter down. "Jilly, there's no reason to be afraid. I'm your husband now. Was it always difficult at home?"

The sheer gentleness of his tone nearly undid her. Jillian sucked in a breath. But he could not understand.

"My life was the typical English girl's upbringing."

"I see. Dancing lessons, embroidery, how to host a perfectly delightful tea, be a perfect model of decorum—and on that perfectly dreadful wedding night, your mother tells you to lie back and think of England."

Startled, she quirked a smile. "That's so odd, you saying that. It sounds so . . . English."

Unsmiling, he studied her. "And I'm not English."

"You're like some forbidden exotic land, calling to me."

"My tutors would faint in disgrace if they heard you, what with all their attempts to groom me for the duchy after my return from Egypt. What spoils it—the accent?"

"No. It's just an air about you of standing apart." She pointed out, "Most dukes don't drink milk from a brandy snifter."

"Or sit about perfectly naked conversing with their wives."

A furious blush ignited her cheeks. Jillian squirmed in her rigid chair. The rich satin caressed her naked bottom, reminding her of Graham's hands. She changed topics. "You mentioned tutors. Did you attend school in Egypt?"

Graham studied his snifter, swirling the milk. "The education I received there wasn't up to English standards. I've always wanted to attend Oxford or Cambridge, like my peers. I suppose I have a great thirst for a standard education that I never satisfied. No time or opportunity."

His confession touched her. "You could go to school now."

"There are too many other duties requiring my attention. No time. Perhaps one day I shall. But I digress. Back to my original thought. You're determined to leave, no matter what. But is it me, or something else?"

For a moment she wanted to confess her secret dream. But would he understand, or condemn her for sharing his longing for education?

"Graham, this marriage was . . . arranged under the most peculiar conditions. I appreciate you feeling honor bound to marry me. But do you truly wish to remain my husband?"

His two dark brows drew together. "Why do you ask that?"

Her lip trembled. "You'll grow bored with me and take a mistress. Many husbands do in these marriages. It happens. I'm not a fool, nor ignorant of the fact."

He studied her intently. She tried not to let her fascinated gaze drift down the smooth, warm skin of his arms, across the dark nest of hair on his chest, lower to the rippling muscles in his flat stomach to his . . . Her breath caught in her throat. Goodness, he was—

Graham caught her gaze. A sensual smile touched his lips. "Although we just finished making love, I already desire you. I will not grow bored with you, *habiba*."

She seized on the term. "What does *habiba* mean?"

"It's Arabic for beloved. An endearment. But you didn't answer my question. Is it me you wish to run from?"

His dark gaze demanded truth. Jillian rubbed her eye with the heel of her hand. She shook her head.

"You're safe from him here," he said gently.

Nowhere is safe from my father's reach except America, she thought.

"You can't run away from what you really are."

The words stirred ancient memories. Jillian felt deeply disturbed and didn't know why. "I can try," she whispered.

Graham abruptly left his seat and walked over to her. Warmth surrounded her in the form of his strong arms. "Jilly, don't run from me," he murmured. "Don't."

He clasped her face in his warm hands and lifted it. His lips touched hers.

He tasted slightly of ginger. She closed her eyes and gave in to the sensual strokes of his tongue. Demanding more, subtle caresses—every silken flick coaxed a re-

163

sponse. Jillian surrendered and joined in the dance, sucking on his tongue with such terror it was as if she were drowning and only he could rescue her.

Or imprison her in his sensual embrace.

She jerked away, trembling violently.

"Jillian," he said quietly. "Look at me."

She shook her head. He turned her to face him. "Why are you so afraid of me?" he asked in his softest voice.

"I'm not," she managed.

She wasn't fearful of her husband; she feared what he could do to her. *You could make me fall in love with you and trap me here.*

Morning broke, washing the large bedchamber in a ghostly gray dawn. Graham slipped from his bed, glancing at his sleeping wife. Spending all night in her arms had chased away his nightmares. He dressed, pressed a kiss to her forehead and went downstairs.

Rising early was a habit learned from years of dawn prayers with the al-Hajid. He could not break it now.

To his surprise, Kenneth sat in the gloomy quiet of the breakfast room. His brother studied him.

"I didn't think you'd awaken this early."

He shrugged. "Old habits."

Graham sank onto a chair, watching Kenneth. Something was bothering his brother, who did not meet his gaze. Instead, he drummed his fingers on the table.

"Actually, I was hoping to catch you before everyone else awoke. I've discovered something. I didn't want to ruin your wedding, but it's time you know. I paid a visit to our accountant last week, and he finally gave me the full statement of our finances that you asked him to tally. The losses we had from the B&O Railroad, and others . . . The news isn't good."

Kenneth slid a paper across the table to him. Graham

slowly read it, a sick feeling gathering in his stomach. He pushed it aside, his gaze meeting his worried brother's.

"But this means we are . . ."

"Nearly broke," Kenneth finished. "All our investments failed. We're on the edge of financial ruin."

Chapter Twelve

Graham stared at Kenneth, feeling sick.

How could this happen? He must have money. The Yorkshire estate badly needed repairs. He had a small battalion of tenant farmers who had done poorly in the last harvest. To compensate, he'd planned to breed Arabians, using Prometheus to breed with new mares he had purchased from the Khamsin tribe.

And of course his plan to ruin Stranton needed funds. For a wild moment he wanted to run back to the harsh sands of Egypt, to being Rashid, the Bedouin warrior who ruthlessly cut down enemies with a sword. But this was England. The only weapons that mattered were money and power. And without money, he had no real power.

"We could always dig for treasure," Kenneth joked. Worry shadowed his eyes.

Graham grasped fleeting hope with both hands. "There *is* something I've kept on the quiet. Something I

GET UP TO 4 FREE BOOKS!

You can have the best romance delivered to your door for less than what you'd pay in a bookstore or online. Sign up for one of our book clubs today, and we'll send you **FREE* BOOKS** just for trying it out...**with no obligation to buy, ever!**

HISTORICAL ROMANCE BOOK CLUB

Travel from the Scottish Highlands to the American West, the decadent ballrooms of Regency England to Viking ships. Your shipments will include authors such as CONNIE MASON, CASSIE EDWARDS, LYNSAY SANDS, LEIGH GREENWOOD, and many, many more.

LOVE SPELL BOOK CLUB

Bring a little magic into your life with the romances of Love Spell—fun contemporaries, paranormals, time-travels, futuristics, and more. Your shipments will include authors such as KATIE MACALISTER, SUSAN GRANT, NINA BANGS, SANDRA HILL, and more.

As a book club member you also receive the following special benefits:

- **30% OFF** all orders through our website & telecenter! (Plus, you still get 1 book FREE for every 5 books you buy!)
- **Exclusive access to** special discounts!
- **Convenient** home delivery **and 10 days to return any books you don't want to keep.**

There is no minimum number of books to buy, and you may cancel membership at any time. See back to sign up!

*Please include $2.00 for shipping and handling.

YES! ☐

Sign me up for the **Historical Romance Book Club** and send my TWO FREE BOOKS! If I choose to stay in the club, I will pay only $8.50* each month, a savings of $5.48!

YES! ☐

Sign me up for the **Love Spell Book Club** and send my TWO FREE BOOKS! If I choose to stay in the club, I will pay only $8.50* each month, a savings of $5.48!

NAME: _____

ADDRESS: _____

_____

TELEPHONE: _____

E-MAIL: _____

☐ **I WANT TO PAY BY CREDIT CARD.**

☐ VISA   ☐ MasterCard.   ☐ DISCOVER

ACCOUNT #: _____

EXPIRATION DATE: _____

SIGNATURE: _____

Send this card along with $2.00 shipping & handling for each club you wish to join, to:

**Romance Book Clubs
1 Mechanic Street
Norwalk, CT 06850-3431**

Or fax (must include credit card information!) to: 610.995.9274.
You can also sign up online at www.dorchesterpub.com.

*Plus $2.00 for shipping. Offer open to residents of the U.S. and Canada only.
Canadian residents please call 1.800.481.9191 for pricing information.
If under 18, a parent or guardian must sign. Terms, prices and conditions subject to change. Subscription subject to acceptance. Dorchester Publishing reserves the right to reject any order or cancel any subscription.

JOIN NOW!

found when I was a boy in Egypt. If I find that, our losses will seem miniscule."

Interest flared in Kenneth's hopeful gaze. "What is it?"

"A fortune beyond our wildest dreams. Buried deep inside an Egyptian tomb."

His brother leaned forward. "Go on."

"Remember the tale Father told of Khufu's magic wishing casket?" When Kenneth nodded, he continued. "The al-Hajid forced me to dig for the Almha, the sacred gold disk of their enemies, the Khamsin. During one dig, I found an ancient papyrus map, torn in two. I remembered the hieroglyphics Father taught me, and discerned it told of Pharaoh Khufu's lost treasure."

Kenneth's blue eyes widened with unmistakable excitement. A small smile touched Graham's mouth. Their father had relayed the tale to the young boys, filling their minds with dreams of great treasure lying buried in Egypt's western desert.

"The first half of the map reveals where the key is that will unlock the tomb containing the casket. The key is hidden inside the Great Pyramid. I was . . . missing the second half of the papyrus showing the tomb's location in the western desert."

"And now, the missing half of the map . . ." Kenneth prodded.

"It was with al-Hamra. I asked Jillian to make a tracing."

Kenneth gave him a wary look. "So the earl could, if he wanted, find the treasure as well."

"He doesn't have the key and has no way of finding it."

Graham's brother leaned back, drumming his fingers against the polished tabletop. "It's a long shot. But maybe it's worth it. You could go to Egypt and take your new bride. Make it a honeymoon of sorts."

Graham stared.

"What?" Kenneth asked impatiently.

"We'll find another way," he said tightly. "*I'm* not going to Egypt, and I'm certainly not taking my wife."

"Graham . . ."

"Taking my beautiful bride into the desert—my *red-headed* bride . . ."

A guilty look crossed Kenneth's face. "The nightmare," he said softly. "I'm sorry, Graham. I forgot. You're right, we'll find another way. Khufu's treasure is a myth, anyway."

"What's Khufu's treasure?"

Both men turned to view Jillian, who was standing in the doorway.

"Hello, love," Graham said cheerfully, giving Kenneth a warning glance. "Come, sit. The servants will have breakfast soon."

She had awoken in an empty bed, missing the warmth of her husband. She had the niggling feeling all was not quite well in this household, and she sensed secrets Graham hid, saw them cloaked in his dark eyes when they made love.

Sitting down next to Graham, she gave him an inquiring look. "Who was Khufu?"

The two brothers exchanged glances. Graham drew a line on the polished table with his finger. "He's the pharaoh concerning the map I asked you to trace."

Jillian's heart sank. "Graham, I meant to tell you. I couldn't get the tracing. I was watched too closely." Her husband's expression tightened, and she said, "I can try again, now that I'm married and have more freedom."

"Try hard," he said softly. "We need it, Jilly."

He looked a trifle desperate, as if it weren't a map he sought but something more meaningful, like his heart's desire.

"Tell me about the story you were discussing," she said.

The duke nodded. "Very well. Khufu is the pharaoh for whom the Great Pyramid was built. His sons liked to amuse their father with stories. One told of a powerful magician who desired revenge upon his wife's lover. He created a small wax crocodile, and had his servant toss it into the lake where the lover bathed. The crocodile came to life and swallowed the youth."

Graham went on, his rich, deep voice lending drama to the tale. She listened, enthralled.

"While supping with Pharaoh Nebka, the magician called forth the crocodile, and out of its mouth it spat the wife's lover, totally unharmed. The magician ordered the reptile to take the boy, and both man and beast vanished from sight."

"Legend says Pharaoh Khufu was so intrigued by the tale he rewarded his son with a magic wishing casket with powers to make dreams come true. Into this box he placed a small gold crocodile with an emerald the size of an egg in its yawning jaws, as tribute to Sobek, the crocodile god," Kenneth put in.

"However," Graham went on, "the clever pharaoh told his son he would receive the treasure only after his death, if he could find it. Khufu buried the treasure in the western desert, but created a map with clues to find it. But first, one needed to find a key to unlock the hiding place, and the key is hidden in Khufu's tomb."

Jillian focused on Graham. "And the map to find this priceless wishing casket . . . this is the papyrus you need?

A strange look entered his eyes. "Yes. And that wishing casket is everything. It's not merely a priceless treasure. Father said it had the ability to grant dreams, even those dreams that seem desperately out of reach." Then he gave an elegant shrug. "It is myth. It could be there. Or not."

"I'll do what I can to trace the map," she promised.

"Do it, Jilly. As soon as possible. We need that map. I need that casket."

For a moment, despair crossed his handsome face. Then the usual blank expression slid over him. She watched Graham help himself to eggs from the steaming trays the servants began to set out. Why was her husband so determined to seek this treasure? Did he truly believe in its magical powers?

And would finding it finally dispel the haunted look swirling in his dark eyes?

Chapter Thirteen

Over the next several weeks, Jillian settled into a pleasant routine. During the day she rode in the park, and sat for hours in her husband's vast library, devouring his large collection. Jillian marveled over his tastes, always taking care to leave before Graham arrived home and caught her reading. She'd learned that lesson from her father, who disdained her thirst for knowledge.

Sometimes she sat in the drawing room, doing needle-point like a dutiful wife while Badra discussed books and nursed her son. At first, Jillian felt shocked embarrassment at her friendly sister-in-law's habit of feeding Michael in front of her. But after a while she realized the viscountess was much more discreet around others. And as she grew to know her better, Jillian realized Badra thought of her as a close sister who shared intimacies. She was deeply touched at the trust the woman accorded her.

Trust and emotional closeness, things the duke did not accord her. Graham frequently vanished for long periods during the day, and when she once timidly asked where he went, he replied curtly, "It's not your business." Hurt, she withdrew, not asking again.

It appeared the only intimacy he would share was in bed each night. There, he made love with great passion. Still, when she clung to him, searching his eyes, he seemed distant, as if he shared only his body and withheld the rest of himself.

Jillian found herself in the peculiar position of becoming closer to her in-laws than her husband. Reticent at first, even Kenneth became friendly. He joined her in the library, explaining he'd only learned to read English in the past year. He talked of growing up among the Khamsin, the Egyptian warrior tribe who raised him, and how he had fallen in love with Badra. Graham's family openly shared themselves. Graham did not.

Jillian tried during dinner to engage her husband in conversation. She dared to comment when Graham and Kenneth discussed investments. But when Graham's piercing gaze locked on her, she quieted and focused on eating her food instead. She did not want to see an echo of her father's condemnation in her husband's face.

Today, she'd actually found herself needed. Jasmine's governess was ill, and Jillian offered to give lessons. In the cheerful schoolroom, the pair skated through reading and sums, and then Jillian decided to stoke the young girl's sharp mind with her own love of economics. Jasmine sat at her small wooden school desk, listening with rapt attention.

"England has been suffering from an economic depression since 1873. Blame it partly on the Industrial Revolution. We are no longer an imperialistic country leading the way in international trade. For example, look at the production of steel. All the new sailing vessels are constructed with it. America produces it far cheaper. And what does it mean when you can produce a product cheaper?" Jillian asked her young pupil.

"You can sell it for less?"

"Exactly—and still make a profit. It's called supply and demand. Buyers want to cut costs; they'll purchase it from the cheapest source. And if there are only so many ships being built, and they all want their steel from America and not England, then it means—"

"Our ship is sunk," Graham interjected.

Cold dread crawled over her at the sound of that deep, smoky voice. Jillian cautiously turned. Her husband lounged in the doorway, arms crossed over his broad chest. He studied her intently. Feeling as guilty as a child caught snatching a cookie, she jumped to her feet, knocking over her chair.

The duke strode into the room, righted the chair. A furious blush ignited her cheeks. "I'm sorry. Er, Miss Hunter is ill today and I . . . I . . . thought Jasmine . . . I mean, economics is . . . and . . ."

She bit her tongue. Would the duke laugh, as Bernard had, or punish her as father had? Surely he would be disapproving of her interest.

"You think England no longer leads the world in industrial growth, Jillian?" he asked.

Wordlessly, she stared. Interest filled his gaze. Heart racing, Jillian waited for reproach, but he parked a hip against the desk. Drawing in a hesitant breath, she explained.

"Mass production has lowered costs and expanded productivity, but demand in England simply isn't enough for what our factories produce. And our overseas export markets are shrinking, thanks to the competition from America."

"But America has suffered as well. Look at the depression of 1883," he countered.

More energized, she nodded. "True, but America is more likely to rebound easier than England due to its competitive pricing and natural resources. As an industrial nation, we are lagging behind. It's the law of supply and demand."

The duke's gaze flicked to his niece. "Jasmine, isn't it time for your afternoon ride? Charles is waiting for you."

The little girl looked to Jillian for affirmation. Jillian nodded and Jasmine scampered out. The duke unfolded his powerful frame and strode toward her.

Oh no, here it came, the lecture and the condemnation, the chiding. She couldn't bear it. Jillian bit her lip.

So expecting was she of criticism, she started when his large, warm hand cupped her cheek. Jillian trembled as he stroked a line along her jaw.

"My wife, the brilliant little economist. I'm fascinated. Whom did you study?"

Jillian stared. He showed no signs of sneering.

"Marshall. *The Principles of Economics* is a book my father bought for his library. He rarely read it."

"Clearly you did," he murmured. "Why are you looking so frightened? I'm not a beast. Didn't you realize when you brought up the topic at dinner I was interested?"

"I thought . . . a woman's opinion about such things matters not to men."

Surely it had never mattered to her father. Her father, who interrupted her mother when she dared to speak. Her father, who constantly criticized her mother until her mother became silent and offered her opinion no more.

He gave a derisive snort. "Some men, perhaps. Not me. I'm not well-educated on investments and economics. Perhaps you'd care to enlighten me."

Her husband sat upon the desk and nodded for her to take a seat. Encouraged by the interest flaring in his eyes, Jillian hesitantly began talking. He asked pointed, intelligent questions. He coaxed answers from her, argued several points. She found herself enthralled, and was surprised to see the little gold watch pinned to her blouse indicate more than an hour had passed. She stood and hastily began organizing papers upon the oak desk.

Graham gave her a thoughtful look. "You're an excellent teacher. Have you ever considered furthering your education?"

Jillian bit her lip. She stared at his kind expression. Did she dare confide in him? She had nothing to lose now. Her hands shook as she smoothed over the papers.

"My heart's desire is to attend college. I had set my sights on Radcliffe College in America." Daring to look up, she saw understanding cross his face.

"Ah, that is why you were running away. Your father wouldn't send you to school."

Bitter laughter rose in her throat. "He sent me to finishing school to learn how to pour tea. He chided me for expressing my opinions and theories. He said I'm a weak woman who prattles about things she doesn't understand. School in America offered the only option."

His warm hand rested atop hers. She stared at the elegant, long fingers pressed against her skin.

"You don't prattle. I find you immensely engaging and fascinating. Why can't you believe me?" he asked quietly.

"Men of rank do not expect intellectual discussions with their wives. They expect them to share their bodies, not their minds." Jillian couldn't help the cynicism inflecting her voice.

"I think men and women can share both," he countered.

"You do?" Her heart thudded wildly at the intent look he gave her, the sultry want in those midnight eyes.

"Take your discussion of gold, for example," he murmured. "Gold, like the color of your hair when the sun lights it. You predict gold will be the backer for currency in America." He plucked free the pins holding her locks captive. They spilled free in soft waves, tumbling down past her breasts, one of which the duke palmed, heat flaring in his gaze.

"The purchasing power of gold continues to rise," she stammered, her gaze riveted to the equally fascinating rise in his silk trousers.

"I doubt it will deflate in the near future."

Desire darkened his gaze to black. Graham very gently pulled her down to the polished floorboards with him. He clasped the back of her neck, drawing her to him.

"Gold, er, gold is much more stable and reliable, and such a . . ." She whimpered as he lightly bit her neck, then chased it with a soothing sweep of his tongue. He pushed her back against the hard floorboards. His hands—oh goodness, his hands were beneath her sensible skirts. . . . Here she was, in a schoolroom, babbling about gold standards while her husband was pushing her skirts up. His hand slid along her inner thigh, teasing and skimming the stocking's edge. His heavy-lidded gaze captured hers as he unbuttoned her white blouse, opening it to reveal the upper halves of her breasts lifted by her corset.

"Do you know how much I adore it when you talk like this?" he asked.

"L-like what?" Oh God, he was running his finger along the edge of her breast. She tensed with sweet anticipation.

"Like the intelligent woman you are. It excites me." He breathed against her ear, nibbling at the lobe.

"I didn't realize you found economics so . . . stimulating."

Graham paused and cupped her cheek. She dissolved at his tender look. "It's you, Jilly, that I find stimulating. Your brilliant mind, your clever wit . . . your passion."

He reached down and loosened her corset, then

popped a breast free. Jillian drew in a breath, feeling her skin flush.

With a slow, deliberate lick, his rough velvet tongue crested her nipple. Graham swirled it round the hard peak, which his mouth then closed over. He suckled deeply.

Jillian arched, gasping, tremendous heat engulfing her with each insistent tug of his mouth. Graham released her nipple and leaned back, a slow, knowing smile teasing his mouth. His wet mouth, reddened and warm. Oh, she needed that mouth, needed it on hers, now. Jillian reached up and wrapped her hands about his neck, dragging him down to meet her.

He kissed her lips, stroked the inside of her mouth, tasting and coaxing her response. Then Graham pulled away, his dark eyes intense.

"Tell me more about Marshall's theory," he demanded.

Talk? Amid this mindless pleasure?

"Ah, um, well . . . Mr. Marshall expresses the logic that man evolving into a more sophisticated being means that even his animal passions need association with mental stimulation. . . ."

"Animal passions," Graham breathed. He made a rough, growling noise deep in his throat as he showered tiny kisses over her collarbone, along the edge of her throat.

"Um, oh . . . *oh* . . . even when he has the means to acquire more expensive food and drink, he still has a restricted appetite, for nature restricts him—oh God," she moaned as his mouth encased her nipple. With long, slow strokes, he flicked his tongue over the hardened peak.

Graham raised his head, his gaze burning into her. "And?" he demanded.

"Graham, please, sod the bloody economics," she begged. She needed him inside her, now.

Deep laughter rumbled from his chest. Graham unfastened his trousers. He leaned over her, his gaze midnight black, as he settled between her thighs and mounted her. She felt the thick hardness pushing at her wet entrance, and with a mighty thrust, he entered her. Her bottom skidded along the polished oak floor; he caught her hips and held her tight as he rocked back and forth, penetrating deep.

Jillian bit back a tiny cry as she clutched his lapels, feeling as if she drowned in pleasure. Giving in, she arched and muffled her cry of release against the black silk of his coat. Her body tensed and convulsed, infused with molten fire. Graham stiffened above her and his jaw tensed as he clenched his teeth, biting back a harsh cry as he violently shuddered.

Releasing a ragged breath, he stared down at her. "Did you enjoy your lesson?" he asked.

Jillian managed to find her wobbly voice. "And . . . and what lesson was that?"

"That, *habiba*, was a lesson in supply and demand. Since I intend to be a very demanding husband, I will supply you with as much pleasure as you can possibly stand, a beneficial trade agreement for both involved parties."

"But at what price?" She held his gaze, feeling him still hard within her.

Graham dropped a light kiss on her perspiring forehead. "Whatever price you desire. How does attending college here in England sound? Would you like that?"

Jillian's heart skipped a beat. "Truly? But the money—"

"Blast the money. We'll find a way. If attending school is your heart's desire, Jilly, then I want to deliver it." He caressed her cheek. "On a gold platter, if I could."

She managed a smile. "Silver. We can't afford gold."

He laughed. "If I find you a school to attend, Jilly, you'll stay with me?"

Haunted loneliness flickered in his eyes. She thought of all he must have lost as a child, and her heart turned. But she needed more from him. She vowed never to have her parents' marriage: two people merely sharing space and not each other.

"If I stay, Graham, things must change," she said slowly.

He loomed over her. The duke's powerful body kept her helplessly pinned to the floor. Her slight, feminine body was invaded, kept at a distinct disadvantage. But she pressed on, knowing she had to speak now, while she had his full attention.

"I can't have a marriage where my husband closes himself off to me. You disappear for hours and don't tell me where you've gone. You build a stone wall around yourself and no one is allowed in. You said men and women can share their bodies and their minds. Share yourself with me, Graham. Everthing."

His gaze went cold. She felt him abruptly withdraw from her, both physically and emotionally. He stood, adjusting himself, brushing off his silk trousers as if their tumble had meant nothing. As if her words had meant nothing.

At the doorway he paused, his back to her, his voice emotionless. "I'll instruct my secretary to begin the search for a university that will admit you. Think about it, Jillian. I *can* give you your heart's desire—if you don't leave me."

But will you give me your heart, Graham, she silently asked. *How can I remain if you insist on shutting me out?*

He left her lying on the floor, her skirts up to her waist, his seed pooling between her damp, trembling thighs.

* * *

With meticulous precision, Graham was setting his plan into action. He'd kept everything concealed from Jillian. To tide his family over, he'd sold one of the four Arabian mares he'd purchased from the Khamsin. He offered half the money to the Khamsin sheikh as a partial payment on the mares purchased from them, but Jabari had written back, refusing payment. Instead, he'd requested a small percentage of money earned from stud fees.

"Your stallion's stud fees, my friend, not yours," Jabari had written. "Speaking of breeding, congratulations on your marriage. Consider the mares a wedding gift."

Graham sighed as he read over the sheikh's smooth, flowing English script. His financial problems were temporarily solved.

Under less pressure now, he'd spent afternoons with Jillian's father at his club—building trust, allowing himself, despite his dire financial circumstances, to lose at cards. Convincing the earl he had taken up his cause.

Only one quest diverted him from his zealous drive to ruin Stranton. Graham sent his secretary to inquire about colleges Jillian could attend. He did it with a guilty pang, knowing Jillian wanted from him what he could not offer. Himself. Share the terrible darkness inside? He couldn't do it. Never again would he permit himself to be vulnerable.

Causing Stranton's ruin took precedence. Graham sent his trusted groom, Charles, to one of London's worst rookeries. The servant finally returned to grimly inform him he had found the type of boy Graham required.

The next afternoon, Graham dressed in clean but modest clothing. He studied his reflection as he slapped on a working man's cap. He must blend in to the surroundings like the panther he was, camouflaged for the hunt.

The rookery of St. Giles nestled in the heart of London like a festering sore. The duke and his groom walked the narrow streets with caution, eyes open and searching. Tucked into the duke's bulging coat pocket was a purse sure to attract his prey. Graham's nose wrinkled at the stench of old gin, sour vomit and urine permeating the streets.

This teeming river of human misery, awash with crime and poverty, chilled his blood. The squirming mass of people reminded him of a nest of black scorpions he'd stumbled upon in a cave in Egypt. Just as ugly, and lethal in their sting.

Trained to scent danger, he scanned the streets as they walked. It didn't take long. Graham felt the slightest tug on his pocket. Catlike he whirled, capturing his prey by the wrist—a tall lad with rags for shoes, clad in a reasonably good coat that was most likely stolen.

"Let go," the boy protested, squirming to free himself.

Older. Perhaps thirteen. None of the childlike innocence he needed. Graham squeezed his wrist in warning and tossed him a coin. "Here, go buy yourself a pair of shoes," he said gruffly.

The boy tore off, disappearing into the crowd.

They continued walking. Graham scanned the terrain, ignoring the dilapidated houses with their windows broken and patched with yellowed paper, the barefoot girls with hardened faces. They passed a man in a tattered brown greatcoat pressing a woman against the wall. The woman's legs were wrapped about his hips as he grunted and shoved into her. She stared into the air with the listless look of an opium user.

Graham forced himself to keep walking. Soon enough, another tug on his coat. He whirled, caught the thief's wrist.

"Hey!" the urchin protested.

The boy in filthy rags had the face of a hungry angel.

His grimy cheeks were hollowed, his eyes defiant but scared. The duke studied him. About eight years old, he had an unearthly beauty with that tousled and dirty black hair and large, dark eyes. Clean him up and he'd present a tempting package.

Self-loathing twisted his guts, but Graham heaved a breath. Nothing would happen, he promised himself. He'd catch the earl before any real physical damage was done.

And the psychological damage?

The boy had lived on the streets. Despite his look of innocence, Graham knew he had seen much—done much, too, most likely. At the age of eight, he was already a weary veteran in the war to claim food and a warm place for the night.

In turn, Graham would arrange to have him brought up by one of his tenant families in the countryside. If one could contain such a wild, untamed boy. If he would not run. But perhaps the promise of warmth, security and food would leash him—as it had finally leashed Graham when he was the boy's age.

The duke took a ragged breath and nodded at Charles. Preliminaries, names—Jeremy—and then Charles made the offer. Jeremy's large dark eyes widened with suspicion and then wonder at the two coins Graham held out.

"Do you understand what I'm requiring?" Graham asked.

The thief held out a dirty palm. "The boys first, guvna."

Graham smiled. Smart child. He handed Jeremy two shiny shillings. The child bit them and stared.

"There's more of that, if you finish the job. Much more. And a home with a bed of your own, all the food you could want."

"A real home?" Then the boy's gaze narrowed. "Wot for?"

A lump rose in Graham's throat. He saw himself, age

eight, dully resigned to never escaping the al-Hajid, offered everything he wanted. Like the feral animal he'd been, he did not want to trust the outstretched hand offering kindness. Like taming a wild animal, Faisal had coaxed him in, little by little. A hot meal, kind words, a place of safety. In the end, Graham had eaten out of that hand.

Of course, he'd found a family to replace the one he'd lost, a place where he had finally felt safe, he reminded himself. Then, swallowing past the thickness in his throat he said, "Because, Jeremy, you remind me of someone I once knew."

It was almost too easy.

Many talks with the earl about his proposed bill had formed a camaraderie between them. Graham informed Stranton he had found a perfect young boy to reform, a victim of the sex trades.

The earl did not know Graham had also been quietly meeting with eight esteemed members of the House of Lords. Lord Harold Bailey was vigilantly campaigning to close London's opium dens. "Halls of iniquity," the peer had brayed.

Graham privately informed Lord Bailey he knew of a prominent citizen who frequented those dens. He then suggested a police raid to catch him, to make a public example to close the dens. The lords could observe the arrest and they would invite newspapermen to record the event. They'd make it known to the public that such raids would become more frequent.

"I will make all the arrangements," Graham had proposed. Bailey thought it a splendid idea.

Bailey did not know what Graham planned was not a police raid on an opium den, but public exposure of Stranton's vice. Graham next penned a letter to Lord Stranton. "I have the perfect candidate, a young boy, for you to reform. But you must go to him. He's too frightened to venture into Mayfair."

He had sent the note with directions and an arranged time, claiming young Jeremy was willing to do anything for money. Graham promised the earl discretion.

The trap waited in St. Giles in a filthy building smelling of old urine and sex. Inside the room, hidden by a large bureau, Graham crouched down and waited. In the room next door, eight esteemed members of the House of Lords, a bevy of police officers and two journalists waited for his signal to storm inside. The duke watched Jeremy sit on a sagging mattress, looking vulnerable and a bit scared.

Hungry greed filled Stranton's face as he entered the room alone. Jeremy looked desperate—desperate as Graham had been.

Stranton's next words did not surprise the duke.

"What do you want?" the earl asked gruffly.

A singular plea of urgency laced the boy's voice. "Please, guvna, Oy've got no one else. I need five shillings."

Stranton licked his thick lips. Saliva made them shiny. "Why should I help you?"

"Oy'll do what you want. Anything."

"Remove your trousers," he said hoarsely.

Jeremey stood and unfastened his pathetic, threadbare trousers. Hard lust gleamed in Stranton's green eyes. He fumbled with the tented dome of his own black wool trousers.

Graham shivered, remembering horrific shame as Stranton told Jeremy in clear terms what was required. *Come now, boy, you're used to this.* . . . His buttocks contracted involuntarily.

Jeremy looked very young and apprehensive as Stranton approached.

Now. Graham rapped hard on the wall. The bobbies burst into the room, followed by the journalists and the eight esteemed members of the House of Lords. They halted, seeing the grown man, the now scared boy.

Aging Lord Baker looked confused. "This doesn't look like an opium den."

Mouth gaping, Lord Huntly stared. "Good God, Stranton, what the hell's going on here?"

Disgust tinged his voice. He knew. They all knew. The journalists scribbled in their notebooks. Jeremy, street-wise urchin he was, had already escaped into the hallway.

"I was setting about to prove the vices of the lower classes," the earl asserted. "These urchins lack morals and would do anything for money. They prefer not to work, but instead desire the corruption of our society and good, decent people."

Graham stepped into full view. "They desire the corruption of our society? Supply and demand, Stranton. Simple economics. He offered you a service you very much wanted. Don't blame the boy," he said in a mocking tone. He glanced at the lords. "Gentlemen, I know I said you would be exposed to the viles of an opium den, but I thought this would more clearly demonstrate a greater vice we should work to eliminate."

"You . . . you liar!" the earl said hoarsely. "Caldwell, you promised . . . You set me up!"

"Promises can be broken, al-Hamra."

Stranton fastened his trousers over his rapidly decreasing erection. Red-faced, dark fury in his eyes, he struggled in the firm grip of the two policemen holding him. Furious green eyes met black. Recognition sparked.

Graham stiffened. Overcome with gloating triumph, he had made a mistake. Stranton knew . . .

"No one's called me that in years. I know you. I *know* you."

The earl switched to Arabic, and Graham flinched. "It's you, isn't it . . . Rashid?" the man breathed.

Graham regained his composure and smiled coldly. "Am I?" he drawled in the same language.

"You'll pay for this, bastard. By God you will. Know this: You're not safe. And neither is your family."

Cold terror struck Graham. He lunged at the earl. Stranton laughed as the police pulled him free.

"You can't deny it, because I know the truth. You can't hide from what you really are. Admit it, Caldwell. Remember?"

Graham went perfectly still, numbly watching his enemy dragged off by the police. But Stranton's low mocking whisper in Arabic taunted him. Words said twenty years ago.

With a dazed look Lord Huntly stared after Stranton, then looked at Graham. "What did he say?"

Graham made no reply.

He went home to find his wife. Jillian, who was reading in the library, took one look at him and cried out. "Graham? What has happened? You look terrible."

Graham grasped her hands. "Did you ever get the tracing of the map, Jilly?"

"Not yet. I haven't had the courage to return there."

"Do it. Now. Immediately. Find a way. You must," he whispered.

Her eyes widened. "Graham, what's wrong?"

"I need to find that wishing casket." He stood on shaky legs. "I'll be upstairs. I trust you'll find a way, Jilly. You must."

"All right," she said, staring at him. "I'll leave now."

When she did, for the first time in his life, Graham deliberately set out to get drunk. He grabbed the crystal decanter of brandy kept on the sideboard and poured himself a large snifter. Taking a gulp, he winced. The liquor burned like raw fire down his throat.

Chilled to the bone, he sat, amber liquid sloshing in the glass as his hand shook. For a long time he sat, staring at the wall in motionless silence. He glanced at the snifter. So very English. So very gentlemanly . . .

With a low cry, he hurled it into the fireplace. Not wanting his family to witness the distress he couldn't hide, he escaped to his rooms and curled into a ball on the floor.

He remained there for a long time, waiting for Jillian to return. Time inched by. The magic wishing casket. How many times had he dreamed about it as a boy, wanting its awesome power to free him? It must have the power to restore hope. And now it was within his grasp—if Jillian managed to get the tracing.

Footsteps outside his doorway warned him of his wife's return. Graham sprang up, stood unsteadily by the fireplace as the door opened. Dressed in her outwear, her cheeks flushed with color, Jillian came inside.

"I have it, Graham. I put it in a safe place, because it seemed so important to you."

"Give it to me," he urged thickly.

Her mouth worked violently. She went to him, clutching his arms. "Graham, please tell me what's wrong. You've been drinking. You never drink. Please, tell me what happened!"

"Go away," he muttered, turning his back.

Resting his head on the mantel, he heard her soft retreat, the door close behind her. She had the tracing. It was safe. Deep down, he knew he must tell her the truth. But not now. He could not bear to see the hurt surface in her eyes.

Hours later, the butler summoned him, informing him Lord Huntly had come to pay a call "of extreme urgency."

He managed to restore himself to rights and hurried to the drawing room. The marquess, standing beside Huntly, looked stricken.

Graham stared in dumbstruck disbelief as the story unfolded. Huntly fingered his bowler hat. "Sorry, Caldwell. I couldn't see him disgraced. Good friend for years. I owed him."

Using his influence, Huntly had convinced the magistrate to release Stranton on five thousand pounds bail. Then the marquess had paid. But when he'd arrived at Stranton's house that afternoon to assure him he would find him the finest legal help, the earl had fled, leaving behind a note addressed to the Duke of Caldwell. The marquess now handed Graham that elegant parchment. The crinkling sound as Graham unfolded it roared like thunder in the empty silence.

His blood froze as he read the Arabic words:

I'll get you, Caldwell. And you'll like it just as you did before. I'll get you. You can run to the ends of the earth and I'll find you. And when I do, I'll destroy you. Your family will be ruined and penniless. You can't hide from what you really are, pretty boy. You liked what I did to you. You know you did.

Chapter Fourteen

Graham knew what he must do. At all costs, he must protect his family from the earl's wrath. And he had the map now. He would return to Egypt, lure the beast away while seeking out the lost treasure. In Egypt, he would kill the earl or be killed.

With a heavy heart, he sat his brother down and told him what had happened. Graham advised he take the family to their remote Yorkshire estate. Kenneth studied him with weary resignation.

"I wish you had confided in me earlier. I'll make arrangements for Badra, Jillian and the children to leave, but I'm coming with you to Egypt."

Emotions clogged Graham's throat. He shook his head. "I'll be fine," he said gruffly.

Kenneth drummed his fingers on the table. "You're my brother. I let you down years ago when the Al-Hajid raided our caravan. I won't do it again."

"It wasn't your fault," Graham said, stricken.

Blue eyes met black. "Yes, it was. Because I was the one

Mother and Father managed to hide and you were left behind. You were the heir. They should have saved you. Not me."

His heart twisted, and for the first time Graham realized that for all he had suffered in the past, his brother had suffered as well.

"What's done is done, Kenneth. Your place is with your family. The best way you can help is by assuring me my wife is safe with you," he managed to say.

Kenneth shoved a hand through his hair. "I wish things could have been different, Graham. For both of us."

"So do I," he said quietly.

Kenneth left, and Graham sat at his satinwood desk, penning a note in Arabic, addressed to the Earl of Stranton.

"If you want me, Stranton, I'm leaving for Egypt in ten days. I'll be finding the treasure of Khufu with the map you took from me years ago. Try to find me, you goat's penis."

Graham sealed the parchment and handed it to his secretary, with instructions to deliver it to Lord Huntly. Stranton had been in touch with him. He felt sure the earl would contact his friend again.

The trap was set with himself as bait. Stranton would not resist.

It wasn't true. It couldn't be.

Jillian had found the newspaper burning on the coal grate of her husband's study, the vile headline screaming out the news as red flames licked the words, curling them into blackened ash. Her father, a perpetrator of such vile crimes? Nonsense.

"Jillian. Ah, good, I've been looking for you."

The deep, smoky voice caused her to whirl with a guilty start. She studied her husband, who entered the room.

"Graham, what's been going on? When I met Aunt Mary today for tea she told me Father was arrested for indecent exposure. Were you trying to hide it from me?" She pointed to the blackened newsprint.

"Yes. Please sit. We've much to discuss, Jillian."

Taking a seat in an overstuffed chair by the fire, she folded her hands. Graham paced the length of the fireplace like a caged jungle cat.

"I've talked with my brother and he agrees it's best to send you and his family to Yorkshire for your own safety. Until the scandal dies down. I'm heading for Egypt to find Khufu's lost treasure, to shore up the family finances. With the tracing you did from your father's map, I'm assured of finding it."

Dumbstruck, she stared at him. *Discuss?* He was giving orders. Something greater than scandal was at stake. Graham, heading to Egypt alone, banishing her to the cold, damp moors? The moment had come to play her trump card. She studied her husband, who was regarding her with that intense gaze of his.

"I'll need the tracing," he told her.

"You can't have it."

"What?"

Jillian tensed, seeing the dark anger flush his face. As he started to prowl toward her, she added, "It's in a place where you'll never find it."

Graham halted.

"So . . . so if . . ." She gulped a deep breath. "If you want to find the treasure, you'll have to take me with you to Egypt. I'm the only person who knows exactly where the key is buried."

"No," he said flatly. "You will tell me where the map is. I'm not taking you anywhere."

Disappointment surged through her. Of course he would not. He'd said no, therefore . . . *No.* She couldn't give in to him. This was much too important, more than a mere treasure. The wishing casket meant something to her husband. Her fists clenched. Jillian took a deep breath for courage. "No."

The duke's dark eyes narrowed. "No?"

"I'm not telling you a thing. Not until we arrive in Egypt. And then I'll give you the tracing."

She stuck out her shoulders. So *this* was what it felt like to take a stand. It felt frightening but oddly exhilarating.

For a minute the hard anger on his face threatened her resolve. She wanted to capitulate. To say "yes," and be the same, ordinary, meek Jillian. But if she did, she'd lose more than the treasure offered. She'd lose everything.

"Take me with you and you'll have the map, Graham."

A muscle twitched in his jaw. "Jillian, there's something you should know. One reason I'm journeying to Egypt has to do with your father's arrest. He blames me, and has sworn revenge. I'm hoping to lead him away from my family and you, into Egypt. He has the map and . . . will know where to find me. For your own safety, you must remain here."

She went still, feeling suddenly sick. "What happened?"

"It has to do with . . . the unsavory circumstances surrounding his detainment. I was present when he was arrested."

She stared. "He was arrested on charges of indecent exposure. Why were you there?"

"Several other lords were as well. It was a raid in which we were present," Graham said tightly. "Your father was caught in an indelicate situation."

He studied her, a defiant glint in his eyes challenging her to question exactly what the circumstances entailed. Jillian closed her eyes, seeing a closed door, hearing a small, frightened scream from behind it.

"I don't want to know," she whispered.

Was that relief in his eyes? No matter. Jillian lifted her chin, meeting his hard stare. "I'm not afraid of my father anymore, Graham. I'm your wife. I'm going with you. If you want to find the treasure, you'll take me."

"No, Jillian. You will give me the map and we will end this discussion," he snapped.

Graham's dark eyes crackled with fury. He strode toward her, every muscle taut with tension. Barely a foot from her chair he halted, his powerful body leaning toward her. She felt the heat of his anger like a live coal. Jillian shrank back, remembering her father's temper. Instinct urged capitulation.

She squeezed her eyes shut, shivering violently. "Go ahead, Graham. Punish me for being insolent, but I will not draw the map. *I will not*," she whispered.

A razor-sharp silence hovered in the air. Then she heard the duke say in a very soft voice, "Jillian, look at me. Look at me. I would never punish you. Don't be afraid of me. Don't."

She dared to open her eyes. His hard anger had faded, leaving behind a weary look.

"You win, Jillian. You shall accompany me. But I warn you, you may end regretting this. We both might."

Egypt, *Ta-meri*, Graham informed her. Land of love. Their arrival in Cairo filled her with enormous relief. It had been a difficult crossing. Graham had run hot and cold. During the day he'd kept his distance, brooding as he paced the ship's deck. At night he'd made love to her with a ferocity she'd never seen him display. Afterwards he'd held her tightly, murmuring soft words in Arabic.

The tension gripping her husband had grown the closer they came to Egypt. Even after they settled into the elegant Shepherd's Hotel and a silent porter unpacked their trunks, Graham paced restlessly. He looked over his shoulder, as if her father were following them close behind.

Jillian took the copy of the papyrus map he'd traced and studied it. She pointed to the intricate symbols. "Where do we look first?"

He glanced over her shoulder at the map. "The key is outside the pyramid. *The key you seek is external, in the position that points to Ra, the chambers will direct you.* The pyramid's exterior western wall."

Jillian studied the map. "How so?"

"I studied Flinders Petrie's detailed report of all the Great Pyramid's measurements. All the pyramid's chambers are west of the vertical passage system. Vertical points to Ra, the Egyptian sun god. But first we need to extrapolate the clues from the pyramid's interior in the King's Chamber. Best to do it that way during the day, looking like regular tourists."

"Fascinating." Jillian beamed at him, but he did not lose the tension riding him.

It wasn't until they set out for a tour of the Great Pyramid that he relaxed. The short camel ride filled her with excitement and left her rollicking as if caught in a great wind. Brilliant sunshine stoked her body and a soft breeze blew. As they dismounted and walked to the pyramid, Jillian ground to a halt. Her mouth parted with astonished wonder. The structure dominated the tawny sands, standing in stark relief against the sharp blue sky.

A deep sense of heady excitement filled Jillian. The Great Pyramid was no longer the majestic temple others had described. It was *here*. She had fulfilled a dream harbored since childhood, when her father had returned from his trip to buy Arabian horses and told her about seeing Egypt's splendid sights.

Her hand shot out, gripping Graham's arm and staying his quick, determined stride.

"Solid. Lasting. Nothing can compare," she marveled.

Graham turned. Appreciation danced in his gaze, momentarily erasing the secretiveness there.

"The pyramid is like you. Intricate, filled with wonders and mysteries. Yet inspiring awe, for all who see it must agree upon its beauty," he murmured.

She felt touched by his poetry, yet disturbed. "Is that how you see me, Graham? The pyramid is splendid yet remote—cold stone. It doesn't invite warmth or closeness." Her chest tightened. "It's built as a *tomb*. Is that what I am, Graham?"

He touched her cheek. "You see it as an Englishwoman does, a monument built to house a dead king. See it as an ancient Egyptian would. Consider its purpose."

"To house the dead."

His expression sobered. "To house new life. Death was only a journey for ancient Egyptians. A journey to new life. This pyramid was fashioned to assist the pharaoh on his way to eternal joy in the afterlife."

Graham moved behind her, wrapping his arms about her waist. His warm breath tickled her ear as he murmured to her, "Look at it. That's what you are to me. A journey to new life."

Disappointment sharp as glass speared her. She had hoped for something deeper, more meaningful, more revealing. But his words, while clever, had not brought about any change. Her attempts to probe this man and discover his layers, to achieve the emotional intimacy she craved, all failed.

Perhaps what she wanted was too much to ask.

Jillian turned in his arms and smiled. "Shall we investigate?"

For a moment, the mask fell from his face and she glimpsed an aching loneliness. Then he returned her smile.

"Would you like to climb it?" he asked. "You should, seeing as it's your first time."

"Oh! May I?"

He escorted her to the structure, eyeing the sweep of her long saffron skirts. Jillian watched with breathless excitement as Graham hired two Egyptian guides. "I'm afraid you'll need help. Some blocks are five feet high," he told her.

"What about you?"

"I can manage on my own." He glanced at her. "Do you mind if I go on ahead? I haven't done this in some time, and I'm anxious to get to the top."

She smiled. "Go. I won't hold you back."

Graham flashed a smile, then took off with the powerful grace of a jungle cat. He hauled himself up each block with seamless grace. He climbed, khaki suit stretching over wide shoulders, black hair gleaming in the endless sun. Jillian murmured her thanks as the two Egyptians pulled her upwards on the higher stones. Determined to do as much possible on her own, she managed the smaller ones.

When she finally reached the top, she saw Graham standing like a pharaoh, scanning the horizon. Tourists flowed past like a stream of water. He seemed so aloof. Something in his stance and proud arrogant carriage reminded her of the ancient kings in this foreign land.

But when she drew closer, a shiver wracked her. Once more she had the eerie feeling her husband was not what he seemed. Witnessing him now, arms folded across his muscled chest, his expression set like grim stone, a flash of insight hit her:

He did not resemble a contented pharaoh surveying his kingdom. He looked more like an embittered invader, determined to conquer. It was as if the sands had scarred him.

What battles raged inside this man, battles he never wanted to share with her? Graham was a fortress built as lasting as this pyramid, locking her out. But the pyramid, like the man, could be invaded. One need only find alternate routes inside, just as explorers had with Khufu's tomb.

Graham shared himself when they made love. He seemed more emotionally vulnerable then. Jillian's feminine intuition told her she had found the way to pry open her husband.

He turned his head and noticed her. "There you are. How did you fare along the way?" he asked.

She stood, slipping an arm about his waist as they both drank in the austere magnificence of the ancient sands. But he seemed stiff as carved wood. Sensing he needed distance, Jillian released him and walked off to be by herself.

When they had descended and joined the line of chattering tourists entering the structure, she felt a distinct change. His aloofness slipped, replaced by thrumming anticipation. Graham did not gasp with awe at the long alley of steps or the oppressive weight of stone surrounding them; he ignored the guide's enthused, halting English explanation of the hieroglyphics etched on the walls. Impatience shadowed his face.

Mindful of the need to cloak their real intentions, Jillian latched onto his arm. When he would have rushed on ahead, she held him back. Caught by her weight tugging at him, he turned and saw her. A rueful smile trumped his impatient look.

Reaching the King's Chamber at last, they milled about with the others, feigning bored interest. Graham pulled her back as the last tourist left the chamber. They were alone.

The lighting in the chamber cast his angular profile into shadow. Excitement danced in his eyes. Her husband looked as enthralled as an ancient explorer first discovering the ruins.

They combed the chamber thoroughly, Graham selecting the west end, Jillian the east. Their search was interrupted by another group of tourists. When the last visitor drifted out, the duke jammed his hands into his trouser pockets and joined her. "Nothing. But it *must* be here."

The map indicated a major clue was specifically in the King's Chamber. Tomb robbers had swept the room clean, picking it over as thoroughly as vultures on carrion.

"There's nothing here."

Jillian glanced at Graham. "Perhaps you are thinking in English terms. Be an Egyptian. Think as they did. Let's take another look at the map. Explain to me the hieroglyphics."

He unfurled the copy of the papyrus he had traced and read aloud: " 'In the chamber of Khufu, the key to unlock the treasure is found, visible to all but hidden from those who would rob the sacred dead. Follow Ra's path, then follow the Nile's opposite course.' "

"The map says to take the clue from the Great Pyramid itself, for it is like the pharaoh: layers upon layers, complex and intriguing."

"So we must look beyond the obvious. But the map indicates the key is found in a very visible spot." Graham carefully rolled the tracing and tucked it away. "I don't see anything clearly visible here."

Jillian studied the empty King's Chamber. "What if the key were not an actual object, but something else? Let's break down the problem. First, what is a key?"

Intrigued, he replied, "It unlocks something."

"You're thinking in concrete terms. Let's view the abstract. A key can unlock a solid object, such as a door, a box, a chest . . ."

"Or a mystery."

Their gazes locked. Graham's filled with excitement as he slowly digested her meaning. "And what if the key to unlock the treasure were hidden in the King's Chamber, but was not actually a physical key, but . . . what? What would tomb robbers be unable to steal? What is hidden and yet visible?"

Jillian began pacing. "If Khufu wished to hide a clue in his burial chamber for his son, where could he order it hidden in plain view?"

Her footsteps rang in the chamber, clicking on the stone in precise movements. Graham looked at her feet. "Jillian! That's it. What is constant and visible, yet hidden?"

She halted, casting him a puzzled look.

He pointed to her feet. "Walk five paces."

Obeying, she carefully stepped five paces and then abruptly stopped. "Measurements!" Jillian exclaimed. "Oh, Graham, yes!"

He rubbed his jaw. "The map says 'Follow Ra's path, then follow the Nile's opposite course.' Ra, the sun, travels from east to west. The Nile's opposite course is north to south because the Nile flows south to north."

Jillian measured east to west of the chamber, then north to south while Graham kept watch out for visitors. "Then outside the western wall of the pyramid, we go ten-point-four-six meters westward, turn south and go five-point-two-three meters," she surmised. "What's the third clue?"

Graham read aloud, " 'In an empty space destined for a king, find the depth of a man's life as he descends into the afterlife.' " An empty space destined for a king. "A sarcophagus intended for a king who was never laid to rest there. But the body was stolen long ago."

Graham gave her a slow smile and went on, "What if it were never there? Some theorize that Khufu's mummy wasn't stolen, but hidden in another burial chamber. If so, then the sarcophagus . . ."

"Would be a ruse and remain empty."

Their gazes whipped to the immense stone coffin. Missing both its lid and the king for whom it was built, it stood out in the empty chamber near the western wall. Jillian measured the depth and wrote the numbers down on a pad kept in her reticule.

"Nearly one meter."

"The key must be buried that far down. We'll have to return tonight to dig," he mused aloud. "Come, let's return to the hotel."

Chapter Fifteen

Back at the Shepherd's, they raced to their suite like schoolchildren, giddy with joy over their discovery. Jillian whipped off her wide-brimmed hat and set it upon a table, eyeing the water closet. A bath before dinner sounded delightful.

Graham's black eyes danced with fevered excitement. "I want to study these measurements."

He sat at the small wood table, armed with paper and pencil as she stripped off her white blouse. Jillian glanced up and saw Graham wasn't studying the figures they had jotted down. His hungry gaze caressed her instead.

"Perhaps we should have an early dinner," he said thickly. His gaze flicked to the bed, covered with mosquito netting.

Jillian smiled. "I'd like that.

After a splendid repast in the hotel's elegant dining room, they adjourned to the immense ballroom for drinks and dancing. The duke ordered champagne for them both. Bubbles tickled her nose as she lifted the flute and sipped.

A giddy feeling, accentuated by the champagne, filled her.

The immense bar and ballroom boasted majestic pillared lotus columns modeled after the ones at Karnak, a ceiling with jewel-toned Oriental murals, and linen-draped tables where an assortment of the wealthy and powerful observed the dancers. An orchestra played while couples swirled by. A balmy breeze floated through the open doors leading to the famous terrace. A delicate floral scent from the blooms in large Oriental vases flanking the columns mixed with the heavier scents of men's powerful cologne and women's exotic perfumes.

Despite her excitement at being abroad, and at the new and fascinating scenery before her, Jillian only had eyes for her husband. The buzz of elegant couples and polite, hovering waiters did not exist. Graham swirled the liquid in his glass, studying her over the rim. His glass remained full, while hers was half empty.

"Do you want to dance, Jillian?" he asked.

She saw him staring at her with avid hunger, and instinctively knew what he wanted.

"The waltz is a fine dance," she said, watching him.

"I did not mean the waltz," he purred. "Would you like to dance with me upstairs?"

He stood and stretched out a hand to her. She put her fingers into his as he pulled her upright.

Clearly the excitement of their find had translated into a different kind of excitement for him. She sensed a warrior's triumph, an eagerness to claim a prize far more corporeal and earthy than the key to unlocking some treasure.

Graham wasted no time as they entered their room. He tumbled her onto the bed, his kiss devouring. The kiss was hard and fast, crushing her mouth against his, his hands roving her body, fumbling at her gown.

Jillian sat up, letting him unfasten it. Cool air billowing from the opened windows washed over her naked flesh as the gown and underlying chemise fell free. Clad only in her stockings, she kicked off her soft kid slippers, smiling.

His gaze darkened and widened as he slid off the bed and shed his clothing. Graham joined her on the bed, kissing her.

She lay beneath him, raising her hips as he opened her legs, his ragged breaths filling the air. In one powerful thrust he was inside her. A startled gasp fled her at the thick pressure in her wet core.

Her hands pushed at the hard muscles of his chest, tangled in the thick thatch of hair as he strained above her. Jillian gripped his muscled arms, hiding her face in his shoulder as he moved. Her scream of pleasure was buried in his skin. The duke shuddered and groaned as he released his seed.

He looked down at her, eyes half lidded and drowsy with pleasure. "Ah," he sighed.

"I do enjoy how you dance," she said impishly. A nasty tug of jealousy filled her. "Did you"—she plucked at the damp sheet—"have many lovers before me?"

To her surprise, he looked sheepish. Graham slid off her, rolled to his side. He rested his head on his hand.

"My dear Jillian, how many lovers do you think I've had?"

Irritated, she pulled the sheet up to cover her breasts. "How should I know? I'm not that experienced. I'd say several. While you were my first," she added sullenly.

"As you were."

Dumbstruck, she stared. Graham reached over and gently tipped her open jaw closed. "I've something to confess, dear wife. That night in the brothel? You weren't the only virgin."

"It can't be."

"It was. You were my first, Jilly."

Deeply touched, she gazed at him. Truly there was something special about his confession. It endeared him to her even more.

"Is there a particular reason why you waited?" she asked.

Tenderness etched his face. "I waited for you. I suppose it was my fate that we would be together. I'm glad it was you. Even with that ridiculous wig."

Jillian smiled. "Even though you explicitly asked for anyone but a redhead with green eyes?" Her smile faded. "Why did you not want that, Graham?"

"I have my reason," he said, his voice a husky whisper. A dark shadow crossed his face.

"Graham, there's something you're not telling me."

"Yes," he said. "Perhaps someday I might tell you. For now, just know this. No other woman but you was meant for me, Jilly. I know that now."

Secrets danced in his eyes and Jillian felt troubled. She hoped he would confess in his own time, and yet when he did, as much as she'd wanted Graham to share himself, she suddenly was afraid of what his secrets would be.

"I have the key to the treasure."

Jillian's pulse quickened with excitement as she stood behind her husband, who was sitting at the table the next morning. She glanced at the papers strewn about. Calculations. From a short piece of wood, Graham had carved what resembled a key.

Last night, they had dressed in dark clothing and set out for the Great Pyramid. Graham had short shovels and an electric torch in his rucksack. The night porter had ignored them as they left the lobby. A short while later, they had arrived at the Great Pyramid. Moonlight spilled over the sand, turning it a ghostly gray. Graham and Jillian measured the distance from the western wall according to the clues they'd discovered. Then they began to dig, and discovered a small stone block with the outline of a key upon it.

This morning, after tracing the outline of the key, Graham had made a duplicate.

"I didn't know they had locks," she confessed.

"They were an advanced culture thought to be inventors of the first locks."

"Are we headed directly to the treasure?"

"No, we need to visit a tribe I know. The Khamsin, who raised my brother, live south. But first, we need to purchase supplies for the trip—and I thought you'd enjoy touring Cairo."

Cairo, with its towers and minarets and Islamic architecture, had Jillian exclaiming with wonder. Graham indulged her in a quick shopping trip in the souks, admiring her womanly curves as she bent over to examine a gold pot offered by an eager vendor. The rich, vibrant emerald tones of her day gown, with its froth of ivory lace, complemented her creamy complexion and vivid red hair. Never again would she wear ugly, repressive gray. Her father had swathed her in it like steel armor. Slowly, Graham was coaxing her true spirit to emerge. He knew she felt unnoticed, unappreciated and unloved, and he wanted to change all that.

But he didn't want her with him while journeying to find Khufu's treasure. At the Khamsin camp, he planned to leave her in his friends' care, while he journeyed alone into the deep desert.

In the desert he would face his tormentor, for while

they had toured Cairo that afternoon, Graham had spotted another redhead ducking cleanly out of sight. And there was no mistaking that face. He knew it too well.

They departed for the Khamsin camp the following day. Graham surprised Jillian by renting a *dahabiya* to travel down the Nile. The two sat on a plush divan on deck as the captain steered the craft. Wind caressed Jillian's cheeks, played with strands of hair escaping their pins. Her eager gaze drank in the sights as the dank smell of river water tickled her nostrils. Donkeys plodded alongside the riverbank, towing carts piled with vegetation. Curious children stared.

"I feel like a redheaded Cleopatra leaping forward in time," she murmured as she waved to the children.

Graham smiled. "Wait until you meet the Khamsin, the tribe that raised my brother. The Khamsin are unlike other desert tribes. Tents are not cordoned off to segregate genders. Men and women eat together, and the men have only one wife."

"A progressive tribe keeping with modern times?"

He chuckled. "An ancient tribe proudly tracing their ancestry back to the times of Pharaoh Akhenaten. The times caught up to them. Elizabeth, the sheikh's wife, helped."

"Odd name for a sheikh's wife."

"She's American. Very spirited, modern and very much in love with her husband. She's a suffragette. She's nearly taught the entire tribe, men and women both, to read."

Jillian hid her surprised excitement. "She did?"

"Elizabeth loves to break traditions. Both she and Jabari are concerned about the Khamsin's ability to merge with modern society and keep the tribe financially solvent. I'm sure they'll be eager to solicit your advice."

"Tell me about the tribe," Jillian urged.

Graham obliged, informing her that the Khamsin lived deep in the desert. "The sheikh has a bodyguard called a Guardian of the Ages, who protects Jabari with his life. I became very close to Jabari and Ramses, his guardian. Ramses is married to Katherine, whose father is an English lord."

More surprises. "Does this Ramses like the English?"

Graham chuckled. "Once he abhorred them. But he's deeply in love with his wife, and has grown to respect the English. He no longer calls them the white-bellied *samak*—fish."

"Good for you he no longer abhors them," she murmured.

"He's a jokester. He teases me about being English."

Her husband looked so very English in his wide-brimmed hat, the cream-colored suit with its ivory tie. Except for one tiny fact. Graham hadn't shaved this morning. A heavy beard was already shadowing his cheeks.

It was as if he had begun to change before her eyes.

They docked at a small village where Graham purchased four camels from local villagers. He loaded two camels with their trunks and supplies he had purchased in Cairo. The Khamsin camp lay deep in the eastern desert, he informed her.

Green lines of vegetation bordering the Nile boasted towering date palms and cultivated fields, but soon they left those behind for the open desert. Sweat trickled down Jillian's neck. Graham guided his camel alongside hers, seemingly unaffected by the scorching noonday sun. Beneath the shady brim of his hat, he studied her with those intense dark eyes.

They took several short rest breaks. Muscles she had never used ached from the long ride in the hard camel saddle. The scent of unwashed animal and desert heat stung her nostrils. Jillian shifted her weight, blinking wearily. It felt as if they had ridden for hours through towering canyons that Graham called *wadis*, and into the high desert. The bleak, desolate landscape depressed her. Surely no life could exist in this arid land flanked by high mountains of limestone and granite. A cloudless blue sky seemed as hard as the rocky sand beneath their camels' hoofs. How could anyone live in the deep desert?

She squinted as she spotted tall date palms and green and yellow vegetation in the distance. Black tents dotted the horizon. Surely a mirage caused by the relentless, burning heat? But she could see tiny figures moving about. The Khamsin camp?

Graham halted his camel and urged her to do the same. Excitement blazed in his eyes. He cupped his hands around his mouth and let loose a piercing, undulating sound.

Startled, Jillian stared. Her husband, with his very English dress, suddenly seemed as Egyptian as the surrounding sand.

Figures stirred in the distance. Wild, undulating shouts echoed back at them. Then she saw several figures grab horses and ride toward them. A cloud of dust rose on the horizon.

Jillian swallowed hard. Graham gave a reassuring smile. "Don't be scared. It's the traditional Khamsin greeting to welcome a son of the desert home."

Despite his assurances, terror gripped her at the wild, warlike shrieks. Jillian sat frozen as a small band of indigo-draped warriors galloped toward them. Warriors on their Arabians hooted and screamed, then pulled to a stop bare feet from them. The warriors wore indigo coats reaching to mid-thigh, and blousy indigo trousers tucked into leather boots. Indigo turbans adorned their heads.

All had short-cropped beards and mustaches. A tall, commanding figure jumped off his horse and strode toward her smiling husband. The two embraced, while the other warriors stared at her.

Graham pulled back, glancing at her fondly. "Jabari, this is my wife, Jillian. Jilly, this is Jabari bin Tarik Hassid, sheikh of the Khamsin Warriors of the Wind."

She didn't know whether to curtsy or salaam. Her nervous gaze flicked to the long scimitar strapped on his belt. To her surprise, the handsome sheikh took her hand in his and shook it. "A western custom my wife likes. She thinks men and women should be treated as equals." He spoke perfect, albeit accented, English. Warmth radiated in his smile. "I am most pleased to meet you, Jillian."

She smiled and murmured her thanks. A shorter, more muscled warrior at the sheikh's side stared with open curiosity. Gleaming white teeth flashed in an impish grin as he glanced at her husband. Graham introduced him as Ramses.

"You have taken a wife at last, my friend. And a most charming one, as well." The shorter warrior swept her an elaborate bow. Mirth danced in his odd-colored amber eyes. "I am most honored to meet you, your ladyship."

"Grace," Graham corrected.

Ramses looked bemused. "I thought her name was Jillian."

"It is. She's my duchess. So the address is Your Grace. Just as I am Your Grace."

"My friend, you are anything but graceful."

"It's an English title." Graham's lips twitched with mirth. "I didn't make up the rules."

Ramses turned to Jillian. "I am honored to meet you, your most graceful gracious ladyship duchess."

Jillian smiled as Ramses winked at her.

"Let's get you settled, your supreme dukish gracious-

209

ness. After that, take your lady to meet Elizabeth and Katherine. They would love to talk with a graceful gracious English duchess."

They settled into a large, spacious tent with soft carpets covering the ground, low tables and a curtain sectioning off a bedroom. A real bed, low to the ground and quite comfortable as she sat upon it, dominated the room. To her shock, Graham quickly undressed. He dug into their trunk and withdrew an indigo outfit matching that of the warriors.

"I wear the *binish* when I visit. The Khamsin consider me a brother and even use an Arabic name for me— Rashid," he explained. He slid a long, lethal-looking sword into a leather sheath attached to his belt. He did the same to a curved dagger.

In Egyptian dress, he looked dangerous. And very much a stranger. Jillian offered a brave if wobbly smile.

"Well, in Rome, dress as the Romans," she said. "Do you want me to find dress similar to what the women here wear?"

"You're perfect the way you are."

"But I should dress for the desert if we're to take the long journey to find the treasure." She poked at her skirts.

A blank look came over him. Jillian grew suspicious.

"Unless you're not planning on taking me. That's why you wanted to come here first! To leave me with your friends."

The duke sighed. "Jillian, it's not safe for you to cross the desert. There are many hazards, and even the hardiest men can die out there."

"Graham—"

"We'll discuss this later," he said firmly. His expression shuttered and Jillian knew he'd talk no more of it. He settled a hand on the small of her back, steering her out of the tent.

Stares accompanied them as they walked through the camp. Jillian dragged in an uncertain breath. Graham took her hand, giving it a reassuring squeeze.

They halted before a stubby tree, its high branches tipped with big spikes. A blond woman and a brunette sat beneath its shade, talking and laughing. A sleeping baby lay swaddled nearby. Children played at their feet. Dark-haired twins, they looked about two years old. A striking, blond-haired, dark-eyed little boy appeared about three. The women glanced up. Graham's expression softened as he introduced them. The blonde was Elizabeth, the sheikh's American-born wife. The green-eyed brunette was Ramses' English wife, Katherine.

"Why don't you sit with them and become better acquainted? Jabari, Ramses and I have matters to discuss."

It was a dismissal, but eager to chat with the intriguing Elizabeth, Jillian nodded. She watched her husband join the sheikh and Ramses in Jabari's tent. The flaps were rolled up to allow in a fresh desert breeze. Graham looked so foreign, as if the sand had swallowed him whole, absorbing and changing him.

Her chances of coaxing him out, of achieving the intimacy she craved were more remote than ever. And now he desired to leave her here, in this camp, while he ventured into the burning Sahara to seek the treasure alone.

Jillian talked with the two women, telling them of her marriage and the quest to find the treasure. And how Graham planned to leave her in the camp.

"I can't let him go without me," she told Elizabeth, feeling a little desperate.

"He wants you here for your own protection."

"What's out there that's so dangerous?"

A thoughtful look came over Elizabeth. "It's said

among the Khamsin that in order to find yourself, you must go into the desert and lose yourself. Our warriors venture into the deep desert to meditate. The desert strips them down to what they essentially are. Sometimes it drives men mad, for they don't like what they find."

Jillian shuddered. Graham, alone in that vast desolation, exposed to the merciless heat and even more merciless ghosts haunting him? A frightful image filled her—her proud, restrained husband howling with anguish as he faced his demons. She could not allow him to face them alone.

"I must go with him. How can I make him take me?"

Mischief filled the American's cobalt eyes. "I have discovered a man can be quite pliant after certain nocturnal activities."

Jillian thought of what her father had done to her. "Or I could hide all his clothing."

The woman named Katherine gurgled with laughter. "That wouldn't stop Ramses. He'd march into the desert naked just to prove himself. Stubborn man." Her gaze softened as she glanced at the tent where her husband sat talking with Graham and Jabari.

"If you wish to go with him, then learn all you can about living in the desert," Elizabeth put in. "Convince him you'll be an asset, not a liability."

Jillian perked up, thinking of learning. "Will you teach me how to manage in the desert?"

The two women exchanged knowing glances. "Of course. We both will," Katherine replied.

Doubt assailed her. "Graham is quite stubborn. Even if I show him I can make the trip, he won't take me," she worried.

A knowing smile touched Elizabeth's mouth. "Stubborn, yes. And very possessive of you—I can tell. Perhaps Graham needs a subtle push to convince him leaving you here may not be to his best interests. An attractive wife alone, surrounded by curious men . . . Wouldn't you agree, Katherine?"

The petite brunette glanced in the direction of the other tent. An impish smile curved her lips. "I'll talk to my husband. I think he can help."

Chapter Sixteen

Jillian stood out from the other women with her delicate alabaster skin, clear green eyes and riot of flame tresses. She wore a wide-brimmed straw hat shading her from the harsh sun. Her white gown had billowing sleeves and an emerald ribbon at the waist. Graham wanted her to look English. She did not belong here amid the sand and hot winds, and amid his murky past.

He sat facing the Khamsin sheikh and guardian. He had told them of his plans to find Khufu's treasure. Ramses gazed out to the horizon where the long stretch of the Nile cut Egypt in half.

"The western desert, the land where the jinn roam. Men die out there," Ramses intoned solemnly.

"I have no intentions of dying," he informed them grimly. "I know how to navigate by starlight. I can identify a camel's tracks no matter how harsh the wind blows to conceal them."

"And you got lost in Cairo trying to find the Shepherd's hotel," Jabari put in.

Graham glared. "A hotel in a city."

Jabari smiled. "A very large hotel in a city. Face it, you could not find the Great Pyramid without a map—"

"And several guides," Ramses finished helpfully.

Graham ignored their jibes. "I have a map Jillian will provide for me. The cave is north of Farafra. If I take the old Darb Asyut route, it will get me there in less time."

The sheikh and his guardian exchanged uneasy glances. "Farafra, land of the cow," Ramses murmured, using the ancient name for the oasis. "I have friends there."

"That route you speak of is treacherous," Jabari warned. "It is a long, hard ten days by camel. The red sand can swallow a man whole if he sets foot into it. There are few wells."

"I have iron water tanks purchased in Cairo," Graham said.

The sheikh looked troubled. "Farafra was long besieged by marauders. There are Bedu roaming the sands who lie in wait for the unwary traveler."

Graham fingered the sharp scimitar strapped to his side. "I'm not unwary."

"But alone . . . ," Ramses observed. "You are not safe, my friend, no matter how fierce a warrior you are."

"I will send several men with you," Jabari decided.

Tension coiled in his stomach. Graham ran a hand over his growing beard. "I will not risk the lives of your men, Jabari."

"You *will* risk it," the sheikh rejoined. "I will not allow you to leave here alone."

Graham studied the pair, wondering if he could trust them—even these, the two men he knew who held honor above all else. A natural caution restrained him from telling all.

But the sheikh's wise eyes searched his face. "You are withholding knowledge. What is it, my friend?"

In the distance, Graham heard the throaty laughter of his wife. Carefree, untroubled. How he wanted to keep her that way, and guard her from the terrible truth.

His gaze flicked to them. "I'm being followed."

Jabari's expression tightened. Ramses put a hand on his scimitar hilt, a gesture Graham recognized the warrior made when feeling defensive. "Who is it?" Jabari asked.

"Someone I know," Graham said guardedly. "An Englishman who desires the treasure and knows it's buried in the cave."

He didn't dare tell them about the fiasco in London with Stranton. Or the real reason he wished to travel alone—to kill Stranton at last, or be killed by him. Graham would not risk anyone else in his personal battle.

"A greater reason to take a band of men," Ramses said.

"No. Traveling with a large caravan is like waving a flag. I must maintain the ability to blend into the sands if necessary, and shift as the dunes shift. I don't wish to attract any more attention than I must." His even gaze met theirs. "Do you remember what happened to my parents all those years ago?" Death screams echoed in his head.

The sheikh glanced toward the women, who were quietly talking beneath the sheltering shade of a thorny acacia tree. "And your wife?"

"She wants to come. She will do as I say and remain here."

"The lady Jillian does not appear to be the type to meekly follow orders," Jabari observed.

Ramses stared with rapt fascination at Jillian as she tugged off her perky straw hat, revealing glossy red tresses coiled into a tight chignon. "Al-Hariia," he murmured. "That hair burns like fire. Does she burn inside as well?"

Graham shifted, narrowing his eyes. He didn't like his friend's interest in his wife. "You'll never find out."

The warrior looked at him and laughed. Mirth sparked his amber eyes. "Ah, so the fair English lady has caught the aloof panther and ensnared him with her fiery hair."

A teasing smile quirked Jabari's mouth as well. "It is about time, my friend. I am most happy for you."

Satisfaction came over Graham as he glanced at his wife and Elizabeth and Katherine. "Enough of me. Tell me of your lives. I see you've increased your family, Ramses. And Tarik looks well, Jabari. He's past three now, isn't he? Why haven't you caught up? Wasn't Elizabeth pregnant when I left?"

Ramses looked uncomfortable. Jabari's jaw clenched as he drew in a deep breath. "Elizabeth . . . was with child. She lost the baby. It devastated her, but she was eager to try again. She became pregnant. Then she . . . miscarried again."

Genuine grief gripped Graham. "I am sorry, Jabari."

Emotion flashed in the sheikh's dark eyes, then he shrugged. "Allah's will. We will try again, if Elizabeth wants to have another child. I told her having Tarik is enough for me, as long as I have her. She is my greatest love."

His friend's open honesty stirred Graham. Deep inside, he longed for the same emotional commitment in a marriage. But he knew it meant sharing the deepest, darkest part of himself with Jillian. He could not.

Relaxing once more, Ramses smiled. "Look at the three of us. Once warriors who roved the sands, free as falcons. Now our wives have captured us and we would do anything for them."

"Even you, my newly married friend. A woman can be most persuasive when you are holding her in your arms. You will see how easy it is for Jillian to change your mind about accompanying you into the deep desert," Jabari mocked.

But Graham could not return their smiles. The premonition danced before him: red hair billowing in the relentless clasp of desert wind, his screams echoing over the dunes . . .

Graham sat in his tent later, honing his scimitar. The blade was dull from lying in an attic trunk in England. He scraped the whetstone along the edge, remembering his other life. He did not want Jillian to blend as he did. He wanted her to stand out, not be hidden in a crowd.

For years she'd hid behind gray silk, high collars concealing her swanlike throat. Jillian, the gray shadow he had coaxed from her self-imposed shell, was no longer afraid to argue with him, to express her opinion. He smiled ruefully. She was stubborn as he, and certain to keep arguing with him to take her into the desert.

Graham realized with a start he had changed. He'd once thought of Jillian as a means to accomplish his ultimate goal. As he had with his family, he'd kept an emotional distance, allowing himself only to be slightly vulnerable when they made love. But now he realized he wanted more. Needed more.

Bringing her to Egypt had been a mistake and a blessing. Graham felt his dogged loneliness forced back by her sweet laughter, stimulating conversation and eager lovemaking. Slowly she was pushing away the darkness inside him. It scared him. The darkness was all he knew. He clung to it like sand clung to skin.

The tent flap opened and Jillian strolled inside. She tossed down her white, floppy hat and twirled, hugging herself. She looked dreamy and delicious and utterly loveable. He wanted to lick every inch of her.

"I've been analyzing the star charts Jabari drew up for me. Well, Elizabeth drew them; Jabari dictated. It's fascinating how the Bedu can calculate how to return home by navigating the stars each hour. He and Ramses are teaching me how to find my way in the desert should I get lost. Do you know that you can literally find your way out of the desert by analyzing latitude and longitude?"

"Yes," he said in a husky voice. Watching her emerge from her gray cocoon had been like seeing an iridescent butterfly take flight. The very stars paled beside her beauty.

Jillian paced, brilliant green eyes afire with excitement. "And the investments the tribe has made—Jabari has the keenest intuition. Yet they could do more. Elizabeth agreed with me that investing in new ventures such as electrical companies will secure the Khamsin's economic future."

"It sounds . . . very smart," Graham murmured.

Once he hadn't cared if she left after their three months were done. Now he couldn't bear to lose her. His thoughts were a maelstrom. Was this love? It wasn't the romance warbled by whey-faced poets. It was burning, like fire. It felt wonderful. And it seared him with pain to think of her leaving.

She whirled, her skirts spinning out like flower petals. She looked stricken. "Oh, Graham, I'm boring you."

He stood and went to her, brushing her hand with his lips. "Don't. Look at me, Jilly. I don't want to restrain you. Don't pretend anymore. I won't punish you for thinking aloud, or for knowing more than I do. I'm not your father."

She seemed to struggle with her emotions. "You know more than I. You can navigate by merely glancing at the stars."

A crooked grin tugged his mouth upward. "I get lost in my own tent. Navigating the desert at night is an art I have yet to perfect. I tend to wander."

"That's not you, that's me. An aimless wanderer."

"You're not an aimless wanderer. You have purpose. Your mind is like an indestructible khamsin, blowing through life, eager to release itself. But you've been restrained, Jilly. I don't want to rein you in," he told her softly.

Her rosebud mouth wobbled. "I'm not a conventional duchess. I don't make scintillating conversation—"

With a finger to her lips, he silenced her. Graham framed her rounded face with his warm hands. "Jillian, I don't want a conventional duchess. Bloody hell, I'm not a conventional duke." He glanced at his indigo *binish*. "I doubt appearing in Parliament like this would be praised."

A light laugh rippled from her perfect, pink mouth. "Just as I must appear an oddity here among the Khamsin."

He shook his head. "Intriguing, yes. But not odd."

Hope filled her gaze. "Then you have no qualms about taking me with you into the desert?"

"We'll discuss it later," he said evasively.

Damn. Somehow he must convince her how dangerous it was for her. But deep down, Graham knew the real danger lay ahead for him. His worst nightmare, coming true.

He held out a hand. "Come, let's go for a walk and I'll explain some Bedouin customs to you."

They emerged from the tent, blinking at the bright sunshine. Jillian clasped her husband's hand, wishing he would cease this remoteness. She suspected here, in this camp among friends, the real Graham would emerge. If only she could coax him out.

Nearby, Katherine's twins, Fatima and Asad, and Elizabeth's son Tarik played in the sand. Fatima glanced up, a cheeky smile on her face. She went to Graham and hugged his knees. "Unca Rashid, play wid us," she said in English.

Graham grinned. He ducked back into their tent.

When he emerged, one of the clean white sheets from their bed covered his body, draping down to the sand.

Jillian laughed. "Playing ghost?"

"I always scared my brother with this as a child." Graham began waving his arms beneath the sheet and moaning loudly.

"You're quite scary," she agreed cheerfully.

"Quiet. You're ruining my act," he replied.

The children stared, bemused looks on their faces. Jabari and Ramses approached, their brows wrinkling. "Ah, Graham, what are you doing?" Jabari asked.

"I'm scaring your son," he countered, moaning more.

"He does not look scared," Jabari observed. "Perhaps if you take the sheet off, he will be more frightened."

Pulling off the sheet, Graham made an exasperated sound. Ramses chuckled and picked up a tiny toy scimitar, its wooden tip rounded. He tossed it over. "Try this instead."

A high-pitched scream, the same the warriors had shrieked, undulated from Graham's lips as he waved the sword. Asad, the boy twin, screamed and toddled off toward his mother, who scooped him up into her arms. Tarik looked bored. Fatima pulled the toy sword from Graham's loose grasp and poked him in the knees. She made a sound resembling a sick goat in distress.

Graham laughed. "A new version of the Khamsin war cry? What a little warrior." He clutched his chest. "You got me." Sliding dramatically to the ground on his back, he closed his eyes. Fatima climbed atop him, solemnly regarding him.

"Unca Rashid crying. Here," she said, touching his chest.

Graham's eyes flew open with a startled look. Then the little girl promptly laid her head upon his chest and yawned, clutching his *binish*. Tarik toddled over and joined her, using Graham as a cushion, his arm slung around Fatima.

"Nap time," Ramses said cheerfully. "She often falls asleep on me like that. Stay there. This is the first my daughter has been quiet all day."

Graham did not smile. He gently stroked the little girl's head with a somber look.

Ramses picked his daughter up and she snuggled into his arms. Jabari did the same with his son. Slowly Graham arose, brushing off his *binish*. The smile he offered Jillian seemed tight.

"I need to check on the camels, Jilly. Why don't you visit with Katherine and Elizabeth a while?" And before she could reply, he strode off, his jaw set.

Despair filled her. The lighthearted moment they'd shared in playing with the children had vanished. She glanced over to see Katherine watching her, Asad asleep in her arms.

"Odd thing for Fatima to say. Why did she?" Jillian asked.

Distress etched Katherine's face. "She was born with a caul. Fatima has the Second Sight. Our shaman says she can see into the hearts of people. Especially those who are troubled."

Chapter Seventeen

After dismissing Katherine's odd remarks, Jillian found herself enjoying the adventure of staying with the Khamsin. She enjoyed talking with Elizabeth. Despite assimilating into the tribe, the woman had maintained her Western attitude. Jillian often saw Jabari looking with loving devotion at his wife. Jillian wished she could inspire the same in Graham.

Two days later, Ramses and Katherine invited them to share what Katherine called "Bedouin English tea." Beneath the shade of an acacia tree, they spread a plush carpet. Katherine boiled water over an open fire, and steeped the tea leaves in a flowered china pot. A plate heaped with scones sat on a low round table. Amusement sparked Ramses's face as he watched his wife pour as formally as if she sat in an English drawing room.

"Do you take milk in your tea?" she asked.

Jillian's brows arched. "What kind of milk?"

"Camel milk," Ramses said, and laughed at her grimace.

"It's quite good," Katherine assured her. "The Bedouin use camel milk to keep alive in the deep desert."

"How do you milk a camel?" Jillian asked.

"Like a cow," Graham cut in, taking his cup from Katherine and nodding his thanks. "Except you stand up, balance the bowl on your left leg and then use your right hand to milk."

Katherine poured a mouthful into a spare cup. "Try it."

Jillian studied the frothy liquid and sipped. It tasted rich and creamy. "It is delicious," she admitted.

"And healthy. On one of my trips to the deep desert, I lived for weeks on nothing but camel milk," Graham said.

"I thought you traveled mainly in the cities, except for visiting this tribe on a brief occasion."

Ramses and Katherine suddenly seemed absorbed in their teacups. A shadow dropped over Graham's face. "Surviving in the desert requires knowledge that will help in an emergency."

"Well, why don't you teach me to milk a camel? I want to be able to help you on the journey."

Graham turned his head, displaying the taut edge of his jaw. "No, Jillian. It isn't necessary. I don't want you milking camels or dressing like a Bedouin woman. You're English."

"And so are you," she said quietly. "Yet you dress like a Khamsin warrior and speak fluent Arabic. It makes me wonder, Graham. Were you truly raised by some doting old English couple?"

The blood drained from his face. Graham's grip on his little teacup tightened. It looked ready to shatter. Like him.

"You're questioning my childhood?" he asked tightly. "If you wish to argue about my past, let's do it in private."

"I won't argue, Graham."

"Nor will I. Excuse me, Katherine, Ramses."

He stood and slipped off, silent. Ramses sighed and followed. Embarrassed, Jillian stammered a polite apology to Katherine. "I just want to help him. How can I?"

The petite brunette looked thoughtful. "Show him you will do anything to go with him. He shouldn't be alone in the desert, Jillian. He needs you."

"How can I change his mind?"

"If he won't teach you to milk a camel, try it on your own. It isn't difficult." Katherine flashed a reassuring smile.

Jillian masked her distress. Graham was more aloof than ever. The change darkening him had become stronger. Her husband was turning into a stranger before her eyes.

Later, as she rested in the tent, fears played over her. Could she do it? Or would she shackle him in her stubborn insistence on accompanying him? The confidence gained in sitting with the great sheikh himself and discussing the tribe's finances faded in light of her ignorance about this hostile terrain. Her fair English skin burned in the sun. Her red hair set her apart. She did not belong here. Jillian didn't know where she belonged anymore.

She rose and freshened up, then went outside. Her husband sat on the ground. An air of fierce concentration shimmered around him as he sharpened his scimitar against a rock. Jillian worked up her courage and approached. He glanced up from his task as she stood over him.

"Graham, we need to talk. You must take me with you into the desert. I'm not staying here."

He could *not* take her with him.

Graham's chest tightened with dread as he set down the scimitar. In the desert, he would confront her father, and it would finally come to an end one way or another. Nothing remained hidden long in the desert. Wind lifted sand, exposing bones bleached by the sun. There were no shadows or darkness in the unforgiving desert. No secrets.

No, the desert would not allow him to stay hidden. It would leech out his blackness, squeeze it like the last drop of water from an empty goatskin bag. He could not allow her to glimpse that terrible darkness inside him.

"You can't go," he said curtly.

"Because you think I'm incapable of the journey? Or is it my father? He won't hurt me, Graham. He never did. Take me with you. I can be your shield."

Irony quirked his mouth. A shield to stave off the burning sun, to hide the darkness? She did not know what she asked. "No."

"Why is my father after you, Graham?"

In the distance, a sheep bleated. In the spring, the air resounded with the echo of squealing lambs. They castrated select males soon after birth.

"He's after the treasure, Jillian. He has the map and wants the treasure for himself."

His answer seemed to satisfy her. "Then you must take me with you into the desert. I can reason with him, talk to him. . . ."

"No," he grated out. "I will not take you with me." Graham paused. He had to tell her something that would push her away. "I can't be burdened by a woman. Stop this nonsense and just give me the directions."

Tears shimmered in her large, green eyes. "Very well. I see you think of me as a liability. I wouldn't wish to encumber you, Graham. I'll draw the map again for you."

She fled into the tent. Pain speared him. He was a fool if he followed her. A bigger fool if he didn't.

He followed. Inside the cooling shade, Jillian sat on the thick, jewel-toned carpet, her head buried into her hands.

Sobs shook her shoulders. Graham knelt down beside her. She struggled against his enveloping embrace. He was stronger. She sagged against him, as if weary.

"Listen to me," he said, his voice trembling as he spoke into the silky softness of her hair. "I want you to stay here and stay safe. Because I . . . care."

"Words, just words. You don't love me."

Graham hugged her tighter. Afraid of letting her close, even more fearful of letting her go.

Two wet emeralds regarded him as she lifted her head. "If you did love me, you'd tell me. You'd open up to me, Graham."

Something inside him stirred. A connection he didn't want. It came anyway.

"Trust me, Jilly," he said softly. "Just trust that I want what's best for you. It's all I ask."

"And all I ask is that you give yourself to me. *All* of you," she whispered. "If you can't tell me, show me how you feel."

He couldn't give her the words she wanted. He could only speak with his body. Graham lowered his head and kissed her. She hooked her hands into his hair, forcing off the indigo turban. Jillian grasped his hair as they tumbled to the carpet. With desperate need, he clung to her as they tangled together, rolling toward the white sheepskin rug near the table. He felt the wool brush his skin. Arousal fled, replaced by fear.

Her soft, pretty laughter mingled with the increased panting of his terrified breaths. The smell of dirty sheepskins grinding into his nose each night. Low laughter echoing in the tent . . . Her father's voice: *"Admit it, you like it."*

He wrenched away, gasping. Jillian stared at him. "Graham?"

He stood on shaky legs, his erection softening.

"I promised Jabari and Ramses I'd meet them at the training grounds," he managed to say. Then he dashed out of the tent, fearing she'd hear the panicked thundering of his heart.

He grabbed his weapons, buckled them to his belt. Fighting to regain his composure, he sped through the camp, passed the grazing grounds, smelled the pungent odor of horses and heard the low bleat of sheep. Suppressing an inner shudder, he skirted the mountain of rock until coming to the training grounds. Bare-chested men slashed blades at each other with grim determination. He spotted Jabari and Ramses dueling, and faltered.

He could not do this. He was not a true warrior. *I am not a man*, he thought in agony. *Am I?* But Ramses spotted him and shouted. Reluctantly, he went to them. Graham shed his *binish* and shirt and unsheathed his scimitar.

"I will take you," Ramses said in English. "Let us see if the English have softened you, Rashid, my friend."

Graham flexed the hard muscles of his biceps. "I am anything but soft, my friend. In the battlefield or elsewhere."

An appreciative laugh escaped Jabari as he stepped back to watch. Graham kept his gaze focused on Ramses. The warrior was shorter, but his fighting skills were legendary among the Khamsin. As the sheikh's bodyguard, he was the best.

As Ramses engaged him, Graham defended himself, feeling confidence flee. All he could manage were weak, flimsy pokes as Ramses took the offensive. Surprise flared in the man's amber eyes. "I don't want to hurt you," Graham said lamely.

"Are you a man or a girl?" Ramses taunted.

Explosive rage erupted. Graham heard the past in a mocking echo. He grunted and lunged forward, filled with violence and the need to crush and pummel and hurt. Surprise flared on Ramses's face, but the warrior recovered quickly, defending himself with adroit skill. Yet the white-hot rage pressed on, until it blazed in Graham's ears with a roaring buzz, blurring his vision as he fought.

"Rashid. Stop it. RASHID!"

The loud, commanding voice of the sheikh cut through the reddened haze. Graham lowered his scimitar. Blood darkened the edge. Scarlet dripped down Ramses's thickly muscled arm.

Horrific shame covered him. "Ramses . . . I'm . . ."

"Good fighting. I do not think I will call you a girl any longer," Ramses joked, but a questioning look filled his eyes.

Covering his discomposure with a wry smile, Graham nodded. "I had to show you I'm no weak-spined Englishman."

The warrior returned his grin, then bound his cut with the silk slash at his waist. "Do not look so alarmed, Rashid. It is merely a flesh wound."

"His hide is too thick, like his head, for you to inflict any real damage," Jabari added, but he gave Graham the same long, thoughtful look.

Graham nodded respectfully, wiped his scimitar, gathered his clothing and left. Hot humiliation at losing control filled him. He fled to a deep *wadi* that had served in the past as a place of serenity. But today, peace eluded him. Graham sank to the hot sand and buried his head in his hands, moaning.

I am not a real warrior, or a man, after all.

An hour after his hasty departure, her husband returned. Bare-chested, he strode into the tent, flinging shirt and *binish* to the carpet. Graham unbuckled his sword and dagger and laid them gently on the table. Jillian studied his tight jaw. Sweat glistened on his powerful chest.

"Did you have a good time?" she asked, uncertain.

He glanced at her and gave a derisive snort. "Warriors don't train for a good time, Jillian."

Filled with enormous daring, she pointed to the scimitar. "Show me how a Khamsin warrior uses that during training."

Startled, he narrowed his gaze. She smiled sweetly.

"It is forbidden for women to visit the training grounds for warriors. They are sacred."

"Then demonstrate it to me here, Graham."

"Do you know why the grounds are forbidden to women? After training, a man is filled with the excitement of battle. The savage need for a warrior to conquer shifts into a different need, in which all he desires is a woman, to feel her soft body beneath his yield in surrender."

Her own body tightened pleasurably at the challenge in his dark eyes. "Show me, Graham," she repeated.

His nostrils flared. The air inside the tent heated, filled with an enticing, masculine scent of horses, leather and sandalwood. He had changed, the refined duke shifting into a dangerous warrior. The weapon he carried reminded her of the perils of this land, where men fought each other, not with dulled foils in gentlemanly sport, but in true battle.

The change had alarmed her before. Now it only served to excite her. Graham slid his long scimitar from its sheath.

An awed gasp of admiration slipped from her as he sliced the air with the sword. Muscle and sinew bulged and rippled as he swirled the scimitar in a series of intricate moves.

Where had he learned? Jillian held her breath, not daring to ask as he sheathed the sword, placing it on the table.

Unsmiling he faced her, sweat beading his forehead, glistening on his sculpted chest. Her hand splayed against the wealth of dark hair there, feeling the firmness against her stroking fingertips. A harsh groan rippled from his lips.

A surge of feminine power filled her as she reached up, sliding her hands around his neck, dragging him down for a kiss. Her lips softened beneath the crushing pressure of his, accepting the deep thrusts of his tongue. Jillian pressed herself against him, cradling the hard bulge of his erection. The soft cotton blouse rubbed against her aching nipples.

Graham tore himself away, panting. Hot desire tightened his face. Jillian backed away slightly, enormously excited at having pushed him into this, a bit scared at his dark intensity.

Could she handle him?

In silent command, he pointed to her blouse. Understanding, she removed it. His gaze widened as it caressed her bare breasts, the reddened peaks of her nipples. She watched him as she undressed and stood before him nude. Graham shed his clothing. His iron-hard penis jutted out.

She sat on the bed, watching him expectantly. Then he pointed to the bed. "Lie on your stomach."

Confusion swirled inside her. His heated gaze transfixed her. "Trust me. This is perfectly normal."

She swallowed convulsively and obeyed, presenting him her backside as she climbed onto the bed. The mattress felt cool and soft. A slight tremor shook her as she felt his hands about her hips, drawing her slightly back. His warm palm caressed her bottom. Jillian didn't know what he expected, but she trusted him. In this position she felt woefully vulnerable.

When his hand delved into the moistness between her trembling thighs, she flinched. He began gently stroking, the thick pressure rubbing against her inner folds. She clung to the pillow, bit it, swallowing a moan.

His voice changed, became deeper and a bit rough. "You like that, don't you? Admit it. You like it."

Embarrassed, Jillian made no reply. His hand between her legs increased the incredibly hot tension as he stroked, culling more moisture. Her bottom lifted as her body instinctively pressed against him. She felt his thick penis begin probing between her legs. Jillian pressed backward, hot with desire, flaming with embarrassment at her feverish need.

Warm breath feathered her cheek as Graham bent over her, whispering into her ear. "Tell me you want me."

She answered with a helpless whimper, aching to have his thickness fill her. Jillian felt his muscled body slide against her, like the leather sheath gloving his scimitar. With one hand grasping her hip, holding her still, the other continued to work dark magic between her legs. Incredible tension flamed as she thrust backward in a silent plea.

His stiffened penis probed against her wet inner folds. Jillian pushed backward again. He withdrew.

Desperate, nearly screaming with frustration, she raised herself on hands and knees, forcing herself back— only to find him forcing her back down. He teased her again, the rounded knob of his penis circling her wetness.

"Graham," she whispered.

With his tremendous strength and weight he kept her trapped beneath him as she wriggled helplessly.

"Tell me you want it," he said thickly.

The hard, thick length of him probed her again. She hid her face in her arms and tensed as he entered with a deep thrust. Jillian bit back a moan as scorching pleasure engulfed her.

"Come on, Jilly, relax, don't fight it." He crooned into her ear as his large body pinned her to the mattress. He began thrusting heavily into her. "You know you like it. You can't hide from what you really are," he grated out.

Pleasure twined with growing fear at his dark intensity. "Graham. Please."

He went absolutely still. Then he moaned softly. "Oh, God, Jilly . . . I'm sorry. What the hell am I doing?"

He slid out of her, panting. Torment swirled in his dark eyes as she rolled over to regard him. He framed her face in his hands. "Jilly, I'm so sorry," he muttered.

"Graham, what's wrong?"

"The past," he said. "I can't let it come between us."

She didn't understand. All she knew was he needed her desperately. Jillian slid her hands around his neck, pulled him down atop her as she feathered kisses over his face. "I won't let it. Just love me, Graham. Make love to me. I need you."

Determined to reassure him, her body needing him back inside her, she caressed him, rebuilt the fire. Graham shuddered, kissed her, traced her body with his hands.

He loved her slowly this time, building the pleasure as she stroked his back. Each deep thrust, each slow stroke increased the tension until she gripped him, crying out with joy. His big body shuddered and he spilled his seed inside her.

An empty coolness surrounded her as he slipped from her body. He fingered her hair as if it were spun silk. "Jilly, I don't ever want to hurt you. God help me if I ever . . . do anything that makes you feel that way again. Forgive me."

"You didn't. You couldn't," she said fiercely.

Her words seemed to reassure him. He fell back onto the bed, pulling her against him, stroking her back in a light caress. Jillian clung to him, watching as his eyes closed. Long, black lashes feathered his cheeks as he fell into a peaceful slumber, his deep chest rising and falling. Jillian studied him, deeply troubled. Why did he seem so tormented?

Chapter Eighteen

Determined to prove her competence to Graham, she set out the next morning for the camel herd. In her hands Jillian gripped the large wooden bowl. She was going to teach herself how to milk a camel.

Accustomed by now to the whispers and stares other women and men gave her, Jillian strolled through the camp. Flames crackled in a nearby cooking fire. A noise filled the air. She glanced at a tent to see a warrior working something in a bowl. The delicious scent of freshly ground coffee filled the air. How wonderful.

She reached the camp's edge and halted, bewildered. The large dromedaries grazed there peacefully. Goodness! Should she just choose one and begin? Was there a certain Bedu protocol regarding this?

Hearing a noise behind her, she turned to find Ramses studying her. His odd amber gaze seemed fixated on her hair. Self-consciously she touched her hat.

"Which ones are the camels for milking?" she asked.

His two dark brows pulled together. He glanced at the

herd of animals, serenely grazing at the sparse outcropping of grasses, then frowned at the camels and selected one. He studied it and said, "Try milking this one."

Deeply grateful, she flashed him a smile. "*Shukran*."

Surprise flared in his gold-brown eyes. "You're welcome," he replied, glancing at the camel. His mouth twisted in a half smile. He strode off, humming a low tune.

Her nose wrinkled at the pungent odor of the dromedaries. They needed baths, all of them. Doubt filled her as she studied the animal's undercarriage. Goodness, the beast certainly didn't resemble a cow. Perhaps the camel was more like a horse. Jillian gritted her teeth and stepped closer. She peered beneath the beast, analyzing its anatomy. Something seemed wrong, but Ramses had told her this was the milking camel. Balancing the large wooden milk bowl on her leg, she went to seize the teat.

Snickering voices murmuring in Arabic echoed around her. Jillian stopped, her hand a hairsbreadth away.

A group of warriors stood nearby, staring and grinning. Embarrassed, she struggled to maintain her composure. They must find it comical to watch an Englishwoman attempt this very Bedouin custom. Well, she'd show them she could do it.

Turning back to the camel, she gritted her teeth. As she reached for the teat once more, a sun-darkened hand seized her wrist. She looked up at her husband's amused face.

"Jillian, what are you doing?"

"You said I needed to know how to survive in the desert. So I thought I'd learn to milk a camel on my own. But I can't figure out . . . well, the equipment doesn't look quite right."

"It is quite right—for a male camel."

Horrified, Jillian stared at the beast, realizing that indeed he was correct. "But his . . . er, his, um, thing, I mean, it's . . ."

"Backward," he informed her. "An oddity of male camels."

Her mortified gaze swept over the snickering men, and Ramses, who joined them. The Khamsin guardian howled.

"But Ramses told me to milk this one."

Graham's mouth quirked into a grin. "Ah, that's why he said I should rescue my wife and teach you how to milk a camel. He must be playing a joke on the *khawaaga*. The foreigner."

Her. The outsider with her odd red hair and pale complexion. Jillian tasted tears in the back of her throat. She was out of place with these people, something she'd anticipated.

But she'd never anticipated being out of place with her husband. Or Graham calling her a foreigner. He blended with them like sand, shedding the regal aloofness of an English aristocrat.

This proved she wasn't strong enough to cross the desert. After all, she was a clumsy, weak female who muddled everything, just as her father had often reminded her.

Jillian handed the wooden bowl to her husband, biting her lips to keep from crying. "Here. You do it. I've changed my mind. I don't want to go with you."

A startled look crossed Ramses's face. Graham studied her quietly. The bowl hung loosely from his fingers.

With all the dignity she could muster and a swish of her English skirts, she marched away. Inside her tent, Jillian tore off her hat and buried her face in her hands. What a mistake, coming here. She had forced him into taking her, and now regretted doing so. For the first time in her life, Jillian wished she were invisible as she had felt all those years. The soft white cotton skirts and the pretty lacy blouse with its vivid emerald ribbons did not suit her. Jillian tore open the blouse, slipping out of it and yanked off her skirt. Opening her trunk, she removed the gray gown from its nest of tissue. Her trembling hand stroked the sensible broadcloth. Dreary, familiar and dull.

Did she truly wish to remain in the gray shadows? Clad only in her chemise, Jillian held the gown against her. She stared at herself in the mirror, the flush of color in her cheeks, kissed by the sun, the tendrils of silky red hair wreathing her face. Graham had yanked her away from the dark recesses and brought her into the light. Hiding in the shadows no longer remained an option. She could not hide from herself.

Absorbed in thought, she did not realize her husband had entered the tent until the gray dress was taken from her fingers and tossed to the carpet. Starting, she glanced into the mirror. He stood behind her, towering over her, a blue shadow still holding the milking bowl.

"The best place for that is the fire. I won't let you hide behind it any longer, Jillian."

Burning her past would not solve anything. Jillian dressed in the white blouse and skirt once more, avoiding his gaze. She spoke over her shoulder.

"I can't do it, Graham. I can't milk a camel, navigate across a plain or any of those things. It's impossible and it's silly to think I could. I'll stay here with the tribe until you return. I don't belong with you out there."

An incredible pain twisted her stomach at those words. Did she truly belong anywhere?

"The Khamsin warriors were right. I'm a woman. Silly and clumsy." She swallowed past a thick lump clogging her throat.

"The Khamsin warriors never said that, Jilly," he said

gently. "That was your father. The men here honor women."

Jillian shook her head. "You don't think I can do it."

He said nothing, those dark eyes calmly assessing her in the mirror. Then Graham captured her hand and led her out of the tent. She tripped behind him, protesting. They passed the long line of black tents, the curious onlookers going about their daily chores, the women baking bread in small clay ovens or tending to their children.

With purposeful steps he went on, stopping only when they reached the herd of camels. Graham went to one and dropped her hand. He caressed the animal's neck fondly.

"This is Sheba. She's lactating." He pointed to her underbelly. "Four teats."

The she-camel with her large, liquid brown eyes gave a soft snort. Graham skirted her with the wooden bowl.

"This is how you milk a camel." With expert ease, he balanced the container on his muscled left thigh, and took one of Sheba's four teats in his right hand. "Just like a cow. Squeeze and pull, aiming for the bowl."

He demonstrated, then handed her the bowl.

Jillian shook her head. "I can't do it. It's impossible."

"Nothing is impossible. Go on." He pushed the bowl at her.

Blinking rapidly, she stared at the bowl, then at him. He gave an encouraging nod. Jillian squared her shoulders and sidled over to the camel. She lifted her leg and with her left hand, balanced the bowl on her thigh. Graham stood behind her, his strong fingers wrapping around hers, guiding.

Together they felt the teat. It felt warm and soft beneath her fingers. With Graham's guidance, she tugged. A froth of white milk streamed into the wooden bowl.

"Now try it on your own." He stepped back, waiting.

Doubts assailed her. Yet running deeper was a determination to prove herself. She took hold of the udder and gently pulled. Warm milk splattered into the bowl. Delighted, she spun around, careful not to spill.

"I knew you could do it." Approval shone in his gaze.

They shared the milk, drinking straight from the bowl. It tasted thick, warm and filling. He grinned at her.

"You have a mustache." As Jillian went to wipe her upper lip, he leaned over and licked it from her in a slow stroke. Need shuddered through her. "Milk is good for the body," he murmured, the husky timbre of his voice matching the sensual intent in his eyes.

A camel the color of fresh cream butted its head against Graham's shoulder. He laughed and patted the neck.

"Easy, Solomon. Did you think I forgot you?" he crooned. Solomon lowered his head, and Graham scratched behind the rounded, hairy ears. "I delivered Solomon when he was born."

Sudden insight struck her. "The birth! That's how you knew how to deliver Badra's baby."

His mouth quirked. "My qualifications were rather circumspect. I'm afraid I don't make a good midwife."

"I think you were wonderful," Jillian said softly.

He studied her a minute, then his hand caressed her cheek. A low cough threw them out of the moment. They turned to see Ramses standing nearby.

"I am sorry for teasing you and making you uncomfortable, Jillian. It was, ah, a little joke." His sheepish look contrasted with his formal tone.

She studied the handsome warrior, wondering why he had done it. "It's all right. I did want to learn to milk a camel."

"And so you did. Your husband taught you. It is a good skill to know . . . in the desert. On a journey." Ramses looked serious, but an impish light sparked in his eyes.

Jillian began to understand. "Yes, it is. I'm glad he taught me. But it was a naughty trick to play, Ramses. Do you subject all *khawaaga* to your little pranks?"

A charming, seductive smile touched his mouth. "Ah, no, just beautiful Englishwomen I like to tease."

Graham narrowed his eyes. Jillian choked back laughter. Now she understood. Katherine had talked to Ramses. And the warrior cheerfully obliged his wife in not only making Graham jealous, but goading him into teaching Jillian to milk a camel.

"I'd hate to see what you do to ugly women," she murmured.

"Oh, those?" He waved a hand with a cheerful smile. "They are boiled in oil. Very tasty with camel milk. Mmmm. But do not fear. You are far too lovely."

Graham made a choking noise and looked away, color blotching his cheeks. Ramses winked. Jillian winked back.

"Ignore him, Jillian. He's a rogue and a scamp, despite the fact that his wife has managed to leash him," Graham grated out.

"A very pleasurable leashing," Ramses agreed cheerfully.

He stared at her with rapt fascination. Oh goodness, this was fun. Playing the part, Jillian touched her uncovered head. "I hope my uncovered hair doesn't offend you, Ramses."

"No. I apologize for staring. I have never seen hair of such color. It is like a flaming Egyptian sunset. If I touch it, will it burn me?"

Beside her, Graham stirred restlessly. "Ramses . . ." he began.

"It's all right. Go ahead, feel it," Jillian told him.

Interest flared on Ramses's face. His fingers traversed up a stray lock to her head, stroking her hair as one caressed a purring cat. "Living flame," he murmured. "Al-Hariia. Like the flush of a woman when a man rouses her passion. . . ."

Graham made a strangled noise in his throat. He stepped forward. "Enough," he said roughly, pulling her back. Jillian sank into the hardness of his chest.

She twisted to look. Graham's bristling look was unmistakable in its masculine possession. *She's mine*, it said.

Ramses gave a wry smile. "It is good to see you back again, Graham, especially with your lovely wife. I think Jillian will prove to be the tempting gazelle that coaxes the shy panther from the safety of its hiding place."

Her husband pinned him with an icy look, which the warrior cheerfully ignored. Sweeping her an elegant bow, Ramses moved off. Jillian wanted to laugh. She pretended bemusement instead.

"What an odd remark," she said, studying the muscled warrior as he wended his way among the dromedaries. "And what does al-Hariia mean?"

His jaw clenched as he glared after the departing Ramses. "The fire."

Later, Jabari invited them to a special feast he'd prepared in their honor. Graham was to leave the following morning for the deep desert. In the sheikh's tent, they sat on plush pillows about a low, round table laden with roasted lamb, rice, flatbread, and other delicious food. Jillian got interested looks from Ramses and Jabari, and knowing smiles from Katherine and Elizabeth, for the two women had worked to fashion her traditional Khamsin dress that she wore tonight. The ankle-length indigo *kuftan* felt comfortable and cooler than her tighter English dress. Beneath the *kuftan* she wore blousy trousers and a loose-fitting shirt. Her flame-gold hair was left unbound like that of her new friends.

Ramses dipped a wedge of flatbread into the sauce and ate, his eyes never leaving Jillian's hair.

"Ramses, it's not polite to stare," Graham commented, sounding irritated.

Mischief sparked in the warrior's eyes. "I was simply marveling, your supreme graciousness, at the deep trust you accord our people in leaving your beautiful wife behind while you trek for weeks into the deep desert."

A barely perceptible growl rumbled from Graham's chest.

"But do not fear. I personally will take charge of seeing to her welfare. She will stay in our tent."

"That is very gracious of you," Jillian told him.

The muscled, handsome warrior waved a hand. "Think nothing of it. Why, I consider you a close member of my own family now. My cousin—you remember him, Graham, the one you always called a . . . what is that word, Katherine?"

"Rogue," Katherine supplied.

"Has offered to teach Jillian how to ride."

"Jillian knows how to ride," Graham grated out.

"Ah, but Kamal will show her the Bedouin way. One has not ridden until one has ridden a Bedouin warrior."

"*Like* a Bedouin warrior," Katherine interjected.

"Of course, my beloved wife." Ramses gave an elegant shrug. "My English, it is faulty."

Scarlet infused Graham's face. A vein throbbed wildly in his temple. He looked murderous. He turned from Ramses and began talking with Jabari about doubling the supplies he needed for the trip. Ramses exchanged glances with his wife.

"You'll need proper clothing for the trip, Jillian. And a good, reliable camel. Above all, you must listen to me at all times. The desert is a dangerous place," Graham warned.

"I'm going?" She tried to keep her excitement at bay.

Graham shot Ramses a murderous glance. "It's safer for you than staying here."

Jillian dipped her head, hiding a smile as she scooped a bit of rice onto her flatbread.

When they bade their friends good night and vanished inside their tent, she sensed an enormous need in Graham. He stripped off his clothing, and she shed hers as well. Lifting her to the bed, he kissed her deeply, his tongue thrusting into her mouth, sweeping inside, flicking in invitation.

After a moment, he tore himself away and began kissing her body, murmuring as his mouth dropped hot, tiny kisses, pinching nips upon her skin, scorching her with his heat. Jillian wriggled.

"What—what is this?" she cried out.

"The Khamsin call it the secret of one hundred kisses," he growled.

Each press of his lips against her aching flesh increased the burn. She writhed. He pinned her down, holding her still. Kissing each inch of her trembling body, nipping in sensitive areas, then chasing with soothing flicks of his tongue. And then he parted her thighs and bent his dark head between them.

Jillian screamed with shocked pleasure.

So delicious. So female.

He bent his head to her feminine core, inhaling the delectable scent of her, female and tangy and spice. Graham studied her, his hunger kicking up a notch as she wriggled in embarrassed heat. His hands pinned her thighs to the mattress. Awed wonder spilled through him at how intricate a woman's body appeared. Filled with soft folds and secret hollows, a complex mystery he longed to explore.

Hidden places, like the thread of caves he'd found once near the al-Hajid camp.

When he was eight, he'd managed to run away and hide there for a precious day, feeling the desert heat lessen as the hard rock interior sheltered him in its rock womb. For the first time since his capture, he'd felt safe. He'd hugged the walls, glad for their protection, their sheltered quiet.

Graham leaned forward and gave Jillian's flesh a delicate, slow lick. His wife wriggled more. "Hush," he crooned against her skin. Here was the greatest mystery yet to be explored. He lowered his head and began to lave her slowly, his tongue running along the curves and folds, tasting her, settling upon her pleasure point. Absorbing her heat, her moistness, her secrets. He longed to hide inside her, pushing back the haunting pain for a little while. To push inside the damp cavern of her warmth and feel safe, to hear her excited, female cries of erotic bliss.

The sweet, excruciating pleasure between her legs intensified as her husband continued to love her with his mouth. Jillian writhed, her breath escaping in a sobbing moan. She clutched his hair but he gave no quarter. Heat exploded inside her as she went taut, screaming his name into the night.

Only then did he cease, giving her shuddering flesh a last, lingering kiss. Graham moved over her, his gaze fierce.

"You're mine, Jilly. Mine. No one else will ever have you." His deep, smoky voice rippled over her and he kissed her ruthlessly, and she tasted her own need on his lips. Jillian clung to him, her limbs boneless as he covered her.

He moved over her, coaxing a response. Urging her on,

he pushed into her, penetrating deep. He took her without mercy, riding her hard. Clutching the hard muscles of his shoulders she melted beneath him. Hard desire glinted his gaze, and he took her hard, thrusting into her welcoming heat. Graham lowered his head and nipped the sensitive juncture between her throat and shoulder. She shrieked, and he followed with a soothing sweep of his velvet tongue.

She realized what had prompted this impassioned response. It was a primitive mating, a claiming of her to announce to all she was his woman. He made love with a fierce urgency, loving her body, telling her with each kiss and lick how he felt. She writhed and moaned under him. With ruthless power, he drove into her. Over and over Jillian arched and met his demanding thrusts, and they clutched each other as they shattered, filling the tent with her screams and his hoarse cries.

Afterwards, he held her tightly in his arms. A dull shaft of lamplight pierced the gloom. Distress filled his dark eyes. Jillian brushed back a lock of damp hair from his forehead. Graham kissed her.

"My Jillian. My wife. Stay with me after the three months are finished. Don't leave me." His voice was low and slightly pleading.

"Graham," she whispered. "Why are you so sad?"

Silence draped them. He pulled her to his side, cradling his big, warm body against her. She lay still a long time until he roused again and made love to her. His lovemaking this time was slow and deliberate. Graham showered hot trails of kisses over her heated flesh until she writhed and begged. He mounted her then, and his strokes were slow, deep and deliberate, his dark gaze capturing.

"Stay with me," he repeated hoarsely. "Don't leave me."

Arching on the edge of a shattering climax, she

gripped him to her. Still he teased, withdrawing, lingering, until she sobbed, begging him to fill her.

"Stay with me," he repeated.

"Help me, Graham," she sobbed.

He drove into her, triggering a cry from her lips as she shattered from the power of her release. Graham tensed above her, his powerful arms taut with strain, his big body shuddering as he bucked and plunged.

She welcomed his heavy weight as he collapsed atop her, resting his damp forehead on the pillow. His words came again, a coaxing murmur. "Stay with me."

Stroking his sweat-dampened hair, she whispered into his ear, "I'll consider it, Graham."

His sleepy, heavy-lidded gaze met hers as he raised his head. "I'll keep you here, beneath me, always, if you dare try to leave."

A shudder of delicious heat wracked her. "Promise?" she asked.

Graham dropped a kiss on her forehead. "Promise."

Chapter Nineteen

Her limbs felt heavy and languid the next day as they prepared to leave. Jillian felt sleepy and sore from the night's fevered lovemaking. They had dozed and then awakened, Graham reaching for her yet again in fierce heat and passion. Each time she went willingly into his arms. He took her time and again, until she sobbed and begged, and then he brought her repeatedly to mindless, boneless pleasure. It was as if he fought inner demons each time he took her.

After a quick breakfast of fresh camel milk, yogurt and flatbread, they washed up. Jillian dressed in the odd, blousy indigo cotton trousers Katherine had made and the loose-fitting shirt. She tugged on the indigo *kuftan* and pinned her little gold watch to it. Next came cotton stockings and boots of the softest leather. Graham outlined her eyes with black kohl, explaining it reduced the sun's glare. Then he wrapped her head in a white turban. He gestured to the mirror.

She saw her reflection. "I look like a walking mummy."

"But at least you won't burn." He unfastened the lid of

a container of white paste. Graham smeared it over the exposed parts of her skin. He waved the container.

"Make sure to pack this. Your skin is like pale ivory. If you don't protect it, you'll burn."

They took with them dried dates and a goatskin filled with butter made from camel milk. Mixed with water, it provided valuable nutrients. Jillian finished packing their things and emerged from the tent, handing her rucksack to Graham.

Other Khamsin warriors had gathered, assisting. The sheikh as well. Jabari gazed at her steadily with his dark, knowing gaze. Jillian felt a fierce flush heat her cheekbones. Surely all the tribe had heard them last night.

But what surprised her most was Ramses. The jocular, teasing attitude had vanished. His odd amber eyes looked troubled as he helped secure her pack to Sheba.

"Thank you for convincing him to take me," she murmured.

Ramses leaned against the camel. He studied her so intently she blushed under his scrutiny.

"It is for his own good, Jillian. Be patient with my friend. Do not leave him, no matter what. He will need all your strength in the desert."

"I have no strength," she protested.

"You are most wrong," he countered. "You have the greatest strength, that of a woman in love."

Jillian worried her bottom lip. "How do you know?"

His gaze softened as he studied his wife, packing a bag of herbs for them. "I know." Then he looked at her once more. "Go with Allah, Lady Jillian. And be careful. The desert can kill the strongest man, but it is the darkness inside a man that can make him lose his soul."

Determined not to be an encumbrance, Jillian began the journey across the immense western desert with cheerful resolve. It quickly melted into grim willpower under the relentless heat.

They had ferried across the flowing Nile in a barge and left behind the fertile green valley hours ago. Their caravan of four camels, one carrying their equipment, the other carrying the iron water tanks, plodded along in a swaying gait. The harsh yellow sun beat mercilessly upon them. No escape. Not even a sliver of shade as they rode across the flat, barren plain. Her buttocks and thighs ached from riding in the wooden saddle. She licked her lips, tasting dryness and grit, inhaling the smell of cotton from the scarf covering her lower face. Jillian swatted at an annoying fly pestering Sheba's ears. Nothing in sight for miles and still there were flies.

When Graham called to take a break, she dismounted in weary relief. He unfurled a small carpet, beckoning to her to sit.

She settled on the rug, eyeing the stretch of sand. No trees. Not even a rock. Nothing but sand, endless sand. Jillian longed for a hot meal, even a hot cup of tea, but was resigned to eating tinned food.

Graham fished something out of his rucksack and tossed it to her. She picked up the two smooth stones and the wood stick.

"Use the stones to get a spark and the wood to catch it."

"And what do you use for fuel? Sand?"

"Something equally as plentiful."

She didn't like the look of impish mischief in his dark eyes. Graham went to another pack and withdrew a small bag. He unwrapped two small brown squares. "Fuel."

Jillian leaned closer, immensely curious. "Peat?"

"Camel dung."

He laughed at her moue of distaste and, using the cloth so his hand didn't touch the bricks, set them on the ground. "Very efficient means of fuel, dried by the sun. The Bedu use it all the time. Nearly as good as coal."

"I'd rather have coal, thank you," she said.

Graham busied himself with setting up a small triangular support, over which he hung a tarnished silver pot with water. "Teatime," he said cheerfully. "All we need now is the fire."

Glaring at him, she sighed and began striking the stones. Over and over. Frustration filled her as he watched, but Jillian doggedly kept striking the rocks together.

Finally, there was a spark and the wood caught. She held the stick to the squares of dried dung, surprised at how quickly the flames took. Soon a fire was crackling merrily away.

Pleased by her success, she glanced at Graham. Mirth danced in his eyes. "Took you quite a long time," he said.

She sniffed, irritated. "I suppose you can do it faster."

"With these, yes."

He tossed a small packet of English matches onto the sand. Jillian narrowed her eyes. "And you watched me. . . . I suppose it was quite amusing watching me make a fool of myself!"

His expression grew somber. "I had confidence you could light the fire. And you needed to do it on your own."

He dropped down next to her, drawing his knees up to his chest. "Jillian, this is a hostile environment. Men, hale and hearty, die out here. To survive you must keep all your wits about you and rely upon yourself."

The idea he had confidence in her left her speechless. Never before had anyone expressed belief in her abilities. She traced a line in the sand with her finger, shyly pleased by his compliment.

"Tea will be ready soon." Graham shook a small box at her. "Purchased in one of Her Majesty's finest shops in London."

Jillian eyed the small kettle suspended over the crackling fire. "Is it . . . different with this means of boiling water?"

He grinned. "It's like sipping tea in an English garden."

She wrinkled her nose. "I daresay an English garden smells more fragrant."

Jillian unpacked a tin of biscuits from the rucksack and set them on the wooden plate, and they prepared the tea. It was a bizarre English tea, the burning blue sky and desolate stretch of sand the drawing room.

They ate in silence. Her husband, who sat next to her, legs crossed, seemed perfectly at ease. He had clearly done this before, not once, but several times. As if he'd lived like this. Was this one of Graham's secrets? The story of a kindly English couple rescuing a frightened boy seemed less and less likely.

"How many years did you live with the Khamsin?" she asked.

He shot her a quick, startled look. "Years?"

"You're too familiar with the desert and its culture to have been a mere guest, Graham. Why won't you tell me about your past with them? What are you afraid to tell me?"

Standing, he brushed crumbs off his indigo coat. "It's getting late. I'd advise you to hurry and finish if we're to make decent time and keep on schedule before dark."

She scrambled to her feet. "Graham, what's out here?"

"Have you ever seen an enemy tribe racing their camels toward you, their bloodcurdling shrieks making terror rise in your throat? Seen their wicked swords flash in the sun just before they cut down their screaming victims?"

"No," she whispered.

"Then pack up and do as I say."

* * *

An hour later, she called out to him, red-faced. He stopped. As they dismounted, he fished into one of the bags, silently handing her the small spade. He then peered into the bag and withdrew two magazines. A teasing grin quirked his lips.

"Would you prefer *Godey's Lady's Book* or *Punch*?"

"*Lady's Book*. That's exactly what I think of modern fashion."

He grinned again, then delicately turned his back as she wandered off to find a spot. A furious flush ignited her whole body. There was no privacy here in the wide open plain. Oh bother. Surely, this would be the least of the upcoming challenges.

Two days into their journey, Jillian made a disturbing discovery. The farther they traveled and the more she tried engaging Graham in conversation, the more reticent he became. She asked questions about his friendship with the Khamsin tribe, but he gave noncommittal answers.

When they stopped for a break, she uncapped the goatskin bag gratefully. Jillian gulped down the water. Graham gently tugged the bag away.

"Slow sips. You'll get sick," he advised.

Licking the last drops from her lips she glanced around at the flat sands, the endless terrain of dust and burning blue sky. A gentle rise of sand from the dune they'd just left seemed tranquil. Goodness, it was so hot.

Graham strapped the bag back onto his saddle. A fierce frown wrinkled his brow. He seemed to go still, listening. Unease pricked Jillian. She craned her neck in the direction they just rode and saw nothing.

"What is it?"

He did not answer. Wind ruffled the hem of his indigo coat. His nostrils flared, as if scenting trouble on the distant wind. Solomon shifted, uneasy, snorting. Sheba raised her tawny head and did the same.

"Do you feel it?" he murmured.

"I don't hear anything."

"You don't hear it at first. You sense it."

"Sense what? Graham, you're scaring me."

His gaze grew distant. "It's coming. The khamsin." He ran to the camels, yelled to her, "Hurry! There's no chance of outrunning it, but perhaps we can reach that rock."

She hurried to her camel and mounted, still bewildered and more than a little scared. "Cover your face!" he ordered, tightening the straps and swinging over the saddle. "Let's put those riding skills of yours to good use!"

Jillian's heart was thundering in wild panic. They rode frantically. She still had no idea what he meant, but the urgency in his tone convinced her. Then she stole a glance over her shoulder. The blood froze in her veins. A giant wave of boiling sand swirled toward them.

Now she knew. The khamsin—Egypt's hot, fierce sandstorm that blew in from the west with killing force.

The roar filled her ears. It rose like a giant wave, rolling toward them, a black cloud like a frenzy of locusts roaring forward, blotting out the burning yellow sun. They needed shelter. It would bury them alive under pounds of stinging, hot grit.

She kicked her camel with feet that shook wildly.

It dogged them, thundering closer. She hung on to the saddle, riding low over her camel's neck, urging her faster. A scattered patch of hard red rock jutted out from the sands. They reached it. The roaring black cloud rolled closer.

Graham jumped off Solomon and grabbed his reins, steering the camels toward the largest boulder. He ran to

Jillian, helped her dismount. He pulled her toward the rock, bade her sit.

"Put your face to the ground. Don't look up, no matter what," he screamed above the thundering roar.

Jillian dropped her face to the ground, wrapping her arms about herself in a ball, felt his hard body and muscular arms surround her. She shook with fear as the roar intensified, and then felt it roll over her.

Hot sand stung her exposed skin. She squeezed her eyes shut, breathing through the scarf. Sand ground into her tiny boots, filtered through her veil. Graham's body sheltered her from the worst. She huddled beneath him, cringing from the sea of sand raging over them.

It seemed hours before he finally stood, freeing her from his weight. Jillian moved her cramped muscles, coughing from the fine dust invading her lungs. She blinked the grit from her eyes and stared in amazement.

Sand covered everything. A fine layer of red dust caked Graham's blue robes, coated his exposed skin. Tiny dunes had accumulated about the rocks. She started.

"The camels!"

"They're fine." He went and patted Solomon's neck, coated with the same fine layer of red grit.

"So that was a khamsin."

"No." Graham was inspecting the contents of their packs. "The khamsin heralds the approach of summer and ends in May. This was just an ordinary sandstorm."

"Why did you call it the khamsin then?"

He stopped and looked at her with a strange expression. "Something that happened long ago," he murmured. Then he assumed his normally tight expression.

Damn the man! Again silent as the desert, refusing to reveal anything. Jillian felt as empty as the vast wastelands they crossed. Would he continue to ignore her day after day, just as her father had? Even though he claimed to care?

Anger fierce as the boiling sandstorm filled her. As Graham tossed her the camel's reins, she unleashed her fury.

"Talk to me, Graham. Stop treating me like I'm a camel. I'm your wife."

He tossed her a quick, startled glance.

"No, it's not like being your camel. You talk to your camel. You never talk to me. You can't know how much it hurts when you ignore my needs. Please, don't ignore me. Yell at me. Please, anything, but don't ignore me." Her voice dropped to a whisper. Her throat seemed full of sand, each pore dry and caked with dust.

He dropped his reins and walked over to her, cupping her cheek, red from the sand's sting. She lifted her troubled gaze. "*Talk* to me," she pleaded.

"What do you want to talk about?"

"I feel like there is this great gulf between us, like a canyon stretching for miles. And I want to jump across it, to reach you, but I'm scared to take the leap. I'm scared that you'll let me fall."

Something unreadable flickered in his gaze. "I would not let you fall."

She reached her hand up to caress his. "Then trust me."

He gazed at the horizon, his jaw tensing beneath the black beard. "I called it the khamsin because when I was younger, the tribe I feared most raided the camp where I stayed. They were brave men, riding like the hot desert wind. Nothing stood in their way. I was standing just outside my tent, watching the scimitars clash, listening to the roar of battle. Then one Khamsin warrior approached, his scimitar drawn. In the heat of battle fever, it is difficult sometimes to discern warriors from young boys. He raised his sword and I knew I was going to die. At the last minute he stopped."

Horrified, she stared. "Were you terrified?"

"No. But I cried when they rode off."

"Why were you so sad?"

The hard, flat look in his eyes made her shiver. "Because they rode off, leaving me behind. Leaving me alive."

But that was all he would say.

Chapter Twenty

They rode in grim silence over the flat sands. Jillian kept casting her husband sideways looks. So many layers and secrets to this man: his manner of dress, the frightening coldness in his eyes as he relayed the story of that Khamsin battle.

Graham stopped and she pulled up alongside him. He appeared to scan the distance. "We should find a place to rest."

Jillian pointed to a wedge of mountain jutting out on the horizon. "Let's aim for that rock. There may even be a water source. I'm afraid the dust may have gotten into our supplies." He gave her an approving look.

As the sun sank into the horizon, shedding a rosy purplish light, they reached the patch of rock. There was no well, to her disappointment. Jillian helped Graham unpack their supplies and set up the tent in the billowing breeze.

Withdrawing a white cloth, he handed it to her. "For

washing," he said gruffly. "You may use a little water. It's all we can spare."

Instead of taking it, she studied her husband. Dark shadows rode beneath his eyes. The fierce-looking turban outlined a dusty face taut with strain.

Jillian had never felt filthier in her life. Sand had crept into her boots, ground into her neck. She could even taste it in her mouth. She looked at the pristine white cloth Graham had kept safe from dust by wrapping it tightly and tucking it away, then she looked at her husband again.

"I've got a much better idea," she said cheerfully. She carefully set the cloth down upon the blanket and then touched his turban.

Graham flinched, his dark brows drawing together. "What are you doing?"

"Sit," she ordered, pointing to the ground. He opened his mouth as if to protest, but she gave him her most stern, governesslike look. "Now."

He sat. She began unwinding the blue cloth, setting it aside. Next her trembling fingers began undoing the fastenings on his indigo coat. Graham stared at her as she tugged it free, helping him shrug out of it. She slipped the underlying shirt over his head, staring at the expanse of dark-haired chest, the grime caked into his throat.

Jillian knelt beside him and took the goatskin water bag. She dampened the white cloth. Then, very gently, she began stroking her husband's hands, wiping them free of grime. Graham started to protest. She laid a finger to his lips.

"Let me do this for you. You've done so much for me."

In silence he allowed her to caress him with the cloth, then a tremulous sigh escaped his lungs as the cooling damp refreshed his body.

"Thank you," he said softly, watching her.

She held up the dirty cloth with a smile. "I suppose it's my turn now. I'll do my face. I'm afraid I must look uglier than the back end of your camel."

He did not smile. Graham studied her with that intense scrutiny of his. "On the contrary, my lady," he said quietly. "I've never seen you look more beautiful."

Then he leaned forward, framed her face with his now clean hands, and kissed her. It was a slow, sensual kiss, and she found herself melting. He tasted of the cinnamon sprinkled into their tea. Jillian groaned and pressed herself against him. Needing him. Wanting him.

He pulled away, his expression tense. "We need to rest." He lay down upon the bedroll, his back turned toward her.

Bemused and hurt, Jillian stared at him. Why was Graham acting like this?

Days later, as they neared the cave hiding the treasure, Jillian found herself totally enchanted by the shifting landscape. The map indicated the cave was in the great white desert, a sea of sand with limestone so pure it stood stark white against the tawny backdrop. She gasped with awe as they approached an outcropping of large stone structures with narrow stems and large, rounded heads.

"We'll make camp here for the night," he decided.

"They're like mushrooms in the desert," she exclaimed.

Graham grinned and began unpacking their supplies, "The Khamsin have a word for them. Al-Ayir."

She tested the Arabic word and gave him a puzzled look as his shoulders shook with laughter. "What's so funny?"

Graham tossed down a rucksack. "It means, the penis."

Her eyes widened as she whipped her gaze to the stones. "Oh goodness, they certainly do look . . ."

His deep laughter greeted her flushed cheeks. "We're going to pitch camp beneath one."

"Graham, you can't expect me to sleep with a giant . . . penis!"

"You should be used to it by now," he replied.

Jillian groaned.

"The Khamsin say it endows the man with strength to last all night," he went on, his dark eyes dancing. "Wouldn't you like me to possess such strength, *habiba*?"

"But dear husband, you already have such strength. And you forget your geology. Limestone is soft."

His crestfallen expression caused her to laugh, then Graham gave a cheeky smile. "Well, perhaps the Khamsin were wrong."

His boyish grin contrasted with his appearance. Dressed in indigo, he appeared a fierce Egyptian warrior. No longer the Duke of Caldwell, he was a terrifying sight, scimitar strapped to his side, lethal dagger stuck in his belt. Jillian marveled.

Surviving here in these dry sands seemed impossible without his guidance. The desert stretched for miles, and her own parched throat ached. And yet, Graham appeared comfortable. Which reinforced her nagging suspicion that he had spent much time among the Bedouin, maybe even grown up as a child among them.

The time was not right to ask. But she would.

They made camp that night and settled into bed. A few hours later, Jillian awoke with a pressing need. Oh, bother. She quietly slipped from bed, but Graham stirred and saw her. He stood as if to accompany her. She shook her head.

"I'd like some privacy for a change. Please?"

He frowned. "Don't go far. I saw tracks earlier, which means there are Bedu in the area. Most likely desert raiders."

"I'm going just beyond those rocks. I won't be long. And I'm taking this." She waved the compass purchased in Cairo.

When she finished her business, Jillian studied the scenery. A pale moon illuminated the rocks, turning them a ghostly gray. Sand eddies whirled, kicked up by the wind. She could understand how a man could lose himself out here. Lose his soul, even.

She stretched, mindful she had been gone awhile, when a slight rustling noise alerted her. Jillian stiffened. Probably just a small desert animal. Yes, of course.

She was laughing, amused by her fear, when a rough hand clapped over her face and cut off all sound.

His wife was gone.

Graham pushed aside the wild panic surging through him. No emotions. Emotion clouded judgment and he needed a clear mind. Graham squatted, staring down at the sand, trying to analyze the patterns. A scuffle. She had been taken, probably by the Bedu whose camel tracks he'd spotted earlier.

He cursed softly. He should have accompanied her despite her protests. And yet, having her separate from him for even a few minutes had provided a bit of relief. He'd needed to be alone with his thoughts, with the darkness gnawing inside him. Yet, at what cost? His blood boiled at the thought of her being held captive. He wanted to howl at the uncaring moon, to race across the sand and find her, to grab her and never let go.

Graham calmed his emotions, willed himself to think. He must find her. Now. Before he lost her for good.

Chapter Twenty-one

In the moonlight, Graham analyzed the camel tracks in the pebbled sand, and by two hours later, as dawn broke over the horizon, his tracking had brought him to a small peppering of black goat hair tents nestled against some rocks, and he also saw the support beams marking a well. As he slid off Solomon, men of the tribe assembled, their faces wary, scimitars drawn. No rifles, he noted with relief. He approached, hand resting on his own scimitar but not drawing it.

Clad in dark robes, the sheikh emerged from his tent. He strode forward with arrogant command and gave a greeting in a desert dialect Graham did not fully know. He returned the polite welcome. The sheikh introduced himself as Mahjub, chieftain of the Jauzi, the people who claimed this land.

Graham wasted no words. "I came for the woman you took yesterday," he said roughly. "I want to see her. She is mine."

Mahjub, an older man with a grizzled beard and cunning eyes, barked an order. Out of the largest tent two women came, escorting Jillian. He studied her anxiously. She was pale, but did not appear harmed.

"Jillian, are you all right? Did they . . . touch you?"

She shook her head, wide eyes full of fear. Her brave smile wobbled precariously. "I'm all right, Graham. Please, just get me out of here."

Relief pierced him. They had not raped her. For whatever reason, he was grateful.

The sheikh watched Jillian warily as the women led her away. "Al-Hariia," he rasped.

Sudden insight flashed. Her hair. It had enthralled Ramses, and here among these superstitious desert dwellers, they called it fire and feared it. He seized that as a weapon.

"Only a warrior with powerful magic can bed al-Hariia, an *houri* from paradise who can consume a man's flesh in flames." Graham struggled with the unfamiliar dialect, praying his words would be clear.

Mahjub's gaze narrowed. He snapped his fingers.

A younger man, black beard shrouding his face, stepped forward. "If you want her, you must fight me for her," the young man asserted to Graham. "She will fetch good money on the slave market."

Mahjub looked amused. "Khamsin Warrior of the Wind. Are you willing to fight for your woman?"

"So be it," Graham said harshly.

No mercy. He could spare none. Jillian's life was at stake.

Graham was ruthless. He slashed and fought with the fury of the Khamsin's ancient Egyptian ancestors—blood not flowing through his veins but blood he claimed by deeds. He was as emotionless as a sandstorm, as overwhelming and complete, engulfing the dirty-robed enemy in a hot, blowing rage.

The Bedu swung his scimitar, slicing Graham's arm. Warmth dribbled down his forearm, but he barely registered the pain. Instinct guided him now, honed by much experience in battle. Blood coated his scimitar as he attacked and whirled, not in the delicate mincing feints of respectable English theater, but raw, powerful and brutal war. He knew he would kill this man. He must. To protect Jillian, the treasure shivering inside the black tent. A deep, primitive feeling surfaced. *She is mine.* Possessiveness as ancient as the sands raged through him.

The killing blow was swift, almost merciful. Graham's enemy gurgled for breath, gasped and fell to the ground, staining it scarlet. An appreciative murmur swept over the watchers. The sand eagerly drank the blood, thirsty granules greedily pulling it down.

Fluid, so precious in these dry, barren lands.

Inner sorrow pulled him. Again, he had killed. He wiped his sword on the robes of his enemy, sheathed it. Then he bound his arm with the silk sash at his belt. The Bedu's respectful nods he met with a hard stare.

"The *houri* is mine," he said in Arabic. "I will take her and leave."

Mahjub smiled, showing a wide horizon of gum and the broken stubs of yellowed teeth. "The *houri* delivered to us enthralls you so much that you kill one of my clan? Then wait no longer to claim her, Khamsin, with your powerful magic. My tent."

And with a grand gesture, he swept a hand toward the many-poled dwelling standing nearby.

Emotion squeezed Graham's chest. For the first time, fear skidded up his spine. What the hell did he want? "I can wait," he grunted.

"You will not," the sheikh countered, his graying brows drawing together. "I insist on the hospitality of my tent to take this virgin. It is our tradition that a warrior who has fought and fought well be rewarded with a woman. Do you refuse my hospitality?"

"I do not refuse the hospitality of Mahjub, the great sheikh of the Jauzi, whose name is honored above all others in this land. But I will not bed this woman here and now."

Graham's formal words made no impact on the sheikh, whose expression shifted to calculating intent.

"I think you are reluctant to bed her because you lied. She is not an *houri*, a virgin from paradise. And if you lied, we will cut out your tongue as we do to those who lie to us. Let us see if you told the truth, Khamsin. Take this virgin and show us your powerful magic. If you refuse, we will take her into the desert as food for the jackals, as we do with all defiled women."

Fear squeezed his heart. "No one will touch her," he swore.

A loud scraping of unsheathed scimitars rang in the air. Graham stared into a forest of gleaming steel.

"A man sometimes may choose his death, Khamsin. He may choose to die in the soft arms of a woman, or he may die with the bite of a blade against his neck. Which do you choose?"

Powerless, he swallowed rising revulsion. He had no choice. *Forgive me, Jilly*, he said silently. To the sheikh he said, "Bring her to your tent. I will claim her there."

Jillian fought the women as they bathed her in the black tent and then dressed her in a gown of green gauze. They covered the nearly transparent clothing with a thick black garment and led her outside. The women shoved her into the largest tent and removed the covering. She stumbled, nearly falling onto the thick carpet. Silks billowed in the desert breeze.

Graham stood before her. A rough beard covered his face. His hair swept past the collar of the indigo coat, a thick mane tousled by the wind. His sleeve was torn in one spot, showing a makeshift, reddened bandage. Eyes darker than midnight silently appraised her.

He said loudly in Arabic and then in English:

"I fought for you. And I shall claim you, in the ancient right of this tribe."

She felt miserable, afraid, and greatly relieved to see him.

And he? He looked every inch an exotic, powerful sheikh, as if he were playing a part upon some stage of windswept sand.

He came to her, black brows drawn together, no longer the duke. She scarcely recognized him. Sun and sand had swallowed him. He'd shifted like the changing, silent dunes.

The women all watched, bright-eyed with speculation. Graham turned to them and barked something in Arabic. The women meekly filed past, marched into a room curtained off from the main tent.

Barely had they done so when Graham began unwrapping the blue turban and shedding the indigo coat. He sat on the carpet and gestured at his boots.

"Take these off," he ordered loudly. "Woman, do as I say before you invoke my wrath."

The thin curtain shielding the women twitched. Biting back a caustic remark, Jillian removed his boots. She stared in astounded shock as Graham stripped down to his bare chest and stood, tugging at the drawstring holding his blousy trousers up. "What in heaven's name are you doing?" she demanded.

"Undressing. Take your clothes off. Now!"

"No." She backed away from him, hands outstretched. Old fears arose—her father, always controlling her, making her feel powerless. Why was Graham doing this? What had happened to the considerate man she'd married?

"Listen to me," he said urgently, gripping her arms. "I've just killed the man who stole you. The tribe thinks you are an *houri*, a virgin from paradise delivered to them. The women back there are watching us. The men are outside, listening. If I don't take you, they'll cut out my tongue for lying about you. If they don't think you're a virgin, they'll let you die in the desert."

"I don't know if I can do this," she whispered.

His gaze softened. He touched her cheek. "Jilly, I don't want to do this any more than you do. But we must. Do you understand? We have no choice."

Swallowing hard, she nodded.

"I'm sorry," he said softly, and suddenly she was reminded of their first time together.

He ripped the thin silk from her body with a rough growl. Jillian shook violently, trying to shield herself with her hands. He took her hands, held them apart, staring at her breasts intently. Whispers flitted from behind the silk curtain.

Her eyes closed in bitter shame. Graham pulled her to him and kissed her, his lips gently coaxing hers apart as his tongue slipped inside, stroking and caressing. It was a sensual kiss, but she felt no desire. She felt rigid as rock. Graham pulled back, determined intent turning his eyes to midnight. He kissed her again, and trailed a line of hot, urgent kisses across her collarbone. His hands caressed her bare shoulders, drifted lower to skim her hips and then slide into the juncture of her thighs.

A jolt of arousal speared her. She moaned as he gently stroked, culling moisture, to prepare her for what lay ahead. He pulled back and shed his trousers, displaying his rigid arousal. She tried not to hear the feminine murmurs and gasps.

How could she bear this? You must, she told herself as he lowered her to the sheepskins, his dark gaze intent as he moved between her legs. His hard male body with its broad shoulders and muscles rippling beneath the taut biceps was as familiar as her own. Yet he was a stranger. She felt him probing her center, which was slightly damp from his ministrations.

"Now. Cry out," he ordered.

He pushed forward, piercing her. Not fully prepared for the shock of his entry, her inner passage resisted. Jillian screamed and arched. A low laugh and words in rough Arabic sounded outside the tent.

Tears blurred her eyes. She felt horridly exposed and humiliated; the act she'd relished as tender and passionate now reduced to crude lust, a private moment stripped down to a public act.

Her husband bent his face close to hers and softly crooned words in Arabic as he slowly expanded her resisting muscles. Then she looked into his eyes and saw tenderness brimming there. Graham whispered into her ear in English, "They're not here. No one else is. Just us, alone. Pretend, my love."

"I can't," she said brokenly. "I just can't."

"You can, Jilly," he said, kissing her tears away. A smile touched his mouth. "Do as every English mother tells her daughter on her wedding night. Lie back and think of England."

His gaze turned serious as his hips surged forward and he thrust inside her. The gentle tone and reassuring words contrasted his pounding thrusts, and the whispers of their audience.

"Look at me, Jilly," he said softly in English. "Come

with me. We're in a garden in England, lush and verdant. There are pink tea roses climbing a white trellis by the pagoda where we sit, sipping tea. A mockingbird is chirping from the boughs of a willow. Can you feel the caress of the cool breeze upon your lovely cheek? You are laughing because I've just spilled crumbs from the delicious scones on my new waistcoat. There's an orange butterfly dancing nearby and you wish to catch it."

Jillian closed her eyes, willing herself into the fantasy as his body slapped against hers. She forced herself to drift. The sticky, harsh heat melted into a delightful English breeze. No odor of stale sweat from the dirty sheepskins beneath them, but the perfume of roses and freshly cut grass from the craggy-faced gardener swiping at it with a scythe.

"My beautiful Jillian, in your green eyes I see the water's reflection. So cool, so serene. Nothing can bother us here."

Jillian willed the images to dance in her mind. She saw Graham's face, smiling and laughing as he chased her and the pumpkin butterfly, dancing out of their reach. His deep laughter sounded as they raced across the soft grass, and Graham chuckled as he caught her in his arms and whirled her around for a kiss. . . .

A harsh groan rasped above her, startling her out of the vision. Her eyes flew open to see her husband stiffen and shudder, his powerful body tensing as he found his release. She felt the warmth of his seed fill her.

Misery swallowed her. But then he sighed and kissed her, his soft murmur caressing her ear as he lifted her hair and kissed the lobe. Confusion swept her as he rolled off, for she could not fathom the words he'd whispered. Her senses were surely scrambled, and she couldn't be sure, but it had sounded like, "I love you."

So many times he'd used fantasy in his own horrible reality of the black tent. He'd dreamed of being anywhere but there—in England, climbing fence posts, or the captain of a pirate ship, sailing to find treasure on tropical islands. He'd fantasized anything but who he was and where he was at that particular moment.

Now filled with self-loathing, he sat up, his back to the wall sectioning off the sheikh's harem. Furtively he grabbed his *jambiya* and cut himself. He smeared the blood on the sheepskins, then quickly dressed.

He paused to glare at the faces peeping out from the thin curtain. "Get her clothing. Now," he barked in Arabic to the women. They scrambled to obey. He picked up his scimitar and *jambiya*, slid them into his belt. His oily rifle he slung over one shoulder. As the women hustled back into the tent, bearing Jillian's clothing, he regarded his wife.

She dressed, shoulders slumped, gaze downcast. Graham held out a hand. Jillian took it as they went outside. Men stood nearby, watching with dark, burning gazes. He felt the wild rage to feel bone and blood beneath his crushing fingers.

Graham suppressed emotions and stood alone, ordering Jillian to mount her camel. He did not dare drop his gaze or let his hand leave his scimitar hilt.

"She's mine now. I will take her with me." His bristling stance and hand on the scimitar hilt said, *Try to stop me.*

Mahjub gave a slight, respectful nod and said in Arabic, "Go with Allah in peace." But Graham could read the sheikh's sly thoughts. A man alone with a woman in the desert was vulnerable.

Instinctively Graham knew they must put as much distance between themselves and this tribe as possible. Violence and greed swirled in their dark eyes.

As he fingered the butt of the rifle against his hip and stared at Mahjub, the sly gaze lowered. Graham nodded and headed for his camel.

Chapter Twenty-two

They did not talk as they traveled, pausing now and then to erase their camel tracks. Graham spoke once, to explain he was trying to confuse the Bedu, should they decide to follow. The wind filled the silence between them, licked her clothing, adding to her internal misery. Graham had remained grimly quiet since his whispered confession of love. It was as if the words were never spoken.

They camped near a remote oasis with a cluster of date palms. There were two springs, one clean and cool, the other bubbling and warm. Jillian sat on the sands and studied the location. Small animal prints abounded. A crow landed nearby, regarded her with black eyes. Black as Graham's. In misery she watched it drink and fly away. Free.

The wild hare he caught with his crossbow he skinned and spitted. It smelled delicious as the grease made the fire spark and hiss, but she had no appetite. She prepared the meal in silence by the light of the flickering campfire.

Shadows danced across the grim set of his jaw as he sat cross-legged, eating.

After the meal, she washed the dishes with water, a luxury, and took a towel and soap to bathe at the spring. Graham's dark eyes burned into her.

"It's not safe alone. There are vipers."

Turning from him, she spoke in a low voice over her shoulder. "I'll take my chances."

But he rose and joined her anyway, trudging over the sands to the tiny spring. Jillian bit her lip as she stared in longing at the clean water. She hesitated at undressing before him.

"Go on," he said gruffly.

While she slipped from her clothing, he whirled. Graham stood, legs outspread, the rigid blue wall of his back facing her. He was giving her privacy.

Hot, soothing water surrounded her as she entered the little spring. Jillian ducked beneath it, swam a little ways out, clutching the soap. Silent sobs wrung from her throat. For long minutes, she cried, covering the sound with sounds of splashing and scrubbing. She scrubbed at her body with fierce loathing, erasing memories and smells.

When she emerged, her body was red from both the warmth and scouring. She quickly dried off and dressed. Graham stood a little ways off, still with his back to her.

She wondered if he'd heard her sobs. She didn't even care.

They walked in silence back to the camp. Jillian took a seat on the striped blanket in their tent as Graham sat beside her. Misery overwhelmed her. She didn't know how to ask for comfort to ease what had happened between them. She felt as if she were losing him. Perhaps she already had.

"I'm sorry I had to do that to you, Jilly," he said.

She hugged her knees tighter, remaining silent.

"It was degrading. I violated and humiliated you."

Her throat tightened. "I suppose you had to do as you must, to save us both. Don't blame yourself, Graham. Your actions were justified."

Dark fire leaped in his eyes as he turned to her, his expression fierce and haunted.

"No. There never is any justification for forcing someone against their will—"

"They forced me, not you. I agreed," she protested, shrinking away from the violence in his eyes.

"I should have killed them."

"You would have been killed. You were outnumbered. Death is not preferable."

"Sometimes it is."

She went still, sensing something haunting in his tone. His eyes were distant as he gazed off into the sky. "Because once, Jilly, the same thing happened to me."

Fearful of shattering the moment, afraid that he would run away inside himself once more, she said nothing. Graham's dark gaze flicked to hers.

"In the desert there is no hiding from yourself. I didn't want this moment to come, but it has. It's time you know what happened when I was six. I wasn't raised by a nice English couple after my parents were killed. I was taken prisoner by one of the men who slaughtered them, taken into his black tent and raped."

The hollow feeling in Graham's chest echoed his desolation. Sweet Christ, it had finally come to this. She would see the blackness inside him and then it would be her choice to walk away or stay. He felt the blackness wrap its inky arms about him like the coldness of a stone tomb. He dully recited the story, not daring to meet her eyes; his gaze riveted to her feet instead, hidden beneath the white robe.

He left no detail out, from the moment his panicked gaze saw the warrior tribe galloping toward the caravan, his mother shoving Kenneth into a basket to hide him and his parents desperately trying to find a hiding place big enough for him. The sun flashed on the steel scimitars as the raiding al-Hajid took lives without mercy, the steel scimitar hovering above him as he cringed. He told of the shining gleam in the eyes of the warrior who studied him and then grabbed his arm, taking him prisoner.

Hidden feet beneath Jillian's white robe. A peep of small, delicate toes, scrubbed pink. Graham stared at them as he relayed the details of the dirty sheepskin grinding into his nose, the nightly torment from Husam, his captor—and Faisal, the man who pulled him from the wretched blackness with a hand outstretched in kindness.

"Faisal saw me taken prisoner and took pity on me," Graham said. He dared to glance at her face. Would he find pity there? Or disgust?

Jillian showed neither. Her expression remained carefully blank. But her fists clenched, showing the little rounded hills of her knuckles.

Graham told her Faisal had lived among the infidel in Cairo and knew English. At the risk of his own life, he'd smuggled sweet dates to Graham whenever his captor let him go hungry. Discovering the boy had a quick, clever mind, he'd taught him as he taught his own sons—how to hunt the wild hare, to analyze camel tracks in the sand, to read in both English and Arabic, to look for signs of water and survive in the desert on nothing but dates and camel milk. He even told her of al-Hamra and the slim hope he'd held out for escape—and the terrible price he paid for such hope and trust.

He did not tell her al-Hamra was her father. Some things were simply too terrible to reveal.

Graham told Jillian how, when he was nine, Husam tired of him. His captor had turned him out into the desert miles from the camp, leaving him to die in the scorching sun. At this, a harsh intake of breath escaped Jillian. Graham glanced at her. Tears shimmered in her eyes. She blinked them away.

His gaze locked on the ground once more. If he looked at his wife, he, too, would cry. Graham pushed aside his emotions, concentrating on keeping his voice steady instead.

He had been left in the desert to die, but returned three days later, crawling on his hands and knees, but alive. Faisal had stepped in and told the sheikh he had learned the ways of the desert and earned the right to live. The sheikh had given reluctant permission for Graham to live with Faisal, but vowed he would never be acknowledged as a warrior.

Faisal taught him anyway. Others ignored him, shunned him. To win their respect Graham became a rogue warrior, joining in the fighting and raiding, but always on the fringes. Eventually they called him The Panther, the cat that hunts alone.

"Faisal told me in the desert, there are no secrets. The desert exposes a man to his deepest core and what he truly is. No matter what terrible things I suffered, no other man could take my soul. And he told me that if I ever got lost within myself, to go to the desert and find who I was again."

Jillian spoke finally, her voice remarkably soft and soothing against his ragged nerves, like the whisper of silk.

"Are you still lost?"

He hesitated and stared out at the sand. "I don't know."

Jillian wrapped her arms about herself as her husband went off to relieve himself—or so he said. She did not dare express sympathy or show it; instinct warned he would loathe pity.

Shocked horror had pulsed through her as he told his story. That little boy enduring so many horrors—flashes of pain surfaced in his dark eyes. She didn't know what to do, how to help him, what doubts and torment he had suffered. All she knew was that she loved him.

Splashing sounded in the distance. Jillian rose and went to the small spring and hovered discreetly behind a palm.

Naked, her husband was immersed waist deep in the warm spring, scrubbing himself with fury. His handsome face twisted in anguish. Just as she had, earlier. Her heart twisted. *I love you*, she thought. *Will you let me love you, Graham? Can you?*

She turned and quietly slipped back to the tent.

Much later, when he felt calm enough, Graham returned to their camp. Jillian remained silent, her gaze following him. He sat on a blanket, cold eating him inside.

She spoke, her voice even. "Were you ignored by the other warriors or . . . ?"

Graham drew a deep breath. "I was seen as an outcast, a girl. I fought to be accepted."

"What did you do to become accepted?"

"I killed my abuser in a duel. Then I cut off his balls and gave them to my sheikh as a trophy." Graham sucked in air, waiting duly to see condemnation or disgust in her eyes. It did not come.

"What did he say?"

Relief stabbed him. Still, he did not lower his guard. "He laughed. Fareeq liked cruelty and sport. He ordered me to be initiated as a warrior."

They had taken him to the sacred grounds where boys turned into men, made him swear the oath of loyalty and circumcised him. The pain had been excruciating. He'd been offered a sedative drink, but Graham had not taken it. He had welcomed the pain.

Respect had flowed then, slowly, like a sluggish river. Always he'd had to prove himself; killing more, risking more. He'd learned to distance himself from emotions. Eventually when Faisal's daughter married into the Khamsin tribe, Graham had accompanied her and become a Khamsin Warrior of the Wind.

"I wanted desperately to be seen as a man," he whispered, remembering his struggles for acceptance.

"How many men have you killed in battle?" Jillian asked.

He tensed, seeing himself in her eyes, a savage raised in a culture of cruelty. "Hundreds. I do not know."

"And how many people have you loved?"

Taken aback, he recoiled. Jillian sat serene, unblinking. "I do not know."

"Less than you have killed."

"Yes," he agreed.

"Less because you wouldn't allow it, Graham. You loved once, and it was taken from you. You were afraid to love again. As you're afraid now. Because you don't want to be hurt again."

His stomach clenched in remembrance: blood flowing like water upon sand, his parents' death screams, the smell of dirty sheepskin in his nose, stares and taunts . . .

A kind hand stretched out. His foster parents had nurtured him, but he did not love them. Did he?

He cherished his family. He would die to protect them, especially Kenneth's new son. But was that love?

"Time grows short. Let's pack up." Graham unfolded his body and turned his back as he began shoving items into a sack. Two arms slid about his waist, hugging him from behind. He tensed.

"Love me, Graham. And I'm not asking for your whole

heart, your commitment. Love me as a man loves a woman in the night. If that's all you have to offer, then give it to me. I need you."

His body swelled even as his mind refused. Emotions fought, clashed like Khamsin steel. He could not love her. He could not burden her with the terrible blackness inside him. Graham glanced down. He was flaccid.

"Night is falling and we need sleep," he said roughly. "Go, get ready for bed." He slipped away to check on the camels. He did not want to turn around and see his wife's tears.

Dry-eyed, Jillian silently assembled the dishes and put them away. His rejection had not hurt her. What hurt was the terrible pain haunting his dark eyes.

Oh, Graham, I've felt your passion, your desire, every time we made love. I know you're every inch a man, the man I love. But how can I convince you?

She had no skills in dealing with inner demons, not even her own. Mocking laughter echoed in her brain, pushing aside a tiny hope of healing him. She wondered if she could reach him at all.

That night, Graham had a nightmare. He woke with a strangled yell and Jillian sat up, shivering. But he pushed away her comforting embrace and turned on his side. She did not reach for him.

In the morning he silently watched her, his gaze wary, as she prepared breakfast. Jillian felt despair push at her. She bit her lip and poured the thick, dark Arabic coffee he loved into a tiny, handleless cup. But he did not drink. Nor did he eat as she nibbled the edges of a flat-bread wedge. Finally she stood, briskly dusting off her hands.

"If we're to reach that cave by nightfall, we should leave."

He made no attempt to pack or move. Dread filled her. He sat as one drained of life, a silent figure in indigo, his arms hugging his knees.

Jillian shrugged, left him alone and went to feed the camels. She stroked Solomon's long neck, watching the beast chew the dried dates. When she returned to the tent, Graham still sat motionless, staring out into the sand.

"Are we leaving?" she asked. He did not answer.

She spent the rest of the day analyzing the map of the tomb where the treasure lay. Despair assaulted her. Each time she attempted to talk to her husband, he made no reply. He sat, a silent statue, staring into the sands.

She did not know what was wrong. Did he think she condemned him for what happened? Jillian gracefully lowered herself beside her husband. She gathered his hands in hers.

"Talk to me. Please, talk to me."

Graham lowered his face to his knees.

"You don't want to know, Jillian. You don't. Go away."

"Is it so terrible that it makes you cry out in the night? I'm your wife, Graham. Trust me. Please."

Turning his head, Graham's stricken gaze met hers. "Do you want to know what I dreamed of?"

"Yes."

"I dreamt of that day. Of al-Hamra's laughter."

She stared in horrified anguish at the sweat breaking out on his forehead. "He laughed after, Jillian. He told me to stop that insipid crying. And that . . . that deep down, I enjoyed it."

"Graham, you mustn't blame yourself," she cried. "You were desperate and would have done anything."

His tortured gaze locked with hers. "Jillian, don't you realize? What if . . . what if I allowed him to do it not because I thought it would free me, but . . ." He whipped his head away from her, his voice so low she barely heard.

"W-what if he was right? What if I did like it? What if my whole life has been a lie?"

She had no answers. Graham seemed remote and distant as the Nile, and Jillian was terrified of losing him, terrified of what he had revealed. She wanted to run far, far away, to put her fingers into her ears and not hear. It was too much for her to bear.

But he had finally revealed his darkest secret. He had turned over his trust and how could she abandon him?

No, Jillian didn't know what to say; she only knew inside his deepest core was a part she needed to reach. She took a deep breath and took his face in her hands. His eyes were blank obsidian, as distant as the boulders they'd left behind in the *wadi*.

She kissed her husband. He did not respond. It felt like kissing dead, ancient stone. Jillian leaned forward, pressing her body against his, desperate to stir life in him. She tangled her hands in the dusty, black locks curling beneath his indigo turban. She breathed into his mouth, begging him with her body to come back to life. To come back to her.

He slowly stirred against her and began returning her kiss, his lips moving subtly, his muscled arms holding her trapped against him. With a loud groan, he squeezed her so tightly she could scarcely breathe. But Jillian did not resist his punishing embrace; she melted into him. Her hands explored his body, pressed against the hard flatness of his belly and daringly slipped lower.

Releasing her, he wrenched away. "I can't . . . do this."

Jillian ached at the wild panic on his face. She braced herself for what she must say.

"The Khamsin say the desert bares a man's soul. There are no dark spaces here, no secrets." Dragging in a breath, she forced herself to continue. "There are no lies here. So tell me, does this man of your past rouse your passion?"

He stared at her in incredulous shock. She pushed further, twisting the knife, trying to break through his fear. "Do you want to fuck him instead of me?"

Fury flared in his dark eyes, turning them to pitch. Like a feral animal, his upper lip curled back, displaying the white gleam of teeth. Graham made a strangled sound. His hand shot out. He seized her by the throat. Breath fled her lungs. She didn't dare move. Didn't dare let her gaze drop. She remained motionless, snared in the grip of his powerful fingers. With one move, he could break her neck.

"You can't kill the truth. So answer me," she rasped.

Silence hovered between them, the only noise the brush of the desert wind skidding across the sand and the wild roar of blood thrumming in her veins.

His grip eased. He did not release her but loosened his hold. His index finger traced a hesitant line across her throat to her trembling jaw. With his left hand, he began exploring her face.

Two lines dented the space between his dark brows. He resembled his nephew, exploring his world for the first time. Graham's left hand skimmed her body and palmed her breast in a light caress. And then Jillian realized what he was doing.

He was touching her as he had their first night together. When they first became lovers. When he claimed her body in passion and torrid heat, and he knew at last the pleasures a woman's body had to offer. His lips parted in an expression of wondering awe. Awareness flared on his face. He knew the answer. And so did she. Moisture carved twin tracks in the grime dusting his cheeks.

Graham released his chokehold on her neck. Jillian took a sweet gulp of air. His tearful eyes widened in horror.

"Christ, I could have killed you."

"You wouldn't. You would never." She picked up the hand that had the power to crush her windpipe and kissed it.

"Part of me wanted to hurt you, Jillian, because I was afraid of the answer. I didn't struggle enough. He told me I liked it because I didn't struggle," he said brokenly.

"You didn't like what happened to you. You were only doing what you had to." She took deep breaths, rubbing her throat.

"I should have fought him. I didn't. Only when he gagged me when I started to scream—and I screamed because I realized I couldn't blame a 'heathen Arab' this time. I let him, an Englishman from my own culture and country, do it. And I accepted what was happening to me."

She framed his face with her hands, her tears blurring his visage. "Acceptance doesn't make something right or enjoyable. My father was cruel to me, and it's all I knew. But I never, ever liked it."

"I'm so tired, Jilly," he whispered. "I'm so very tired."

She kissed him tenderly. "Then sleep."

Like a young child, he curled against her and lay his head on her lap. Jillian choked back a sob and her trembling hand stroked his head.

The burning sun scorched the land. Heat filled the inside of their makeshift tent. For a long time Jillian sat on the striped blanket, oblivious of everything about her but the sound of her husband's deep, slumbering breaths.

Eventually she lay down and slept. She did not know what time it was when she opened her eyes. Starlight glittered in the heavy black sky above. A pale silver moon washed the sand and the little lee of their dune with grayish light. Something had awoken her.

Jillian glanced down and realized that, during their sleep, Graham had curled his body about hers, tangling them together like twisted rope. His muscled thigh pinned her legs to the blanket, his arm draped about her shoulders. His eyes were open. They studied her with unblinking intensity.

He shifted and pulled her closer. His lips sought hers, his tongue caressing the inside of her mouth. Fire leaped inside her veins as she hooked her arms about him, kissing him back. Graham fisted his hands in her tousled hair, groaning as he kissed her. She felt the pressing hardness of his erection.

His hands roamed her body, shoved up the *kuftan* and tugged at the blousy trousers beneath the long dress.

"Take them off," he said.

She did. He hitched up his indigo coat and opened his trousers. Graham rolled her onto her back and mounted her with heated urgency. Unprepared for the force of his entry, Jillian cried out in shock. He stopped, kissed her, coaxing her response until she writhed against him in need.

His thrusts were hard, fast, the implacable pressure stretching her until finally her body accepted his intrusion and bathed him with her arousal. Jillian bit her lip as he released the fury of the past, his hands pinning her wrists to the blanket, his heavy weight trapping her beneath him. She met each violent thrust by tilting her hips upwards in welcome.

There was nothing gentle about his taking her. It was a rough, primitive claiming as he overpowered her like a khamsin. His flesh pierced hers, taking by rights what was his. Taking back his past and starting anew.

The sensual onslaught gripped her. Her body tensed and she cried out, stiffening beneath him, her hands gripping the hard muscles in his back. He climaxed just as violently, his body bucking and then suddenly turning rigid, a feral growl ripping from his throat. His breath came in harsh, ragged pants. Graham collapsed atop her, his heavy weight trapping her, his head buried in the soft hollow of her shoulder.

For a long moment Jillian lay still, not daring to breathe, reluctant to disturb him. Then at last he raised his head, supporting himself on his elbows. A fierce male satisfaction glowed in the dark depths of his eyes. He kissed her, a slow deep kiss filled with tenderness.

"I love you, Jilly," he whispered. "I think I always have."

And she knew then that his demons had been vanquished and would never return.

Chapter Twenty-three

The cave on the map was within half a day's ride of an oasis and a small village. After they found the treasure, Graham promised they would visit the village for a real meal and to replenish supplies.

They reached the cave by midday. Had they approached from the east, they might even have fallen into it. The opening was nothing more than a slit gaping in the flat terrain. Graham unpacked their supplies while Jillian peered dubiously at the yawning shaft. Sand spilled into the darkness. She shivered.

"We can slide down," Graham offered. He took her hand with one of his and grasped an unlit lamp with his other. "Come on. Together."

They slid down the deep sandy slope. She felt as if they tumbled into a yawning darkness with no end. When they struck hard turf carpeted by thick sand, she released a breath.

Graham stood and helped her up as she shook her

robes. When he lit the lamp, an awed gasp escaped her. The cavern was enchanting. She thought of the Arabian tales in her father's library and knew the true magic of the desert.

Hundreds of giant conical forms dripped from the ceiling, crystallized water frozen into immortality. The delicate ice crystals hung in a lacy arrangement, their translucent twists delicate as fairy wings. Light played over the chalk-white and tawny forms as Graham lifted the lantern.

"It's like the enchanted cave I once dreamed about," he said, his face rapt. "When I was a boy, I used to escape to a place like this in my mind."

Love washed over her. Jillian squeezed his hand. "Aladdin's secret cave, filled with treasure. A place where you could feel safe."

His jaw tensed. "Let's do this quickly."

Minutes later they'd assembled their gear: a sturdy rope, their rucksacks, the rifle and jugs of water. Graham reached into his belt and withdrew the wooden key he had fashioned in Cairo.

He shouldered the rifle as they went searching for the door. Low-lying ceilings, too low for a man to squeeze under, prohibited them from exploring some portions. It was a small cave, and Jillian began growing frustrated. Her nose wrinkled at the odor of bat droppings.

But Graham insisted on thorough, slow searching, cautioning her to avoid a large crevice splitting the floor. They peered over the edge. Jillian shuddered as they dropped a small broken piece of stalactite into the darkness and did not hear it hit bottom.

Graham looked at her. "Slow and steady."

After about an hour, they came upon an opening in which they both had to squat. Graham pointed to a small cartouche, barely visible, carved into a delicate stalactite.

"Khufu," she breathed. "This must be it!"

She felt like Alice squeezing into the tiny house in Wonderland as they progressed. Finally reduced to crawling on her knees, Jillian wondered if the oppressive weight of the confined space could actually squeeze her lungs.

They came to a dead end no higher than three feet. Frustrated tears burned her throat as she stared at the limestone wall. Nothing. No keyhole.

But Graham showed no such emotion. He merely studied the wall, running a hand over its surface. The blank wall slid back, like a panel. It revealed another wall beyond. There was a large keyhole.

He turned to her, a boyish grin filling his face.

"Old Egyptian trick," he said.

"Taught to you by an old Egyptian?"

Laughing, he produced his wood key and, with a firm click, drove it home. A perfect fit. The door unlocked and swung open into velvety darkness.

Graham crawled through the doorway. When Jillian hung back uneasily, he glanced over his shoulder. "Come, *habiba*. We're nearly home. It's all right," he said soothingly. "I won't let anything happen to you."

Taking a deep breath and shoving aside her panic, she followed.

Graham assisted her, then helped her stand. She protested, fearing they would bump their heads upon the ceiling. He told her quietly, "Look up." She did.

The room they had invaded was even more a spectacle than she imagined Aladdin's cave. Graham went to one of the iron sconces on the wall and lit a torch—a torch that had not been lit in more than four thousand years.

The room was small, irregularly shaped and filled with geodes. Spikes of crystals—purple, deep blue, translucent, red—littered the ground. The same spectacular stalactites that were in the main chamber hung like crystal chandeliers here as well, but the ceiling was triangular instead of a dome shape.

"Like a pyramid," she realized aloud.

Graham laughed. "The old sly dog. He created his own pyramid out here in the desert."

Upon a small stone table fashioned from limestone, resembling an altar, an alabaster box resided. Graham's hands shook as he approached it.

The magic wishing casket! Jillian held her breath and nodded as he shot her a questioning look.

Graham broke the lock.

Inside the long, thin casket lay a gold crocodile bigger than a man's fist. In its yawning jaws rested a glittering emerald.

"Oh," Jillian said faintly. "Oh my."

Graham could not move or speak. Before him lay a childhood dream. He caressed the alabaster box, stroking its surface as if it were a woman's thigh.

"The legend about this casket," he mused. "If you put a slip of paper into it that details your greatest wish, then put the casket under your bed at night as you sleep, in the morning your wish will come true."

"I don't believe in magic. Of course, I almost don't believe this is real." Jillian touched the emerald with a trembling finger. "With treasure like this, who would need to wish? These riches could buy any heart's desire."

"Some things in life cannot be purchased, Jilly."

She pressed his arm. "True. If I could, I would purchase your past, Graham, and give it back to you anew. But I can't."

Solemn, he locked gazes with her, then brushed a

kiss against her cheek. Jillian smiled. They turned to leave.

As Jillian pushed open the door and crawled through, Graham took a last look then dropped to his knees to follow her. But the door suddenly closed. His stomach clenched. He pushed the door. It would not give. A worried frown creased his brow. He pushed again.

Dull panic spread through him as he settled his powerful weight against the wood, but the door did not give. It remained locked. He was trapped inside, without the emerald.

From the other side he heard a low, sly chuckle. "Come out, Caldwell. Slowly."

Graham froze. That voice from his deepest nightmares. Stranton.

The earl had clearly taken the map and gone to the village, lying in wait for his arrival. Stranton likely needed the treasure as much as he wanted Graham dead; it would provide enough money to live in anonymous comfort for years.

But Graham didn't plan to die today.

He slowly opened the door, crawling out on his belly. A light shone ahead in the distance. He kept crawling through the tunnel until he reached the open cave. There the sharp, pungent scent of bat droppings stung his nostrils.

He stood, glimpsing his enemy. Graham tucked the casket into his binish, raised his rifle to his shoulder. Head shot. Easy enough. But Stranton pulled his daughter closer, using her as a shield. Graham's finger hesitated on the trigger.

Jillian shook. Her face appeared pale and pinched.

"Let her go, Stranton," Graham ordered.

"Put the gun down, Caldwell. Do you really want to risk shooting her?"

"Stop hiding, bastard. This is between you and me. Neither of us wants to see her hurt."

"I have nothing left to lose now."

Graham felt a moment's despair, then he made a choice. "I'm putting down the rifle. Don't hurt her."

"Slide it over here to me," the earl ordered.

Stranton advanced with Jillian as Graham did as he asked. His gaze never leaving Graham's, the earl kicked the weapon away. It fell with a clatter into the crevice.

"She deserves to know the truth, Caldwell. About what you truly are," Stranton sneered.

Graham went still, his heart racing. *And so it goes,* he thought in anguish. Jillian would know the truth at last. . . .

Panic shredded Jillian's composure. She had emerged into the cavern to find her father standing there, cutting off her scream, a pistol at her temple. Her heart thundered faster. "Father, please. Leave us alone," she whispered.

"It was your husband who propositioned that boy, Jillian. He thinks he can get away with his vile crime. I'm taking him back to London to face authorities and put the blame in its rightful place. You liked it. Admit it, boy. Admit it. I want to hear the truth. It was your fault, Caldwell. Tell her the truth. *You liked it,*" the earl taunted.

Graham sneered. "That's what you wanted me to believe. But you and I know the truth, *al-Hamra.*"

Jillian stared at her father in horror, her stomach lurching. Oh dear God, it couldn't be. Her father was the one who tormented Graham's nightmares?

Graham's expression became carefully blank once more, devoid of emotion. Jillian recognized that tight control, for he was artful in cloaking his thoughts. Yet a pulse still beat wildly at the base of his throat. Dark turmoil swirled in his gaze.

"Are you ashamed, Jilly?" he asked quietly.

"How can I not be?" Her own father, taking advantage of a child who had trusted him? A desperate, small boy?

"Stop stalling, Caldwell. Hand over the treasure."

From inside his binish, Graham pulled out the alabaster casket. He stared at it. "No. It's mine," he said.

The earl laughed. "I had the hieroglyphics translated. You're a fool if you think that box has magical powers."

Jillian watched her husband's expression shift into a woebegone look. He looked like a lost child.

"I don't believe in the magic wishing casket's powers." The duke paused, his face stricken. "But I always wanted to. Long ago, when I found the map. It gave me hope. I dreamed there was such a magic box and it would change . . . everything. Including me."

And she knew then what this quest was about. To find the box had been a childhood dream—not merely to secure the treasure inside, but to possibly reclaim what he'd forever lost: his parents, his innocence—all those things in childhood he'd watched slip through his fingers.

Sweat glistened on his brow. His expression became as barren as the sands. He did not even regard her father, standing with a pistol in hand. Her husband looked terribly alone.

Her father shook his head. "Wish all you want, Caldwell. It won't change what you really are. There's no escaping the truth. Admit it to my daughter. You were just using her to get to me. She deserves a real man." Regret darkened his expression. "In America, where the scandal won't follow her, I'll give her part of the money I get from selling this treasure. Let my daughter find some happiness."

A huge weight pressed on her chest. For so many years she had longed for her father's affection, for a small sign of trust, of caring. He had never even embraced her. He'd kept her chained in the house, imprisoned under the harsh restraints and rigid rules. Now he was giving her, finally, what she had sought? Freedom to choose her own path?

Graham remained silent, but the plea in his eyes was all but a shout. *Don't leave me, Jilly. Trust me.*

Jillian struggled to breathe. The two men stood still as the stone columns nearby. Two different futures. She could easily now, with this money, seek her old dream in America, attend Radcliffe and never look back. *Isn't this what you dreamed of all your life?*

But when she looked at her husband, whom she loved, she realized sometimes dreams change.

No, she couldn't leave him. Nor could she repair the damage her father had done. But she could erase the horrible doubts she knew were tearing Graham apart. Especially since she remembered something else.

"Don't listen to him, Graham. He talks about himself, not you. Father is the one who can't escape the truth. He's always hiding from it, but he can't hide any longer. That time when I was six—do you remember, Father?"

The blood drained from the earl's face. His grip on his pistol wavered. "Jillian, stop."

"I didn't want to remember. I shut it away but it came back. Mark, the son of the head groomsman. We were playmates. Mother frowned at me playing inside with the servants' children, but you never protested. And that day upstairs, you took Mark down the hall and brought him into that room and you closed the door. You told me to go away and forget anything happened. I remember Mark's face, so pale and scared as you started to close the door and told him to remove his trousers . . ."

"*Jillian,*" the earl began.

"And the key turned in the lock and I couldn't move, my feet would not obey. I listened outside and I heard him scream and cry, and you were saying . . . you were saying . . ." She gulped down a trembling breath. " 'Such a pretty boy. Come now, admit you like it. There's no escape from the truth. You can't hide from what you really are.' "

Her words broke Graham's inertia. His eyes blazed fire. "You sick bastard," he rasped. "How many lives have you ruined?"

But Jillian's father ignored him, his stricken gaze riveted to his daughter. "I told you to go away, Jillian. I told you . . ."

"I wanted to," she whispered. "But I can't hide from the truth any longer, Father."

A huge weight pressed her chest. It felt as if the cave itself was collapsing, squeezing the air from her lungs. Jillian could not look away from her father's face. The anguish there once would have broken her. It did not any longer.

In that moment, Graham stormed forward. Her father swung his pistol up. Jillian cried out a warning and grabbed his arm. Thunder exploded. Ancient crystals splintered as the bullet struck a stalactite.

Graham ducked and rolled, his motion propelling him forward toward the crevice. Jillian's screams echoed through the cavern as he scrambled to stop, failed, and in one fluid motion, disappeared over the edge.

One hand clasping the treasure, Graham wildly grappled for purchase as he slid down the rock wall. A narrow ledge stopped his fall. Forcing calm, he struggled to maintain footing on the shelf. Above him, the slit showed light from the cavern. Crystals in the dome ceiling sparkled. He had never seen anything more spectacular. A fine sight before he died.

And so it ends this way, he thought with dull resignation.

Does it? a mocking voice asked. *Isn't Jillian worth fighting for your life?*

Graham sucked in a breath. His ribs hurt from scraping down the rough rock face.

Two heads appeared above, both red. Both with green eyes. One filled with wild panic, the other with grim satisfaction. Graham turned his gaze to the wall. He would not look up and see his enemy gloating.

"Graham, oh, Graham, hold on, I'll get a rope."

He glanced up to see Stranton restrain her. "Only if you toss up the treasure," the earl shouted.

"Never!" Graham cried. Sweat dampened his palm, loosening his grip on the box. His fingers desperately grasped it.

His future? His hope?

Shame filled him. He was a coward, and he could not bear the look of condemnation in Jillian's eyes if he looked up.

"Graham, please, look at me. *Graham*," she called out. "Don't give up. Hang on."

"Jillian, I forbid it," her father yelled.

"Quiet, Father," she snapped.

Graham heard the sounds of a scuffle, of her father pleading with her to listen to reason.

Squeezing his eyes shut, he gripped the wall. His hand splayed against it. His heart thudded dully in his ears.

Minutes crept by, then suddenly a rope slapped down next to him.

"Let go of the box, Graham," Jillian pleaded. "You'll need both hands to climb."

He could not. "No, Jilly. I can't."

"Please, let it go. I love you. I know you think the box will make everything bad go away, but it's not your fault what happened to you. You don't need magic boxes. I can't erase your past, Graham, but together we can build a future."

"You're ashamed of me."

"I am ashamed of *him*, and of what he did to you. Please. Come back to me."

"You've no reason to be ashamed of me, Jillian. It's his fault," Stranton rasped.

Graham's fingers curled around the alabaster case. His treasure. His shield. He could not release it. But Jillian's voice again came to him.

"Look at me. Look at me, not the box!"

Somewhere inside he found a thin thread of courage. Graham looked at his wife. He looked into her green eyes, shimmering like emeralds. He shifted on the ledge—and nearly slipped.

If he didn't release the box, he could die. But why not die? He had been ready before. He just wanted to end the pain.

But then he looked up at her again and saw her eyes shining with tears. "Please, Graham. Please come back to me. You asked me before not to leave you. I promise I won't leave you. Don't leave *me*."

He held the treasure. The box would give him money—money that would have satisfied Stranton twenty years ago and prevented the vile deed the earl had done to him. Money meant power. It always meant power.

"I need this," he grated out, gripping the box.

"Graham, you don't. You want it to protect yourself from anything bad ever happening again, and I understand. But I don't care about money or your title. I'd love you even if you were a poor chimney sweep. Ramses told me the darkness inside a man can make him lose his soul. Don't keep the darkness inside any longer. Let it out and let me in."

He looked up and saw Jillian, and his heart went still.

Here was the real treasure. His wife openly stated her feelings. She loved him, despite all his many transgressions and what he was. She was living flame to his darkness. And for the first time, he felt the darkness pushed back, fleeing from the living light she shone inside him.

Yes, the real treasure was his wife.

But for so long he'd held onto his pain and his fury, intertwined like threads on a carpet. Could he finally release them? Graham looked at her and the pain in his chest eased. At last he had something worth living for instead of something he wanted to die from.

His fingers uncurled around the box. Peace settled over him as he felt its heavy weight fall into the darkness. It slid down, crashing onto a jutting shelf mere feet below. Jillian's father screamed.

"No!" Stranton grabbed the rope and scrambled down. Landing on the shelf below Graham, he reached wildly for the box. But the ledge cracked and the earl lost his balance and fell. At the last moment, he caught himself.

Stranton grasped the ledge with his fingertips, dangling. Great gasps of panic shredded the air. Graham stared down at the man who had abused him, who violated his trust, who was now in mortal peril. He looked up at Jillian.

Cautiously, he reached for the rope that she swung toward him. Catching it, he wound it about his waist, tied it, then reached down to the earl. "Let me help you," he said harshly.

Stranton looked up at his daughter. Something dark and haunting touched his face. "I never wanted to hurt you, Jillian. I tried so hard to keep you away, to keep you from being tainted. That's why I always disciplined you.

You were the only good thing in my life, so pure and beautiful. I was proud of you, and kept thinking your goodness reflected me. But now . . . I can't hide behind you any longer. I can see it in your eyes. They're like a mirror . . ." His voice dropped to a whisper. "I see what I really am."

Graham felt brief sympathy for Stranton, forced to confront the darkness inside and seeing only the ugliness of his soul staring back.

The earl's pleading gaze met his. "I'm sorry," he whispered. "Forgive me."

Graham squeezed his eyes shut. He thought of the pain of his past. He thought of Jillian and the hope of his future. Opening his eyes, he managed to utter words he'd once thought impossible. "I . . . I forgive you."

Peace settled on the earl's face. "Take good care of my little girl." Then Stranton released his grip on the rock, falling into the darkness. Jillian screamed.

Graham knew he must get up to her. Dear God, she was all alone, and she needed him. His muscles clenched and strained, but he pulled himself up slowly to his wife. He pulled himself slowly back to life.

Through her tears, Jillian saw Graham emerge from the crevice. He pulled her into his warm, strong arms. Laying her head against his broad chest, she sought comfort in his sheltering embrace. For several minutes she sobbed and he simply held her. When she finally pulled back, he touched her damp cheek, brushing a lock of stray hair from her face.

"I'm sorry, my love," he said softly.

"I can't believe he's gone. I . . . I'm relieved he'll never hurt you or anyone again, and yet, oh God, he was my father. All those years wasted, thinking that I could

299

never be good enough to meet his rigid standards. All I wanted was for him to love me, and he couldn't—not the way I wanted. In a way, he used me like a shield to hide behind."

A troubling thought struck. She looked at Graham beseechingly. "What did Father mean when he told you to stop using me to get to him?"

Blood drained from her husband's face. His throat muscles worked as he swallowed. "I don't quite know."

A sudden sick feeling hit her. *I don't want to know. But I must.* She worked up her courage and whispered, "I think you do."

Graham drew in a ragged breath. He looked her directly in the eye. "Yes, Jillian. No more hiding from the truth. He reasoned that I used you to become friendly with him, to devise a means to ruin him."

Her heart shattered. "*Is* that why you married me, Graham? To get at my father? Was I a pawn to you and nothing more?" *Please, tell me the truth. But I don't know if I can bear it if you used me as Father did, the lies and betrayals. . . .*

"I married you for many reasons, Jilly. But yes, to get at your father was a main purpose."

"Did you want to kill him for what he did to you as a boy, Graham?"

A muscle twitched in his cheek. "I wanted to kill him that night at the ball. I had planned as much. But . . . I saw you and I changed my mind."

Oh God, it was worse than she had imagined. Jillian's lips trembled. How could he have done this to her? "You changed your plans? You wanted to ruin him and I was your pawn? That's why you didn't want me coming here with you!"

Graham looked ashamed. "Yes. I arranged for him to

be caught with a young boy. After he was arrested and fled, he left a note swearing revenge. I taunted your father into following me to Egypt. I knew he had the map and could find the cave. He would kill me or I would kill him. But I never meant to hurt you, Jilly. Never."

Two large tears slipped down her cheeks. "But you did. Bastard," she whispered.

He went toward her. Deeply anguished, she put out a trembling palm. "Don't, Graham. You lied to me. You used me—oh God, you used me just as Father did. He didn't really love me and you never did, either. You publically ruined me by telling everyone I wasn't a virgin, all to trick me into marrying you. You did it for your own vile purpose! You didn't want me to produce an heir, and not even my"—her voice dropped and became a mocking imitation of his—"my intellectual abilities. You merely wanted revenge."

"That *was* why I married you, but I fell in love with you. I love you now, Jilly."

Jillian presented her back to him. "All I ever wanted was you to share yourself with me, Graham. Not your wealth or your title. I wanted the truth. Even now, you wanted to lie to me about what Father said."

"Forgive me. Please." His voice was broken.

"Forgiving you isn't the problem, Graham. How can our marriage work if I can't trust you? What kind of man are you?"

"Don't leave me, Jilly," he begged. The tremulous note in his voice lashed her as much as his betrayal.

She clenched her hands, and fresh tears flowed. "I promised I'd stay, but I can't ever believe anything you tell me again. You can say over and over that you love me and I'll never know if you really mean it. *Never*."

Silently she walked to her rucksack and fished for a

clean cloth to wipe her face. Her father was dead. Her marriage was dead. She had lost everything.

But she had never really had either of them to lose, had she?

Chapter Twenty-four

Jillian did not talk as they made their way to the oasis village of Farafra. It stood on a small hill of white chalk, surrounded by barren desert and the jagged edges of three mountains. Dominating the terrain was an ancient walled fortress. The village itself appeared quaint and primitive, but Graham barely noticed. In the square, men sat spinning wool and gossiping. All heads turned curiously at the newcomers. Graham greeted them courteously and asked directions to the home of the family Ramses knew.

The house of Abdul Al-din was stark, its owner courteous and friendly. Abdul's dark eyes lit when Graham mentioned Ramses. He beckoned to his wife to assist them. They were shown to a small room with a low bed and a small table, and given water for washing their hands and faces. Abdul's wife and daughters dragged a large copper hip bath into their room, offering to get hot water from the nearby hot spring. Graham politely refused and

303

did the task himself. When the tub was filled, he looked at Jillian.

"I'll bathe when you finish," he said quietly.

They were served a delicious dinner of rice, bread and, in their honor, stewed goat. Graham dipped flatbread into a narrow bowl of tomato sauce and ate it. Abdul was eager to hear of his friend, Ramses. Graham made polite conversation, all the while painfully aware of Jillian sitting silently beside him.

The women had crushed flowers and rubbed them into Jillian's hair, scenting it. The fragrance tormented him. Fresh, clean—like her. He longed to bury his face in her hair. He knew he could not.

That night they lay together in the narrow bed. He listened to Jillian's anguished sobs. A gulf larger than the Sahara stretched between them. He ached to hold her in his arms and comfort her. Graham turned over. With a trembling hand, he gently touched his wife's shoulder.

Jillian flinched. "Don't," she rasped.

Graham's shoulders sagged. He rolled over, inching toward his edge of the bed, staring into the darkness.

She'd promised she wouldn't leave him, but this limbo was far worse. He had coaxed her out of the grayness of her life, allowing her to see the vibrant living flame inside her, and now the grayness was back. He had a marriage of grayness, as ugly and stark as London fog.

It would almost be better if she left him.

Bitter irony poisoned him. After a lifetime of never trusting anyone, he had become untrustworthy. He couldn't win her back. Sweet Christ, how the hell could he expect her to simply open her arms and welcome him with fervent kisses? Had *he* been able to forget? Stranton had won after all, in a way. Graham was the one who was ruined.

Tears rolled down his cheeks. For a long time Graham lay there, silently sharing his wife's tears.

The next morning Jillian drowsed in bed. When sunlight speared into the room, pooling on the floor, she sat up and dressed. Abdul's wife told her Graham had taken the camels to water.

Jillian settled herself on a pillow on the floor, and the woman placed a short table before her. It was laden with bread, cheese and honey. A small cup of sweet tea accompanied the meal. Jillian ate quickly, profusely thanking the woman for her hospitality, then went in search of her husband.

She found him at the watering trench. Seeing her, he gave a curt nod. Jillian hovered, uncomfortable with this new tension between them but still heartbroken by his betrayal.

Graham was winding lengths of rope about the feet of their camels, hobbling them. He poured water into the basin used for watering animals, and Jillian watched with avid interest. To her amazement, he crouched by the basin and began slapping the water's surface with the flat of his hand. He sang, making odd smacking noises with his lips.

Goggle-eyed, she stared at him. "What are you doing?"

"I'm encouraging them to drink their fill."

Graham continued his peculiar song, warbling as he stared at the dromedaries. Jillian looked. All three beasts had their ears pricked forward. They began making an odd whining sound, straining toward the water.

"It's an old Bedu trick," Graham explained. "The camels are trained to respond to the song, and the slapping of the water. They know they are to leave for a journey where they will lack water, and they must drink. When they have drunk, I'll let them graze for about an hour, then repeat the same."

Jillian squatted down beside him, smelling the delicious dampness of the fresh water in the basin. She studied her husband, this stranger, yet so familiar to her, with his black beard, penetrating eyes dark as the desert night and his muscled frame hidden by his foreign clothing. He was a man of the desert, at ease with these people who shifted like the sands. A man who had used her for his own means.

She hugged herself, trembling. Oh God, she loved him. But had he ever loved her? He said he did. And yet she had trouble believing him. Actions spoke far louder than words.

Graham unfolded his powerful frame and went to the camels who were whining now and straining toward the water. "Get back or you'll be trampled," he advised as he untied them.

No sooner had she skirted the edge of the basin and stepped away then the beasts raced in and drank with great gulps. Graham joined her by the trench, speaking to the camels in Arabic and pouring water as fast as the level in the basin was lowered.

"How long can camels last without water?"

"Seven or eight days if they've had their fill. They're like walking water tanks. A man could live off of them." His jaw tensed beneath his black beard. She sensed something greater was at stake.

"Graham, what do you mean, live off them?"

He looked somber as he scratched Sheba's long neck. "The Bedu consider the camel their lifeline. If caught without water in the desert, you can survive by slaughtering one and drinking the water it has consumed."

"Goodness," Jillian said. "Are you afraid we're going to have to resort to such measures?"

A reassuring smile touched his mouth. "No." Then he

riveted his gaze on the bleak, wide expanse of the eastern horizon. His smile faded. "I hope not."

A few hours later they had saddled the camels and were headed due east. Graham kept them at a steady pace as he and Jillian progressed across the desert. She sensed something dark and forbidden lurking on the horizon.

Jillian adjusted her white scarf more securely across her face. The sun beat mercilessly down upon them. She thought of being stuck out in the vast wasteland and suppressed a shudder. The trip had been a waste. Her father was dead, the treasure lost forever. And she had lost Graham, if she ever truly had him.

They pushed farther ahead, making camp for the night before the great, jagged peaks of several mountains. Jillian watched Graham roast a rabbit he'd caught earlier for their dinner. Conversation between them remained strained. It was as if he had given up and accepted.

Jillian ate the rabbit with her fingers. It was hot and delicious but she had little appetite. She glanced at the flat, barren horizon.

"If we get lost, will the Khamsin come for us?" she asked.

"They're coming already. Jabari gave us twenty days and then said he would send a party of warriors after us."

The thought gave Jillian a little comfort.

The next three days proceeded as smoothly as the first. Jillian felt fresh hope they were going to make it. That hope faded as her husband stopped abruptly. One tanned hand shaded his forehead as he scanned the horizon.

"What is it?" she asked, fearing to know.

"Dust in the distance. Could be another caravan. Or not."

Graham removed the veil covering his face. Cold dread filled her at his expression. He muttered what sounded like an Arabic oath.

And then she saw them, too, approaching fast. Four riders. Her heart slid into her stomach. Dear God. The raiders who had first taken her captive—they had followed.

"They probably think we found treasure"—he cast a worried glance at the iron water tankers—"and that we're hiding it inside those tanks. Can't make a run for it. Our camels are tired. We're going to have to face them."

"Where's the rifle?"

"Down in the crevice with your father," Graham reminded her. He slid off his camel and ran over, assisting her down. "Get behind me," he said tightly. He unsheathed his scimitar and stood in a defensive position away from the tankers.

She had to help him. Two against four desert raiders if she helped, they stood a fighting chance. Jillian's frantic gaze raked the ground looking for any kind of weapon. Nothing but pebbles and stones. She unwrapped her emerald scarf from about her neck and gathered the fist-sized rocks.

He threw her a quick, startled glance. "A sling," she explained. "If you think I'm merely standing here and watching us die, you're quite wrong."

"We're not dying," he replied hoarsely. "Not like this."

The raiders' wild, ear-splitting hoots rose like an angry wind. Jillian clapped shaky hands over her ears as the men dismounted, running toward their camels. Sunlight glittered off their swords as they swung.

Jillian screamed and Graham cursed. Three of their

camels screeched in pain and collapsed, their blood flowing into the sand. The iron water tanks one carried hit the ground. Water sprang from the leaking container. Solomon staggered from a glancing blow, but he galloped off.

Graham faced his enemies, his expression fierce, sword held with practiced ease. With whooping screams of triumph, the dirty-robed, dark-bearded raiders rushed forward, swords flashing. Graham did not move. They were nearly upon him when he lashed out with the fury of a boiling sandstorm.

Graham the duke melded into Rashid the warrior, executing deadly moves, whirling and pivoting with lethal grace. Three raiders attacked in violent strokes, but he fought with unwavering resolve, relentlessly dueling his attackers. The fight became a deadly ballet of steel against steel. The harsh, undulating cries of the Bedouin raiders rang in Jillian's ears.

She took a large stone, put it into her scarf and lobbed it. It slammed into one Bedouin's temple. He staggered. In the next instant, Graham's sword struck him down. Now it was three against one.

Jillian danced away and tucked another stone into her scarf. A whistling cut the air as she whirled the fabric then let fly. *Whap!* It struck a Bedouin on the hand.

Not good enough. He turned and charged, sword held aloft. Graham spun, saw her predicament and raced over. A different Bedouin picked up a rock and threw it. It clubbed Graham on the head with a loud thwack.

"Graham!" Jillian screamed.

Scarlet ribbons of blood streamed down his face. He staggered and the two raiders on him rushed forward. One grabbed his sword. They were trapped.

Jillian rushed to Graham as the last raider approached.

309

She recognized him—the sheikh who had shown no interest in raping her. Would he do so now, then leave them both in the sand for the vultures?

While the sheikh and another Bedu held swords to Jillian, the third went to the iron water tanks. Disgust filled his face as he kicked at the empty containers.

Mahjub, the sheikh, looked at Graham.

"Since you have no treasure, we will take your woman. She will fetch a good price at the slave market. You fight bravely, son of the desert, and I will set you free. But I will strip you of power. You will return in shame to your people, knowing you were unable to help your woman."

One man slammed Jillian downward. She fell on her back. "Take her," the sheikh ordered. "So he can watch."

Fear blossomed in their eyes. The men looked down at her. "She is fire. I will burn," one protested.

"Do it," the chieftain snapped.

The men exchanged glances, muttered something. One turned Jillian over, forcing her to her hands and knees. The other fumbled with the drawstring on his blousy trousers.

Graham's heart dropped. They were going to rape Jillian. He had never believed in a no-win situation, but never before had he faced such desperate odds. Silently he cursed bringing her with him. If only he had left her back at the village for the Khamsin rescue party to find, then she'd be safe.

Mahjub's dark gaze lingered on him. Something other than triumph flared there. Graham recognized it immediately. He had seen it in the eyes of his Egyptian captor. In Stranton's eyes. No wonder the sheikh wasn't interested in Jillian.

"Yes," the sheikh said smiling cruelly. "You wish to save her, Khamsin? Then take her place."

I can't do it, Graham thought frantically. *Oh God, I just can't. Not again. Never again. I'm sorry, Jilly. I'm so sorry.*

Emotion closed his throat. He clenched his grime-streaked fists. Jillian's terrified eyes pleaded with him as the Bedouin yanked down her trousers, exposing her rounded bottom.

Agonized, he stared at his wife. He knew what this would do to her. Jillian would become a wreck, shutting out everyone, becoming distant. The feelings of shame, bitter humiliation and anger—emotional scars that lashed deep. Darkness would take her, extinguishing the living flame he had helped bring out. He couldn't bear for her to become what he had been.

I love you, he said silently. *I love you more than life itself*. And then suddenly, he knew he must do, despite the terrible price he'd pay. . . .

"Yes. Take me," he said hoarsely, revulsion and nausea rising in his throat. "Take me and spare her."

Lust blazed in Mahjub's dark eyes. "You give yourself willingly? If you do, we will release her and take you to the slave market. A eunuch is worth many camels."

Graham swallowed hard. He knew what they would do to him. He wouldn't die. But he would fervently wish he had.

Yet it meant giving her a chance at survival.

Inhaling a ragged breath, he repeated his words to Lord Stranton twenty years ago: "I will not struggle."

The sheikh gestured to the man positioned behind Jillian, who yanked up his trousers. The other man released her.

Mahjub's hungry gaze caressed Graham. He gestured to the ground. Graham understood. His trembling fingers fumbled with the buttons of his *binish*.

"Go," he said harshly to Jillian, who scrambled to her

311

feet. "Find Solomon. Ride hard and fast to the east to find the Khamsin. And don't look back."

Jillian watched in dumbstruck horror as her husband began to undress. The thin, tall sheikh watched Graham intently, his breath quickening, an odd look in his dark eyes.

Oh God. Suddenly she understood why the sheikh had never raped her. And Graham now offered himself to spare her.

Bile rose in her throat. And she knew then how deeply he loved her. Actions spoke louder than words.

I won't let him do this to you, Graham, she thought fiercely. *Together we can defeat them.* She remembered the men's fear when they saw her naked body and the red curls covering her sex. One had used the Arabic word for fire, and she knew they were afraid to rape her. Afraid . . . they would be consumed because she was a jinn? Sudden inspiration struck.

"Go, Jilly," Graham ordered, his voice thick. "I told you to go. Run as fast as you can."

"No," she said in English, "I won't let him do this. At worst we will die together. Graham, remember when you told me how you defeated your Egyptian captor when he was distracted? We can do the same."

Understanding flashed in his eyes.

"Take off your trousers, my love. You will need your legs and arms free," she said softly.

He did so. "When you say *now*," Graham agreed. He dropped to his hands and knees.

Jillian tore off her turban, shook free her red-gold hair and removed her clothing. She stood before the men fully nude. She screamed the English word. *"Now!"* Then she made a shrieking sound like that of a desert spirit.

One of the Bedouin glanced at her in terror. "Al-Haiira," he screamed. "Jinni!"

All three stared.

With lightning speed, Graham kicked out, catching the man on his right behind the calves. The raider toppled. Next he lunged upwards, grabbing the man's scimitar. In one expert stroke the man fell silent, scarlet gushing from him. Graham struck the Bedouin on his left, killing him, too.

Alone now, the sheikh stared at Jillian's enraged, naked husband, scimitar in hand. Bloodlust shone in Graham's eyes. Terror shone in the sheikh's. He had made a grave mistake.

The sheikh yanked up his trousers, turned and ran. Graham gave chase. In a minute he was upon him, his sword glinting in the sun.

The sheikh's high shriek was suddenly cut off. Savage, angry grunts issued from her furious husband. Jillian cried out as he continued to strike. Again. Again. Again. Dark blood flowed into the sands, a sluggish stream.

"Graham, stop it. Stop it! He's dead! He's dead!"

Panting, Graham lowered the reddened scimitar. Blood had spattered his naked body. He dropped the sword, put a hand to his head.

"It's over, my love," Jillian said softly. "He won't hurt you. No one will, ever again. Come to me."

She held out her arms and he embraced her in a crushing hug. Warmth trickled onto her naked shoulder. Jillian cried out in alarm.

"Your head is bleeding."

She ran to her nearby rucksack, grabbed a towel and ran back. Her shaking fingers held the cloth over Graham's wound.

He said, "We've lost camels, and I don't know how

badly they hurt Solomon. We have to find him." He winced at her gentle touch.

She anxiously examined the laceration. "The bleeding's slowed, but I'll have to clean it."

He studied her. "We should put some clothing on first."

Flustered, she glanced at him, feeling horribly shaken. "Oh, Graham, he would have . . . You were going to let him . . ."

His mouth tightened. Then he glanced down and smiled. "I wouldn't advise walking naked through the desert. There are some parts of me that wouldn't do well with a sunburn."

Tremendous love for her husband rushed through Jillian, feeling like warm sunshine after a dark, dreary night. He jested after nearly suffering his worst possible nightmare? All for her.

And then she realized the deep inner strength of this man she'd married. This man who truly did love her. Enough to sacrifice himself for her.

Jillian struggled for words. Her mouth worked. Graham touched her cheek.

"Don't say anything. All I ask is for you to give me another chance, Jilly. I love you. I'd die for you."

"Or worse," she whispered.

He nodded. "Or worse."

A somber look covered his face. "Thank you, Jilly. Thank you for saving me. In more ways than one. Do you remember when we saw the pyramid in Giza?" At her shaky nod, he continued. "I told you it represented new life for the pharaohs, and you were just like the pyramid. New life, for me. Your strength gives me strength." Jillian grasped his hand, the momentary rush fleeing her, leaving behind shaky disbelief. She shuddered as she glanced at the Bedouin bodies. "What will you do with them?"

"Leave them for the jackals," he said roughly. "And the desert wind. We need to keep moving if we want to live. We have little water and I don't intend to die out here."

Chapter Twenty-five

At noon two days later, Graham collapsed. Jillian screamed. She slid off her mount and ran to his side. Her husband lay on the sand, prone. He raised his head and moaned.

"My head, it hurts."

She gently examined the healing purplish bruise on his head. The blow must have injured him more than she'd realized.

"Graham," she called. "Graham!"

A deep groan rumbled from his throat. "Must . . . find help. I think we're lost."

They had recovered two of the Bedouins' camels and a weakened Solomon, who had suffered a gash to his hind leg and limped. The other camels had run off. Graham had not expended precious energy running after them. Now Jillian wished he had. Yesterday one of their two camels had collapsed and died. The other was weakening fast. The iron water tanks were empty, their contents spilled onto the sand.

Graham promised they could make it. But as time wore on, Jillian had begun to wonder. The trail he followed meandered, plus the sun's position seemed wrong. But what did she, an Englishwoman, know of desert travel and following camel tracks in the sand? He was an experienced desert traveler, and, doubting herself, she had said nothing. Now she sorely regretted not speaking her mind.

Jillian glanced up. All she could see was a wide horizon of burning white sand. Disoriented from his injury, Graham had surely miscalculated their route and gotten them lost. Lost in the desert, with only half a goatskin of water.

Katherine's advice came back to haunt her. "If you're struck in the head and later have a headache and disorientation, stop and rest. It could take three to five days to clear."

Three days of rest when they barely had two days' worth of water? Jillian acted quickly. She unfurled a blanket on the hot sand and rolled Graham onto it. Next she erected a small tent to shade him from the broiling sun. She touched his cheek, feeling the skin hot beneath her fingers.

Rescue was on the way. Surely the Khamsin could find them. The Bedouin could track a camel in a sandstorm. But they were running out of water. By the time their rescuers arrived, she and Graham could be dead. She knew what she must do.

She had to leave him, had to go alone and find her way back to the main trail of Darb Asylt and leave a sign for their rescuers to follow. Jillian thought frantically. The raiders had stolen her compass when she was first captured. She sucked in a breath. Jabari and Ramses had taught her how to find her way in the desert. Her sense of direction was excellent. She must finally believe in herself. No choice left. Stay here and die of dehydration, or try to find the caravan route and leave a sign for the Khamsin.

All around her lay open terrain. No landmarks. They had wandered south, but she wasn't sure which direction to head. If she could find her way north, Jillian felt confident she could find the caravan trail. But which way was north?

She remembered what Ramses had explained. With a twinkle in his amber eyes, he had said, "Jillian, my friend tends to get lost. He has the sense of direction of a blind camel. I'm entrusting you to show him the way, should this happen."

Then the Khamsin warrior had proceeded to show her how to figure out direction by using the sun.

Recalling his words, Jillian fetched the camel crop and spade and dug a small hole. She plunged the crop into the hole. The long pole made a distinctive shadow on the rough ground. She marked the spot with one of the wood matches. This was west.

Next she fished a hair ribbon from her rucksack and tied it to the crop's bottom, and drew in the sand with Graham's blade a circle exactly the radius of the shadow the pole cast on the ground. Jillian retrieved one of the wooden matches and marked the spot on the circle of the shadow. Consulting the little watch pinned to her robe, she waited fifteen minutes.

Jillian checked the shadow and marked the new position. Then she drew a straight line between the two marks. East–west. Standing, she positioned the west mark to her left. West to her left, north to her front. Her eyes scanned the horizon, looking for markers. A distant clump of rock hovered ahead to the northeast. Of course. The route.

Hesitating, she glanced at the resting camel. Weakened

from blood loss, Solomon might die if she took him with her. If she left him here, as a last resort for Graham, for life . . . The thought was too terrible to bear.

Gulping back tears, she gave the camel a reassuring pat and went to her rucksack. She scribbled a note on the back of the map tracing, and tucked it beneath Graham's sleeping body. Then Jillian emerged from the tiny, makeshift tent. Squinting at the burning sun, she wrapped the emerald scarf about her face, leaving only a slit for her eyes. She took one quarter of the water, leaving the rest for Graham, kissed his cheek and mounted the last Bedouin camel.

Ramses had told her a man could live without food for weeks, without water for only three days. With dogged determination, her feet aching, her throat parched and dry, she pushed on. Jillian rationed the water she'd brought with her, taking only sips. She navigated at night by studying the stars as Jabari had taught her.

Late the second day, she came upon the unmistakable signs of camel tracks leading in an east–west direction. The caravan route. She slid off the camel, licked her parched lips and began piling stones into a cairn, forming an arrow pointing in the direction she had come. Her bones ached and her throat cried out for water. When she finished, despair flooded her. How would the men know it was them? She needed another marker. Her scarf.

Jillian tore off the emerald garment. It hung from her fingers, fluttering in the wind like a flag.

Her scarf, the one Graham had purchased in the souk in Cairo. "Green as the quiet grasses in an oasis, quiet pools of refreshment." He had given a self-mocking grin at his poetry. He had told her she should always wear jewel colors to complement her spirited nature. "You're not gray, Jilly. You're flame, the energy of roaring fire.

You're verdant grasses. You're the deep blue of a turbulent ocean. But you're not the gray of silence anymore."

Emotion clogged her throat. She unwound the scarf and secured it to the stones, praying the Khamsin riders would see it before the desert wind carried it off and left only their bones bleaching under the sun's relentless lash. The endless wind slapped it like a Bedouin woman pounding dust from a rug. Would frayed tendrils remain a month from now, if no one came and she and Graham died out here?

The thought was too horrible to bear. Jillian fisted away sudden tears springing to her eyes. She blamed the wind and sun, and began the journey back to her husband. When the Bedouin's camel collapsed, Jillian struggled on alone, staggering back to Graham while the sun beat mercilessly down upon her.

Sick with worry, Graham scanned the horizon. The note Jillian left increased his anxiety. While he had slept, she'd been trying to find the caravan route to leave a marker.

He saddled Solomon and urged the beast on, groggily following her tracks. He wanted to race after her, but prudence checked him. Solomon was severely weak and limped. His wife's tracks in the sand were difficult to follow, and if he lost his head, he'd be wandering in circles, never finding her.

A lone figure appeared hours later on the shimmering horizon. Graham urged Solomon into a gallop. Dust kicked up behind him as he pushed the protesting camel on. Reaching her, he jumped off, grabbing his goatskin bag of water. Jillian lay prone upon the burning sands. He raced to her limp form. Deep, gasping breaths rasped from her parched lips. Dehydration had set in. But they had no water.

As he stared at her lying on the ground, the wind lifted

a corner of her white scarf, licking her face and teasing out a tendril of flame-gold hair. Red hair, billowing from the force of the wind whistling across the desert plain. Just like in his nightmare.

Jillian's eyes fluttered open. Those green eyes, brilliant as glossy emeralds, stared at him, not in scornful challenge but with resignation. Her eyes closed as if it were too much effort to keep them open. She was dying.

"No, no, Jilly. Don't leave me," he moaned. The harsh yellow sun grated on his body, mocking his pain.

Graham threw back his head and screamed and screamed. His screams echoed over the barren plain, disappearing into the dust.

Chapter Twenty-six

The tent he erected on the sandy plain shielded his parched wife from the yellow sun's harsh embrace. Graham knelt beside her, his throat raw. The woman he had loved in the night, who'd coaxed him into facing his darkest demons, lay on a blanket. So dry. Her pale, delicate body was so dry. Squeezing his eyes shut, he saw her desiccating like a mummy, forever preserved, the moisture squeezed out, each precious drop of life drunk by the greedy sands.

His hand touched her hips, slightly rounded. She wasn't pregnant. He thought about her carrying his child, imagined her grunting and straining and sweating to bring it forth, just as they had grunted and strained and sweated in passion.

Gently, as carefully as Badra had done with her new son, he handled her, uncovering her body, tugging the grimy dress from her shoulders, removing the loose trousers and boots. Naked, she lay upon the blanket, her skin slightly shriveled.

There was no water left. None but in his own parched body. Graham licked his cracked lips, summoning saliva. He kissed her, his slightly moist lips to her dry ones, passing on his precious fluid. Harsh, ragged breaths labored in her chest. In. Out. Barely moving. Life slipping away from her, like water into the sand.

His parched mind began seeing her body as fruit. The small, delicate breasts in their roundness were apples. He imagined the tart sweet juice running between his lips, sharing, passing on moisture to her—to refresh, to give life.

Her navel was a pitted date, easing the ache of his dry throat, soaking the cotton in his mouth, refreshing his arid body. Wetting his fingers, he touched her belly, leaving twin tracks of moisture like footprints. He was passing on his moisture to her, willing her to absorb his life. His fingertips trailed her pale skin, that freckled skin dotted here and there like strategic geographic points on a map. He delved briefly into the tangle of red curls between her thighs, tunneled to the hollow his body had eagerly sought. Dry there, too, as the hot sands. He imagined the rosette of a dewy pomegranate half, its plump moistness beckoning him to sink inside and refresh his parched body and spirit.

Graham took an empty water bag, squeezed it over her parted lips. One last droplet fell onto her mouth. He pushed it with his finger past her lips onto her tongue.

Clutching both goatskin bags, he emerged from the shallow protection of the tent into the glaring sun, the brightness hurting his eyes, threatening tears. No moisture should be wasted in the desert. He was a survivor. No tears in the desert.

Graham envisioned Jillian on the sand, its caress dry and hot upon her dying flesh, enveloping her like a lover. Her body, bleached dry and so alone, covered by sand as he had covered her body in the dark night, sand thrusting into her secret hollows, invading her sweetness, knowing her intimately, claiming her in ways he could not. He felt jealous of those hot, greedy sands. They would swallow her whole as he had always wanted to do, sinking into each cell, burrowing into her in ways he could not. Knowing her in ways he could not.

No. The sand would not claim her. "*Jillian is mine,*" he roared. "Mine! I will not allow you to have her!"

The silence taunted him as the wind blew the shifting sands into his face. Words roared back, *Then a sacrifice must be made.*

His gaze fell on the camel lying near the tiny tent. Solomon. His friend in the desert.

I cannot. I must.

He remembered Solomon's birth, pulling the beast from its mother, naming him after the legendary king. He recalled the stubborn way Solomon resisted the harness. Taking dates from his hand. Nudging him as he slept once in the deep desert, warning him of the danger of marauders who desired to rob and slay him as he slept.

Solomon saved his life once. Now, again. Graham clutched his two empty water bags and removed his *jambiya*, stroked his thumb along the sharp edge. He approached Solomon, who raised his head weakly. Graham knelt beside the wounded camel.

Large, liquid eyes held his. Solomon lowered his head, butted it against Graham's thigh. Then he studied his master. Knowledge seemed to burn in his ageless, wise eyes.

No tears in the desert. Graham held up his knife to heaven, an offering to the hot wind, the burning yellow sun, the uncaring sands.

A short prayer and a swift stroke later, Graham held out one bag to catch the blood. Liquid was life in the desert. He drank the blood, forcing himself not to gulp. To sip slowly.

A single drop rolled down the camel's neck. Graham took his finger and captured it, bringing it to parched lips to taste.

When the blood was drained, he tied off the bag and set it down. As his Bedouin family had taught, he slit the animal's belly, found its paunch and drained the water into the second bag. Graham did all this with numb detachment, setting the liquid aside. In a few hours, it would be drinkable.

He took the bag of blood and went into the tent to bring life to his beloved.

Darkness surrounded her, dragged her down. Jillian let herself slip into it, wanting to slip away into blackness for good.

The commanding male voice had not allowed her to. It had urged her to drink the thick liquid she wanted to spit out. It kept forcing her to drink. She had drunk, fell asleep, only to be woken and forced to drink again.

Now a bevy of new voices rang in her ears. Distant shouts, Arabic words she didn't understand. She felt herself lifted, carried off into the scorching sun, then the blessed relief of shade. The hardness of ground was beneath her, cushioned by a thick blanket. The murmuring voices faded. Her body was an iron weight. So tired. Jillian struggled against opening her eyes.

"Shhhh," a different male voice crooned. "Drink."

Her lips parted as liquid was forced past. Jillian eagerly gulped the refreshment, then gagged on the salty-sweet taste. A firm hand closed her mouth.

"Swallow, Jilly," ordered the same deep voice that had not let her sleep, had forced her to drink earlier. A voice with authority. Jillian swallowed, then coughed.

"Good girl," it murmured. "Again."

A cool, wet cloth stroked her skin. She shivered and

tried to pull away. The voice murmured reassuring words, crooned for her to remain still.

Why was she feeling so sick? Her head pounded like war drums. She just wanted to slip away and sleep forever.

"Don't you die on me," the deep voice ordered. "Don't you dare die. Not now. You're going to live. Fight it, Jilly."

The instinctive need to obey could not be pushed aside. It mandated she struggle against sinking deep into the peaceful sleep and leaving behind the pain. Deep inside, a spark flared and caught. As the cool, wet cloth caressed her naked flesh, Jillian began fighting to live.

Graham stared down at his wife as he stroked the damp cloth over her bare torso. A swath lay across her breasts and hips for modesty's sake. His anxious gaze sought Ramses.

"If you hadn't arrived . . ."

"But we did. Thanks to the marker she left, we knew how to find you. It saved both of you, my friend. As did your sacrificing Solomon to give her fluids," he said calmly.

Ramses raised Jillian's head again, pressing a small cup to her lips. He forced her to drink the mixture of salt and sugar that would replenish her body's fluids. Heartsick, Graham stared at her lying nearly lifeless on the blanket.

"Jilly, I love you. Don't leave me. I don't know what I'll do if you don't make it," he whispered, stroking her hair.

Jillian's eyelids fluttered. Ramses smiled. "I believe she will. She has something to live for, my friend. You."

When Ramses left the tent, Jillian tried to speak. Graham laid a finger upon her sore, cracked lips. "No, love. Don't speak." He stared in awed wonder. Life. Such a precious gift. "You have an amazing will to live, Jilly."

She struggled to speak. "For a weak Englishwoman."

Graham brushed her mouth with his. "No, not weak," he said quietly. "I knew you had it inside you—the inner strength you kept seeking. It was there all along."

"You saved me."

"You saved yourself, my Jillian. All I could do is point the way." He felt his chest compress with the awful truth. "Had you not been so strong . . . you would have perished long ago."

Her gaze sought his. "You . . . knew I'd make it?"

"I knew it," he said solemnly, stroking her forehead. He looked away for a moment. "I didn't want you with me because I knew out here, there are no secrets. I didn't want you discovering mine."

Cradling the back of her head with one hand, Graham lifted the cup to her lips. She drank, her gaze locking to his.

"I'm glad I know," she whispered. "You're free now."

Free? He didn't want to be free, not of his wife. He pushed aside the thought, concentrated on her.

"I was confident you could make the journey across the desert. You're a strong woman. You needed to believe you could do it on your own. That you could endure the worst the desert had to offer, and emerge victorious."

"You believed in me?" she whispered. "No one has ever believed in me. Father said I was a weak woman. Like all women, I needed a strong husband to lead me."

Graham's jaw tensed beneath his black beard. "No, Jillian. Not to lead you. To walk with you, not in front. To allow you to be who you are, not push you into the shadows." He paused, struggling with his pride and dignity. "To remain at your side. Please, forgive me for being such an ass and lying to you. Trust in me and let's make our marriage work."

The duke glanced down, studying the sweep of red-gold lashes feathering her pale cheeks. She made no response. There was time enough later for her to make that choice.

And if she couldn't trust him after all? He must deal with it as he had dealt with all the other painful events in his life. But deep down, Graham knew this would hurt worst of all. He loved her.

He just prayed she felt the same.

Chapter Twenty-seven

Slowly Jillian recovered from the devastating effects of dehydration. They remained at the Khamsin camp, giving her time to fully recuperate. Graham hovered, attending to her with fervent devotion. As she recovered, Jillian felt fresh guilt. Her father was dead, but she couldn't forget the damage he'd done to her husband. How could their marriage work? Every time Graham saw her, wasn't he reminded of the horrors of his past? She didn't dare ask.

Finally they prepared to depart for Port Said. Jillian bade good-bye to her friends. Emotion overcame her as she hugged Elizabeth. She had spent several hours with the sheikh's wife, confiding in the older woman her father's shameful past, her own torment about it. Wisdom flared in Elizabeth's blue eyes.

"A man's love can help you get through your own darkness."

Jillian studied her. "I don't know . . ."

Elizabeth's smile faded. "I do," she whispered. Then

she glanced at Jabari, her eyes shimmering. "Trust me, I'm right. And trust in Graham's strength. Give him a chance."

Doubts filled her. Could they make it work? Or would the pain of their individual pasts prove too much to overcome?

It was a quiet, uneventful journey back to England. Graham retained his distance from her, even booking separate cabins for them. He said it was to give her enough rest. Jillian suspected otherwise. Pain speared her, but she graciously smiled and thanked him for his consideration.

Now she stood quietly in her husband's London study, watching as he pored over paperwork at his satinwood desk. He scribbled in bold, masculine handwriting on an official-looking document. Graham tore the paper out and handed it to her.

Jillian took it, her eyes never leaving his. "What's this?"

"I had two of my Arabian mares sold at auction. They fetched enough money to provide a small living for my family."

"Oh, Graham—the horses." She knew how much he loved those horses. He gave a dismissive wave.

"One must make choices. They will be well-treated."

A gasp fled her lips as she stared at the amount. "A bank draft for one thousand pounds?"

"For you. Enough to purchase passage to America and attend college. Enough to pursue your dreams of attending school." His expression remained impartial, but dark torment swirled in his velvet brown gaze. "It's your choice. You know everything about me now. You'll always know that . . ." His fists clenched. A muscle in his jaw jumped as he stared out the window. "You'll always be aware of my past, and what your father did to me. It's not an easy thing to live with, and I understand if you choose to leave. If you do leave, I will not try to stop you. You can run as far as you like, if this is what you truly want."

Torn by indecision, she stared at him, the check gripped in her fingertips. "Do you want me to leave?"

Graham looked directly at her. "No. You *can* leave me, Jilly, but in the end you can't hide from the truth. It will not change a thing. And neither will my love for you. Try as hard as you like, it will follow you. My love will not change. It's a fact you can't escape, even across the Atlantic." Then he assumed an impartial look. "It's your choice."

He stood and pushed back from the desk. "I will await your answer in the drawing room."

The bold letters on the bank draft stood out in stark relief. A violent trembling seized Jillian's hand. The paper fluttered as if caught in a windstorm. Money. Enough to achieve her dearest dream. Education. A new life, far from the tawdry scandal dogging her footsteps. Far from Graham.

Whether it would fail or not, did she truly wish to leave the man she loved?

Pacing the length of the drawing room, Graham fought the tumult of emotions rushing through him. Dimly he felt grateful Kenneth and his family hadn't arrived back from Yorkshire. He needed to be alone to gather his composure if Jillian left.

"Graham? I'm ready to give you my answer."

He jerked his gaze to the doorway. Jillian stood there, her long, curly red hair falling softly about her shoulders. A forest-green day gown draped her lush figure, matching her sparkling green eyes. His desperate gaze hungrily drank in the light sprinkling of amber freckles across her cheeks, her rose-petal soft lips. One last look—he'd have one last look before she left him.

Graham watched cautiously as she held up his check. Pieces fluttered in the air as she ripped it to shreds.

He didn't dare stir, fearing it was a dream and he'd awaken. "You're not leaving me? Despite everything?"

Her emerald gaze briefly mirrored his past torment. She hung her head, staring at the carpet. "Only if you truly want me. I love you so much it hurts. Every time I think of what my father did to you, I feel guilty and ashamed of myself, but . . ."

Stricken, he approached. Putting a hand beneath her chin, he tilted it upwards, forcing her to look at him. "It's not your fault, Jilly."

"But he was my father," she whispered. "How can you not look at me and see him?"

Graham cupped her cheek. He wasn't Stranton's only victim. "How, *habiba*? Because I love you. When I look at you, you're all I see. The beautiful, warm flame that lit the darkness inside me and allowed me to leave behind my past." A single crystalline tear spilled down her cheek, splashing hot wetness onto his hand.

"Can we get over this, Graham?"

"You never get over it," he said somberly. "You get *through* it. And you go on. It's possible, Jilly. Will you try with me?"

A tremulous smile touched her lips. "In Egypt, I received some wise advice from a smart woman. She told me a man's love can help a woman heal from her own darkness. All I had before was gray shadows. I didn't even wish to acknowledge what deep inside I knew was true. Now I need to push on. But I need you by my side."

Graham clasped her hands. "I can't promise it will be perfect. I'm not perfect. But I'll try."

"I don't need a perfect husband or a perfect marriage. I just need your love."

"That's perfect enough for me," he said softly.

He crooked a finger. Jillian went to him and he enfolded her in a tight embrace, then tipped her face up. A feeling so intense, so powerful, overcame him and he wanted to shout for joy. He kissed her gently then and she responded, deepened the kiss. His now. Forever. This redheaded witch had turned into his beautiful angel.

A delicate cough drew them apart. They glanced at the doorway and a red-faced butler. "Er, begging your pardon, Your Grace, but you have a caller."

"Blast it," Graham muttered. "Can't we be alone?"

The butler ushered in Jillian's aunt. Jillian beamed and ran toward her. Graham hung back, uneasy. He hadn't killed Mary's brother, but would she find him responsible anyway?

"I'm so happy you're back," the woman said, lifting her frail, rice-powdered cheek for a kiss.

Jillian's somber gaze met Graham's. "I'm afraid I have rather horrid news, Aunt Mary. Father is dead."

No emotion flickered over her aunt's face as Jillian slowly relayed the tale, leaving out the more lurid details. When she finished, Mary sighed. "At least he's at peace now."

Tension fled Graham. He studied his wife's aunt, wondering uneasily about her reaction. It was almost as if she knew what her brother had been.

Her aunt showed no grief at Father's death. Bemused, Jillian watched Mary wave a hand, as if to brush aside the news.

"Now, the reason for my visit. I heard of your financial circumstances, Jillian. I need to hand over your money."

"But I don't have any money," Jillian protested.

Mary offered a serene smile. "Mr. H. M. Pepperton does." As she stared, her aunt explained. "Jillian, when my Horace died, I longed to return to England. But your father was a spendthrift. I was afraid he'd misman-age my money, so I told him I had very little. That wasn't exactly true.

"Every time you gave me advice about what Mr. Pep-perton should do with his finances, I passed it along to my solicitors. Some of the results are sitting in an account for you, my dear. You are the child Horace and I never had."

Jillian blushed. "Why did . . . why did you tell me to go to Madame LaFontant to sell myself if I had money?"

A twinkle sparked in Mary's eyes. "Not just sell your-self to anyone, but the duke. Catherine, the brothel's owner, is a friend. When she told me about how the duke was searching for an articulate, pretty virgin, I immedi-ately thought of you. I'd met him at the Knightsbridges', was charmed with his directness and warmth, and knew you two were perfect for each other."

Graham stared. "She told me she was discreet!"

"My dear duke," Mary said with mirth, "you should know nothing is discreet in a brothel."

"Why are we perfect for each other?" he asked. Jillian felt him reach for her hand. His fingers laced about hers.

Sorrow etched her face. "Because you both had that same haunted look. Years ago, I overheard our father ar-guing with Reggie. Papa had caught him with . . . one of the stable boys. Totally classless, Papa shouted. Reggie had laughed and said he did the same to an English boy in Egypt who was clearly an aristocrat. The boy was being held captive by a hostile tribe. Papa was horrified. He'd said the boy could be one of the Duke of Caldwell's miss-ing grandsons. Reggie had said the boy only endured what he himself had in childhood. And then I knew . . ."

Graham fell silent. Sweat coated his hand where it rested in hers. Jillian gave his palm a reassuring squeeze.

"I'm sorry, Your Grace, for all my brother made you suffer."

"Graham," he corrected quietly. "Please call me Graham. We're relatives now. And I wouldn't have it any other way."

Mary nodded. "Now, about Jillian's inheritance—"

"Keep it for my wife to draw upon as she needs in college."

Jillian stared, not daring to believe. "Did you . . ."

"I sent my secretary to someone knowledgeable about which English colleges are open to women. He tracked down Emily Davies, a suffragette. She recommended University College."

Fresh hope filled her as she regarded his tender smile. "Then you must take the rest of the money, Graham."

Two stubborn lines furrowed his brow. He shook his head. "It's your money, Jilly. We'll manage, somehow."

Mary looked thoughtful. "Your Grace—er, I mean, Graham—I understand you're quite an expert on horseflesh. I have two Arabian mares, recently purchased from your stables, but would like to breed them."

"*You* bought my horses?" Understanding dawned on his face. "Ah, I see. Mr. H. M. Pepperton did."

"Good horses, too. I understand you have a fine stallion with blooded lines. What would you say to joining forces and entering into a business together in breeding Arabians? I'll be your financial backer," Mary proposed.

"Only if you take twenty percent of the profits. I don't want charity, even from family."

"Fifteen," she shot back.

"Twenty-five," he countered.

"Twenty, with the stipulation Jillian reinvests the funds."

They shook hands. Mary smiled. "Well, I'm pushing off as soon as I visit my solicitor and have him send you a bank draft. I'm taking your mother to America for a visit, Jillian. I haven't seen her so animated in years."

"Aunt Mary, one question. How did you become friends with a brothel madame?" Jillian asked, deeply curious.

Mischief sparked in her aunt's dark eyes. "For her to find me male companionship, my dear. I may be old, but I'm not dead."

Then her aunt swept out of the room, chuckling.

"The last word, as always." Jillian shook her head. "Male companionship!"

Heat flared in Graham's gaze. "I'm quite ready for some female companionship. Would you care to engage me in a dance?"

She tugged at his hand. Laughing, they sped up the stairs toward his bedchamber. Graham closed the door with a firm click, locking it. Heat flared in his eyes as they undressed and tumbled onto the bed. He showered her with tiny, hot kisses. She clung to him, arching as he entered her.

"Look at me, Jilly," he said softly. "Look at me."

She had seen passion, tenderness, stark male possessiveness, but always it seemed something was missing from his gaze. As if a protective shutter dropped, a barrier preventing her from seeing inside him. Now Jillian looked up into her husband's face and found what had been missing.

Graham made love to his wife with exquisite tenderness, and they wrapped around each other in a desperate attempt to become one. He held nothing back. Every raw emotion was clearly expressed, from awed wonder to heated desire.

They shattered together in a blinding explosion of heat. For a long moment he lay atop her, gasping as she pulled him closer, then he rolled off. He pulled her to his side, needing to feel her softness. He relished her heat, her proximity. Truly now, he had found what had been missing.

Jillian gazed into Graham's eyes, heavy-lidded with satisfaction. A soft smile quirked her mouth. "We should send a thank-you note to Madame LaFontant for bringing us together," she mused. "I knew you were special from our first moment alone. When you handed me those roses and gazed into my eyes, it was like . . ."

"Destiny. One red rose and one white rose," he said softly. "I didn't know then what the colors meant. I do now."

"What, my love?"

"The red stands for passion and love. The white for purity and innocence. Combined, they symbolize our differences and unity."

His lips were warm and firm against hers as she surrendered to his kiss. How perfect. He had chosen well, her husband. Two roses, two innocents, bound together. United in past torment. Unified now, in love.

Burning Tigress

JADE LEE

Charlotte Wicks wants more. Running her parents' Shanghai household is necessary drudgery, but a true 19th-century woman deserves something deeper—her body cries out for it! Through a Taoist method, her friend Joanna Crane became a Tigress. Why should Charlotte be denied the same?

Her mother would call her wanton. She would label Charlotte's curiosity evil. Certainly the teacher Charlotte desires is fearsome. Glimpses of his body inspire flutters in her stomach and tingling in her core. The man had a reputation among the females of the city as a bringer of great pleasure. There is only one choice to make.

DIANA GROE

MAIDENSONG

When Rika sings the Norse legends, her beautiful voice captivates all who listen. But after a raid on her homeland, she finds herself the captive—a slave to the powerful Bjorn the Black. He is the one man who can destroy her life, yet the only man she can truly trust. The only man who has ever ignited the passion in her soul…and introduced her to the pleasures of the body. But Bjorn is duty-bound to bring her to wed another. And thus they begin a perilous journey to a foreign land, a voyage that will test their courage in countless ways and challenge the strength of the love that is their destiny.

Jennifer Ashley

Penelope & Prince Charming

His blue eyes beguile. His muscular form can satisfy any fantasy—and to top it off, he's royalty! What woman would dare refuse the most sought-after lover in Europe? Miss Twice-a-Jilt Penelope Trask, that's who. And, unfortunately for Damien, marrying Penelope is the only way to inherit his kingdom. Good thing this enchantingly infuriating woman doesn't seem *completely* immune to his many charms. But wooing is difficult, and a strong desire threatens to overwhelm them every time they touch. Why hasn't anyone mentioned the road to happily-ever-after is so difficult?

ATTENTION
BOOK LOVERS!